ONE NIGHT

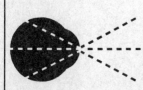

This Large Print Book carries the
Seal of Approval of N.A.V.H.

ONE NIGHT

ERIC JEROME DICKEY

THORNDIKE PRESS

A part of Gale, Cengage Learning

GALE
CENGAGE Learning·

Farmington Hills, Mich • San Francisco • New York • Waterville, Maine
Meriden, Conn • Mason, Ohio • Chicago

LIBRARY OF CONGRESS CATALOGING-IN-PUBLICATION DATA

Dickey, Eric Jerome.
   One night / Eric Jerome Dickey. — Large print edition.
      pages cm. — (Thorndike Press large print African-American)
   ISBN 978-1-4104-7771-2 (hardback) — ISBN 1-4104-7771-1 (hardcover)
   1. African Americans—Fiction. 2. Large type books. I. Title.
PS3554.I319O54 2015b
813'.54—dc23   2015009336

Published in 2015 by arrangement with Dutton, an imprint of Penguin Publishing Group, a division of Penguin Random House LLC

Printed in the United States of America
1 2 3 4 5 6 7 19 18 17 16 15

To Dwayne Orange.
Run with the angels, Poppa.
Run with the angels.

After all, we are nothing more or less than what we choose to reveal.

— *House of Cards,* Season 1, Episode 7

We are our choices.

— Jean-Paul Sartre

I only sleep with people I love, which is why I have insomnia.

— Emilie Autumn,
The Asylum for Wayward Victorian Girls

6:31 P.M.

. . . and then sirens interrupted my unlawful transaction. Law enforcement sped in our direction. I winced, cursed, and shivered. The Hawaiian Gardens Police Department and the sheriff's department were coming to arrest me. The abruptness of the sound of so many sirens caused my body to shake, caused adrenaline to rush, triggered my fight-or-flight mode. The prolonged scream of sirens became louder. Came closer.

The darkness that had arrived long before five o'clock in the afternoon deepened as a perpetual winter rain, cold as ice cubes, intensified the misery on this frigid, colorless night.

I turned and confronted the man in the expensive gray suit. He was tense, twitching as if he had also experienced the sudden heat that comes from fear, from fight-or-flight, but a man dressed like he was would

9

never have anything to run from. He looked like he knew the cops were coming here.

I snapped, "Are you with the police? *Are you a friggin' cop?*"

Winter rain was being spat from the miserable skies, traffic was bumper to bumper; there was no way I could get to the truck that fast, nowhere to run, and the sirens called my name as they sped closer.

Closer.

The truck. They were coming for me because of the goddamn truck.

Brow furrowed, the well-dressed man made fists and turned toward the incessant wails.

I wasn't ready for this. I didn't have an exit plan, not under these conditions.

A winter storm had been going since morning and had caused at least six hundred traffic accidents in three hours; at least five of those were within spitting distance. Traffic was a bitch with PMS, and all the die-hards were out Christmas shopping. Cars, SUVs, pickup trucks, minivans, and hearses clogged the entrance to the Long Beach Towne Center, Hawaiian Gardens Casino, and every strip mall that made up this waterlogged city. That made it impossible for me to get back in my ride and speed away. And if I did manage to get to the truck, the world before me crept toward the 605 at three miles per hour, and traffic heading in the opposite direction on Carson Boulevard couldn't be breaking five.

And as the sirens sang, my frustration was like a slow ride to hell in a flooding dystopia.

Closer. Closer.

He remained tense, his jaw tight, not blinking, his body language speaking of nothing but trouble.

This was unexpected. Fear arrested me. I almost let my weapon slide down to my hand.

Closer. Closer. Closer.

Patrol cars sped by with their fiery lights flashing, raced toward Lakewood, toward Long Beach. We were underneath the shelter between two gas pumps. Behind us was a nonstop line of traffic, a line that stretched both in the direction of the 605 freeway and deeper into Hawaiian Gardens.

The man in the suit took a hard breath, opened and closed his right hand, his face thunderous

Voice trembling, feeling my fear, I asked, "Now, where were we?"

"You parked your truck and came to me with an interesting proposition."

"I can let the MacBook Pro I have go for

seven hundred. Cash."

He said, "Really? Seven hundred dollars for a stolen MacBook Pro?"

"Once again, it's the fifteen-inch, and this sells at the Apple Store for over two thousand dollars. If you get it for seven hundred, you've saved at least thirteen hundred."

"You don't save money by spending money."

"Well, that'll never be on a billboard on Sunset Boulevard. Saving is bad for the economy."

"Really? You're expecting to get that much for a stolen computer that has no warranty?"

"Well, how much are you willing to give me?"

"One hundred dollars."

"Dude, you're crazy. This has the latest-generation Intel processors, all-new graphics, faster flash storage, and retina display. This bad boy has over five million pixels. That's better than HDTV. The battery lasts up to eight hours. Don't tell me you're a PC guy? You look too hip to be a PC guy."

His left eye was bruised. Maybe he had been mugged, or involved in a Christmas brawl. Customers throw hard blows for two-dollar holiday sales at Walmart, and there was one up the street, its lot packed — but his suit and car were made for Rodeo Drive. He considered something beyond me, glanced at the battered old white Nissan truck I was driving.

He said, "Best Buy sent you to do deliveries in that truck?"

"I had to drive my own vehicle tonight. Company cutbacks."

A few minutes earlier I had driven from my resting spot by the Towne Center and the Edwards Cinema into a Chevron station. There were seventeen gas pumps, all but three occupied, and the twenty-four-hour Subway attached to the gas station was just as busy. I had pulled up to pump number 17, stopping opposite pump number 12 and a brother in a modern gray suit. When I eased out of the truck, he was holding his gas hose, his shoulders hunched like he'd never been rained on in his life. I put on a cheerleader smile, walked halfway to him — bouncy and perky like Katie Couric — told him that his whip was very nice — used that praise as an opener — then engaged him with a flirty smile and started a conversation. I eased closer, whispered that I had a MacBook to sell, asked him if he might be interested in a deal. He had paused, inspected me. My wig was long and loose, like a bad-hair day, and I wore a stolen yellow polo shirt and Dockers that had come at the same five-finger discount, both too big, and a stolen Best Buy badge on my jean jacket. He stepped closer and asked me to repeat what I had said. I told him I had a new laptop in the truck, asked him if he wanted to buy it before I sold it to someone else. I told him the price. Then sirens had echoed and passed. Now we were back to haggling in the rain.

He evaluated me from shoes to eyes and asked, "Are you Egyptian?"

"Am I Egyptian? Are we in Egypt?"

"You look Egyptian."

"I'm part broke and part black, all mixed with hard times and frustration."

He looked down his nose at my uniform, my face. "Your tongue is pierced."

"Yeah. So what?"

"What do you do at Best Buy?"

"That's not important. You want to buy the MacBook or not?"

A frigid breeze kicked in and chilled his condescending attitude.

His phone buzzed. He held it up, read a message, then scowled at the traffic.

I asked, "Need to go so soon?"

"A long text message from my wife."

"You okay? Look like you just received bad news."

"She's just arrived at a hospital."

"Is she okay?"

"Distraught. Family friend had an accident. Someone close to both our families."

"Do you need to go to her?"

"I'm not a doctor. Nothing I can do but watch her break down and cry."

"Need to text her back?"

"She's type-A, not a woman that many men can date, let alone marry, because she is always stressed out. She will have a fit if I don't respond right away. For her, everything's urgent. So I won't."

"Type-A. She's the type of person who loves to win at everything."

"She is."

"You know how she is, and you're going to leave her anxious. That's cold."

"Cold like winter in Siberia."

"So do you want the computer or not? You're making me miss out on other customers."

"Tell me again, how did you manage to get a brand-new MacBook Pro?"

I turned up my jacket collar, shivered, shifted from one hard-toe shoe to the other, and told him I worked the stockroom over in Hawthorne, just east of the 405. It was a rainy Wednesday night and I had been sent on deliveries. Despite Amazon running the

15

world, I told him, Best Buy still did drop-offs.

The man in the gray suit asked, "How'd you manage to come across that . . . that laptop?"

"Told you. They had an extra one. I went over the electronic invoice and it wasn't listed. So it fell into a black hole. I never signed for this one. It won't be reported. It will simply vanish from the database. My dilemma is trying to decide if I am going to take it back and get somebody in trouble for the screwup, or see this as a sign and sell it and make enough money to pay my rent this month."

"You're short on your rent."

"Most of my income goes to paying frickin' rent. Like everybody else in L.A., I'm always short."

I had said too much. That admission gave him bargaining power.

Another police car zoomed by, forced angry people to pull to the right, made a bad traffic evening a lot more frustrating. The siren was so loud I had to wait for the downside of the noise to go on talking.

He asked, "How much is your rent?"

"Dude, it's cold out here, and it's raining. Half the people in L.A. are coughing and the other half have the flu. So before I end

16

up getting sick as a dog, do you want to buy the MacBook Pro or not?"

"Might be a way that I could help you out."

"I'm only bargaining with the laptop. Nothing else is for sale."

He said, "Three hundred. Take it or leave it."

"Six. That's my bottom line."

"So you better take that stolen computer to eBay."

I was about to curse him, but he pulled his wallet out and let me see a fresh row of greenbacks inside. Couldn't remember when I'd had that much cash and it wasn't being used to pay a bill.

I said, "You can afford the six. This laptop cost over two grand. Don't rip me off."

"I could afford to go the Apple Store and buy one brand-new with a full warranty."

"Do better than three hundred. Three hundred is below Black Friday prices."

"You're a pretty woman."

"I'm almost as pretty as that silver wedding ring on your left hand."

"You're wearing a pretty nice ring as well."

"On my right hand."

"Why is it on your right hand?"

"Because it won't fit on the middle finger of my left hand."

"But that is a wedding righty, right?"

"Your ring is on your left hand. That means you bought the cow."

"Yours on the right hand means?"

"It means I'm no one's cow. So where's your cow? Where's the woman you make go moo?"

He said, "We're estranged. I guess that would be the best way to put it at the moment."

"At the moment? What, you're estranged until you get home? Then you make her go moo?"

"It's been a long day for me; a long day with lots of driving and lots of stress, and anger, and too much drama. This traffic is starting to look like they're evacuating Los Angeles. We're both going to be trapped in this dull city. Let's go somewhere warm and dry and grab a bite to eat and talk about it."

I said, "Buy your wife this laptop, maybe stop by 7-Eleven and pick up a hot dog, find her some crotchless lingerie at the ninety-nine-cent store, go to redtube.com and look at some hot porn by Belle Knox or Lisa Ann, role-play, and I guarantee you that by tomorrow evening you two will be tight."

"Mind if I take a look at the merchandise first?"

"It's hot off the press and still factory-sealed. So, yeah, I mind the box being opened."

"Mind if I check out the five million pixels and retina display that's better than HDTV?"

"I'm in a rush. You can open the box when you get home."

"I can't do it now? I can't open what you're selling me from Best Buy now?"

His tone darkened, sent a chill up my spine.

He repeated, "Open the box. Let me turn the computer on."

I didn't back down. "Open your wallet."

"Show me what you're selling."

"Show me the money."

"Let's see the laptop that Best Buy lost in the system."

"I'm not opening the box for you until I have the money in my hand."

"Two thousand. I'll give you top dollar for a stolen laptop."

I paused, nose wanting to run, shivering, hunger pangs gripping my belly. "What's the catch?"

"If I open that box and there is actually a laptop in there, a brand-new MacBook Pro, and it has the paperwork, and it turns on, you get the two grand. If it doesn't power up, or if you're trying to do a version of the old rocks-in-a-box scam, then it's a new game. So, who's zooming who here?"

"Nobody is trying to run game."

He said, "But if it's not a laptop, two

hundred for a blow job."

"You're disgusting. And someone married your ass?"

"You're leaving? I thought we had a transaction going on here."

"Have a good life, and tell the cow you make go moo I send my sympathies."

"Hold up."

I said, "Don't come any closer."

He put his hand on my jacket. I thought he was attacking me, but he just stuck something in my jacket pocket. His hand felt my breast when he did it. I went ballistic.

I snapped, "Don't touch me. I don't friggin' know you like that."

I allowed what I had in my jacket sleeve to slide down to my hand. The box cutter.

If so many people hadn't been around, if it had been only him, I would've cut him deep.

There was a camera. Traffic wouldn't allow me to escape. I wasn't much of a runner.

I snapped, "This is America, asshole, and touching me like that is sexual harassment."

He said, "Look, I might have come at you wrong."

"*Might* have? Really? Your disgusting ass tries to get a blow job for two hundred and you grabbed my breast and you *might* have come at me wrong?"

"By accident. I touched the tits by accident."

"What is your issue? I'm not a whore. Go screw your goddamn mother, asshole."

I reached into my pocket and looked at what he had crammed inside. It could have been scraps of paper with less value than shinplaster, as worthless as a Canadian twenty-five-cent bill. But it was American money; hundred-dollar bills. I counted them quickly. Twenty one-hundred-dollar bills.

My hands and voice shook. "What the hell are you expecting for this much money?"

"Merry Christmas."

"You're serious?"

"And I hope you have a happier New Year than I'm going to have."

This was a setup. I knew this was a setup, but I didn't know what kind of setup this was.

I said, "Damn. I knew it. You're an undercover cop."

He reached into his pocket, and I waited for him to flash his badge and ask me to turn around so he could put me under arrest. But he took out a gray business card and handed it to me.

He loosened his tie, took the box, said,

"Sure this isn't a MacBook Pro?"

"Disgusting. You're disgusting. You should drop to your knees and apologize."

"For what? Looks like you came out on the winning end of this con game."

"You insulted me. Suck your pathetic dick for two hundred? I don't care how much money you give me — that was the most insulting thing you can say to a woman, besides calling her a cunt."

He barked, "You insulted me first."

I barked back at him, "How did I insult you?"

"I saw you across the street. You watched me. You picked me to be your target."

"You saw me?"

"You pulled up into the gas station, eyes on me. Twenty other people here buying gas, and you looked at my car, jumped out of your pickup, came right to me, hurried to get to me before I left, came to me smiling like an innocent little girl, all fake, trying to be a sweet, sweet, sweet grifter. You picked me. So give me a goddamn break. You tried to con me. You insulted me first. Act like a con, and then expect to be treated like what, a lady? Act like a con and get treated with the respect you deserve."

I snapped, "Take your money back."

"The box is mine. I'll go home, give this

to my unworthy wife as a Christmas present. She loves presents more than anything in the world. I'll watch her open it and see what it does for our marriage."

"You're going to give it to your wife?"

"Perfect timing. She surprised me with one of my Christmas presents this morning. We usually do that twelve-days-of-Christmas thing, but we're skipping it this year. Got mine early. So this will be one of hers. Was going to try to get to our cabin in Big Bear and go skiing — lots of snow coming in. Was going to be me, her, her second dad, and his new girlfriend, but I think this will be a better present."

"You're joking. You are not giving that to your wife."

"Unopened. Might slap a pretty little bow on it and buy her a nice Christmas card to boot."

"No. Don't. Look."

"My wife loves presents more than anything in the world."

"It's two kitchen tiles with a printout of a computer on both sides."

"You should've used one tile. Then the weight would've been about right. Don't quit your day job."

"Give it back."

I stood there with his money in my hand,

angry, now all but begging him to give me rocks in a box for a smooth two grand. Wasn't a thrill; there was no win if he knew it was a con. Honestly, I would've taken three hundred for the box, but he looked wealthy, so I had played hardball and doubled my price the way stores at The Grove overcharge for the same rags that will sell at T.J.Maxx in six months.

He asked, "Which one of these guys pumping gas here is your accomplice?"

"I'm alone. This was a spur-of-the-moment decision."

"That's not smart."

"I'm tougher than I look."

"A lot of dead women have said that."

"I'm more vigilant and tougher than a lot of dead women."

"How much is your rent?"

"Not as much as your car note."

"How much?"

After a few stubborn breaths, I said, "Eight twenty-five a month."

"How far behind?"

"Two months."

"That's rough. You're about to be evicted."

I said, "Was about to be. I just need to get my second wind, time to think, that's all."

"Then you'll be able to pay your rent."

"Don't do this."

"Do what?"

"Go from being the King of the Assholes to being . . . being all nice."

The rain fell a little harder. Cold, damp wind blew the disgusting flavor of the city in my face, sent drops of rain into my open mouth. Tonight this area tasted like tongue-kissing a girl with bad breath while she had mushrooms, eggplant, and semen in her mouth. Even in the rain the streets smelled like dogs humping, a pack of lions, butt crack, and a cheap dentist's office in the far reaches of Pacoima.

He took a breath. "Ever heard of a place out in the Valley called Houghmagandy?"

"Afraid not. I don't party out that way anymore. Don't really party at all."

"Ever heard of a place called Decadence?"

I said, "Why do you keep looking at me like something is wrong with me?"

"Does that piercing hurt your tongue?"

"Stop looking at my mouth. Eye contact or look at the ground — those are your options."

"Part of me just wishes that I actually had a chance to have a conversation with you."

"Why would a guy like you want to talk to a girl like me on a night like this?"

"To vent. To see if I'm wrong."

"You probably are, but I'm sure you can

afford to hire a professional to sort that out."

"Would rather talk to you, a regular person, to get a woman's perspective."

"To talk down on your wife with the same mouth you eat her hairy pussy with?"

"Just to talk and figure out things. For a moment, part of me wanted to talk."

"The part of you that needs a two-hundred-dollar thrill from a woman on her knees."

"Look, if I wanted to get sucked off, I'd stay in the 714, not come up to this filthy county. And she would be much prettier than you. Okay, I shouldn't have said that. Despite you coming at me like you thought I was an idiot, I should not have offered you cash for fellatio. At least not that much cash. Fifty is the going rate for a piece of ass; less if I went to Santa Ana and picked up a Vietnamese whore."

"Go to hell."

More sirens. This parade of police more severe, a carnival of bad news approaching. The man from Orange County reacted with heavy breathing, more intense than before, like he had a fear of sirens. Only he was tense, like he was witnessing a balloon being blown up, watching it get overblown, and waiting for it to explode. His eyes followed the police cars until they disappeared.

My eyes did the same.

The man from Orange County didn't move. His cell phone rang, and that broke his trance, but he didn't answer, only hurried away from me. He took his package and opened his vehicle, dropped the box inside, then hopped in his car without looking back. His car started, the lights came on, and then the engine revved and he pulled away, into the mess of vehicles on Carson Boulevard, but ended up twenty feet away. He was stuck. His lips moved rapidly, expressed bottomless anger as he talked.

6:42 P.M.

L.A. was a beautiful woman with a complex soul, a woman who had good intentions but had learned to be loyal only to herself, because she was all she had. L.A. was a bitch, and I related to her. I really did.

I sat in the battered white truck for a moment, in shock, two thousand dollars in my right hand.

Christmas songs came from every car that pulled in at the gas station. Sensory overload. This whole season was sensory overload, and was hitting me harder than it had last year. I just wanted to get to the twenty-sixth, wanted to get to the other side of Christmas and Christmas trees and joy and excited children.

I didn't want to be around people, and at the same time I didn't want to be alone.

The white truck at my disposal, I started its engine with a screwdriver. The truck's radio played an all-news station. Same news

I had heard ten times since I had been in the streets this afternoon. A thirtysomething woman in Torrance had stabbed her three children. The oldest of the brood was only three years old. I spaced out. The news went on, said that near Malibu an older hotshot businessman — a prominent gentleman in his fifties — had been found beaten. It was the time of year for robberies, a Christmas tree being a sign of brand-new goods in the home, and they thought the guy had walked in on someone trying to burgle his home. Teenagers in the Dominguez Hills area had been arrested as masterminds of a sex-trafficking and prostitution ring; they had used social media to bait Asian girls. There were more horrid stories like that, the rest mostly shootings, because people in California love their guns as much as they love their cars. I sat staring at the rain, stuck on the news about the mother who'd broken down and killed her kids. Three babies had been slaughtered. All I could wonder was what could make a mother harm her children like that, when being a mother was hard, but the best thing in the world.

I turned the radio off. Didn't care about that bad news because it wasn't my bad news.

Moments later I ditched the stolen truck

— dumped it about a block away, closer to the casino. I had stolen it from the grounds of the casino, so I wanted to go a few more blocks, but the traffic had a mental disorder, and I didn't want to be in a hot ride too much longer. That jerk from Orange County could've been on his phone calling the local police, could've been giving them all my info.

I still wouldn't put it past him to claim he had been robbed. Two thousand dollars would make me a felon, and being a felon would send my life on a trajectory I couldn't imagine, so I remained on edge. California lawmen are as nice as rattlesnakes, only there is antivenom for rattlesnakes. There are still a few loons with badges putting people into permanent sleep in both L.A. and Orange County.

Like I'd been taught by Vernon when I was growing up, I wiped away my finger-prints, then hurried back west. Accident up ahead. Two cars. One on fire. Plenty of looky-loos. I didn't gaze at the accident as I walked by. Didn't want to see a dead body. Didn't want to see anyone on fire, never again. I held my breath, averted my eyes, moved as fast as I could. Hot and sweaty, heart beating like a beast demanding to be freed, I caught my breath at the Denny's parking lot. That was where I had left my true ride, my first car note, my candy-white convertible Beetle. The filthy car was four years old. I bought it when it was a year old from a certified pre-owned VW dealer. That car had been an important purchase, the only serious purchase I'd ever made in my life; probably more important today because it was a safe car. And it was a convertible. It made me a true L.A. girl. My entry into the world of ragtops. Only had forty thousand miles on the odometer. I had been approved for my own loan. Didn't need a cosigner. Was independent. We loved that car. I still did. I still loved the car.

More sirens came closer, then the sound faded. More flashing lights did the same.

I went to my VW, removed my ratchet wig, let my long, healthy dreadlocks hang, ran my hand over my damp hair and evened it out. My mane had been washed and braided until yesterday, so now my locks were *über*-curly. I called them my Ledisi locks, like the badass singer. I fixed my hair, then tossed my damp jean jacket into the backseat; it landed in the child seat, then tumbled to the floor, where it mixed with about two dozen Barbie dolls, broken Happy Meal toys, stale french fries, and only God knows how many types of crumbs.

I looked at my phone. No call, no text, no Facebook, no tweet, no Instagram, nothing from my boyfriend. Anxiety, irritation, and disappointment combined and changed into anger, mumbles, sighs, curses, and head shakes. I was about to text him again. Was tired of chasing him, like cat chasing dog. Had texted him so much I felt like I was a stalker. Was going to ask him to meet me at Roscoe's Chicken & Waffles, tell him the Obama Special and Arnold Palmer would be my treat tonight. He'd complain about the rain. He wouldn't want to meet me in the rain. But I was antsy. Couldn't stand this weather, couldn't bear the combination of dreariness and yuletide solitude, so as the world shopped to buy Jesus nothing for his birthday, I texted my boyfriend and told him that chicken and waffles would be my treat. I told him that I wouldn't talk his ear off tonight about Natalie Rose, told him I was in a good mood and really needed to see him this evening, then added a few *X*s and *O*s.

I waited two minutes. No response. That was my third message since eight this morning.

Yesterday was no more. Today was what it was. Tomorrow could only be better.

I pulled the money out, looked at the

twenty hundred-dollar bills, counted them twice.

I had money. I could pay my friggin' rent. I could by a tank of gas for my goddamn car. Could get my hair done by Sheba. Could buy two-ply. Could splurge at Whole Foods before I settled my big bills. I wanted to live and eat like I used to live and eat for a week. Needed to let food be my medicine and let my medicine be healthy food. No. I wanted Whole Foods, wanted that status, but Whole Foods took up whole paychecks and was too expensive for a chick like me. I'd use my Whole Foods bags and go to the Food Barn and buy survival food at reasonable prices, let my malicious neighbors see me coming back home with three Whole Foods bags filled to the top. If I played it smart, I'd survive another month.

The rain. The wintry chill. The desire to not be alone until the sun came up.

But sometimes it was better to be alone. Nobody could hurt you.

My boyfriend. I broke down and called him. No answer. Didn't leave a message. I took out the card from the guy at the gas station, ignored his name but looked at his number.

I called him. No idea why. But I looked at the digits, at that area code from a faraway land, and I dialed his area code, exchange, and number, and listened to it ring once before he answered.

"Good evening. How may I help?"

I said, "It's me."

"Who is 'me'? This call came up blocked."

"Guess I'm lucky you answered."

"Who is this?"

"The girl you just met at the gas station."

"The grifter who tried to con me, threatened me, and cursed me out."

"The one and only woman who went off on a well-dressed insult in a suit."

"What can I do for you?"

"Wanted to say thanks."

"Still think I'm disgusting?"

"Men are worthless, so that hasn't changed."

"We may be, but you can't live without us."

"You love your wife?"

"Love is a fire. But whether it is going to warm your heart or burn down your house, you can never tell. Joan Crawford said that. And that is where I am now, in a house that is burning down."

"I don't care for that quote."

"It's true. For me, it's true."

"How did you mess up?"

"What do you mean?"

"There are two hundred and ninety-two ways to make change for a dollar using pennies, nickels, dimes, quarters, and half dollars. There are twice as many ways to piss a woman off."

"Then there must be three times as many ways to make a man walk away from a woman."

"You have an answer for everything."

"Actually, no. I have more questions than answers. I'm good in my office. I'm great at work. My problem has always been in the social arena. I really don't know much about the heart of a woman."

"Anyway, I just wanted to say thanks. And wish you a Merry Christmas."

"Do you really work at Best Buy?"

"No. And don't give that present to your wife. That's why I called. That's really bugging me."

"Didn't think you worked at Best Buy. The outfit really doesn't fit you."

"Stole it. Some Mexican guy left it in the laundry room where I live."

"Well, what you're doing now, give it up. You're too pretty for jail."

"I'm too pretty to catch a city bus, but I do take that risk from time to time."

He asked, "Since you're not Egyptian, where are you from?"

"I grew up on a farm in Kansas, but before that, after my mom and dad were killed in a dark alley following a night at the theater, I was put inside a spaceship and sent to this planet, where I was bitten by a radioactive spider, so now when I get mad I turn green and get as big as the Jolly Green Giant."

"Yeah. Right. Just when I felt bad and wished I had met you at Starbucks."

"Do you really wish you had met me at Starbucks?"

"Would've been nice to have met you and maybe chatted over coffee."

"Was nice of you to say that, if you meant it."

"I meant it."

"If not, still nice of you to tell that lie. It's the time of year when people lie a lot, so it's cool."

"A chance meeting at Starbucks could've been a much better first impression for both of us."

"That's another part of the reason I called you."

"What do you mean?"

"I called you because . . . this version of me . . . tonight . . . this is not me at my best."

"Not me at my best, either. Today is not

37

the day you'd want to be my friend."

"Life has been hard on me. The last couple of years, maybe three, have been trying."

"Sorry to hear that."

"In public, around people, you at your best, me at my best, would you have approached me?"

"No. But I would've spoken, been friendly and said a thing or two, nothing remarkable, then would've sat down and enjoyed looking at you, admired you until someone better-looking walked in."

I said, "I probably wouldn't have noticed you."

"Probably not."

"Where are you right now?"

"On the 605. Was trying to get to the 91. Only made it to the next exit."

"There is a Denny's off the 605, city of Lakewood side, at the Carson exit."

"What's up?"

"Want to eat, but don't want to sit in a restaurant and eat alone."

"Is that an invitation?"

"I get migraines real bad if I don't eat, and I feel silly sitting in public places by myself."

"Do you want company? Is that why you called?"

"What's the real deal with your wife?"

"What do you mean?"

"Is it that you're not getting any? You're rich and think you're entitled to any poor chick on the side of the road? You want to know if you've still got it? You couldn't control yourself? Or is it that your wife disgusts you because she gained weight and can't get her chi together? Or you just don't love her anymore?"

"That sounded personal. Was that your issue with whoever you were seeing?"

"No reverse psychology. Answer me. How did you get to your current state of misery?"

"I'll sum it up. She pushed for commitment. She got what she wanted. She lost interest in sex. I began to wonder if she was interested in someone else a long time ago, wondered if she was either physically or emotionally cheating. The marriage has basically been vacillating for the past few months."

"Is your little Ann Coulter attracted to someone else?"

"I married a good girl. I married a church-going woman. I married the perfect résumé."

"What did you do to make the marriage get that way?"

"Always the man's fault. Men are blind to

the things that women can do."

"Always *is* the man's fault. Cause and effect. So, entertain me with your tale of woe."

"You want me to sit in traffic and have this type of profound conversation?"

"If you feel like coming back this way, to casino town, it's an invitation to talk face-to-face."

"You're not planning on robbing me, are you?"

"I've already robbed you."

"I was robbed long before I met you."

"You haven't been robbed until you're robbed by me."

"You plan on robbing me again?"

"Come back to Denny's and see."

7:27 P.M.

As rain flooded the parking lot, I sat in a pleather-covered booth at the Denny's in Lakewood.

Two thousand dollars were in my pocket. I still expected the money to be counterfeit.

I was wearing a golden Lakers jacket. Had owned it almost five years and it showed. I dug in my purse, took out a worn paperback by Asimov so I'd look like a studious, rather than desperate, chick. And it gave me a reason to keep my head down, mind my own business, and not make eye contact with random guys that could be misconstrued as more than two people in the pointless universe who happen to be looking in opposing directions at the same moment. I had come in alone and a couple of guys had checked me out, had looked at me like they were thirsty and wanted to sip from this Coke bottle. Those guys were with girls. They were disgusting for doing that. There

were a dozen booths and tables. I wasn't
the only person who was alone, but there
were plenty of people rushing to grub. Gear
associated with every university or junior
college or sports team that had ever been
part of Southern California covered the
heads and bodies of most, that gear being
the tuxedos and suits of the area.

The news was on, and I was once again
pulled in by the story of the mother who
had killed her three babies. I fell into that
story, into a trance, wondering what the
mother's mental issue was that she would
do something so horrible at this time of the
year, wondering if that monster called
Depression had its hooks so deep in her that
she lost it. I was in a zone of numbness until
a server passed by, shocking me with the
heat from a flaming meal being carried on a
tray. The fire felt like it had leapt and taken
to my skin. I screamed, threw my book
down, jumped up, slapped my arm a dozen
times, checked my dreadlocks, looked for
the flames, and made sure I wasn't being
burned alive.

The smell of burnt flesh.

Fire ignited a memory that sent a chill
down my spine. I stood there, in front of
everyone, eyes wide, the news mixing with
chatter and clatter from utensils against

plates. I wasn't on fire. I picked up my book, pulled my dreadlocks from my face, checked them again. There was no fire. I sat back down. The waitress dropped off her order, then hurried back, apologized for startling me. By then I was back in control, but still off-kilter and a little ashamed. She wore dark makeup and dark lipstick and had dark tattoos, body piercings, and a rebellious, gothic appearance. She was sexy. I liked her look a lot.

I said, "No problem. I think I startled you as much as you frightened me."

She ran her hand over her blond-and-red Mohawk, studied my face, and said, "You look familiar. Wanted to say that when you came in. Now that you've put on makeup and stuff, you really look familiar. I know that face from somewhere. Swear I do."

I fake-grinned a bit. I had gone to the ladies' room and transformed from hard grifter to very feminine. MAC Strobe cream. Nivea eye primer. Garnier BB cream. Estée Lauder Double Wear Stay-in-Place concealer. Chanel Vitalumière Aqua. Had used powder to set the concealer. MAC bronzing powder. Lumene brow gel. Cranberry lip liner. Snowberry lipstick. Mary Kay berry fresh lip gloss. Added length to my lashes with Clinique extreme. The cosmetics I had

had been bought on Crenshaw Boulevard after somehow falling off the back of a Macy's truck. Being broke and looking broke are two different things. I had styled my dreadlocks, made them look a little wavy, loose, and fancy. I looked like a hipster, a professional hipster who lived on the West Side or in Culver City. I did it to be ready to go see my chicken-and-waffles-loving sex partner. Plus, if the man from Orange County returned, I didn't want him to see me as feral, as savage.

I told the waitress, "Sweetheart, I've had more than a few jobs. Way more than a few."

"Were you in a film?"

"Did student films at UCLA, USC, and all the community colleges. Few small nonunion movies. Had parts in a few indie projects. Did a commercial for the Gap about four years ago. Nothing major."

"Something is different about you, and it's not the hair. You gained a little weight?"

"I was a size zero back then. Was either a vegan or juicing and living in 24 Hour Fitness."

"I knew you were an actress. I mean, everyone around here is, but you carry yourself like one."

"Based on my W-2, not really. I'm a substitute teacher."

"At least you have a job. All the other actors I know work here or at Starbucks."

"Sweetheart, I've worked every restaurant from the Valley down to Crenshaw Boulevard."

She laughed. "You should be a comedian, I love the way you say things."

"I was a comic. I gave doing stand-up a shot. Went at it hard for three years. Made it to being a middle act at some spots, meaning I was on stage for thirty minutes. Hard business for a woman."

"You're a natural. I bet you had everybody applauding your jokes and stuff."

"Behind the scenes ain't fun. Promoters fail to pay. Men try to screw you, and women are jealous if you get two laughs more than them. Did lots of stage time in dive bars that run blenders over your setup and punch line. Some nights it would have been easier to teach a dog to meow and a cat to bark."

"You are too funny."

"I have my moments. I was a huge fan of Leonard DuBois. Modeled my career after his, but times have changed. Anyway, haven't been on stage or inside a comedy club in over two years."

"Wait a minute."

"What?"

"Was your hair long and blond back then?"

"Yeah. It was. That was back in my Brazilian hair days."

With a quizzical look on her face, she said, "Is your name Jackie?"

"Yeah. Wow. You know my name?"

"I saw you do comedy before. Oh my God."

"And you remember my weave and my name?"

"Because my name is Jackie, too. We have the same initials — that's why I remember your name."

"We have the same initials? What's your name?"

"I'm Jackie Faye Stevens. And your name . . . is it Jackie Francine Summer?"

"Close. Jacqueline Francesca Summers. But people call me Jackie, as you know."

"You said you worked in the Valley. My God, you're the one with the kid. The little girl that died."

I paused, lost the faux happiness in my tone. "Yeah."

"Your daughter, Natasha, in the fire up in the Valley or something."

"Natalie Rose. Her name is . . . was . . . Natalie Rose. I didn't think anyone noticed."

46

"Lord, how did that fire happen? I'm sorry — is it okay to ask you that?"

I nodded. "A Christmas tree. A spark from faulty wiring. A drunk father."

"That happens a lot."

"She was with her father. She was with my husband. Well, we had split. Divorce was in process. We divorced and contributed to the population of disassembled communities and broken families from coast to coast. So I guess that I could say she was with my estranged husband when it happened."

"You were supposed to be the next big thing in Hollywood."

"In black Hollywood. You can be famous in black Hollywood and no one in the world knows who you are. Anyway, before my daughter died, I was doing so much. Acting, stand-up, theater, auditioning, and still had to have a full-time job to pay the bills. And I was trying to be a good mommy. I was trying to do it all, be successful, and make money to care for my child. I had a . . . breakdown . . . when she died. None of that seemed important anymore. Nothing did, actually. Everything seemed so false."

"You were good, talented, and you're more beautiful than anyone on television. You should've been on one those shows

47

right now. Right now they love smart, strong black women on television."

"Thanks. Gabrielle Union took my spot for one television show."

"That wicked bitch."

"Then Lola Mack beat me out for a big part in a sci-fi film."

"Hollywood really should be after you."

"Hollywood, if they want me . . . I'm not hard to find. It's a different world for a black woman in Hollywood. Black and Hollywood have always been oil and water. The odds are never in our favor."

"That's too bad. How are things going?"

I shrugged, smiled, tried to not have a saturnine expression, said, "One day at a time."

"Every week, the same bullcrap all over. It's so damn hard to make it in America."

"So damn hard."

"Maybe you'll meet another nice guy and start over."

"I'm done with love, and not for the lack of trying. I've kicked the habit, and now I am free. Love ain't nothing but another progressive disease."

"What does that mean?"

"Progressive disease? That's like a physical illness whose development in most cases is the worsening, growth, or spread of the disease. Every day you're more dependent than the day before."

"Like an addiction?"

"Like alcohol. Like crack. Like cocaine. When we buy love we purchase our own pain. When you fall in love, you're depending on the person on the other side of the table to feed that addiction."

"That's weird."

"I'm weird."

"I like you. Stay weird."

"You do the same."

"Again, sorry about what happened to your little girl."

"Thanks, Jackie. Means a lot to hear you say that. Especially this time of the year."

"You're on Facebook?"

"My name on Facebook is Natalie's Mom."

"When I get to my phone, will look you up and send a friend request."

"I'll look for it."

"I'm getting off work. Have to do some Christmas shopping for my boys. I tell you — and I'm being honest — if I lost my boys, I'd buy some rope, or step out in front of a truck, or lie down on a train track."

She hurried away. Book lowered, I looked across the room, saw a young man with his little girl.

I almost started crying. Almost grabbed my things and left the joint. But the little girl smiled at me, made playful faces. I focused on her. I peeped through my fingers, made a dozen silly faces. She laughed. I made my lips move like I was singing the alphabet up to the el-em-en-o-pee part, then changed and lip-sang to her the Strawberry Shortcake song.

She laughed a little more before she went back to her father. He played with her.

I wished that she had come to me, to sit with me, to play with me.

I looked inside my bag, moved things aside, and saw what I was looking for — a bag of balloons in a rainbow of colors. Had been in my bag for more than two years. I was going to give the bag to the little girl, was going to lighten my load, but she was focused on her daddy now. I didn't intrude.

Time moved slowly, and I watched them for a moment. Watched with mild envy.

My father never played with me, not like I saw other dedicated fathers playing with their children. He never taught me to ride a bike. I had to learn on my own. I had to fall on my own. Get up on my own. Even when I lived with him, his second wife became the one in charge of my existence, and when he was around it was more like living with the friend of an uncle, and that friend of an uncle never gave me hugs and kisses. I was an inconvenience. Wasn't pretty enough for him. That was my foundation.

This rose grew from that rock in a world of backhanded compliments.

Backhanded compliments are as valuable and useful as a bag of three-dollar bills.

I saw Jackie moving around behind the counter. We made eye contact, smiled.

She put on her coat and hurried out the front door, to her family, to her boys.

I ran my hands over my dreadlocks, remembered when my hair used to be pressed, or permed. Conformity. Had to rub my eyes. I rubbed the tattooed flowers on my shoulder, and then I sighed.

I was starting to think the arrogant, affluent guy wasn't coming back to my world. I couldn't call him again, because after I had called the number on the business card, without reading the rest of his info, I had thrown it away, then had deleted his number from my phone. I did it in case later on I hooked up with my boyfriend and, for whatever reason, he decided to creep my history while I was sleeping and went through my phone, then woke me up wanting to know whom I had been calling. The man from Orange County had said that my number had come up blocked, which meant if he had changed his mind there was no way he could call me, either. He didn't have my name, didn't have my number — he only had the box of tiles I had sold him. I was about to get up and leave when xenon lights exited the 605 at Carson, turned right, and pulled into the parking lot. Those headlights announced the arrival of the luxury car. I saw him when he pulled up and found a place to park right out front. Lucky bastard wouldn't have to walk far in the weather. Seemed like the rich got all the perks. I sat back down. Wished I hadn't called. I put my Asimov away, saw a wealth of red and blue flashing lights, heard more sirens shrieking this way, and felt high-strung, like a reluctant criminal. Imagined him arriving with the police. Imagined him bringing them inside and pointing me out as the con, the thief. This was a random dude, the man I had tried to run a con on. This was the man who had offered me two hundred dollars to perform fellatio.

The clock on the wall announced that it was 7:35.

7:36 P.M.

The man from Orange County came in from the rain, brushed water from the shoulders of his gray suit coat, wiped the soles of his deep-brown shoes on the dirty mat. Sartorial elegance. He handled himself with a self-assurance that made him stand out as he stood near the cash register like he was a damp bawcock, a handsome rooster. A couple in the first booth was loud now, the woman louder than the man. She wasn't happy about something, and he was unhappy that she was unhappy while he tried to eat his dinner. The man from Orange County looked down at them, shook his head, then took a step and scanned the room. The wail of sirens faded, as did the illumination of their red and blue lights.

I took a breath, sighed, regretted that I had called him, then put on the golden no-nonsense Jackie face, nodded, and waved for him to come over. He still didn't realize that I was the same girl. I had changed my clothing; rather than an oversize Best Buy uniform, I had on glasses, purple Timberland Nellie Chukka Doubles, and black jeggings under a fitted, sleeveless, flowered dress, so he could see my true shape as well as my eclectic style, which gave the middle finger to the coldness of winter. I stood up for a moment. I waved at him again. His eyes locked on me, and he saw that I had dreadlocks, black, a few light brown and Rihanna red, all down and loose; most cascaded down my back. He did a double take, still wasn't sure. I stuck my tongue out, showed my tongue ring. He nodded, then came from the counter area past three booths and just as many tables. I stood. We shook hands, like it was a business meeting, then he stared at me. He still wasn't sure it was me. He evaluated my dreadlocks, my face. Was taken aback. I felt like I was at an audition. I became a new kind of uneasy, felt my heart in my mouth, experienced a heightened state of anxiety, experienced fear, and to hide that sensation I created a smile.

I sat down and said, "You came back. I'm surprised."

He said, "At least three games are on, and they're playing the local news in here."

"I would think they'd be playing a basket-ball or football game."

"So you don't think they will change the channel?"

"Not with all these people so into the news."

He unbuttoned his suit coat, eased into the opposite side of the booth, and said, "You look different."

I stuck my tongue out again. He saw the piercing.

He nodded. "Still wouldn't have recog-nized the new face."

I said, "Going to see my boyfriend in a little while. Had to change and put my face on."

"Pink fingernails are the only things that look the same."

"Oh, yeah. My favorite color. I always wear a splash of pink."

"Didn't see your white truck in the park-ing lot."

"Wasn't my white truck. I borrowed it for a while."

"A night of crimes and cons."

"Walk into any store. Shoplifters galore. Seems to be the season made for breaking the law."

He said, "Rocks in a box."

"You said that someone got to you before I did."

"Ten years ago. I was in Newport Beach and a white surfer guy approached me at a strip mall and offered me a bargain on a brand-new VCR, microwave oven, and TV. Said he worked for a trucking firm. He showed me what looked like good merchandise, all of it still packaged in the original boxes."

"All of these boxes were sealed in plastic, with a picture of the item on the box."

"Just like yours. Of course he was in a hurry, just like you were, and we made the transaction fast, the same way you wanted to make your exchange. The déjà vu inspired some of my anger."

"Which did you buy from the white surfer guy? And saying *white* and *surfer* really sounds redundant, by the way."

"Everything. I bought everything. VCR, microwave, and a TV."

"Damn. You are a low-level con man's dream date."

He nodded. "It was close to Christmas, so I went home and wrapped everything up without opening the boxes. I took it to my girlfriend's place, put it under her Christmas tree."

"Oh, no."

"She opened the boxes on Christmas morning, in front of her family, and found a lot of rocks."

"What did she say?"

"She called me that morning screaming, and I hurried to her place. And as Mariah Carey sang a Christmas song, I stood between my girlfriend at the time and her parents and relatives, looking down at a mountain of dirty rocks. They had made a pyramid. I thought they were joking with me, but the way she was crying, telling me I had ruined her Christmas, all I could do was tell her what had happened. When I told her and her family what I had done, how I had been conned, she told me I was stupid and cheap. That from a woman who had a bootleg of every movie made since *Gone with the Wind*."

"What you lost in money was worth it. You learned a lot about her that day."

"Learned she was self-centered and immature and had no empathy. That's funny to you?"

"Hell, yeah. Nothing like a breakup on Christmas morning. Crying over her presents like it was her birthday? She forgot who died for her sins. Hypocrites. You and your rocks in a box. Her with all those bootleg movies. Stockpiling bootleg movies? You dated a felon. And you're judging me? Both of you were hypocrites. Honest, law-abiding citizens will put their morals on hold to get a good deal."

"You've done it before."

"Few years ago, I did a little thing in Santa Barbara and sold an iPad for two hundred. Did a fifteen-hundred-dollar notebook for a couple hundred. Had both in shrink-wrap, so they looked legit."

"People are pretty stupid. If I hadn't been taken before, you would've had me tonight."

"People don't care where it comes from. They're as bad as the ones who steal it. That's how Bernie Madoff scored billions, and that's how every other pyramid scammer got his cash. From the honest, yet greedy. From hypocrites. People know it's too good to be true, but fall for it anyway."

Feeling warm, I took my Lakers jacket off. The sleeveless dress allowed him to see that my left arm had tats of roses from my shoulder to just below my elbow.

He nodded, took a breath. "You've turned your body into a canvas."

Again uncomfortable, I asked, "You have tats?"

"Nah. My family thinks tats are for sailors, convicts, and the lower class."

"Your family — are they Christian?"

"They are. And to prove it, they go to church every Sunday, except Easter."

"Funny how the most agreeable people you meet will have body art, will be covered in tattoos, and the most judgmental assholes in the world are the first to run to church on Sunday."

"Except Easter."

"Except the day the ones who don't go to church buy new shoes and suits and dresses and go like they're going to a prom featuring Jesus. Yeah, that really changes my perception of them."

"Guess I'll change the subject."

"Would hate to have to call your wife and tell her you were crucified in Denny's."

He looked at my midsection. "Your waistline."

"It's small. Makes it impossible to buy jeans or slacks that fit me properly."

"Gives you incredible definition."

"Raise the level of the conversation, or go back to Orange County."

"You upgraded yourself. Mind if I get over looking at you? Beauty can be shocking."

His phone buzzed. He lowered his head and looked at it. Became uneasy. He read the message, remained uneasy. He put his phone down and made himself as comfortable as he could.

I said, "Your shirt is pink. Wasn't it white at the gas station?"

"I changed shirts. Had the other one on all day."

"Pink looks nice on you."

"Is that a compliment?"

"Not really. I still think you're disgusting."

I took my glasses off, put them away. Didn't want to look too nerdy.

I said, "Your right hand. Your knuckles look bruised."

"Hit a wall."

"The eye?"

"Caught the edge of a racquetball racquet early this morning."

"You play?"

"Not that well."

"Obviously."

The waitress came and rushed us to order; overworked, under-tipped, and possessing no social graces. She left and we looked at each other and shrugged at the attitude of Miss Bah Humbug. We started talking like we were normal people. He was a tech head, and within three sentences he learned that technical advancements didn't interest me. He'd rather talk about the astrophysicist Neil deGrasse Tyson than a Sunday-morning speech from a pulpit. I'd rather have a serious talk about independent films and the history of Hollywood or existentialism or Sartre. Within five minutes we knew we were extreme opposites, yet we enjoyed each other's company, and I found it humorous. Left-brain thinkers and right-brain thinkers — that intellectual arroyo is so wide. He glanced at the television off and on as we talked, and it felt like politics and culture were the things that he liked to talk about. These were my Poverty Soup days. Politics and pointless conversations about self-destructive cultures didn't interest me. Then we moved on and talked about art. Something he said about a trip to Cuba triggered that conversation. I told him the sculpture of Rita Longa fascinated me, how she had dedicated her entire life to her work, how she knew where she belonged in the world, and how I had always wished that I had that kind of talent. How I hadn't found my purpose yet. I mentioned creator Juan José Sicre and the studios of Isabel Chapotin before I moved on to painter Eduardo Abela, then René Portocarrero.

I said, "Once upon a time, before the tattoos, I posed nude for an art class."

"How did you pose?"

"Was in a position like the sculpture *Triángulo* from 1936. Google it."

He used his iPhone to pull up the image. Then he held the phone between us while we chatted.

My hand accidentally touched his. Then his hand unintentionally grazed mine.

It was his second time touching me tonight. This time, it wasn't offensive.

His energy was strong, sent currents, made the fine hairs on the back of my neck dance.

He said, "Your callipygian backside fits your frame and definitely makes your body look like art."

"For me it's all in the spine."

"What do you mean?"

"I have what you call swayback, so that mild curve makes my rear more pronounced."

"We called that saddleback when I was growing up."

"Same thing. I hate it because people say the exaggerated curve resembles the back of a horse, right about where the saddle fits. Mine isn't that exaggerated, but it's there, and I've heard all the jokes. Yeah, you could make a lot of jokes about *saddle* and *rear end* and *riding*. Lots of jokes that would not be funny. Anyway, this dirty old man once told me that I had an ass like an ecdysiast. I cursed him out."

"Ecdysiast. That's just a fancy word for *stripper."*

I said, "An ecdysiast is a striptease performer or exotic dancer, not a two-dollar stripper."

"But you cursed an old man out for saying that? You curse out old people?"

"Old people used to be young people, and just because you have age doesn't mean you have wisdom or tact. I didn't know what the word meant at the time. If I see him again, I might apologize. Maybe not. Not cool for an old man to walk up to me, then start talking about my butt. Not cool at all."

"When I said your callipygian rear was nice, it was a compliment, an observation, not a come-on."

"Callipygian is just another five-dollar word for *ass."*

"It's not a noun; it's an adjective used to describe shapely buttocks."

"What so funny?"

"Buttocks is a funny word. Butt. Tocks. Sounds funny."

"When Forrest Gump says it, and you're no Forrest Gump."

"You have been blessed with a voluptuous form and an especially callipygian backside, one that no doubt makes and leaves an impression wherever you may sit. See?

Adjective, not noun."

"Change the subject or go dance in the rain."

"I made a joke and complimented your *callipygian* figure at the same time."

"It wasn't funny. And for the record for all I know that word could mean anything."

"And for the record, at Syracuse they named the statue of Aphrodite *kallipygos*, and that word comes from the Greek adjective *kallos* meaning *beauty*. *Pyge* is a noun that means *buttocks*."

"I don't care."

"I like that word."

"I don't. You don't just meet a woman and start talking about her ass."

"Saying a woman has a callipygian backside is not the same as a cheap lust-filled compliment. I am only acknowledging that you have the callipygian rondure observed in the islands and Africa."

"Stop making an ass of yourself and making me become the butt of your intellectual booty jokes."

"I digress. And as the statue of Aphrodite raises her robe to reveal her true charms, you have raised your fetching voice and shown me you have some serious issues, other than needing rent money."

"*Enough.* Back to our regularly scheduled

programming about art or go sing in the rain."

He took a breath and shrugged. "Which other artists do you like?"

"I adore Frida Kahlo as well. One day, when I have the funds, I would love to travel to where she was born. I also love neoclassical art. There aren't enough blacks represented in neoclassical art, so when I saw this bad stone sculpture, this portrait by Philippe Faraut, I said one day, when I had mo—"

I was interrupted as a big fight broke out. The angry, loud couple sitting at the booth closest to the cash register had an all-out argument. They cursed each other in Spanish. She threw a steak in his face. He threw a glass of water at her. She threw food. He threw food. They grabbed each other and wrestled. Nobody jumped in. He let her go. She stormed out. He threw money on the table and went after her.

I said, "Guess they won't be having a merry Christmas."

"Not many of us will."

"Where were we?"

"Art. You were telling me who you liked, what you would buy if you had money."

"That is a long, long list. If I was filthy rich, my crib would be a museum filled with art by Michelangelo, Rembrandt, Picasso, da Vinci, Turner, Donatello, Monet, Rodin, van Eyck —"

A loud crash from the parking lot jarred everyone in Hawaiian Gardens and Lakewood.

Customers jumped up. Waitresses stopped waitressing. The damaged car's alarm went off.

The man who had left after arguing with his wife had backed out of his space, no doubt still in a rage, and slammed into the rear quarter panel of the luxury car. They pulled back in, adjusted, accelerated, backed up fast, and slammed the luxury car again. They were fighting, had been slugging it out like Rihanna and Chris Brown on repeat since they'd left. He reversed again, and it looked like he was about to rip away the whole side of the luxury car.

I said, "Oh my God, they hit your car, they hit your car, they hit your car."

They rammed the car again. The driver fought his wife as he backed out of the parking space.

I said, "Damn, they're about to do a hit-and-run."

His hands were fists and his jaw was tight, like he was about to change from Don Draper to Samuel L. Jackson in *Pulp Fic-*

tion. His body language said he was about to sprint out there and kick ass. Only he was looking at the news, not the accident. His attention went against the current.

The driver backed out, threw his car in drive, turned his lights on, and sped away.

The man from Orange County did nothing. He stopped watching the news and did nothing.

I said, "Aren't you going to get their license plate number and call the police before they —"

He used his remote to turn his alarm off, then looked around at the people in the restaurant.

I ran to the front door and came back, said, "I'm calling the police."

He glanced up at the surveillance cameras. "No police. Not yet. We're not ready."

He said that like if the police came, they'd take me away. I didn't know if that meant he'd turn me in, so I put my phone down. He didn't bother to go look at the damage. The rest of the people in the restaurant had their eyes on us. The rich man. The brown girl with dreadlocks. They waited for one of us to do something. I sat back down, watching him, but his eyes were back on the television and the news.

A guy ran in from the winter rain and hurried to the waitress, and she directed him to our table. The guy had seen the accident and had written down the car's make, model, and tag number. He ran and handed the information to the man from Orange County, who thanked him and shook his hand. The guy stood there for a moment, waiting for his excitement to be reciprocated, and when it wasn't, he lost that expression that said he was a hero, looked perplexed, then scratched his head as he walked away, left the restaurant, got into his car, and drove away. The man from Orange County tore up the information.

Everyone kept looking at the damaged luxury car. A few people went out to inspect the damage themselves. Amazed, people inside talked about the fight, regretted they hadn't had their phones ready to record and post it, and continued to rubberneck at someone else's personal tragedy. A man and a woman had had a fist fight in front of us, and since it was no one famous, it was just entertainment. I thought it was a great time to talk, to take the opportunity to scrutinize the forces of culture, gender, and race, but he wasn't talking. He had gone dark. We looked out the window. Sirens and flashing lights lit up the Christmas season. He looked down at his hand, over and over, like he could see its pain.

I sat back and counted the cars creeping by, many with Christmas trees on their roofs.

He said, "It's my wife's car."

"That's your wife's car? Someone just jacked up your wife's car and you don't care?"

"Ordered it for her back in June. One of her Christmas presents."

"That's a two-thousand-and-this-year car? And it's *one* of her presents? Just *one*?"

"It's a two-thousand-and-next-year automobile with all the overpriced bells and whistles. Leather-lined wooden iPod drawer. Teak decking. Has pop-up dash speakers. Rear-seat champagne cooler."

"Has she been inside the new car yet?"

"Not yet. Hadn't officially given it to her yet."

"Now it's damaged."

"It lost its value the moment it left the car lot. Just like my marriage did when I left the church."

"I still would've chased those jerks and run them into a ditch."

Food arrived.

I had wanted a fried cheese melt, the one that clocked in at about thirteen hundred calories, but he ordered a low-calorie salad, so I ordered the same, thinking I could eat salad now, then stop at Roscoe's and get chicken and waffles with the guy I was dealing with, when he finally called me back. Chicken and waffles and some private time until sunrise. I was lost in thought for a moment. The man from Orange County started eating.

I blinked and adjusted my focus, asked, "Aren't you going to bless the food?"

"Jesus wept."

"The shortest verse in the Bible."

He said, "One noun. One verb. A complete sentence in my book."

"Don't plagiarize. Be original. That was written over two thousand years ago."

"But I guess nowadays if Jesus wept,

everybody would call him a punk, like they did that Republican guy. Mary can weep, but if Jesus came back to this world and shed a tear —"

"Whatever. Bless the food."

"Bless the food we're about to receive for the nourishment of our bodies. Amen."

"Amen."

"And Jesus wept."

"Whatever."

He stabbed his salad with a fork and asked, "Where do you live?"

"Where people don't let other people hit their cars and get away with it without a body bag."

"East L.A.?"

"Leimert Park section. Heard of that area? Middle-class blacks live there."

"Where the body of Elizabeth Short was found?"

"When white people lived there. My apartment isn't far from where they found the Black Dahlia."

"Never been to that area. They did serious damage up there during the last riot."

"You heard of Leonard DuBois?"

"The comic?"

"I live in the same apartment he used to live in. Was hoping it would bring me good luck."

"Small world. I used to do business with the guy who was his best friend. Tyrel Williams. He was my mentor back in the day, during my college days. He helped me get my company going."

"You own a company?"

He nodded as he asked, "Why are you looking at me like that?"

"Oh. Sorry. Your eyes. The colors. Didn't see them when we were at the gas station. They're interesting. Just an observation. Not flirting. They caught me off guard. Didn't mean to stare like that."

I blinked, felt my heart beating faster, like drummer Buddy Rich was doing a number inside my chest. Butterflies broke free, moved around my stomach. That rarely happened to me.

I shook off the butterflies and asked, "What's your situation at home? You're not telling me something; that much I see in your body language and eyes."

"You're reading my body language?"

"The black eye? The bruised knuckles? Did you beat your wife and go get dinner? Is that why you don't care about your wife's new car getting banged up in the parking lot? Is this about your wife?"

"Haven't seen my wife today, and again, she hasn't seen what was her present. I was in D.C. I had business in Gaithersburg, but we wrapped up a day early, and everyone was ready to get back to his or her family. I was, too. So I rebooked, flew back into John Wayne Airport this morning. Got home and she was gone. She didn't expect me in so early, I guess, and had left her iPad on the kitchen table. She went to work out early. So I guess you could say that I did the same."

"She wasn't home and you went to play racquetball."

"Got in the way of a racquet. And I did hit a wall with my fist."

"Fingers tapping the table — that means you're not comfortable."

"You're reading too much into a little tapping. Keeping time with a song inside my head."

"Don't talk to me like I'm a yokel. You're lying about something. A lot of something."

"Am I? Are you a mind reader as well?"

"You're not giving me much direct eye contact. You're a liar."

"If I look at you, you get offended. If I don't, you think I'm a liar. Which should I do?"

I laughed. "You got me on that one. I still think you're lying. I pick up on other people's feelings. No matter how hard they try to hide what they're feeling, I pick up on it."

"That's how you know who to con."

"You're a liar."

"Same for you. I met you as a liar, so as far as I know, every word from your face is a lie."

"I lie all the time."

"That was probably a lie, too."

I chewed my salad and looked into his eyes. Time slowed down. That is why people don't look at each other. Eye contact does things, causes changes in the atmosphere. Eye contact creates wars, creates fights, but eye contact also creates arousal. I felt the weird, pointless tingles, and I read his face and his smile. I tried to look inside him, see what he was feeling, while at the same time guarding myself.

I cleared my throat, maintained a straight face, asked, "What's the big issue at home?"

"Who said it was a single issue?"

"Fine. Is it a bunch of small issues?"

He stabbed at his salad, hardly took a bite. "We have issues large and small."

"What's the primary argument all about?"

"We argue over dumb things. Every day she has to create a fashion video of what she's wearing — clothes, makeup, the whole nine — and upload her never-ending vanity on both YouTube and Facebook."

"Vain, or just very confident. I can't call that one. How's the communication between you two?"

"Every conversation becomes an argument that ends up being a mudslinging match."

"I understand that. I totally understand that. I was with someone . . . six years ago . . . and that was the way it was. Started off on that high, then after a year we hit rock bottom and crashed."

"I can relate. She went from her actions showing me she loved me to saying she loved me, but her actions no longer lined up with the conversation."

"Showing is always more important than telling. Show me and I'll never ask you to say it."

"She no longer loved me as I was, and wanted me to change. I gave up a lot to be with her."

"We all give up part of ourselves to be with anyone. Relationships change our trajectories."

"I guess we do. But with a good love, we could gain even more than we'd ever imagined."

"Are you heading toward indifference and just saying it is what it is, and doing what you have to do on the side?"

"Nothing on the side. Not for me."

"Kids?"

"No kids. We tried the second year. At least I thought we had tried."

"You're confusing, and I think you're lying. Do you cuddle?"

"What?"

"Cuddle. Do you and your wife cuddle at night? People should cuddle naked. I'm a cuddler."

"Not anymore. She turns her back to me."

"Maybe she wants you to snuggle up on her booty and get it from the back or something."

"She sleeps downstairs in the family room, on the sofa in front of the television, most nights."

"Sounds like, as they say in the Caribbean, pussy gone frost. Sex got boring?"

"Not for me. When you love someone, sex never gets boring."

"When you don't?"

"It's just a way to ease the tension built up inside your body."

"Oh. Hmm. Is she a lesbian and pretending to be straight?"

"None of the carpet in-house has been munched, as far as I can see."

"How often do you have sex?"

"Very seldom. But when we do, it's a real quick event, like wham, bam, thank you, roll over, wash up, and she's on the iPad playing Candy Crush and I'm surfing Netflix, looking for a movie."

"I guess the honeymoon phase has ended."

"Most people should get a divorce right after the honeymoon. Some should during."

Then he gazed into my eyes. I tried to read him but was fascinated by the colors of his eyes.

In a tender voice, I said, "You have one bluish-green eye and one brown eye."

"Oh. Yeah. I do."

"Both have gray circles around the iris."

It was a mutual gaze. People around us probably misinterpreted it as the look of love.

The direct eye contact caused arousal. But it also created hostility.

I felt both. It was a hostile arousal.

I didn't know how to respond to that sensation.

I asked, "So are you unhappily married, or regretfully married?"

"What's the difference?"

"Unhappy is how the other person makes you feel. You want it to work, don't want to divorce, live day to day in a comfortable state of distress and embarrassment, and you have hope, so much hope, but it's hard. You're not going anywhere, and it's more about the hopeful heart than divorce court."

"And regretfully married?"

"Regret is when you wish you had never married. You hate yourself for your choice, and for that you project that hate and animosity and anxiety from your black heart to your partner. You punish them day in and day out because you want them to be as miserable as you are."

"In that case, I am the unhappy one, and I think my wife has always been the regretful one."

"And you don't have a girlfriend? I'm going to ask you that over and over."

"I've realized there are many types of women — two in particular. When I was single, a certain type of woman was attracted to me: the single woman. But there were a lot of single women who had boyfriends, but wanted something better, or were experimenting with their desires. Now, my wedding ring attracts married women. So I guess there are a lot of unhappily married women. A lot of women living with regret."

My tone softened. "Take up many offers from those living in Unhappyville and Regretville?"

In what sounded like a tone of regret, he said, "None."

"Other people know you have problems at home?"

"No one has a clue. In pictures, around friends, we seem to be the perfect couple."

We held eye contact. My nostrils flared and my pupils dilated. His pupils dilated.

He played the stare game. I played the stare game.

The stare remained unbroken. We gazed. Inhaled. Exhaled. Gazed. Inhaled. Exhaled. I wanted to lick my lips, but I didn't. His cell rang and that broke the stare, ended the challenge. He looked down at his phone, saw the number on the ID, but he didn't answer. He shifted with the energy of the restless, his mind on something powerful. At last, I could breathe. I managed to lick thoughts away from my lips. My nipples ached, and I could barely breathe. I swallowed and looked away from his eyes.

Susan was smiling.

She hadn't smiled in a long time, and rarely with that much enthusiasm.

I kept my knees together, legs closed like Chick-fil-A on a Sunday.

I asked him, "Okay, black man from Orange County, the land of John Wayne, the man who probably didn't vote for Obama because of what his white friends would think, what kind of women do you like?"

"I voted for Obama the second time."

"You saw the light."

"Hated Romney more than I disliked Obama. Hillary had earned the spot, and the nation betrayed her by turning it into a political version of *American Idol*. They went for race and popularity over politics."

"Why, in all of your négritude, would you want to vote for her and all her Bill Clinton baggage?"

"Get over it."

"And the women? What kind do you like?"

"Why? What does that matter? How does that change the universe?"

"My dream guy'd be a combination of Idris, Denzel, Blair Underwood, Michael

Ealy, the guy who plays Thor, the guy who plays Captain America, Prince, Bruno Mars, and Brad Pitt."

"You chose celebrities and fictional characters, not anyone who has provided anything more than entertainment. Not one Einstein. Your reality is to salivate over being with an unattainable fantasy."

"Damn. Never felt this shallow in my life. Not. And he would be able to converse about geometry, science, probability, calculus, biology, and statistics, and he would speak Spanish, Italian, and French."

"Now you want a polyglot with a mind like Einstein who looks like a centerfold for *Playgirl.*"

"Then I would be stimulated and satisfied in all arenas. Play the game. What's yours?"

"When I was in undergrad, even before then, all I dreamed about was marrying a sorority girl."

"Overrated, but you like what you like, for whatever reason you like what you like."

"That's the type of woman that attracts me. I went to a Greek show when I was in the tenth grade, went to a step show and saw the black fraternities and sororities stomp the yard. But the women, those women . . . I had never seen women like that in my life. They weren't like the stereotypical black women on television. That brand of woman was like a Bentley: unadvertised. It was like a certain type of black woman was being hidden from regular society, ignored by media. So many sorority girls, women who were on a mission, women who changed my idea of what a real woman was in this country. They changed my views of black American women."

"Looks, on a scale of one to ten? What does Miss Mensa have to look like? Halle or Beyoncé?"

"To be clear, on my scale, Beyoncé is about a six."

"What about Halle?"

"Halle is about a four."

"Damn. That's cold."

"She's aged out."

"You're not giving them extra points for being light-skinned?"

"Giving a black woman extra points for being light-skinned is like grading on a curve."

"Hold up. Let me get my phone and post that on Facebook. If you have to get a next one, what would she be like?"

"I'd prefer sweet juice from a well-educated, very dark berry, and I'd be open, so that berry could come from Mississippi, New York, Nigeria, or Peru. Wait. No. Actually, I don't think I want her to be American."

"Why so extreme? You look like a Spain, Greece, and Italy kind of guy."

"I loathe what the black man's journey has been in America, what that has done to his soul, so I would want someone with a different perspective, someone less brainwashed by these ideologies."

I asked, "Where are you from?"

He took a breath, hesitated like it was a big reveal, and said, "I was born in Vicenza."

"Italy? You're Italian?"

"American. Dad was in the US military. Grew up in Colorado."

" 'Grew up in Colorado.' That's a sentence I've never heard a black man say."

"Well, I said it. What do I win? More ridicule and sarcasm? More stereotypes?"

"You're from the land of pot smokers."

"The land of 4:20."

"Why do they call it 4:20?"

"That was the time people used to meet to get high. At 4:20 A.M. or 4:20 P.M."

"You had 4:20 moments?"

He gave me half a smile, then asked, "Where are you from?"

"Here and there and here. Was the oddball. I grew up hiking to Forbidden Island

and windsurfing under the sun of a tropical paradise. A place no one is really aware of, and I like it like that."

"You're not American?"

"I was born in Saipan, but came to America right after, with my mother, so I didn't know the place at all. I lived here for years, then went back and spent two years in Saipan with my dad, then came back here after my dad remarried. Didn't like my dickhead stepmom. Came here and finished high school."

"Just north of Guam, south of Japan, east of the Philippines, west of Hawaii."

"Smart guy. Bet you could make a mint on *Jeopardy!*"

"Maybe that's what's different about you."

"What, exactly?"

"You were socialized a little differently."

"Some. My experiences aren't those of the typical black woman in America."

"Different than the average American. But not enough."

"Meaning?"

"You've been in bad company most of your life."

"You don't know anything about me."

"Am I wrong?"

I said, "Since you're judging and dissecting and looking at me like I'm weird, let's

84

talk about you. Your hair — it's kind of wavy. Indian in your blood, or are you a hypocrite and texturize your hair?"

He hesitated, appeared uneasy, then said, "My mother is black and my father is white."

"You're a brown-skinned Drake and didn't vote for your cousin Obama?"

"Your attitude changed when I told you I was biracial."

"I'm surprised that you're part black, that's all."

"You're hilarious to be so bigoted."

"Well, America's attitude changed when they found out Obama was biracial and married to a dark-skinned black woman. If being American means I'm bigoted, then blame the cult, not the members."

For a second we gazed at the parking lot, at his damaged ride. Someone else entered the lot, ran over broken car parts, and took the space next to his car, where the hit-and-run driver had parked. He stared at his car. Angry. But he did nothing about it. I ignored him, absorbed the sounds of conversations and the clanging of silverware against plates like punctuation in many of the conversations. Inhaled the aromas.

He said, "Your boyfriend, the one you have now, how did you meet him?"

"Started off as a Facebook relationship. Around the time Solange went Mortal Combat on Jay-Z, around Mother's Day. We had mutual friends who were going back and forth about that incident, and we both ended up on their pages. Yeah. Around . . . Mother's Day. I'd gone on a rant about the Solange thing, said the situation was vile, yet had gotten more attention than the missing black girls because it appealed to everyone's prejudices, ignited emotions, and was satire in a way that showed people are devoid of intellect and reason."

"Welcome to the Internet. No IQ test required."

"Anyway. He saw my posts, clicked like on things I had posted, and somewhere down the line I clicked like on what he had posted, which was like initial contact, and then he sent me a request. I almost declined it, but we had mutual friends. Good-looking guy. Smart. Great body. I checked out his page first. Nothing weird. Nothing perverted. I found myself reading all his posts. Could form complete sentences. Didn't use ROFL and OMG and LMBAO and HBD, or overuse silly emoticons like a third grader."

"HBD?"

"Happy birthday, which really should be

HB, unless you're saying 'Happy birthday, Dickhead.' "

"Tell me about your boyfriend."

"Where was I? Oh, right. He had actually in-boxed me a very thoughtful note, and I was impressed by his use of the English language, so I added him. See, I like considerate people, too. Every day he clicked like on my posts. He liked my opinions. My jokes. He clicked like on a lot of my photos. Gave me compliment after compliment. Then down the line he put another message in my in-box, and we started exchanging private messages, and so it became a hi and bye friendship, one where we exchanged innocuous messages, and soon we clicked like more and more, practically on every post, and then we started leaving public comments as well."

"Comments are like getting attention. It's a form of nourishment a lot of people need."

"A comment says you are there right next to somebody, paying attention, and soon a stranger becomes part of your world and important to you, someone you look forward to seeing online every day."

He said, "He felt important to you."

"Yeah. Guess a little attention goes a long way. The next thing you know we'd graduated to WhatsApp, then, you know, you're exchanging cell numbers, testing the next level by texting. Then you might call and leave a voice message, then talk for real, then you're on Skype, taking it to the next level, kind of like being face-to-face, flirting, being a little bit naughty for each other, feeling the vibe, being excited. And then you're meeting at Roscoe's Chicken & Waffles on Pico, finally face-to-face, and you can see, smell, hear, touch each other, but it's like you've never met and have already known each other a long time at the same time, and then after doing that three or four times, you're ready for the next sense, want a taste, want to feel, and after dinner at Roscoe's you're on the sofa making out and then waking up on the carpet naked, sucking leftover waffles and fried chicken wings from between your teeth."

"Sounds like you had the thrill of a lifetime. On the sofa making out after chicken and waffles. I like kissing."

I grinned. "Me, too. People should kiss more."

"People should kiss and laugh, especially when everything seems dismal."

"Kissing makes things better."

He said, "The best relationships have lots of profound kisses."

"They do. It all starts with a kiss."

88

"Kissing is where it all begins."

I said, "And telling them to kiss your ass is how it ends."

"Starts and ends with a kiss."

"And hopefully one tastes better than the other."

"Hopefully."

I asked, "How long have you been married? Forgot to be nosey and ask you that."

"Twenty-eight dog years."

"So that's four years you've made the cow go moo. How long did you date?"

"We were married within a year."

"You were engaged soon as you met."

"She met me, said she was madly in love, then was in a hurry to go buy a ring."

"Pregnant?"

"Wasn't pregnant. Said she was ready to be my wife."

"Because you're rich."

"Stop calling me that."

"It takes a long time for people to get to know each other — between two and four years. People who are patient and don't rush it, take their time, they are less likely to get divorced."

"I've learned the hard way."

"Where is your first girlfriend? Tell me

about your first heartbreak, or the first girl who had her heart broken into a thousand pieces by you. I assume it's not the woman you married. Am I correct?"

"Ladies first. And since there are no ladies, you can go first."

"You're disgusting."

He said, "Tell me about your first."

"Let's see. Hmm. Used to hang out with this older guy, Vernon. I was thirteen and he was sixteen, and both of us were in the same grade. Vernon didn't get the benefit of social promotion — better known as letting dumb motherfuckers go to the next grade — not back in the day. Vernon turned me on to the good stuff. Weed. Triple Peach. Wild Irish Rose. Mad Dog 20/20. Nothing but the best of the cheapest."

"You were a regular Rizzo when you were thirteen?"

"Was a latchkey kid from the age of ten, so I had the house to myself from when school was out until my mother and step-father came home from work, about five. I used to come home, clean up, vacuum, and cook dinner before I sat down to do my homework. If the house wasn't clean and food wasn't ready, I would get a serious whooping. *12 Years a Slave* had nothing on me."

"What happened to Vernon?"

"Ended up robbing liquor stores, doing break-ins, in and out of jail. He taught me how to break into cars with a coat hanger, and how to steal a car with a screwdriver. He taught me how to drive, too. Taught me how to burn up a car with gasoline. Dude had sickle cell, too. Sickle cell is what did him in. But he was the boss while he lived. He died before he made it to twenty, but he squeezed sixty years of living into those two decades. He knew his time was short, so he said to hell with the rules and did all he could."

"To hell with the rules. Don't be afraid. Live in the moment. I've never lived that way."

"He was an exciting guy. Always up to no good. Always in a fight. Never a dull moment."

"Interesting friend. Loved him?"

"He was my first sexual partner. Awful sex. Didn't love him. We only did it twice, but I won't ever be able to forget him. He was having sex with everybody, mostly women out of high school. College girls thought he was in college because his old ass always carried books. He even slept with a few teachers."

"I knew guys like him when I was growing up. Women loved those guys."

"How many girls like me did you know when you were growing up?"

"None, really. From what I see and hear, none. They didn't live in my area."

"Now it's your turn. Tell me about your first love. How did it end?"

Half of his smile went away. "We almost made it, but broke up before we went to university."

"Where did she go?"

"Princeton."

"Smart bitch. Bet she lives in a mansion now."

"She's at a top law firm and resides in a mansion that rivals a governor's mansion."

"How did you lose her?"

"At the end, well, let's just say one night she came home smelling like Trojans."

"The football team or the condoms?"

"The condoms. But then again, I have no idea what a football team smells like."

"Wow. In high school?"

"We misbehave and get wild in Colorado, too. Half of the state should be on *Jerry Springer.*"

"So she cheated on you and came home smelling like a Trojan factory."

"Trojan condoms. They have their own unique smell. At least they do to me."

"She should've used Durex. Those smell better than Trojan. Trojan makes it smell like you had sex with the Michelin Man. Durex smell like Hubba Bubba bubble gum and don't taste so bad."

"Yeah, she smelled like a used tire factory."

"Trojan is definitely a no-blow-job condom. The flavor is horrible. Someone should come up with a barbecue-flavored condom for the hood. But greedy bitches would probably start chewing dicks."

"That's gross."

"Anyway. The Colorado girl — tell me, how did that go down?"

"I got off work early; I used to deliver pizzas, and it was a slow night, so they sent me home. I stopped by her house, was on her porch waiting for her when this guy dropped her off about midnight. I knew who he was. White guy named Jerald. Jerk looked like Eminem, with ginger hair in braids."

"She was . . . is . . . was a black girl? Well, Colorado's version of a black girl."

"Looked like a more elegant, more sophisticated version of Gabrielle Union."

"Gabby again. You're the second person to mention her name tonight. Gabby, Gabby, Gabby."

"Will never forget that smell. She stank.

Like weed, cigarettes, white-man come, cheap liquor, and Cool Water cologne. I smelled her and I knew she had been with him. Knew it before she said."

"Okay. But how could she smell like come if she used a condom?"

"He didn't put it on at first. She made him put it on after."

"She told you?"

"That was the way we did it. She refused to start with a condom, but wanted me to stop and have it on when I was ready to come. She did the same with him. I know she did. I knew her."

"Speechless on that one. Guess her pamphlet on safe sex had a few pages missing. Sounds like she was the type to put her seat belt on after an accident. Sponsored by Unplanned Parenthood."

"We had planned to go to the same college, Princeton, declare the same major, graduate together, backpack together for a year, then marry, work for three to five years, then have a lot of babies."

"I know you did something to make yourself feel better, or make her feel worse."

He grumbled, "The first heartbreak is the one we never forget."

"So what did you do with that anger? What did you go home smelling like?"

"I went home smelling like a sweeter pussy than she had."

"Damn. That was raw. I thought you were going to say you kicked the dude's ass."

"That, too. But I had popped two of her girlfriends by the end of the next week."

"Look at you. Kicking ass and getting laid. So motivated. You were on a mission."

"Would've been three, but her sister was on the rag, so she just gave me a blow job."

"It traumatized you. Mentioning that now, looks like it reignited an old fire."

"Still reading my body language?"

"Like an eBook."

He said, "So, those are my details. Not proud to have been a fool, but it happened."

"Happened to me, too. I got played bigtime."

"Guess it happens to us all once or twice."

"Guy I was crazy about slept with a couple of my girls, and a couple of their girls."

"What did you learn?"

"That men are men. To not trust bitches. To not broadcast your business. If you have some good wood, they want it. My friends smiled in my face and had my man behind my back. Tricked me."

"A con woman tricked by deception experts, or was a deception expert conned by two women?"

"Anyway."

"I understand how to run a business, but never have really understood a woman."

"You don't understand women? As dapper and well put together as you are?"

He said, "Sometimes it feels like I only understand a woman when my dick is inside her."

"You only understand a woman while your cock is inside her?"

"Feels that way."

"Takes more than two minutes to get to know a woman."

He nodded. "I know. A man can know a woman for years and never really know her."

"A woman can only know a man if he wants to be known, and how he wants her to know him."

"We trick ourselves. A man can fall madly, deeply in love, marry a woman almost as soon as he meets her, with each breath feel as if she is his soul mate. But she breathes for someone else; someone else may be her soul mate. There is always someone in the shadows. Always someone on standby."

"If you're not the one, why wouldn't she just marry her true soul mate?"

"No idea. Maybe because the other guy was already happily married."

"Maybe she didn't want to marry him, just enjoyed the sex with him."

"Could be."

I said, "Maybe she doesn't want to see the lover every day, not like husband and wife.

Some people are good company; others are good to have in your bed for a little while."

He nodded.

I asked, "You okay over there?"

"The girl from Colorado, my first love . . . I had never seen her look so ecstatic. She left that guy's Mustang and danced her way to the porch. She danced until she found me waiting on her. As he drove away, when she saw me come from the shadows — I hadn't ever seen a girl look so remorseful. Didn't get it."

"You never let that go, did you?"

"Not sure. But I moved on. I moved on, met someone new, and married."

"How did you end up with your wife? Where did you meet the Republican?"

"Was on the third level at Barnes & Noble at The Grove. I was at the top of the escalator, flipping through a Harry Potter book, and saw her coming up. It was like she was an angel coming to meet me."

"The Grove? Nice. Classy area. Wife was a sorority girl in tight jeans and high heels?"

"That first look, that first eye contact — bet it was that way the first time Adam saw Eve."

"Adam had never seen a woman before."

"That was how I felt. Like God had created a woman just for me. To be mine forever."

"In the beginning there was lust, and lust was good."

"It was love."

"Keep it real. It was lust. She got your dick hard."

"She stimulated my mind. Intelligence excites me. She impressed my friends. The day we met, we talked Harry Potter, law, business, physics, politics, family, college, everything. She is articulate, well-read, and very ambitious, and most of all, she told me that she was loyal. Jealous and loyal."

"How jealous is this one? On a scale of one to ten?"

"She's a ten. Jealousy is her dark beast. She loves a good confrontation."

"Jealousy for the preservation of the relationship, or a control freak?"

"If she thinks she has a sexual rival, if she feels an interpersonal boundary has been crossed, even a compliment from a woman left on Facebook, she can become a bit extreme."

"She sounds like a loon. Still, jealousy comes from the fear of losing something of value to us."

"Maybe I was just as jealous, and twice as loyal. She came from a good family. My family had the same structure. It was the right recipe. She was perfect. It was love. I know what it was for me. I know what I felt. We sat in the café and talked Harry Potter like we were middle school children. Of all the things in the world, we talked about Harry Potter the longest. We sipped tea and talked about wizards and fantasy. Didn't want the moment to end, so I invited her to come out on my boat the next day."

"You popped the panties the next day."

"We made love for the first time. We were on my boat. I docked us at Catalina for the night."

"*Bow chica bow wow.* She broke out the lingerie and hooked you up."

"It wasn't planned."

"She planned it. Trust me. She shaved the cat and climbed on the boat ready to freak."

"It was spontaneous. We were only going to meet for lunch. One thing led to the next."

"She stepped on the boat, saw you were rich, and the doors to her church opened."

"She told me I was the man of her dreams. I felt love when she touched me."

"Lust is a master showman who disguises himself as love, and love is a mythical creature who keeps habitat with the Easter Bunny, Santa Claus, the Tooth Fairy, and other lies we have been fed."

He shook his head, rubbed his hands together, said, "Funny."

"What?"

"It started off that she was the only woman I wanted to look at. She was the only beautiful woman on the planet. When love goes in the other direction, every other woman on the planet is more attractive than a man's wife; more attractive because he does not judge his wife from the outside in, but from the inside out. In the end it will always be about character over beauty."

"Marriage made you hard."

"It's not marriage that makes us callous. Marriage, that spiritual union, will always be beautiful. It's the people who marry and don't take marriage seriously; it's other people who make us coldhearted."

I asked, "How educated is she?"

"She went to University of Pennsylvania, graduated magna cum laude."

"Her major?"

"International law. She modeled to pay her way through university."

I nodded, let that end right there. His wife had serious credentials. Had married smart. I imagined his intellectual trophy, nicely dressed, magnificent, with cascading blond hair; the kind of woman who can walk into Starbucks on Centinella and suddenly every black woman in the room feels invisible.

He said, "Eyes averted. Shoulders dropped. Biting lip. Your temperament has changed."

"I'm like the people sitting here in Denny's. This is as close to Dubai as most will ever get. I'll never be mansion-smart. Best I can do now is pass by mansions and throw rocks."

I pulled my lips in. The baby across the room cried like it was colicky. The man across from me saw me look at the kid, saw my discomfort, saw me adjust my body language. I had studied him and now he had turned the tables, and I didn't like being studied, didn't like being dissected.

I asked, "Why are you looking at me like that?"

"Answer a question for me. It's about your boyfriend."

"What about him?"

"Tell me the truth. How does he treat you?"

I shrugged. "I'll be honest. Some days, like today, I feel ignored, like I need to be with someone worth being faithful to. Some days being faithful to him makes me feel like I ain't doing nothing but cheating myself of the next opportunity that could present itself to me. Kind of stuck where I am right now."

"How many years have you and the chicken and waffles guy been together?"

"We might be at about six months now."

"Might be? You're not sure?"

"Well, I'm confused about it most of the time. We've never really discussed the anniversary, or which anniversary should be the official anniversary. Women, we have first-time-we-talked anniversary, first-time-we-went-out anniversary, first-time-we-went-to-a-movie anniversary, first-time-we-kissed anniversary. Didn't write down the day I think we became an official couple. Actually, I wouldn't know how to figure out the day — if I should go by when he first liked my comments, or when we starting talking on Skype every day, or when we met face-to-face, or when we kissed, or when we did it the first time and woke up buck naked on the carpet with chicken and waffles on our breath and between our teeth. Women, we kinda go by the moment we first felt like we were officially chatting. We go by the moment we feel a connection."

"Men go by penetration."

"That's jacked-up."

"That's reality."

"Well, for a woman, or most women, the relationship starts before the sex."

"You only had one good month? It lasted as long as the life of a few butterflies."

"You've been married how many years and have had how many good marital months?"

"Good point. What changed? After your good month, how were things different?"

"Hmm. After penetration, there was less Roscoe's, fewer phone calls, less IMing, less checking on me by sending texts. Now it's cold, silence in between last-minute texts trying to hook up hot booty calls. We haven't broken up, so I guess he's still my man. He says he is. After the first month, he'd be over at my place by six, then gone by eleven. I stopped cooking elaborate dinners for him, since I knew he'd be leaving. I don't run a fuck-through restaurant."

"Why does he leave by eleven?"

"Never asked. He'd look at his watch about ten thirty, then exit stage left by eleven."

"Why are you tolerating the situation?"

"Guess I'm still basing everything on the energy from a month that went by, basing it on a few good nights on the carpet, the way we see an actor in a movie and that role hooks us in."

"So the first month was like the original

Matrix movie, the rest like the crappy sequels."

"Well, it feels like it's been a lot longer. More like how the first season of *Lost* was the bomb, then the rest was torture, but you keep hoping for a good episode, for good moments, here and there."

"And you're sitting here, waiting on him, looking like a lost puppy."

I shrugged. "It was a good month. I'm hoping for more five-cups-of-coffee moments."

"Five-cups-of-coffee moments?"

"You know. That serious high you get after you've had five cups of coffee."

"You have to keep feeding love what it needs to keep it feeling like love. Drink a lot of coffee every day, and you'll need to drink more coffee to get the same effect."

"Caffeine and love. Both are drugs. You become dependent. It starts to own you."

"Your relationship with Chicken and Waffles sounds as miserable as my marriage."

"I'm not hooked. We're just ships docked at the same port for now, that's all."

"You're restless. Aggravated. Your expression says you're in pain and ready to jump."

I frowned at my phone. "Hurts when he doesn't call or text me back."

"The guy you're chasing . . . is Chicken and Waffles the type of man you'd want your son to be?"

"I'm not chasing him. I'm not chasing any man."

"Play the game. What you have described to me is an abusive relationship."

"I'm not in an abusive relationship."

"People who are in bad relationships, abusive relationships, know that they aren't good, yet they stay. I could be wrong. Tell me the good things about this chicken and waffles guy."

"Maybe instead of trying to analyze my life, you should ask why your wife is with you. Sounds like she's done. Did she do the math and decide to stay married because she's found the cash cow of all cash cows? Go to hell. Yours is the abusive relationship you need to worry about."

"The question is if I have reached my goddamn limit."

"And she, the one you picked: Is she the type of woman you'd want your daughter to be?"

"I would hate to have a daughter like her."

"Then abort your relationship. Pay the piper and move on."

"Don't judge me."

"If anyone at this table is in an abusive

relationship, it's you, not me. I don't go home to that kind of craziness every night. Mine is jacked-up, yeah, but this is my choice. Maybe this is where I am the most comfortable right now, in a comfortable state of discomfort. I'm not married and miserable, not like you."

He slapped his keys down and gave me hard eye contact.

I reciprocated.

He asked, "Want coffee?"

"Thought you were ready to get rid of me so you could get to your wrecked car."

"Coffee or no?"

"Phone hasn't rung, traffic is still horrible, so I can blow time and have coffee."

"You're not chasing him."

He flagged down the waitress.

We looked away from each other, having nothing to say at the moment.

Truth is a burden.

I didn't like him. I didn't like the things he said, hated the way he made me feel.

I hoped my words gave him ten times the grief.

His cell blew up and he checked his text messages.

Then, suddenly, my attention was somewhere else. The man with the little girl was leaving. The little girl waved at me. I wanted to go meet her, hug her to my chest, wanted to give her a Barbie doll. I should've given her hugs, kisses, two Barbie dolls, and my bag of colorful balloons. I wanted to run after them and give her presents — might even have given her the balloons and walked out of Denny's and left the man from Orange County sitting alone — but they arrived at that moment. Red and blue lights fired up the parking lot. Four police cars pulled in from Carson Boulevard, sirens on. Everyone looked outside. The police went to the end of the lot. I saw their lights brightening up my car. Fear crawled up my back. I was trapped inside my head, replaying when I dumped the stolen truck. I was sure I had wiped it down. Was sure that my prints were gone. I became antsy, my leg bouncing, wanting to run to the door and see if the cops had gone to my car.

I asked, "Did you set me up? Is that what the text messages are about?"

"Shut up."

"Did you contact the cops, then come here and have this long talk to delay me and set me up?"

"Yeah. I'm angry and today the world is my enemy."

"I will give you the money back."

The man from Orange County reached

across the table, grabbed my hand.

His grip was strong, like manacles. Shaking, eyes wide, I looked at him. I tried to pull away from him. He held on to my hand. Held it firmly. The sirens stopped singing, but the lights kept on flashing.

He said, "Shut up."

"Answer me. Is that why you came back here? To have me arrested?"

8:04 P.M.

He said, "What other crimes have you committed?"

"Are you a peach?"

"What's a peach?"

"A snitch. An informant. I've never committed a crime a day in my goddamn life."

"That's a lie."

"If the police come, after I throw coffee in your face, that will be my story until I get an attorney."

"You sure? Never committed a crime? Not one?"

"Cheated on a boyfriend when I was in high school, but he can't prove it, and neither can you."

"That's it?"

"He deserved it."

"You said you stole the truck tonight."

"What truck? I don't see any truck. Do you see a truck?"

"You were talking in code. You stole it."

"Bloody hell. You took the rocks in a box. It has my fingerprints all over it. You can't prove that, either. I won't admit to anything, you hear me? Wait. Have you had your phone on the table so you can record this conversation? You can't record me without my permission. It won't be admissible in court."

His fingers rapped against the table. "The cops are coming inside."

I twisted my body so I could see behind me. Six police officers came into the diner, guns holstered. Orange County focused on the officers. Sweat appeared on his nose. His breathing slowed. His brow furrowed. He reacted the way I had felt when I heard sirens while I was doing my rocks-in-a-box con. The police marched toward us, all muscles and badges, handcuffs, stun guns, and real guns.

I opened my mouth to scream. Again he reached across the table, grabbed my shaking hand.

He said, "They're coming for me, not for you."

8:05 P.M.

The police glowered at people, then sat at the two booths behind us, the larger corner booths closest to the Carson Boulevard exit from the 605. They were behind Orange County. They sat facing me.

I looked at the man from Orange County.

I said, "That wasn't funny."

"Guess I was mistaken."

"I'm not laughing."

"Neither am I. I'm ready to get out of here now."

"We ordered coffee. Sit. Don't rush. Take a breath. Act normal."

A couple of the officers gazed at me. I had tried to con a few people that evening. Had been in the parking lot at the casino. Had stopped by two Chevron gas stations, then at the Cash for Gold at Makena Plaza. Had stopped and tried my luck at two Starbucks, Walmart, and a dozen other stores. I'd been all over Hawaiian Gardens. Someone could've called it in. Hoped there wasn't a BOLO out on me.

The man from Orange County had gone cold, hard, angry, his jaw tight.

Coffee came. He sipped. While I sat trying to pretend I wasn't on edge, every ten seconds the waitress stopped and refilled the cups. I gulped and gulped and gulped. Within moments, there was so much caffeine in my body, each time I blinked I saw God. The man from Orange County drank coffee like it was water. He wasn't talking. He was distracted. He stared at the television at times; other times he checked his phone, or just spied around the room. Something was pulling at him, pulling hard.

He said, "Local news is about to come on."

"Do you want to tell the cops about the hit-and-run?"

"Why don't you walk over there and tell them?"

"Is that really your wife's Christmas present? Is that car stolen? Who are you?"

"I gave you my card."

"I threw it away."

"Too bad."

Police radios squawked and added noise to the sudden din in the den of bottom-feeders.

From the speakers on the wall, Frank Sinatra sang a classic Christmas song.

Now anxious to leave, the man from Orange County said, "Let me handle the bill."

"I invited you back to this five-star joint."

"You're used to picking up the tab for your boyfriend, aren't you?"

"And you're used to paying for everything for your wife, aren't you?"

He said, "We could flip for it."

"Heads."

The coin went high, landed, and I slid the tab to his side of the table.

He stood up, regarded the police officers, made direct eye contact, and gave them all season's greetings. The long arm of the law reciprocated. He stood and scowled as if they should know him.

The cops went back to talking to one another.

Then the man from Orange County followed me as we left. Spoons clanked, chatter rose, radios squawked. I felt like I was being watched. I looked back. Every police officer's neck was stretched near to breaking, their eyes glued on me. Men. Easily distracted from what is important.

The night my ex had his daughter, our daughter, when it was his weekend for court-ordered visitation, she had stressed him. She had cried because she wasn't feeling well. A Lakers game was on. He couldn't watch it in peace, and that had stressed him. I was in Canada working on a film. The last film I'd ever worked on. Hollywood can kiss my ass. I should've been with Natalie Rose, not chasing a stupid dream. He had taken a drink to calm his nerves. Once the bottle was opened, the demons had him, and, as the Lakers went down in flames, he drank the river dry. I should've been with Natalie Rose. Or she should've been with me. I failed to protect her.

The thought hit me hard. I stopped walking and my hands became fists. I wanted to scream my child's name until my throat bled from the pain. Then I felt so angry I quivered. So friggin' angry. Had been so angry that I had stopped speaking to the father of my long-dead child; had refused to acknowledge he ever existed. After we buried our daughter, I shut him out of my life. Seeing the boys in blue gave me a jolt. Seeing them look at me and grin felt disgusting.

My chest rising and falling, I turned around, stormed by the man from Orange County, hurried over to the officers, and snapped, "Stop looking at my ass. I know you're saying foul and disgusting crap as I walk away. How about some respect for the people who pay your salary? You see me with a man and do that mess? Half of you are wearing rings. Stop being disgusting and do your damn jobs."

One of the cops said, "Jackie Summers? I was just telling them that I knew you."

"Do I know you?"

"No, but I used to work with Ricky Summers."

"You know my ex-husband?"

"Yeah. We know Ricky. I haven't talked to him since I went to his wedding back in July."

"He's remarried?"

"He married another police officer. They're having a baby soon. You didn't know?"

A fist closed around my heart and a leviathan of animosity and hurt and resentment came down on me. I turned away from them, almost ran away from them, and headed back toward the register, marched up to the man from Orange County. Body tense, I stood close to him, real close, and allowed the men with badges and guns to see me with a handsome man in a tailored suit. I put my hand inside the man from Orange County's hand. Surprised by my touch, he looked at me. I didn't care that he wore a wedding ring. He was a man of quality. Let the cops gossip like bitches. Let them tell Ricky.

The man from Orange County asked, "What just happened?"

"Nothing."

"Something happened. What did you say to the cops?"

"Nothing that I haven't said before to a thousand and one disgusting men like them."

"Should I go have a word?"

"Time on the clock only goes forward. I just need to get away from the past."

Behind us, the preview for the local news came on — again the story about the mother who had lost it and killed her three children. She had used a knife. Again I experienced coldness and lost focus before the news said the next story would be about the old businessman who had been robbed and beaten half to death during an apparent home invasion. It seemed trivial when they said the old man might not live until the sun rose tomorrow. I tried to speculate what could have happened to the mother of those children. Couldn't imagine. The kids would never be able to experience a full life, their lives taken before they could have fun in school, date, go to prom, and marry. Was going to be a bad Christmas for more than a few families. There is never a good time for bereavement, but deaths at Christmastime are the absolute worst. I thought about my child, how I had felt, what I felt now, and I felt for those families. Someone changed the channel, brought me out of my trance, and suddenly the game was on.

They did that for the police, did that for the men who were still watching me.

They stared at me because they knew me.

They knew my story.

They knew my truth.

Behind my smile existed so many levels of pain, so much hurt, and sleeping hostility.

I checked my phone for the umpteenth time, in vain.

God had stopping crying and the ice water from heaven had been put on pause.

We stood in the frigid air and he inspected his damaged car for a moment. There was enough light to see that beauty had turned into a beast. It hurt me to see an expensive car like that damaged.

I took a deep breath. Calmed down. Wasn't my Christmas present; wasn't my problem.

I said, "That's at least eight thousand in damage."

"More like twenty-five. I have insurance."

"Oh, right. What was I thinking? People like you have full coverage and not just liability. I'd have to take my car to a shop in Hawthorne and let an illegal immigrant fix it, and I would have to pay cash."

"I still have to pay the thousand-dollar deductible, and the value will take a dive."

"So that means you want half of the two

grand back?"

"I don't care about that money. Means nothing at all to me."

"Good, because I've gotten kinda used to having it now."

He set free a few curses, kicked away broken parts, squatted, took out a white handkerchief, covered his right hand, then ripped away parts of the fiberglass that would have rubbed against his tire.

I asked, "Is it drivable?"

He nodded, stood, took a deep breath.

I asked, "Heading to go see after your distraught wife?"

"Edwards Cinema is right there. Might take in a movie, blow some time."

I looked at my phone, said, "I might need to blow a little more time, too."

"After I see a movie, after I take a moment to de-stress, then I'll go find my wife."

"Which movie are you going to see?"

He looked at a movie app on his phone and said, "The remake of *Annie* just started."

"I should head toward my boyfriend's area, but I want to see *Annie.* Movies make me happy."

"I don't mind the company, but we'd need to rush."

I said, "Let me get my car."

He looked at the traffic and said, "It's right there. We could just walk across the street."

"Nobody in California walks. It makes you look homeless or poor."

He started walking toward the street and said, "We'd only have to find another parking space."

I pulled my jacket tighter, my breath fogging out in resentment and abhorrence as I strolled.

My ex-husband had remarried. Our child had died, and he had moved on so damn easily.

At the crosswalk, we had to wait for the light to change. Cars drove close to the curb, sent spray our way. He took my hand, pulled me back from the curb. I was about to pull away, but I didn't.

The traffic was as cold and mean as his expression.

He said, "Wind is picking up. Let's jaywalk."

"You're going to break the law?"

"You're bold enough to run a scam, but scared to jaywalk?"

"Whatever. If we get a $250 ticket, you're paying for mine, too."

He held my hand with his injured hand, protected me, put his body on the side of stopped traffic and shielded me as we crossed the street, walking around slow-moving cars like we were in New York. When we crossed the street, I thought the man from Orange County would let my hand go, but he held it, had me walk on the inside, the position a lady walked in, not on the outside, the position where a man puts a woman who is for sale. The man I'd thought was a disgusting asshole was a gentleman. I thought about my boyfriend and felt guilty, but I adjusted my hand until our fingers were interlocked. We remained that way until we made it past the line of traffic struggling to get into the Long Beach Towne Center, down the sidewalk, through frigid air and drizzle, past shopping madness, past waterlogged Christmas trees, past signs that read "Happy Holidays," none saying "Merry Christmas" because they were cowards who didn't want to offend those who had different beliefs. When we made it to the front of the cinema, he let my hand go so he could take his wallet out. Just like that, I sort of missed the connection. Missed the sensation of touch. He had already given me money and a meal, and now he was going to pay for the movie.

I told him, "No. This is on me. It's my turn."

"We could flip for it."

"Does your wife ever pay for anything?"

"Not even Decadence."

He put his wallet away. I bought the tickets, paid for popcorn, bought sodas. It felt good doing that. It felt good not coming off like I was a freeloader or a gold digger. I appreciated what he had, but what he had belonged to him. It belonged to him and his wife. My life would change. I'd get past the grief and be able to function on the level I used to function. I would get my own townhome one day.

We entered the crowded theater, where we were forced to sit down front, and we had missed the first ten minutes of the movie. We sat down, heads back, and watched the movie, casually eating popcorn, without talking, but we shared the armrest between us, sat with our arms touching. A guy in front of us was sending text messages when we sat down. The man from Orange County made a negative sound.

I guess he was used to going to the opera, or to the theatre on London's West End.

The seating was uncomfortable, and I leaned toward the man from Orange County because a fat dude was on the other side of me and I didn't want a stranger touching me. I was so close to the man from Orange

County that my head was almost on his shoulder. Seconds after we sat down, we were laughing at what was funny, being quiet during the serious moments. We shared moments created by Hollywood, and it felt as if there was a thin psychological closeness between us. I bit my bottom lip; I hadn't been to a movie in a while. I used to take Natalie Rose to the movie theater at the Baldwin Hills Crenshaw mall every weekend. She could watch the same kiddie movie every week; she didn't care. She would memorize the dialogue and start to talk along with the actors, and she would sing with every song to the point of distraction. Now I looked around the theater, looked for children, looked for her.

He asked me, "You okay?"

I pushed my lips up into a faux smile. "I'm great. What's the problem?"

"That bright light from that big phone isn't bothering you? It's like the sun in my eyes."

The guy in front of us continued sending text messages, text after text. Orange County was very agitated, and that energy moved from his body to where we were connected, rolled into my system. He pulled away from me, leaned forward, grabbed the headrest of the guy's chair, pulled it all the way back, then made it throw the guy forward. The rude guy jumped and looked back.

Orange County leaned forward and said, "That's what it feels like to have you in front of me sending text after text after goddamn text. Turn the damn phone off or I will keep popping your seat."

"Don't come at me like that. You don't know me."

"Did you not see the message that said to turn off all phones and not text? Or do they need to put your goddamn name and photo in the announcement so your dumb ass will know you're included?"

The rude guy looked Orange County up and down, saw a man who was pissed off to the max, then told his date to not worry about the assholes behind them. Orange County sat back down. I sat back down. The guy in front of us mumbled something, some insult to his date, directed at us, then got up and left. His date and two other friends followed. They said some vulgar things on the way out — had to get in the last word. Orange County was about to get up, but I held his hand and he sat back in his seat.

The rude asshole who had been in front of us came back with security. They came in like Nazis with flashlights and pulled the man from Orange County and me from our seats, escorted us to the lobby, and asked us to leave. I was about to pitch a bitch, but Orange County just smiled at them and told them to refund my money for the tickets, popcorn, and soda. I gave them back the change they had given me and they gave me back my same hundred-dollar bill. I wanted my damn c-note back. I pitched a fit and made them find the one I had given them, just to give them some trouble.

We were led to the front door like illegal aliens from south of the border being deported back into Tijuana. I bounced my body like I was in a hip-hop video, threw up two stiff middle fingers, and shouted over and over like I was Iggy Azalea in a bad mood, "Merry Kiss-My-Ass, bitches."

We moved with excitement and anger through the yuletide crowd, and went back out into the darkness. I turned my cell back on; still no return message from Chicken and Waffles.

I said, "Well, that was the best ten-minute date I ever had."

"It wasn't a date. And I think that was about five minutes."

"Oh, yeah. Right. We're just holding hands and kicking it like homies."

Orange County turned his phone back on. It buzzed with messages. His jaw tightened again.

I asked, "Any messages from your distraught and jealous skinny white wife?"

"She's called and sent quite a few texts, and so have a few other people we know."

"Everything okay?"

"As good as it's going to get until something changes for the better or the worse."

"Guess you won't be getting her over-the-top luxury car fixed before Christmas."

"She doesn't deserve it."

My box cutter was in my hand. I expected to see the assholes we had had a moment with following us. Orange County was tense, his hands in fists, and he kept looking back. No one was there.

I asked, "Are we jaywalking again?"

He took my hand and mocked my tirade, "Merry Christmas, bitches."

"It's Merry Kiss-My-Ass, bitches. If you're going to steal my punch lines, get them right."

"Whatever."

He held my hand and it felt natural. My hand slid into his. The warmth of his hand surrounded mine and made me wish Carson Boulevard was miles more than six lanes wide. He let my hand go when we made it to the sidewalk. I put my hand in my pocket, missing the sensation of being touched.

8:34 P.M.

Shoulders hunched against the cold, he said, "Thanks for the movie."

I laughed. "Whatever. I really wanted to see that movie, too."

"Never been kicked out of a movie theater before."

"Movies, libraries, church — I've been asked to leave everything at least once."

When the man from Orange County escorted me toward my candy-white convertible VW Beetle, we stood in the chilly, damp darkness. I had parked in the back of the Denny's lot, close to a used car lot that had cartoonish, colorful walls. I paused and gazed at a large image of Betty Boop holding a steering wheel and waving as she drove. She was painted on the fire-red, sky-blue, and yellow walls. It definitely stood out and made drivers pause. The disgusting police had parked back in that part of the lot as well. We stood at the rear of four police cars and continued making small talk in the dank weather made for creating colds, flu, and pneumonia, as if we were on the beach on a sunny day.

The temperature was in the forties. I pretended I wasn't freezing from the walk back.

He said, "Before you go, may I ask you two questions?"

"Sure."

"Your hair."

"You prefer it long and blond?"

"It was against my neck at the movies. Felt nice."

"You hate it and are about to give me a speech about conformity, right?"

"On the contrary. I admire the history that it holds."

"Thanks. That caught me off guard. What's the first question?"

"May I touch your dreadlocks?"

That made me pause and tilt my head. "Why would you want to touch my hair?"

"I've never touched dreadlocks before, never experienced the texture."

"Ever gone out with a black woman who has natural hair?"

"Never."

"Wow. But why am I not surprised? Seems like white, Indian, Spanish, and Asian men are more accepting of a black woman with natural hair than most black men are. Dude, you disappoint me."

"May I touch your dreadlocks?"

"Sure you want to do that? Last guy who touched my hair died of sepsis."

"I have insurance. I'll rush to Kaiser and let them fill me with antibiotics."

"You have insurance? Must be nice. I break a leg, it's bankruptcy for me."

"Break your leg, buy some duct tape, and you can use my staple gun."

"Whatever. Letting someone touch my hair, that's a big thing — monumental, dude — because letting someone put their unwanted energy in my hair, that could change my energy for life, could change me."

"Okay. Was just asking. No problem."

"Now I have a question."

"Okay."

"When you see a black man or black woman with dreads, what is your first thought?"

"They are Rastafarian. And the hair is nasty, ugly, unkempt, dirty, and probably has lice."

"You're living up to the black-hating stereotypes in Orange County."

"A lot of people think that way."

"My hair is not nasty, not ugly, not unkempt, not dirty. My hair is clean."

"Your hair is amazing. It's beautiful. Smells very nice. Your dreads are like very fine braids."

"These are sister locks, but I still call them dreads. I have no hang-ups about the nomenclature used in the science of hair. *Dread* might sound negative to some, but I really don't give two poots and a biscuit what anyone thinks. Nasty? Never. I put a lot of work into maintaining my hair. My hair smells very nice. My body always smells nice. I'm not a nasty woman. I dab when I'm done."

"Dab?"

"After I pee-pee. I don't use the bathroom and just get up and walk away. I use wipes and dab. And you want to know what nasty hair is? Weaves. You have some women who will leave weave in their hair for six months, and when they go to remove the mess, they have mold growing in their real hair."

"Wait. Women will pee and walk away without . . . dabbing?"

"There are some nasty bitches out there. If they don't dab the front end, they probably don't wipe the back end. That's women of all colors and races. Guess what? I'm not one. I smell nice at all times."

"Didn't mean to offend you. I will take

that lecture as a long way of saying no."

"No, I wasn't saying no. You can touch my locks, but I wanted you to know that it is a big deal for me. I don't want you to think I'm the kind of woman who lets any man, some stranger, touch her locks."

"You sure?"

I nodded again. He came closer, entered that invisible three feet of personal space, and ran his fingers through my locks, then across my hair. I thought that he would just take one and feel its power and texture, but he touched my roots as if he were trying to read my history, touched my roots and massaged my hair, massaged my scalp. It felt good. I licked my lips. He ran his fingers across hair that held the strength of a thousand ropes, of a thousand ancestors who won a thousand battles before they lost a war on the shores of Africa, a war that sent many into the Middle Passage, a lost moment that had sent a culture into an unrecoverable depression, and he smiled like he understood, this man who lived behind the Orange Curtain, away from the poverty of people who looked like him, away from the culture of men who had hair like mine. Then I reached up to him, touched his face.

I did it without thinking. I touched his

face and looked into his eyes.

I took a step away, gave him an uncomfortable smile. He smiled back.

Then he looked into my eyes, and his expression seemed to say that watching me was like smoking opium.

When we made decadent eye contact, he laughed like a shy boy. I almost laughed a little girl's laugh, too. I laughed, but I remained cold, an ice queen. Had to keep my walls high or the enemy would try to climb over. Cold rain fell again and he looked at me like I was beautiful, as if he were an ancient explorer who was desirous of crossing the Bering Strait and venturing deep inside another country. I was beyond my age of innocence, self-indulgent games no longer new or surprising to me.

Then he broke the stare, shut down the moment, and checked the time on his cell.

I looked at the time on mine, again checking for a text message, freeing myself from his gaze.

When I raised my eyes from my Samsung, his erotic eyes were waiting to see mine.

I tried to read his body language. I had lost that ability. I was without power. As we maintained eye contact, he confessed that he had wanted to feel my hair from the moment he had seen my locks. I nodded, told him that I was glad to fulfill that small wish, and said that I was glad that he had asked first or I would've been offended. Someone touching my hair — it was a personal thing.

He said, "There was a second question."

"What do I win if I get the answer right?"

"I'll go across the street to TGI Fridays and buy you cheesecake, if you like cheesecake."

"Oh, hell yeah. I love cheesecake. My thighs want the best cheesecake in L.A."

"Sure you want to know the question?"

"Dude, we're talking cheesecake. What's the question?"

He asked, "May I kiss you?"

I stopped blinking. The six lanes of traffic stopped moving. That question made the world stop spinning. A chill ran up and down my spine. My hands opened and closed a thousand times.

I cleared my throat, took a step away, and shook my head, folded my arms across my breasts.

I said, "That came out of nowhere."

"Not for me."

"Well, it did for me. Why in the hell would you want to kiss me?"

"Have you seen you?"

"I'm not big on looking in mirrors."

"What did you think I was going to ask?"

"You have a wife."

"I do. Somewhere out there, I have a wife."

"I have a boyfriend."

"I know. You have Chicken and Waffles."

"Whatever. We have people to kiss."

"Regardless, before I go away and never see you again, I want to kiss you."

My breath fogged in front of my face, telling me the temperature had dropped.

I looked at him. Tall. Well dressed. Intellectual swag. Successful. Professional.

And he had some edge to him; some academic, lack-of-self-control bad boy was in his blood.

I glanced at his car, then at his wedding ring. He had a cow to make go moo. I had someone to get the milk for free. I was an L.A. girl and he was an O.C. dude. We had nothing in common.

I said, "Convince me. Tell me why you want to kiss me."

"You're a person of great wit, of great intellect."

"But?"

"There is no but. You're a beautiful bel esprit in dreadlocks."

"Wow. That was a real compliment."

"It was."

"And why should I want to kiss you?"

"Because we'll never have the chance

137

again. This is our once-in-a-lifetime moment."

We stared. He had held my hand. He had
touched my hair.

I said, "It would be just a kiss."

"Can I? May I? Will you? Can we?"

"Are you a good kisser?"

"Don't know. Never took kissing classes
in university."

"You have to kiss the right people. Other-
wise you just end up with spit in your
mouth."

"You get cheesecake."

"Just one kiss?"

"Just one."

"For how long?"

"Ten seconds."

"Five. Take it or leave it."

"Okay. Five. Up to you."

I nodded. "Guess a short kiss won't hurt
anybody. It's almost Christmas. All the palm
trees — we can say those are mistletoe, and
it will be a kiss based on custom and
culture. It can be our secret."

He asked, "You okay?"

"I need to floss."

I reached into my purse, took out floss,
pulled him a long strip, did the same for
myself.

Then I said, "I don't like bad breath. I

have a fear of bad breath."

I dug in my purse and pulled out two individually wrapped, melt-in-your-mouth hospitality mints that I had left over from eating breakfast at Chick-fil-A about two weeks ago.

I handed him one. "Suck on that first."

"Seriously?"

"I want you to suck it. Or there will be no kiss."

He unwrapped his and I unwrapped mine.

He sucked on his and I sucked on mine.

He asked, "How do we do this?"

"Dude, you're the one who wanted the stupid kiss. Make it happen or say good night. And let me put down the rules. No sloppy tongue, no ass-grabbing, and no grinding. I'll slap the Jesus out of you."

He took my hands and eased me closer. His touch, my fingertips in his hand, made me tingle, and that tingle ran across my lower back, startled me, and I almost tripped, felt aware, clumsy. Then we were close, bodies touching, adjusting, trying to figure who should put their hands where, how close we really needed to stand, like we were middle school kids getting ready to start their first slow dance.

"Dude."

"What?"

"To the right. You're supposed to turn your head to the right when you kiss, not to the left."

"It looked like you were turning your head to the left, so I mirrored your movement."

"I was adjusting my dreadlocks. Don't want one to end up in our mouths."

His finger touched my chin and I turned my neck, angled my mouth toward his.

His lips touched mine and I felt a mild jolt. His tongue touched my lips and I jumped.

He asked, "You okay?"

"Let's try that again."

"We don't have to."

"No, I want to."

"You're falling apart."

"Trying to not freak out. I can do this. I can. I can do this."

My mouth opened, not all at once, but it creaked open and accepted the tip of his tongue.

The tip. Just the tip. It always starts with them whispering they want to give you the tip.

I felt the tip of his tongue. Our tongues touched. And we were connected.

My mouthed opened a little more, then a little more.

Our tongues intertwined.

I opened my eyes. I saw that his eyes were closed. Then I closed my eyes again.

My heartbeat accelerated. My hands held him to keep steady. My breathing thickened.

I was nervous. I exhaled tension, unable to relax, like I was having sex for the first time.

Then it felt like summer. The tension dissipated. Kissing him became a meditation. His tongue moved in and out of my mouth, tasted me in a slow, easy, unhurried, perfect rhythm, hypnotic and smooth, then he sucked my tongue, sucked it softly, and, without warning, I imagined other things.

One minute. Two minutes. Three. Four. I fell into a sweet, warm haze. Dizzy, I eased away from the kiss, from him, moved five steps back, put a safe distance between us and caught my breath.

"Damn, dude."

"What?"

I looked down at the ground, looked at the dark, damp asphalt under my Timberlands.

He asked, "What happened?"

"I'm checking to see if my drawers came off. That kiss was a panty-dropper."

He came back to me. My head tilted to the right and my mouth opened as my eyes closed. Our tongues reconnected. Soft.

Sweet. It became a hungry embrace, and at that moment everything in this world seemed all right. Another minute passed before we paused. We stared at each other. Tilted heads again. We kissed again and I felt a strong, unexpected desire; I felt famished for this. My clit began to twerk. The taste of his tongue was like a brand-new type of sweetness, and I couldn't get enough.

I said, "Don't kiss me like . . . like . . . like this."

"I could tell you the same."

We kissed again.

I said, "Jesus . . . you can kiss . . . you can kiss . . . damn you can kiss."

"Your tongue-piercing — it gives something extra to the kiss."

"You like that, don't you?"

I sucked his lip and my body quaked, and I felt the earth move beneath my feet, felt the ground shift like it was about to break apart and separate us, move him away from me for my own good.

I drew in a deep breath, many deep breaths, curt exhales, gasped as my breath fogged from my mouth, then panted, actually snorted, and let out one long exhale as I sang, "Damn, damn, damn."

I eased away, light-headed, but he pulled

me back to his tongue. The kiss became so intense, too passionate, too hungry, too greedy. I imagined the collapse of every building from West Covina to San Ysidro to Santa Monica, imagined the earth swallowing every man-made structure. The kiss set off landslides, snow avalanches, tsunamis, and volcanic eruptions of ice in my head, inside my body.

I whispered, "You're grinding on me. Told you not to grind on me."

"Sorry about that."

"No, don't stop. Just position yourself . . . little this way . . . little that way . . . right there."

If I had a fault line, he was definitely on my fault line. He was on my focus, on the spot where it all begins, moving against me. It felt so good. Like we were in a club slow dancing to a love song.

He kissed me and I kissed him and I was shaking, shaking and moving against him. He moved his cock clockwise, and my callipygous backside joined in, only it moved in the opposite direction.

I didn't know how to stop. I didn't know how to end this moment. The twitches were small, but he felt them, could tell by the way I moved that his serenade had me wanting to sing him a lullaby.

I enjoyed the moment for what it was, something that shouldn't be happening, yet it was.

People walked by. Cars started. Horns blew across six lanes of traffic.

I said, "Okay, okay, okay. That's enough. No more kisses."

Out of breath, we stood in stunned silence. Twitches continued. Then I held his face and pulled him back to me. It was another slow and easy kiss. He stirred me. The kissing had me starry-eyed.

Chest rising and falling, my voice heavy, I said, "Curiosity satisfied?"

"Not really. May I move your hair back away from your neck?"

"Whatever you're thinking will cost you more cheesecake just for thinking it."

He pulled my dreadlocks back, sucked my neck for a while. Sucked my neck, sucked my ear, sucked my neck. For two or three minutes, my toes curled inside my Timberlands.

He created an earthquake inside me, and earthquakes cause damage.

He stopped. Kissed me again. Soft kisses. And again. And again. And again.

Eyes closed, feeling him as I kissed him, I asked, "Don't you need to get to your distraught wife?"

"Your voice is husky; sounds like honey and bourbon."

I whispered, "Time out, time out, time out. What the hell do you think you're doing?"

"Your tongue tastes so sweet."

"It's the candy."

"This is sweeter than candy."

We kissed. My brain, the same region that is affected by addictive drugs like cocaine, was flooded with dopamine. Sweet dopamine spiked. My brain was stimulated. My body was stimulated.

This wasn't right. Sentiment covered the logical part of me, came like a harbor wave.

And as we kissed I pulled him closer, and my inappropriate thoughts became words, rolled off of my tongue, sounded heated and felt like fire when I asked, "Do you have to go to your wife right now?"

"What else is there to do in the rain?"

"You have an hour?"

"I should be able to manage an hour. What do you want to do?"

"We could go drive Sunset Boulevard and see the ex-men."

"The movie?"

"No, real ex-men. We can go watch the transvestites; we might see Eddie Murphy."

"I was hoping you'd want to go bowling."

"We could stop grinding and playing kissing games and you could go buy condoms."

That caught him off guard. I felt exposed, like I had crossed a line.

He kept his face close to mine, his lips on mine as he asked, "Are you serious?"

"You want some of this tonight? Guilty pleasure with no strings attached."

"Are you teasing me?"

"Who jokes about condoms this close to Christmas?"

"You're trembling."

"Because I think I just put myself out there and made a fool of myself."

He sucked my bottom lip. "You're interested in me in that way?"

"Dude, I think I just asked you if you wanted to have sex."

"Why would you want to have sex with me?"

"You're turning this around? What, am I the dude now? Don't make me the dude, dude."

"I'm surprised, that's all. Girls like you are never interested in a guy like me."

"You're hot. Disgusting, but hot."

"Since when do you think I am hot?"

"So do you want some of this or not? And you're old enough to know what *some* means."

He pulled me back to him. "I think that we are attracted to one another."

"The way you kissed my neck, I wanted to rip your freakin' clothes off."

"Are you serious about condoms?"

"Do you have time? I have to be somewhere soon, so cut to the chase."

"I'll find time."

"Take me to Pompeii, find us a romping shop in a comfortable fornicave."

"I can figure out the word *fornicave.* Romping shop?"

"A bed. Do you want to get us a warm, dry place to kick it for an hour?"

"You're smiling and laughing a little, so I can't judge how serious you are."

"I mean, you don't have to. You have a distraught wife. I don't want to be out of line."

"I want you, too. I don't know this area. Where can we go?"

"Don't even think about the Crazy 8 Motel or Lakewood Inn. No trucker-hooker hot spots."

"No problem. Any other suggestions?"

"There's a La Quinta Inn about a mile up the road."

"No. You deserve better than a place where you park right outside your room."

"Wow. Okay. Then we'll have to leave the

area to make that happen."

"I'll use my phone and ask Siri for a list of better hotels."

"I'm a Samsung gal, but I'm not going to hate Siri for helping us out right now."

"I'll get directions. You'll have to follow me."

"First order of business. Condoms?"

"Have to buy them."

"I'll follow you to get the condoms. I have to choose, not because I don't trust you or think you're not competent enough to choose a rubber, but because certain types make me itch like hell. Another brand makes me . . . break out . . . down there; that spermicide stuff, that spermicide nonoxynol-9, not only makes my vagina have a very bad reaction, but causes a smell, and that odor will stick around."

"Understood."

"I don't want to be alone. It's so Christmassy and cold and wet and dark, and I want to be warm and dry and not be so alone for a little while. Christmas is not an easy time of the year for me."

"Understood. Winter and Christmas are hard times for a lot of people."

"Christmas a bad time for you, too?"

"Right now, this is a bad Christmas season

for me, but, like you, I don't want to be alone."

"I'm talking too much, but how does it feel? Asking you to chill with me for an hour or so, how does that seem to you? I feel like a dude all of a sudden, and I am not a girl who wants to be a dude."

"It feels like I just exited the nightmare of all nightmares and fell into a fantastic dream."

I said, "Kiss me again. Let's make sure this is the real deal."

Then he gave me the tongue again. I was more relaxed, more open, and could feel all that he transmitted. It was a song, a movement, passage of light, a playful character, like the second or third movement of a sonata or a symphony. It was poetry. I felt like I came. He rubbed against me and it felt like I was having small orgasms. I held him, shivered, became a storm, revealed how passionate I could be, tried to turn him out. He let loose and showed me the same. Another handful of minutes went by.

I blinked a dozen times, in a trance.

He asked, "Are you okay?"

"You're wearing boxers."

"Boxers don't leave much to the imagination."

"Oh, I'm imagining things I really

shouldn't be imagining."

He walked with me, held my right hand, that act telling me that he had claimed me, that he desired me in a sexual way. I didn't let him walk me all the way. Didn't want him to see the mess inside my VW. Didn't want him to look into my dilated pupils and ask me questions that would take me back to anger. I had been stressed. I had been anxious. I had been depressed. I had been hostile to the world.

I pulled my seat belt on, and then I checked behind me, looked for Natalie Rose. I expected to see my daughter in the backseat holding a doll in each hand. Old habit. The car seat was in my rearview. Too many Barbies scattered on the floor. They looked at me like I was being irresponsible, like I was being a bad mommy.

I hesitated. Turned the signal light on to go in the same direction as the fancy car, then aimed the steering wheel to go the opposite way. I could take off, zoom away, never see him again in my life.

I could end it at the kiss. I touched my dreadlocks. He had touched my dreadlocks. He had kissed me. After kissing someone like that, with that much passion, he was part of you. His DNA was inside my mouth. Philophobia, the fear of becoming attached, the fear of falling into something that felt like love, rose inside me. I shuddered like I had an acute case. But that was impossible. Orange County and I had nothing in common. It would just be sex; one night of bad sex with a handsome guy. It would be amusing. And since there was no sunshine, it might improve my dark mood for two minutes.

He wasn't husband material for me, and I wasn't wife material for him. This wasn't about anything beyond the next couple of hours. Those were the reasons to go with him and the reasons to run away.

Then I saw a break in traffic and pulled out as well, followed his trail, sped up, caught up with him. Whatever happened next wasn't about him. This was a decision. I made sure none of the Barbies could see me. Turned their heads to the side. It was about me, what my soul needed more than what my body desired. There wasn't any way I would end up drunk and wake up married to a stranger. I checked my cell again. No message from Chicken and Waffles. That confirmed my decision to walk the road less traveled. Everyone vanishes from life every now and then. I needed to vanish from the dystopia that existed both inside and outside of me. I could be a bad girlfriend for once. I could be a naughty mommy.

Again I looked back at the child's seat. Had thought I'd heard her laughing.

A block later, he left the slow-moving traffic and pulled into the turn lane. I thought he'd had a change of heart, that the distraught wife had called him sobbing and needed him by her side.

Part of me was hoping that she had.

He could engage me in conversation. He listened and had things to say worth hearing.

He had held my hand. Touched my hair. He had kissed me. Without warning, he had aroused me. He was very handsome. He was married; miserable, but married. He could talk about how unhappy he is, have sex with me, and be back between his wife's legs in time for Christmas, the memory of me forgotten, as if I never existed. I would be back with the guy I was seeing, possibly tonight, as if he never existed.

I should not follow him, but Susan was at the wheel now. Susan was determined to satisfy her curiosity.

He pulled back into traffic, fought rudeness and fought his way to the right lane. Now I assumed he had car problems, that the hit-and-run had created a mechanical issue. His turn signal illuminated and he pulled over. He'd located a 7-Eleven. And where there was a 7-Eleven, there were condoms.

I guess he had asked Siri for the closest place to buy prophylactics.

A Nissan filled with guys was in the turn lane right behind, also pulling into 7-Eleven.

In a few seconds, I'd wish we'd never gone inside that convenience store. There are more than fifty thousand 7-Elevens in sixteen countries, and those assholes chose to rob the one I was in.

When we arrived, the 7-Eleven was empty. One cashier. The man from Orange County was looking at bottles of wine. I was near the front, browsing fashion magazines. Thirty seconds after we arrived the double glass doors opened and bad news hurried in from the rain. Two pants-sagging fools. Could've been Asian or Mexican, or black guys who had one white parent. Same hue, same hair. One of the hoods turned, looked around. The other hood checked the aisles, passed bottled water, iced tea, energy drinks, crackers, cakes, and yogurts. I kept my eyes averted, silently told him I knew what was up, and didn't make direct eye contact. I knew that move. He was the lookout. Baggy pants and hoodies. It was the way they kept their dark hoodies over their heads after they entered the convenience store that announced this was going to be bad. Bad luck had followed me. This was going to be an act of violence. Then the third guy rushed in, armed with a gun, and ordered the store employee to open the register. I tried to signal to Orange County, wanted to scream, but he was walking toward the register.

He looked down at his watch, ignored the bad news waiting at the front of the store.

The one with the gun was busy making the store employee empty the cash register.

I hurried that way, out of instinct, wanting to protect, to stop Orange County.

Orange County glanced at me and shook his head.

He wanted me to stay where I was. He strolled right by the two lookouts.

They looked at the brown-skinned man in the nice gray suit like he had lost his mind.

He casually went toward the counter like he was about to pay for his two bottles. I thought he was going to put his bottles of wine on the counter. Then he gritted his teeth, became Denzel in *Training Day,* Idris Elba in *The Wire,* and, with the bottle in his right hand, pulled his arm back the way I imagined a man playing racquetball pulled back his racquet when he was about to execute a kill shot. Energy crackled as it passed from his legs and hips to his wrist without dissipating. The kinetic links never broke. He had perfect form. He held the neck of the bottle and brought the base across the left temple of the man holding the gun. The impact was fast and wicked, a dull thud, but it was loud. He followed through with his strike, his body twisting. He hit the man and the gun went off, exploded and echoed, sent a bullet into the cigarettes. The cashier screamed. I think I screamed, too. The other two guys ducked and yelled out in their native tongues. The wine bottle that the gunman had been hit with spun on impact, bounced off the back wall, hit energy pills, crashed to the floor and broke, that, too, sounding like a gun-shot. There had been so much force behind that blow, plus kickback from the gun. When the gun had gone off, I had blinked, had recoiled and felt the energy from the blast roll through my body, awaken whatever part of me was still asleep, stimulate what had been numb. The gun tumbled behind the counter and fell into the hands of the cashier. The cashier screamed over and over, screamed like he was falling from the top of the Empire State Building. Gravity pulled the gunman to the tiled floor. He landed on his face, another dull thud.

Orange County turned and looked at the other guys, the second bottle now in his right hand.

They had seen the way he had hit their coworker.

Orange County gritted his teeth and nodded as if to tell them the next move was theirs.

They would've attacked him by now, like wolves, but I had come to the front of the store and I had my box cutter in my hand. Before they could rush him, they'd have to get by me. I was a wolverine, and a wolverine could run animals ten times its size out of the woods. They saw me, anxious, eyes on them, my blood now whisky and ice. They had paused, and in that pause they lost their advantage. The cashier had the gun. He was shaking, yelling in Arabic, but he had the gun in his hand. The thugs screamed in their thug language, barked at us like we had no right to interrupt them while they worked. They turned over stands filled with chips and junk food, bolted out of the store and left their friend behind, ran to a waiting car. Tires spun on damp pavement. Headlights came on after they took to the streets. They didn't come back with guns. Where they had been stood fear and anger wrapped in silence. The energy was powerful. My heart beat strong. It beat so damn strong. I floated over the scene, lived outside of my body.

I looked at the thug on the tile floor. Kicked his foot. He didn't move.

The man from Orange County smiled at the cashier, calmly said, "This the best wine you have?"

"Uh . . . uh . . . uh . . . we got chardonnays, merlots, and cabernets."

"Is this the best sweet red wine you have? This one from Argentina?"

The cashier snapped, *"He pointed a gun in my face."*

"How much is the wine that I have in front of me?"

"For you? Anything you want is free. You saved my life. Both of you saved my life. You are a great couple. You are the best husband and wife in the world. I will give you what you need for free."

"No. I'll pay. Would hate for you to lose your job over a bottle of wine."

"I'm calling the police."

"No police. Not yet. Let me finish shopping."

I said, "His car just got wrecked, so he's very irritable. He's having what seem like mood swings, and might be depressed because of his marriage. So, basically, he's PMSing and having a really bad night."

The clerk was wide-eyed, on autopilot, his

voice at a pitch higher than Mike Tyson's, he was talking so fast. "Anything else? Slurpee? Glazed doughnut? Milk? *USA Today* newspaper?"

The man from Orange County took his time and said, "Condoms."

"Condoms? You need condoms?"

I said, "We just met and we're about to go have sex for the first and last time."

The man from Orange Country said, "She has a boyfriend who loves chicken and waffles."

I said, "He's married to a rich, distraught, jealous chick who probably loves oysters and caviar."

The cashier trembled and said, *"That man on the ground pointed a gun in my face."*

The cashier dumped all the condoms on the counter, dozens spilling to the damp and dirty floor. Then he manically dumped energy drinks and cartons of U.S.A. Black Gold natural enhancement sex pills, Vigour Gold, Wolf Shark, and a dozen other penis-hardening pills in front of us as well.

He took deep breaths, and, with tears in his eyes, said, "Take them all. You can have all of them."

Orange County displayed his trademark frown, aimed it up at the store's security camera.

I picked two packs of flavored Durex, fruity flavors, both claiming to have an ingredient that kept a man from coming too soon. I dropped both boxes next to the red wine. Since my vagina didn't have taste buds, the flavored condoms implied something that wasn't going to happen. Unless he did something first, I'd never go down. I'd fallen for that trick before. But this guy wasn't going to be around tomorrow. He was as disposable to me as I was to him, so fellatio wasn't an option.

While Orange County wasn't looking I palmed a small package of stay-hard pills. The package said that it was the top-rated erection pill Zytenz. I eased that inside my pocket and winked at the cashier. He was too traumatized to care. I picked up an energy drink, too. While I did that, the door swung open and I tensed. But it wasn't more thug-stateers. A group of old people arrived, flooded inside the 7-Eleven, and started shopping. Thug on the damp tile, the store in disarray, the old folks marched in and stepped over everything. Blacks. Asians. Spanish speaking. Casino crawlers. Like the casino, they were all nitty-gritty and in desperate need of face-lifts. The legion of losers stormed in in search of lottery tickets and food cheaper and better than what the casino had to offer. This world was dull, possessed no elegance. They wanted cigarettes and beer so they could get back to the ocean of green tables in a third-rate casino where people from all walks of life gathered to play poker. I'd spent many nights at that poker table when I wore my ring on my left hand, had spent too many days and nights married to the wrong man.

Orange County handed the shaken cashier his American Express charge card. He paid for the wine and the condoms. We left, went back out into the brisk air and rain. We stood at the front of the store, in a cramped parking lot, in an area populated by vagrants. Orange County massaged his right hand.

I dropped the box cutter in the pocket of my Lakers jacket, then opened the energy drink.

He said, "You're still trembling. Thought you were tough."

"I'm at my toughest when I'm scared."

I handed him the energy drink. His hand was shaking a little.

Then I opened the Zytenz. I handed him two pills.

He asked, "What's this?"

"Aspirin."

Without questioning me, he opened the energy drink, then threw the pills in his mouth and washed both down. I took the energy drink from him, took a nervous sip. We'd kissed; we'd shared fluids by kissing. I wiped my nose, wiped sweat from my forehead, pulled my dreadlocks from my face, threw my scarf around my neck, and then three-pointed the energy drink into the garbage bin not far from us.

Over the sound of traffic and rain, again, like clockwork, sirens came alive in the distance.

His voice trembled when he said, "Everything that just happened, it's all on the security video in the store."

"Just like the car accident at Denny's. They have us on video eating inside Denny's."

"This is different. Way different than a hit-and-run."

"But if we run, this could be considered a hit-buy-condoms-and-run-so-you-can-hit-it-too."

"You never stop with the wisecracks, do you?"

I told him, "If we stay, you might get a key to the city in a ceremony. Would be a small key."

"Still wisecracking."

"Could be a big Christmas reward. You'd be online and make the local paper."

Orange County wanted nothing to do with the police.

The sirens came closer.

With my Lakers jacket shielding me from the cold winter rain, I hurried toward my VW.

Condoms and wine in his hands, Orange County jogged toward his injured luxury car.

I led him down narrow, urban side streets, shortcuts known to taxi drivers, cops, and criminals who specialized in carjacking, navigating us through a hundred and one gang zones. I am a fast driver, L.A.-style, and I rolled though stop signs and red lights, barely touching my brakes, and he kept up with my wicked pace. When I looked in my rearview, I saw his silhouette driving in the ultimate comfort, could tell he was yapping on his cell the entire ride. He had called the distraught wife. His hand was moving like he was arguing. Twenty-five miles later we arrived at Century Boulevard. He hung up his phone and took the lead from there. For the next two miles I followed his dented luxury ride, until we arrived at a five-star hotel near LAX. He went to the best hotel on the strip. I didn't hang out on that level. That was intimidating. Made me question what kind of sex he was expecting. I was curious about him, wanted to salve my loneliness for a few minutes, then resume my life. We valet parked. Before I got out of my car, I moved the ring I had worn when I was married to Natalie Rose's father to my left hand. Felt wrong doing that. Orange County waited for me. Again, I looked at him, at the debonair man in the suit of all suits, at his shoes. I wasn't in clothes on the level of his, but I wanted the hotel staff to regard me with respect. I grabbed my bag, hoping he wouldn't say anything about me carrying so much, but I wanted it to look like I was arriving as a guest, not as rented coochie. He carried my bag in his left hand. He brought nothing with him — a man with no luggage, with no baggage, just an eclectic woman with her pink-and-green oversize bag of a generic brand, and a bottle of red wine from South America. The condoms were anxious, dancing in his pocket.

The lobby of the magnificent edifice that catered to the vices of its clientele was marble and glass. It smelled like hopes and dreams and silent immigrants who worked for barely enough to get by, and was filled with simple creatures avoiding complex lives. Dozens of hip professionals were at the bar having a bodacious Christmas party.

Music jammed, Billy Idol singing "Jingle Bell Rock." Top-shelf alcohol flowed like a river. It was the kind of party that started after work and went on until last call. Drunken women in very sheer catch-a-cold-or-catch-a-man dresses were acting like they were on spring break in Cancún. Inebriated men in dark suits were having the time of their lives, making passes and grabbing asses and refilling glasses. I was nettled because my clothes weren't on their level and the high and lofty airs of those alcoholic assholes reminded me of all that had gone wrong in my world. Didn't matter. Soon executives would be stoned, revert to being frat boys, and the women would revert to being sorority girls, and the lot would be getting screwed inside out in executive suites. An emotional season was always the season of sex. Many affairs would happen tonight, a lot of first-time, onetime sex. Everybody wanted to let loose and feel good and make the commercialized season one worth remembering. A hip-hop group was staying at the hotel, too. That party of about thirty congregated near the bar, bottles of the latest trend in urban alcohol on their tables while they all spat out vulgarities, sullying their parents' culture, a culture that had survived the Middle Passage, and committing verbicide to the wicked beats inside their misguided heads. They glanced at me with the same regard the police officers had at Denny's. They opened their mouths and revealed teeth covered in ornate grills; a mélange of architectural styles decorated each mouth. They judged me by my company, and I judged them in the same fashion. They had brought their own pride of fair-skinned video girls and created a stripper parade featuring J. Lo, Beyoncé, Iggy Azalea, and Nicki Minaj clones. Female hustlers. The lowborn and the highly educated were docked at the same port, a mixture of classes, all feral. But a savage in a suit — or a savage in an expensive dress and heels — would never be seen as being feral because they had better grammar and were better tippers.

A drunken white frat boy was more crass than any sober hip-hop star I'd ever run across.

I gave all the disgusting men who stared one second too long a peace sign with the index finger down. I'd seen them all before. Men were with women and still lusted after the next hole to fill.

The man from Orange County and I walked like we were professional husband and eccentric wife, were treated like we were

Brad Pitt and Angelina Jolie. Wedding ring on the left hand, feeling odd, remembering those times, I stayed to the side, took in the lobby and the people while the man from Orange County booked the room. As the tipsy crowd sang "Rudolph the Red-Nosed Reindeer," we took to the elevator. Once the doors closed, the noise ended. A dozen people were on the lift. Everyone paused to say happy holidays. Usually the custom was to not speak, to exhibit a lack of tact, to be inconsiderate and not hold the door open if someone else was running for the elevator. But this was the time of year when strangers actually spoke to one another. It was the only time of year that it was cool to say hello and not get the side eye. One amorous, giggling couple was going to their room. Only one of them wore a wedding ring. Coworkers. A fling. We rode the crowded elevator in silence. I'd just met Orange County and was inside a high-priced fornicave going to a romping shop, where many had done only God knows what before. My heart thump-thump-thumped. With each second, I was a second closer to adultery.

With each passing second I was a second closer to losing this feeling of emptiness and pain.

My ex had moved on. Married. Had a

replacement child on the way. I still lived with Barbie dolls and woke every morning wishing I could go back in time and change one day. Or just not wake up at all.

Inebriated and frisky people entered and exited the elevator at the second, third, fourth, and fifth floors. When the doors closed and we were stuck in the crowd, the man from Orange County pulled me to the back of the elevator, with my butt to his groin, then turned me around to face him.

He asked, "You're still with me?"

"I'm here. Just taking it all in."

"Strange. I could see your reflection in the door. Do you want to be here?"

"I want to be here."

"My wife has that same empty, distant, regretful look when I'm with her."

"I'm not your wife. And stop trying to read my body language."

"Second thoughts?"

"Of course not. You? Second thoughts?"

"Shoulders slumped. Eyes on the ground. Heavy thoughts. What are you thinking?"

"Something the cops at Denny's said stuck in my mind."

"What?"

"Nothing important. Let's not spoil this before we get to the room."

"Was one of the officers someone you

used to date?"

"Of course not."

"Then do me a favor. Try to be here with me. For this hour, stay with me."

"Okay. Sorry about that."

"I miss you. Your mind left me, you left me alone, and I missed you."

"I need you."

"You're silly."

"I'm serious. I need you."

We held each other like we'd been lovers many times over, kissed like we were two sixteen-year-olds during a summer we would never forget. The elevator doors gently opened and some people stepped inside, some people exited. The doors closed again, and we stayed in the back corner of the elevator, eyes closed, kissing. We kissed like the art of the tongue dance was something we had invented and patented and wanted to keep to ourselves as long as we could. We stopped and saw that new people surrounded us.

I kept his mouth on mine and said, "Damn, I need that. I need those kisses all over me."

"Love your lips and kisses and how you respond to me."

"What else do you love?"

"The look in your eyes when you're turned on."

"Jesus, I want to wrap my legs around you and see what you feel like inside me."

"Under one condition."

"Which is?"

"I'm going to ask you some hard questions."

"Oh boy. Okay."

"What's your favorite color?"

"Pink."

"Tea or coffee?"

"A complicated order from Starbucks, just to piss them off."

I put my head against his chest and could hear his rapid heartbeat.

I asked, "What are you afraid of?"

"Besides you, nothing."

"Thought you were going to ask me my favorite position or if I'm into S&M."

"What is your favorite position?"

"As long as the wood is inside, no matter how you bend me, it's all good."

"Like getting your hair pulled?"

"Won't be a problem."

"See? Now you're here with me."

"I'm here with you."

Then the doors opened at the seventeenth floor. We stopped talking and kissing and he led me through the people who were left on the elevator with us. Kissing had made me dizzy, and they were all a blur.

Everyone told us good night and wished us a merry Christmas.

We told them the same.

We walked the carpeted hallway without talking. My palms were humid. I was aware of every step I made, of every breath I took. He had to flip the key card and turn it to figure out how it went in, and I hoped he wasn't that clumsy in bed, could imagine him flipping me over and over, looking confused, trying to figure how to put it in. I was here, I was at the door of the hotel room, but still couldn't imagine us having sex. Kissing, yes. Sex, no. He swiped the card three times. Nothing but a red light illuminated. His frustration returned. He had a short fuse. He swiped the card again. The red light taunted us. Maybe that was a negative sign. I told him to give me the key card. I swiped it once and the red light finally changed to green. That had to be a positive sign. The light was red for him, and green for me. He pushed the heavy wooden door and I walked in before him, stepped into the suite. My boots felt so heavy. I had to remind myself to breathe. I walked into darkness and silence. I walked into an abyss of quiet. I hadn't heard silence in forever. It was tranquil. I hadn't felt peace in more than a decade.

A warm room and no traffic sounds, no wail from sirens, no frustrated drivers blowing horns.

I felt like I had gone to another country, one that existed inside another dimension. I turned the lights on and my eyes ignored the art, the contemporary glass desk, and the white leather sofa. There was a thick white comforter on pure white sheets covering a beautiful king-size pillow-top, our romping shop. It was so much larger than my twin bed that it looked like a playground.

I wanted to get on that bed, jump up and down and do flips.

He opened the wine and found two glasses at the minibar, washed them out, then placed them on the dresser. He reached into his suit coat, took out the condoms, placed them next to the wine. He looked at me. I grinned. We were moments away from infidelity. While he opened the bottle, I went to the bed, pulled the covers back, and inspected the sheets. I went into the bathroom, gazed at shiny marble and silver and glass. Big shower. The dim light above made it look like paradise. Separate bathtub. I went back to the romping shop. He waited for me to finish, his tie loosened.

He had turned the television to the news. I wanted to see if there had been an update about the mother and the three kids who wouldn't experience this Christmas, but I told myself to stay focused.

He asked, "To your satisfaction?"

I nodded. "Checking to see if the attempted 7-Eleven robbery is on the news?"

He turned the television off. The room darkened when he turned the light off. Eroticism rose. We became silhouettes. I wasn't good at having sex without being attached. I wasn't Britney Spears in brown skin, dreadlocks, and tats.

We sipped a little wine, then put our glasses down. He held me. We kissed to keep the fire from going cold. I ended up on the bed, him behind me, pressing his entire body against my backside.

He was hard. That wood would go inside me, all the way to the root of that tree.

Then I was very nervous, breathing through my mouth. Not wanting to go on.

He put a trail of hot, wet kisses along my neck, sucked my ears again, playing in my dreadlocks, then gently rolled me over and eased his warm tongue into my mouth. It was sizzling. Energizing. I was wet. Susan was lubricated, as if she were sending me a signal that he was the right man for me. Susan wanted to bond, and she sent tingles up my spine, tingles I couldn't ignore. Heightened anxiety remained. I convinced myself that the doors of the church were ready to open. He was married. Tonight he desired me more than he did his wife. He desired me more than he did a successful, educated woman of a different class. In a flash, I wondered if he could be mine. Angelina Jolie stole Brad Pitt. Elizabeth Taylor took everyone's husband. Even Jerry Seinfeld stole his wife, took a woman who was on her honeymoon, made another man's wife his own. The morally challenged prospered, as did those who lacked a social understanding of ethical behavior. The world loved a bitch. The world praised bitches. Bitches were the new goddesses. In my heart, I wanted to be good, but my mind told me that the world loved a good girl gone bad. Maybe he was a good man, because no one was born bad. Bad was how the world turned us, how nature or bad nurturing made us. Or maybe he was a man who was doing bad because good men who play by the rules finish last. Maybe this unpaved road of deceit could lead to our happiness. That made me laugh. It was a small laugh, but I laughed. I would be out of here in less than two hours, all my silly thoughts in tow. An hour was all I had offered; an hour of sweet regret that would last a lifetime. Sex was all he wanted. Those were not his words; those were my feelings, my experience with men. All I thought about was love. Love was all I wanted. Yet part of me was here because the confines of love were what I didn't want. Love wasn't rewarding. It couldn't pay my rent. I had no control in my life. But here, in this bed, with him, I was a goddess. I controlled him. I would rule him until he came. Outside of my child, I'd never been loved before. I'd had sex, but I'd never been loved. I was never loved as a child, never experienced the love of both parents, had never been in a relationship where I was needed for more than my body. This yearning for love was so deep that I would trade a truth for a lie, knowing that this moment of sex with a man was just sex with a man, but the physical things were never as deep as the spiritual. We have so many needs. The soul needs what it needs. The body desires what it requires.

And the mind needs what it needs. Mine needed a distraction. It needed to feel free.

I sat up, took a long sip of wine, smiled, and whispered, "Let's get cleaned up."

"That was abrupt."

"The whole night has been abrupt, unexpected, odd, and so damn wonderful."

He stood up. I stayed on the bed, my head hanging over the edge, viewing him as if he were upside down. It was a blow-job position, but that wasn't going to happen, not without him making me his Happy Meal first. That was on my mind; that naughtiness was on my mind, and I grinned up at him. He smiled. He would be naked for me very soon. Soon I'd be naked as well. My heart skipped a beat. I wanted to move, but was frozen where I was, staring at the dick print of a man who wore boxers. He got on his knees, his face upside down to mine. Kissed me again. It was an electrifying upside-down kiss.

I said, "I want to do this all night, but I can only be here until he calls."

"I'll need to leave soon, too."

"What's the next move? How do we move from the fantasy of sex to the reality?"

On his knees, kissing my cheeks, he whispered, "Flip to see who showers first?"

10:09 P.M.

He showered first, did whatever he had to do to relieve and clean his body, did what he had to do to prepare for intimacy, and came out with a towel around his waist. I stayed on the bed, resting on one of the pillows, the covers pulled back, and while he showered I sipped red wine from Argentina.

I moved my ring back to my right hand. I became an ex-wife, a former single mother.

He dropped his towel. He showed me what I had gotten myself into, what wanted to get into me.

He looked at me, nude, his dick exposed, on display. I nodded in approval, nodded and licked my lips with a different craving. It was nice, more than capable of growing to be a span, the width of a man's hand with the fingers spread apart. I shifted, swallowed, grinned, took in his nakedness, let out an abrupt sound of surprise, a short sound that lasted no longer than a hemidemisemiquaver.

He came to me, kissed me again; two minutes went by like two seconds. He felt what his kiss did to me, what sucking my ear did to me, what sucking my neck did to me, saw the change in my eyes, heard the change in the sound of my voice. I almost let him have me right then, almost took him.

It was going too far, too fast. I wanted it to go there, I think, but not before I was proper.

I stood up and nodded at the way his penis stood halfway up and bobbed at me. Its stiffness made me nervous. Looked like he was ready for some sort of sexual training camp, like he had a clear mind, a mind free of guilt, and was here in this hotel room in preparation for a long, rigorous season of fornication. But I knew I'd only be here an hour, maybe less. He had a wife. I had a boyfriend. We had other lovers to spend the night with. Well, for me, most of the night. There would be no breakfast at sunrise for me. I'd leave Chicken and Waffles and return to my own apartment, where I'd wait like a lonesome queen. This was my gift to me. This was a night that no one would ever hear about.

This was for me.

I took my bag and my glass of wine with

me, passed by him with my tail wagging, my face grinning. He pulled my arm, stopped me. Kissed me. Made me want to get naked and dance on the ceiling.

I said, "Let me get cleaned up."

"I want you like this."

"Look, about one hundred and sixty-six thousand people are having some form of sex at this very moment, about a fourth of them cheating on spouses and boyfriends and girlfriends and mistresses, so if you want to join them, let me shower, because now you have my clit so swollen I can't stand this heat."

We laughed. He let me go. His one-eyed friend never stopped bobbing and staring at me. Then I touched his cock, touched that flesh with one finger. He jerked and made pained sounds like he was super sensitive. Super excited. He looked embarrassed. His embarrassment made me bold, made me comfortable, made me become the aggressor. I intimidated him. He wanted me, but was afraid of me. My fingers closed around his long and strong cock, held it gently, massaged it, felt his energy. His eyes closed and his hands grabbed at the bed covers. I held his energy in my hand. When it was firm, when it was rising, I let it go, eased it down to his inner thigh, watched it spring back up. I took my hand away, dragged my palm to my fingers across that part of him, broke away, and walked backward.

He opened his eyes, whispered, "Jesus. That was nice."

I nodded. "You haven't been touched in a while, have you?"

"Not like that."

"I'm really nervous."

"I know."

"I'm not a one-night kind of girl. And you're a married man. Can't get past that right now."

"You can change your mind anytime."

"You've had one-night stands?"

"A few. In college. After that high school breakup, I was detached for a long, long while."

"I do relationships. They're not the best, but I'm a relationship kinda girl."

"I do marriage. I'm that type of man. Dating many women and sleeping around doesn't thrill me."

"You kiss your wife the way you kiss me?"

"Not anymore."

"Why not?"

"The first thing to end is the kissing. You kiss less and less."

"Not even when you're having sex?"

"No."

"She sucks, you eat, but you don't kiss?"

"The ancillary part of sex, the fellatio, the cunnilingus, that becomes less and less, and soon it's just basic sex. Man on top. Woman on bottom. We have sex without kissing, when we have sex."

"You have sex with no kissing. You become each other's whore."

"We become each other's whore."

"I should stop talking."

"We should."

As I went into the bathroom, the man from Orange County turned on the local news again. The volume on the television rose and I could hear the reports. The same news regurgitated itself. The mother who had killed her three children was being analyzed, her entire life torn apart, the father of those three children gone mad and crying, their family members being interviewed, each with more tears in their eyes than raindrops in the sky. I wanted to know all about that woman, wanted to know what led her down that dark road, but that story was ending and they went into the update I didn't relate to, the news about the old businessman who was robbed and beaten in Santa Monica. They said that it looked like a home invasion, that his children and ex-wife were now being interviewed. The update said he might not live to see Christmas, but those three children from the previous news report had barely begun to live and were already gone to play with Natalie Rose. That wasn't fair. He turned the television off and the bad news went away.

I took a dozen deep breaths and wiped tears from my eyes with the back of my hand.

While the world outside the hotel room fell apart, I sipped my wine, knowing that in a few minutes I'd be on that comfortable romping shop, inside this comfortable room, having sex with a stranger.

My knees trembled, my head felt light, and despite being unsure, I smiled.

10:16 P.M.

I locked the bathroom door behind me, turned the handle to make sure it was secure, and then felt weird for doing that, but he had done the same, as if he thought I would break in to rob and rape him, so I followed protocol. Made me think that he was closed off, that this experience would be horrible, that despite the good kisses, he would be done in a couple of minutes, five minutes of me staring at the ceiling and wishing I were somewhere else, then I'd lie and tell him how good he made me feel, how he was an awesome lover, and we'd talk a moment, he'd fall asleep in the middle of the conversation, then see the time and jump up ready to kick me out of the room so he could go home. Men were different creatures after orgasm arrived and lust was erased by satisfaction. The urgency to have you changed to urgency for you to leave. They were different after curiosity had ended. Every hunter was a new man after the end of the hunt. He'd be ready to kick me out, then change the sheets and call the next chick over to his room. That was assumed, but I knew while I was staring at my nudeness with the water running in the sink, while I was checking for a message from my boyfriend, that the man in the other room was messaging his distraught wife. I needed to shave my legs, but that would take too long. And I had some hair outside the door to the church, but it wasn't much; it looked womanly, not like out-of-control foliage. I didn't want to use a razor — I preferred to wax — and all I had was a razor, so I might have to take a chance on getting bumps, then having to tweeze them out. I cursed and looked at my nude reflection. Outside of war paint, I had a toothbrush, toothpaste, and lotion. I had fake eyelashes, tea tree oil, rosemary oil, L-Lysine, mascara wands, wipes, cod liver oil, castor oil, hydrogen peroxide, Diflucan, Sporanox, B-12, novels, green tea, kale chips, and more clothes in my bag. I always kept a bag in my tattered and ragged car, kept a bag in case I ended up at my boyfriend's crappy apartment in his crappy neighborhood down off Crenshaw and Adams. I took out the peroxide and wiped down the countertop to kill all the germs, then took a plastic cup and soaked my toothbrush in peroxide, then sprayed some peroxide into my nostrils to kill bacteria, help clear out the passageway, and loosen any stalactites or stalagmites, then took a mouthful of peroxide and held it for a moment to kill germs, something I did every once in a while but not too often, then I used a towel and wiped the bottom of the shower with peroxide, in case he was the type of guy who pees in the shower. Men can be so damn nasty. And while I showered, I multitasked; I had coconut oil in my mouth, to kill more germs, and at the same time I poured peroxide in my hands and rubbed it across my hair. The peroxide helped keep my hair light naturally, and I didn't want to do that before having sex with a stranger, but had done that ritualistic motion before I could stop myself. I spat out the coconut oil and cursed again. Said two tears in a bucket, fuck it, then put toothpaste on my electric toothbrush.

To get to all of my things, I had taken the stash of balloons out of my bag. They had been on top of all my mess. I still wished that I had given them to the little girl at Denny's. My daughter would have loved to share with her. I took them out of my bag, placed them on the bathroom counter. Was going to drop them in the garbage. Didn't. Stared at the colors. Would get them before I left the room. Give them to a child.

When I was done, I inspected my butt, made sure it was presentable and didn't have ass acne like Montana Fishburne. I reached into my bag and pulled out a pair of red pumps, a pair of just-in-case-I-saw-Chicken-and-Waffles-and-we-actually-went-out-to-someplace-nice pumps, put them on, looked at myself in the magic mirror on the wall, asked it if I was the fairest of them all, then tried to decide if I wanted to walk out wearing only high heels and brown skin, then decided to not model the birthday suit. Then I changed my mind about the heels. Too slutty. Too much like that regrettable night in Las Vegas.

I looked at my right hand, at the wedding ring that rested on the wrong hand as if to symbolize that once upon a time I had been drunk in love and crazy about an alcoholic. A highly functioning, fun alcoholic, but an alcoholic was what an alcoholic was. I took the ring off, put it inside my bag, then looked at my hand, at my bare hand. I nodded. A wedding ring worn on the wrong hand meant that once upon a time a woman had married the wrong man. My life had been filled with encounters with the wrong boys and men. Tonight didn't need to be any different. Would be nice if it was, but not necessary.

I wouldn't be Mommy tonight. I'd get some pain for a while. I'd get some sweet pain.

Tonight I could put on red lipstick and pretend to be a dreadlocks-wearing Cinderella again; a woman with strong hair, not nappy hair, never nappy, hair with strength that has intimidated too many in the world. I could be Barbie with tats and brown skin, one that should be on the top shelf, and never on Black Friday special or marked down any other day of the year. I deserved attention, if only for a little while. I'd step out and be positive, would smile, laugh, wink, be sexy, not be a fussbudget.

I nervously left the bathroom with a towel wrapped around my body, followed protocol, went to stand before Orange County like I had been created from his rib. There was music. Lights were off. Television was on a station that played music to make love by, music to make babies by, music to fall in love by. Would've preferred the blues, some John Lee Hooker groaning "I Cover the Waterfront" on repeat, but the music was nice. The television created an ethereal glow, a mood, brightened shadows without revealing the details of my imperfections. He evaluated me, then took his wedding ring off, as if he had meant to do it while I showered, then put it on the nightstand, as if that was all it took for a married man to become unmarried once again, as if that kept him from being culpable.

He stood, naked, looking like a professional had arrived and fluffed him before his performance. Holding a condom in one hand and his cell phone in the other, he saw me exit the bathroom.

We inched toward the big moment. We were about to cross that line.

I blinked and my mind spiraled in a hundred directions at once.

Online I had read why men had affairs: for more sex, for new experiences, to boost ego, for the thrill of the chase, to be opportunistic, to sabotage a current relationship, for revenge, out of entitlement. The same bloggers said that women had affairs when they wanted to improve their self-esteem or have new and better sexual experiences, when they felt lonely or wanted to explore their own feelings through sex.

Some women wanted to feel younger. The fear of aging, the fear of no longer being attractive, made many women reveal their secrets to new men. Money and power, the hard reasons that motivated many to barter with sex, and desperation and hormones — all those reasons were excluded from a woman's list. A woman's list was a record of lies made of sugar and spice, made us victims, fallen angels, spoke nothing of many of us being just as unscrupulous, self-centered, and vile, lacking in compassion and sans foresight and pessimistic and shortsighted with goals as our sperm-carrying counterparts.

Nuts or tits, we were all the same: same needs, confusions, fears, emotions.

On those pages of hackneyed logic that made men evil and manipulative and women saints deprived of what their souls needed, I had no idea where I fit in. It was probably a combination of all the darker reasons. It was almost Christmas. I had met Chicken and Waffles and fallen into bed with him near Mother's Day. That had been a hard time for me. I had been given the right to celebrate that day, and it had been snatched away, leaving the scars behind. I had been very emotional that season; I knew I probably would always be very vulnerable, or try to hide from the world, on that holiday. Last Mother's Day, I didn't want to be alone, and that was how the relationship with Chicken and Waffles had started.

That same energy was in my body now. That same need for distraction was just as strong.

I looked at the man from Orange County. I looked at the married man I'd just met. Ten million people were in L.A. County, and we had ended up at the same cardinal points. I was a woman and he was a man and there was some need and attraction and that was that. I didn't know if I would do this once. Or twice. Or if this would start me on a long spiral into hell. I wasn't verdant enough to think that he would want me only once. No man wanted me only once. All I knew was that I felt good in his presence, and I deserved to feel first-class, and he made me feel superior. Two hours from now this would be done, and I'd end up in my apartment, alone, surrounded by photos of Natalie Rose, Barbie dolls on the twin bed we once shared, as I rested on my side, watching the rain, watching God cry the coldest tears.

L.A. was flooded. I'd never learned how to cry, not like that, not so freely.

He asked, "Are you okay?"

I blinked again, only two seconds having passed since I had exited the bathroom.

He said, "You had that distant look again."

"No, I didn't."

"What were you thinking?"

"Was feeling more than thinking. I was thinking about how I love to make love when it's raining."

"Do you?"

I whispered, "It's like God is crying."

I left my thoughts and over-examination and self-awareness behind and nodded. I took three more steps, stopped just feet away from him, then grabbed at the carpet with my toes. He stopped texting and put the phone down, but kept a loose grip on the prophylactic. He saw me with no shoes on my feet to boost my height, my dread-locks down and framing my face, saw the gloss on my lips, then licked his own lips and glanced at the towel that stood between me and nakedness, between him and sex with a stranger.

One thing that I had learned since my weight gain was that skinny girls look good in clothes, as does any mannequin, but curvy girls look good naked. He looked at me the way I look at art.

He looked at me like he wished his bony wife would give up tofu for Popeye's fried chicken.

He looked at me like he understood the power of a great ass.

t me like he couldn't wait to
et.

lligent, had his life together,
ortable in his own skin.

And he looked at me like he appreciated and craved what others had taken for granted.

I said, "That expression on your face."

"What about it?"

"That smile. That is a big smile, like a ray of sunshine. Plus, you're holding your cock."

"Why are you so goddamn beautiful, sexy, and intelligent?"

"I want the truth. I think I'm going to need some thought bubbles."

"Physically, you're intimidating. You look like a woman a man should both desire and fear."

"Desire me now. Desire and comfort me before you go to your distraught wife and comfort her."

"You are better than Bettie Page. I'm intimidated."

"Fear me later. Once I'm in that bed, two minutes from now when you're sleeping, fear me."

"Two minutes."

"Three, tops. You'll get thrown and need a rodeo clown to come and rescue you."

"Let this begin."

I grinned. "You make it sound like we're going to battle."

"Maybe we are. You are equipped for war of all wars."

"Am I supposed to be afraid?"

"Maybe. That's what fear is all about."

I said, "I have to warn you. I'm very sexual, and when I get like this, in this mood, I need to let loose and express that side of me, need to veer off into the darkness."

"We're on the same page. I'm very sexual. I'm not kind in bed."

"This swive could be a contest."

"Swive?"

"Means to do the nasty."

"Yeah. This is going to be a contest."

I said, "Is that a challenge?"

"Sure is."

I grinned. "Are we betting cheesecake?"

"Which flavor of cheesecake are you willing to lose this round?"

I hummed. "Caramel-pecan. I think I'll bet the slice you already owe me."

"I see your slice of caramel cheesecake and raise you a slice of chocolate chip, cherry, and blueberry, plus chocolate-chip cookie dough, key lime, pumpkin, Oreo, red velvet, and Reese's cheesecakes."

Again laughter. Again bonding through laughter.

The laughter faded and he said, "Drop the towel."

I let my towel drop to the carpet. Nakedness stared at nakedness, and nakedness smiled.

"Why are you looking at me like that?"

"Noticed your incredible figure at the gas station."

"You looked at me like I was the ugliest bitch on the planet."

"Quite the opposite. Beautiful face, your hips, your breasts, the swayback. Some package you have there, and I mean that in the most respectful way. Even wearing that Best Buy gear and that other hair, no matter how ill-fitting, you couldn't hide your shape. One glance at you and I'll bet men turn temporarily insane. Guess that's why I made that awful offer. Temporary insanity. That's the story I'll use in court."

"Looking at you naked, all tall and toned, yeah, I'm curious about you. Guess I'll have to plead the same temporary insanity."

"Your breasts. Nice. Amazing."

"Left is a little bigger, right is more sensitive. The left one is called Tina. You touched the right one once, without permission, but now you have full permission to enjoy her texture and taste."

"The one I touched, does it have a name, or is that one not speaking to me?"

"The right one is called Marie. And yeah, she's speaking to you."

"Tina and Marie."

"Marie has freckles and my birthmark, and the nipple is slightly bigger. Both love to be sucked."

"You've named your breasts."

"Tits this hot deserve to be named."

"Tina and Marie."

"Named my ass, too. I have a pretty hot ass."

"What did you name your ass cheeks, Rick and James?"

"Ophiuchus. This sweetness you can't keep your eyes off is called Ophiuchus."

"You named your butt after the thirteenth zodiac sign?"

"Wow, you're smart. Might have to rename it Callipygia. Starting to like that word."

He smiled. "And your vagina?"

"Susan. I call her Susan."

"Your vagina has a Hebrew name."

"Means joy of life, and she is always joyful, bright, and cheerful."

He laughed. "You know I could say a lot about the falseness of the zodiac and then give you a lecture regarding the name you gave your vagina. Joyful, bright, and cheerful? How about horny?"

I laughed, too. "No more long Obama-Clinton speeches, okay? Not when Tina and

Marie are looking at you and wondering when you're going to introduce yourself and make Susan sing a melody."

"I will meet them in a moment. Let me pretend I'm in a museum enjoying the art."

"We don't have that kind of time."

"Never rush art. Never. Especially when you will only be able to see it once."

"We have places to be very soon, so the museum will have to close if you want the legs to open."

He looked at me, eyes filled with wonder and lust. "More tattoos. Very sexy tattoos."

"That's where too much of my money has gone the last two years."

"You have a piercing in your belly button, too."

"I do."

"But I love the tongue ring the most. It feels a like a cute little pearl. It's like a clitoris — small, cute, and hidden in warmth. You have to find it to appreciate it."

"Wow. Is that why guys and girls who like girls always hit on me? I have a clit mouth?"

"Any other piercings?"

"Nothing else. No clit piercing, if that's what you're asking."

"You're addicted to the tats and body piercings."

"The pain."

He asked, "You like pain? Something happened to trigger the need for pain?"

"It was life-changing."

"That was a lot of pain."

"I could tattoo my body ten times over and it wouldn't be enough pain."

"What happened?"

"So instead of pain, let's see what an hour with you can do."

"You don't want to say, I will drop the conversation."

"Why do you keep talking?"

"Nervous."

"Why?"

"Have you seen you?"

"You can't be more nervous than I am."

"You come across as cool, smooth, like this is no big deal for you."

"Are we going to be naked, in a nice hotel room, start talking, and ruin the mood again?"

"Swive."

"Swive. Give me a deeper pain."

He came to me, a man who reminded me physically of da Vinci's Vitruvian Man, and kissed me, picked me up. He picked me up, and that did it for me. Butterflies told me that this wasn't going to be a mistake. He carried me to the king bed, laid me down, studied my nakedness as Anita Baker sang in the background, this nakedness that was new to him, and he made a grunt of amazement. He massaged my body from my feet to my neck, then across my back, then my butt, massaged me so well that I didn't want him to stop. Then he turned me over and massaged my legs up to my breasts, stayed with my breasts as he stared into my eyes. My dreadlocks were open, loose, wild like Medusa, a beautiful Medusa, a sensual Medusa. One of three sisters in Greek mythology known as the Gorgons, Medusa had a destructive effect upon humans, and I wondered if I would have a destructive effect on him, if I would destroy his fragile marriage, if I would best an unseen foe, or if he would be my Perseus and destroy me. My mind went dark, had mean, devilish thoughts. I grinned, took many breaths, allowed myself to become his nymph, his young and beautiful goddess, a toy that would make him her plaything as well. I masturbated him. He massaged me. I was nervous to touch him again, because this was the start of the transition to the official invitation to enter me, but I did. I touched him as a signal that it was okay to do other things to me, a signal that trust had entered the room; therefore, soon, he could enter me.

I held him, stroked him, made him rise again, and made his hood vanish.

I whispered, "Nice. This is nice. Jesus, this is a nice piece of work."

He made another sound of approval and arousal. He hardened in my hand. That turned me on. Soon I answered him with my own keen, a soft cry. He put his nervous hands on my damp flesh, touched each part as if each was a separate work of art, not combined into one sculpture, then tasted my neck, sucked my neck, made me tense, made me let out a stronger sound of arousal, made my back arch. He licked my breasts, kissed my stomach as if he were afraid, as if he were afraid of the consequences of adultery, and he put that damp fear on my sensitive stomach, fueling my arousal, my wickedness, his eyes searching for mine, searching for my satisfaction before he slipped his tongue inside my navel, moved his tongue into my navel as if he were trying to break into my body, and that faux penetration excited me, made me become wet with the anticipation of wrongness, then took his tongue to my thighs, sucked my inner thighs, moved his tongue across my vagina, used his tongue, opened me.

He opened that empty space, unlocked me with his tongue. With his fingers, he parted my walls, then with his tongue he painted my vagina, repainted its walls, then slid all of his tongue inside me. He sucked my clit like it was the cock of a woman. Legs trembling, muscles tense, I took a deep breath, one that rose from me between the sacrum and the diaphragm, and like I was the fat lady in the last act of an opera, I called out to heaven, then covered my mouth with my hands, tried in vain to silence myself.

He tongue swiped my sex like he was licking the frosting off a cupcake. I called out to heaven again. Then he gave me a strong lick, using the width of his tongue, licked me the way Huck licked Quinn. He licked in a hungry way that said I appealed to his palate. He was voracious. Rapacious. The greedy bastard devoured me. Seism after seism rolled through my body, tiny earthquakes, the warnings that preluded orgasm. My sounds encouraged his tongue to torture me. He dragged his tongue across my vagina. He took a mouthful of me, sucked, gave a little pressure, and woke up so many nerves. I quivered, cooed, held his head. Without embarrassment he sucked me like I was a man, made my back arch, and as I swallowed a dozen heated sounds, he ate me. Made slurping sounds. Glanced up at me as I looked down at him. Made his tongue dart in and out. Made circles. Then put all of his tongue deep inside me again. I lost it. People in planes, and on Century, Sepulveda, and Airport boulevards, heard my sexual pleas.

He stopped and whispered, "This is beautiful. So beautiful."

I shook and gasped. "Your mouth, your mouth, stop talking and use your mouth."

"What do you want me to do with my mouth?"

"Oh my God, Jesus Christmas. You know

what I want, so stop talking and quit play-ing."

"Tell me. Tell me what you want me to do. Be explicit."

"Suck and lick my pussy the way you sucked my tongue in the parking lot at Denny's."

He turned me over, made me raise my ass, and put me in doggy position.

10:41 P.M.

Bent over on all fours, my spine arched, in a passive position, I didn't know what he was going to do, or which part of my real estate his tongue would regard as open house. This was *coitus more ferarum,* Latin for describing sexual intercourse in the manner of wild beasts. All sex is animalistic. The positions don't matter; that is when we are primal. Again his fingers opened my lips, exposed me to his breath, to a long stream of air being blown across my folds. He blew and blew, then painted his name on my sex. I eased down on my shoulders, reached back and spread my cheeks. Showed him what he wanted. He licked my sex with trills, rolled his wicked tongue in a vicious way, like the Spanish letter double *R — rr, rr, rr, rr* — written a hundred times in a row, and cameras flashed behind my eyes. My heart rate elevated and my sexual sounds, the vociferation of pleasure, expanded.

It was fanatical, heated, and lovely.

The eight muscles of his tongue were strong, like he did a hundred tongue push-ups every morning, and twice as many every night. He inserted his tongue, gave me its length. I felt beautiful and out of control. That tongue. He played with me, changed the shape of his tongue, lengthened it, shortened it, curled and uncurled its apex and edges, and flattened it out, licking me along my sex. I couldn't take it; I lost the ability to speak, could only breathe and swallow. The sounds he made while he was eating drove me mad. His tongue flitted in and out of me, moved with the speed of a hummingbird, and I grabbed the sheets, became the bird that hummed. It was light and swift, the way he darted, the masterful way he fluttered and trilled, and I couldn't stand it. His tongue was the bee, and my flower was in bloom, was wide open. Nerves danced and it ached so good, the itch and sweet irritation magnified, and I heard them calling, heard a fusillade of orgasms begging for me to surrender to the power of his tongue. I tried to hold out, wasn't going to let him make me lose control, not so soon, but I couldn't take it. It felt too damn good, and I wanted to burst. I collapsed and lay there smiling, eyes wide, the words I said all indecipherable. He fingered my sex as he massaged a nipple, then massaged my buttocks, gave each cheek a playful spank, a sting, then pulled my hair, turned my face toward him, kissed me, saw I was okay, then flipped me on my back and opened my legs wider than before. I was as flexible now as when I was a size-zero girl with long, straight hair, the kind Hollywood adored. Again his tongue came toward me. I adjusted my body, directed my sex, wiggled toward his tongue, and moved with a shameless urgency to put him back on the right spot. He made me hold both legs up in the air, pushed them back over my head, my bottom high in the air, like I was doing sexual yoga. He licked, suckled. I trembled. My body heated up more; I imagined flames coming from my pores. His hands cupped my butt, new fingers on my ass, strong hands. Then he moved his hands, moved them back to my breasts, and pulled at my hard nipples. That hurt so good. His cunnilingus was so good; the tongue could make me give up the need for good wood.

Breathing concise, in a throaty voice, I panted, "*Damn.* Do. That. Again. Again. Again."

With a grin in his voice he stated the obvious, said, "You like that?"

"Damn that tongue of yours."

He savored me. Made me squirm. Beg. Made me fall madly in love with tongue. Made me feel like misbehaving was worth the cost. I pulsated; the start of aurora borealis and contractions.

This was therapeutic. This was curative. This made all wrong seem right.

He tasted me rapidly, and I lost control, began to orgasm, as I processed the moment.

I was who I was, and he was who he was, and in life we were where we were.

He whispered, "Stop moving."

"I can't."

His tongue searched for that position that would make me confused and turn sex into love.

When his tongue was inside me, I felt as bright as the sun, and when he stopped, when I felt the darkness again, when I descended from heaven, I held his head. When I slipped away from what felt like the edges of love, I made him put his tongue back, until it was time for me to experience nirvana again.

When I had stopped trembling, I looked to the windows, looked at the dark skies and rain.

He spanked the side of my ass. A shock

rolled through my body.

I panted. "Harder. Spank me harder. Make it sting. Please, make it sting."

He hit my ass over and over, gave me lashes like I was a child.

The bright flash of pain. Pain covered other aches.

I lost my breath. Couldn't breathe. Had to inhale slowly through my nose. Tried to relax. Tried to exhale slowly through my mouth. He spanked me more. I squirmed. With his hands he opened my legs as wide as he could. His tongue played me like I was a piano with one key, strummed that magical key, sent me to a wonderful place, a place where I had no hardships, no overdue rent, no issues, a place I didn't worry about high gas prices. I licked my lips, squeezed my own breasts, trembled, danced, tried to suck my own nipple, but he moved my hand away, continued to squeeze one nipple as he rubbed the palm of his hand across the other breast. He gave me good head, and I lost control. He paused. Backed away. Stared at me. Watched me tremble and try to regain control. When I had stopped writhing, I looked toward the windows, looked at the dark skies, landing planes, and rain.

He whispered, "Are you ready for all of me?"

"You know what I want. You know what you kissed me and made me want."

"Tell me."

"Come put it in me. I want you in me until I can feel your balls tapping against Susan."

"Dirtier."

"Come screw me with that big cock. Give Susan that long, stiff dick."

We laughed. It was fun, sounded ludicrous, was sexy, and we laughed.

"Dude, quit the madness. Stop making me become a parody of myself, and put it in."

"So it's like that?"

"That kinda talk sounds so silly and contrived. I'm not a porn star."

"Tell me what you like."

"When it feels good, I'm an *oooh* and *ahh* kinda girl."

"Really?"

"But it's up to you to make me go *oooh* and *ahh.*"

He came toward me. I pushed him away, pushed him hard, like a dominatrix.

"Put a hat on the soldier. The soldiers don't need to have an egg for breakfast, unless you want to buy breakfasts, lunches, and dinners for the next eighteen years. Let's have fun, but keep it safe."

He backed away, ripped open the condom. I touched myself. He watched me touch myself. I wanted him to see me touch myself. My lips were swollen, open, glutinous; sticky, thick with honey.

He touched himself, prepared himself, then came toward me, ready, anxious.

Then my phone vibrated. My siren screamed. It was him.

It was the man I had been waiting to hear from since early morning.

It was Chicken and Waffles.

I jumped, felt exposed, like the Moral Police had arrived with leg chains, tar, feathers, and scarlet letters, like I had been caught in bed with a married man. I became aware of everything, of every breath, of my nakedness. The spell was broken and I was anxious to get to my phone. Orange County looked at me, raindrops tapping against the window, the O'Jays at the top of the song "Stairway to Heaven."

He said, "Damn."

"Sorry."

"Just like that?"

"But you knew I was waiting on this call."

"You have to bounce?"

"He's available. He wants me to come to him now. Wants to kick it for a while."

"This late? Takes him this long to call you back?"

"Guess I get the late shift tonight. He'll want me from now until just before sunrise."

"He makes you leave his bed, in the cold, in the rain, before the sun comes up."

"Don't judge me."

"And you'd rather be in the streets doing a con and risk going to jail than to ask your boyfriend of six months for some help? He can call you this late, and you can't turn to him when you're in need?"

"Don't spoil the evening."

"I think it's already spoiled."

"Look. I really enjoyed sitting in Denny's talking with you. Almost felt like I was out on a date. Almost feels that way now. My boyfriend and I rarely do anything together in public."

"Do you have a drawer at his apartment? Has he made space for you, or do you have to leave early in the morning in the same sullied clothes, doing that Walk of Shame women talk about?"

"None of your goddamn business."

"Does he at least allow you to leave a toothbrush at his apartment? Or do you have to clean up all evidence that you exist before you bounce? Do you have to clean every pubic hair you leave behind?"

"You're judging me."

"He doesn't care about you. He would have called you long before now. I'll bet he does as little as he can in order to get as much as he can. One call, you go running. Those five-cups-of-coffee moments are over, and you know they're over. He wants the benefit of your sex without the effort."

"How do you know it's him and not me? Maybe I'm just using him to get what I need. Maybe that's as much as I can handle right now. Maybe I can't handle any more than the little he offers."

"Get your phone. Answer him. Crawl to the phone like you're crawling to him."

"Don't judge me."

"Get your phone. Get dressed. I'll walk you downstairs to your car."

He stood up. Went to his clothes. Picked up his pants, stood at the window, his back to me.

I said, "You're mad."

"Not mad."

"Then what are you?"

He sighed. "Just thinking. Sitting here questioning my life."

"What are you thinking about?"

"I was thinking about love. Every other woman I have ever been with. Angela from Miami. Greta from San Diego. Kate from Puerto Rico. Another one, a medical student from Haiti. One from Botswana. Lori. Peggy. Pretty girls wearing pearls. At this moment, looking at the rain, not wanting to go back home to the life I have now, I miss them. I miss how my life was with them. I can hear their laughs. Remember how good the sex was. More than the sex. Some did amazing things, were uninhibited in bed and were very adventurous, but I'm not counting orgasms. I'm remembering how they made me feel as a human being. I miss how they made me feel. I do miss the sex, and lately I think about them, one of them, maybe imagine two of them at once when I masturbate. Maybe not at once, but the face changes with the act I am remembering. Life was exciting then. And those rare moments I'm with my wife, I have to confess, I'm no longer with her, but stuck in time, drifting on a memory, still with one of them. One I used to come with. We would orgasm at the same time. We didn't worry about brushing teeth before the morning kiss. I miss her scent. To be with my wife, I have to think of a love gone by, one of the women who were spectacular lovers, to keep myself sane. When I'm alone during the day, I miss how good the friendships were. I want to call them the way a person in a 12-step program has to call every person he has wronged. Want to look for them online, but I don't. Life goes on. People marry. Get new lovers. Have babies. We change. World keeps spinning. All the clichés. But that doesn't make me stop wondering why I chose this woman and not one of them."

"You chose the jealous one. Jealousy can be confused for caring and passion."

"I chose the one who would confront any woman she ever thought was interested in me."

"She ran them all away."

"She called them all. Sent them all e-mails. Even made a few threats."

"Damn."

"She told them I was married and their carnal or emotional services would no longer be required."

"You had to think of the women you still lust for, you thought of them, to be with me?"

"No. I was focused on you. I was here with you. You weren't here with me. So now I am thinking of them to take my mind off you. I am trying to forget you. I just want to forget I ever met you."

As he glowered at the rain, my body language and temperament matched his. I did the same, stood up, stood next to him, stared at the rain and thought of pangs and love, of boys since Vernon, of men since I'd become a woman, that total low, and my mind settled on the man I had thought I would love forever. Ricky was on my mind. That was back when in I lived in the Valley, off Sepulveda, the longest boulevard in Southern California. I thought about love, spring break and trips to Vegas, gambling, too much partying, and vodka on the Strip, where there were no clocks in casinos, where many woke up broke and with hangovers and realized that somewhere between the blackjack and poker tables they had been diverted to a drive-thru wedding chapel and had given vows before a cockeyed, imitation Elvis Presley wearing blue suede shoes. Love and alcohol could make you wake up married in Vegas, and you'd think it was the best decision you'd ever made. It wouldn't matter if your parents disowned you for that. It shouldn't matter that he had moved on, married, was expecting a new baby.

That had been part of my journey.

The man from Orange County picked up his boxers.

I said, "Don't."

"Don't what?"

"Don't leave."

"You're leaving."

"Don't leave like this. I don't want to . . . break up like this."

"You're leaving to go to him, right? You're

choosing him over me, right?"

"Wow."

"Wow what?"

"Rejection. Since that bitch messed you over in Vail, you've had so much rejection."

"As much as you have had pain."

"What did the wife do? Tell me."

He took a deep breath, scowled at the rain. "Have you heard of a place called Houghmagandy?"

"You asked me about that at Denny's. Is that another country club?"

"Heard of a place called Decadence?"

"No. Is that an underground club in Hollywood? I don't have a budget like that."

My phone sang and sang and sang, became my personal siren, my personal warning.

He said, "She has memberships to Houghmagandy and to a place called Decadence."

"She belongs to a couple of country clubs — so what?"

I paused, relaxed, ignored my phone, smiled, and took his hands. Pulled him back to the bed. I touched the side of his face, his injury. I kissed his wound, asked no questions.

I had a gut feeling that his wounds had nothing to do with racquetball.

The way he had handled the thug at 7-Eleven, I could only imagine what had happened.

I said, "You exploded at 7-Eleven."

"I did. I lost it. I really lost it. Lost it the way I did when I found my ex-girlfriend's lover."

"You left that part of the story out."

"I know."

"What you did tonight was brave, foolish, and arousing. My nipples stood up and applauded."

"You became a butterfly with a box cutter that looked like a wicked switchblade."

"Somebody had to save you."

We laughed soft laughs.

"Do you and the wife make sex tapes?"

"What?"

"Wanted to shock you. You were getting too down in the mouth. That nice smile went away."

"I haven't made any movies. If she has, only she would know."

"What's the point of marriage if you can't finally be a slut and no one can call you a whore? I'm joking about the slut thing, but serious about the sex-tape thing. Never been a slut, have to say that. Mickey Rooney had more wives than I've had lovers. That doesn't include guys I've made out with, just the ones who made it to the middle of the middle with more than a finger or a tongue. Anyway. I'd love to be married, to have a true husband. I'd write love letters every day, and every night would be the biggest freak for my husband. If I were married and my husband loved me like I loved him, I would want to record almost each time we made love. It would be like a video journal. We wouldn't do it in a pornographic way, wouldn't be no 'Mimi and the shower rod' thing. I would be with my husband in a more artsy way, so we could see ourselves expressing that love over time. Real love expressed by intimacy. Us in bed, on the floor, in the shower, in the car, outside at some place being naughty, wherever, whenever, laughing, being silly, being serious, being lovers, being friends, being a husband and wife in love. We'd sit up and sip red wine and review our love history from time to time. Might record fellatio and cunnilingus here and there for kicks, a recording that showed me praising my husband for being my man, and record him praising me for being the awesome woman who gives him unconditional love, but what I would want to see is us as a couple, nurturing each other, bonding, being spiritual and inseparable, like we shared one heart, would want to see us aging in the arms of love and friendship. I'd want to see us go from being young lovers to an older couple with grand-kids, still making love like we were newly-weds, bad hips, arthritis, and all. The camera would be on our faces, capturing our sounds, our words, not taping cocks and cunts and tricks for kicks. I'd want what's in our eyes. I'd capture that part of us, that private part of us on film. I'd want to capture the love and passion. You never wanted to do that?"

"Maybe I should've become a swinger. Maybe that would have excited my wife."

"That's disgusting. People who live like that are infected with the devil."

"Yeah. It is disgusting."

I said, "I'm sorry. For jumping when he called. I really messed up the night."

"It's cool."

"Need you to kiss me again."

"Why?"

I said, "Kiss me. Make me stay. Kiss me and make me forget about the rest of the world."

We kissed. It was different. It was awk-ward.

He asked, "Who are you? You're not a real grifter. You're a brilliant, beautiful woman."

I almost told him that I had been married, that I had married a man with a substance problem, and I thought that I could fix him, but in the end I was the one who ended up broken. After I had put a small coffin in the ground, I almost didn't make it to the next sunrise. Didn't want to go down that road, a road that ended in flames. I poured myself a glass of wine, drank it all in what felt like one gulp.

Rocking, gazing at him, hoping he couldn't see the real me, I asked, "Who are you?"

"Just a man who wishes he had met you earlier today. I saw your physical beauty, and my dick jumped up and slapped me upside the head and gave me brain damage, added to the temporary insanity. But your mental beauty, your voice, your mind, your humor — it has all gotten under my skin."

"And my tongue ring."

"Yeah, that, too."

"Be honest. You saw my tongue ring and thought about two-hundred-dollar blow jobs."

"All men look at tongue rings and think about blow jobs, only they want them gratis."

"Why?"

"Because we're men. Same reason women

look at Idris and their clits do the River-dance."

"It's an involuntary reaction with Idris."

"Well, your tongue ring is to me what Idris is to you."

"And my hair. You approved of my hair."

"Your hair is simply amazing."

"You became enamored by me one aspect at a time."

"You're one helluva package. You don't see art all at once. Art has many levels, and many never comprehend the depth. They only see one color. You have to sit with art, gaze at art, take in the aesthetic beauty, and each time you discover something new. As one listens to you with his heart, he has to feel you with the eyes. See how your eyes are drawn to particular areas. Take in the composition, shape, shades, and shadows, see how you're well-proportioned. The raw-ness is beautiful and the depth cannot be ignored. The way you move, the way you dance, is amazing. You're shapely, art come to life, well-decorated intellect. Your voice — it turns husky, then becomes melodious, like honey at times. Each word you speak, no matter how vulgar, sounds like a song. You have character. You make me laugh."

"Wow. If Hollywood saw me that way, I'd be the next Regina Baptiste — the brown version."

"You almost made me wish you were my wife."

"Jesus. Stop. I don't need you to start lying. You went too far."

"I said almost."

"Still too far."

"That's how I was feeling. Now I just wish I had never turned around on the 605."

I pulled at my dreadlocks, absorbed his sincerity, softened my tone, and said, "Can we start over?"

"Can we?"

"May I kiss you?"

"Your boyfriend might not like the taste of me on your tongue."

"Forget him. You're right. When I need him most, he's never by my side."

We kissed. Did our best to get back to where we were. The things he had said . . . I wanted this man. This stranger, this warrior, this vulnerable and wounded bird, I wanted him. Tonight he deserved me.

I said, "I think I was just feeling a little scared."

"Of what?"

"I never meet guys like you and they dig me. Brothers want me, but they don't like me. For guys like you, men who have their lives together, men with your disposition,

I'm not the girl who's supposed to be in the picture frame with the family and dogs. I have dreadlocks and tats and I'm not fat, but I'm not skinny, and guys who probably don't have either the physical or the mental equipment to get the job done attack me in some fashion: the hair, the weight, talk about my ass, say the same trite, disgusting bullshit. They attack what they fear, what they can't comprehend. So, to them, that made me the girl no one wants to read about or see as the lead in an A-list Hollywood movie. I'm not the girl next door."

"You are the girl next door. Every girl lives next door to somebody."

"Yeah, someone has to live next door to Bates Motel and the Groovie Goolies at Horrible Hall."

"Your uniqueness. You woke up something inside me. I was on the way home to a new problem, had a crisis to deal with, ran into you, became distracted, and meeting you made everything else going on in my life, made everything bad that had happened since sunrise, seem irrelevant and small."

"Well, I think you're a pretty smart guy."

"I like you from the inside out."

"You want to give me some of that intellect from the inside out?"

"I want to get some of that intelligence

while you get some of this intelligence."

"Fair exchange."

"A fair exchange is no robbery."

He came and rested behind me, moved against me again, clockwise, then the opposite direction of the rising of the sun. I moved against him, moved counterclockwise when he moved clockwise, and clockwise when he did the opposite. I pressed into him and he pushed into me. He hardened again, cock poking at my ass. I felt that he still wanted me, felt how much he wanted to have me.

I rolled over on my belly and he rolled with me, moved my hair, and kissed my shoulders. I loved when I was on my stomach and a man was lying on top of me. I felt his weight on my body.

He grabbed my neck in a chokehold, gave me roughness, but soon became kind, nuzzled my neck. I imagined getting it doggy style with him grabbing my hips to really give it to me; imagined him grabbing my dreadlocks, pulling my head back. When I was getting wood like that I felt complete. That position allowed a man to have depth, and that gave me sweet pain, took me away from all my worries.

He said, "Be explicit. Tell me what you want to do. What you want us to do."

"You be you. I'll be me. No pretending. No dramatics."

"Okay."

"I want you to stop talking and put that inside me."

"I'm ready to be inside you."

"No, you're not."

"What's wrong?"

"I'm not that girl from Vail, so we start the way we end it."

"What does that mean?"

I said, "Put the helmet on the solider first. Not in the middle of the war or just before the cannon is about to blow. Put the condom on Mr. Happy and then we can play war, and no one gets hurt."

"Let me put it on."

"No. Let me do that for you. Let me show you how it should be done."

11:00 P.M.

He handed me the flavored condom and I put it inside my mouth, pressing the reservoir tip against my tongue and the ring against my teeth, then used my hands to hold the base of his erection while I pulled his foreskin back, pressed the tip against the roof of my mouth, and used my lips to roll the condom on. I made sure my teeth didn't rip it, and dressed him that way. I had warmed up to him. I was revealing more of my true self. He might find out some of the things I did when alcohol was in my blood. He set free low, sustained, mournful cries, hums that told me he loved what I had done.

He eased on top of me, anxious, yet reserved, and the doors to the church opened. My legs opened automatically, slowly, in invitation, in consent, opened like there was a sensor that caused them to accede just for him. He lay on top of me, settled his warmth on my warmth as the television supplied a baby-making song by Marvin Gaye, telling us to go ahead and get it on, to find that sexual healing, and as our bodies touched, everything about him felt powerful. He kept the bulk of his weight on his elbows so he didn't squish me. The body of the strong on top of the body of the feminine. But the body of the strong was always weakened by the softness of the feminine, always weakened by the gifts of the feminine, forever weakened by crossing the folds into a secret place. New sex. Unknown sex. Fantasy sex. I was so over-wrought. I couldn't be still. I shivered with anticipation of the best part of sex. I antici-pated him sliding inside me, the first con-tact, the connection when the real sex started, being opened and stretched. Every-thing that had been hard about me, all that had been difficult about me, no longer existed. I was woman. He was man. He kissed me, teased me with his cock, teased me by moving it up and down against my damp slit. I wriggled, bit my lips, bit his lips, put my nails in his back, breathing like I was drowning, embarrassingly excited. His mouth was on mine, his tongue moving with mine, and he teased me, sucked the long, distressful, dismal erotic cry of sexual distress out of my mouth. I needed to be penetrated, opened, and taken back to the land of orgasm. Over and over I wiggled underneath him. It went on and on until I wanted to scream for him to put it inside me, wanted to scream for the long and strong cock. Then he backed away. He backed away and grinned.

He was toying with me, enjoying my misery.

He came back to me, and I pushed him away.

I said, "You had your chance. Playing games like that, you blew it."

He came back to me, smiling.

I smiled, too. We kissed again. I could hold out as long as he could.

I would play the game, would win the game, and would eat cheesecake while he had none.

He eased on top of me again, and my legs reopened for him like a gate to his home, gave one last chance, a final invitation into the other parts of my temple, and he lay on top of me, weighed me down, powerful, the body of the strong again on top of the body of the feminine.

He kissed me.

I reached down and touched his long, sweet dick. That was like LSD. Long, solid dick. I made sure that LSD was still covered, felt comforted when I made sure that he hadn't tried to do a trick and slip it off. Men would do that, try to sneak and remove the condom, try to lose the barrier because the rubber stole sensitivity and gave more than a few erection problems. He was covered, and the erection had no problem. Long, strong dick. It amazed me and made me anxious.

God bless *aspirin* and how it made what was malleable become as strong as wood.

We were here, had arrived at the last exit before creating our own little Sin City.

I held on to his erection, felt that power in my hand, felt what would be inside my body, imagined this moving in and out of me, and I became dizzy thinking about the moment he would be inside me. My belly filled with butterflies and as I stroked his cock I couldn't wipe the silly smile off my face. I was giddy with anticipation. I took a breath. He moved inside me slowly at first, and as moments went by, as his breathing thickened, as he thickened inside me, he sought to own me with each stroke, but with my every soft sound, while he was inside my feminine place, even as I trembled, I owned him.

Twenty comprehensive and unwavering strokes later it felt like he was trying to earn the pink slip to Susan's heart. From the first stroke it felt that good. We had had so much foreplay, and the prickling in my body needed to be scratched in the worst way. I wasn't going to give in, wasn't going to be weak. Wanted to act like I didn't want him more than he wanted me. Had to be a lady and let the man lead. My hand betrayed me. My fingers wiggled and reached down. My body joined in the conspiracy and betrayed me as well. My ass shifted in order to line up my vagina, and my hand held his latex-covered erection, measured it the way a woman measures an erection when she holds it the first time, its weight, its power, its stiffness. New pussy had him in heaven. New dick had me hot as hell.

My phone buzzed again. Chicken and Waffles' ringtone. Again it was ignored.

The man from Orange County bit my lips, sucked my tongue, and gave me another kiss that felt like nothing I'd ever felt, a kiss that shortened my breath. I wanted more. He kissed me like he'd wanted to kiss me all his life. Each kiss was better than I could have ever imagined. Had forgotten how good a moment like this could feel. The suspense was powerful. It had been that way with my boyfriend the first time. When it was new. But he had rushed inside me, hadn't taken his time, had put his dick in me and started pumping before the gun had gone off, had raced toward orgasm. Now my eyes opened. I was moments into cheating on my boyfriend, and I craved having this new man deeper inside me. I craved all of him. I craved his cock. I craved this strange cock. And now this man was dying to know me, dying to be deeper inside me, to be all the way inside a woman who had been a stranger to him a few hours ago, a woman the universe had placed at the same gas station at the same moment to make this possible, as if it were already written. So I arched my body, helped him be able to explode deeper inside me. Being opened, feeling total penetration until his skin rested against mine — it hurt and felt good.

I whispered, "Jesus Christmas."

"What?"

"You're all the way inside me. All of you, all of your cock is inside me."

At an unhurried pace, he moved in and out and in and out. Each time I moved away from him, then toward him. It was an unhurried dance between people who did not have the luxury of time. I purred. He moaned. Moaning was nonverbal direction, said you were on the right road, doing it the right way. The auditory battle escalated.

We'd only started and I became a little louder, cries of sexual ecstasy rising from my body, trying to lose control. It felt so good. From the first lick, this had felt too damn good.

I whispered, "We're having sex; we're having sex; we're having sex."

"Yes. We are having sex."

"How the hell did this happen?"

"Don't question it. Enjoy it."

We were having sex. I was having sex with him. We were together, yet separate. My mind raced. I felt what I felt, while he felt what he felt. Our experiences were independent from each other, yet here we were, pleasing each other in the absence of love. Sex was sex. He was so into me. It felt like he was here with me. Lovemaking is divine and soulful, yet he put himself completely into the act of faux love, maybe the start of what to him would feel like true love, a place where I wanted to be, but I keep it on the physical level, because there, in that shallow place, I will not drown, so I am safe.

He whispered, "You okay?"

"My heart is racing."

"Are you freaking out again?"

"I'm fine; I'm fine."

"You're okay?"

"Overwhelmed with emotions."

"Should I stop?"

"How does it feel to be inside me like that?"

"You feel so warm and nice inside."

My insides took on the shape of his erection, opened to fit its form. He took his time, and that was driving me fifty shades of crazy. As I opened up, I cursed. I panted as I felt his erection filling me, stretching me, moving deeper. Color came in waves like an ocean. His tongue had been bliss. But his erection was the top floor of heaven. Then I was underwater, floating in space, swimming in serotonin and dopamine, all at once, my sounds low and strong, but relaxed, happy, alive, dancing against his LSD.

He asked, "You're okay?"

I whispered, "Don't move. Let me absorb this moment."

"Okay."

"Pull back out to the tip, then wiggle back in; move like you're waving at me."

"Cheesecake."

"Yeah, cheesecake. The bet is still on?"

"The bet is still on."

He pushed in deeper. It hurt. I smiled and clutched his shoulders. He pulled all the way out, then moved inside me again, did that over and over and over, and as moments went by, as the torture went on and on and on, as once again his breathing thickened, as he again thickened inside me, as he opened me up more, I stretched to accommodate his enthusiastic dick. He sought to own me with each eager stroke. Each stroke felt indelible, like none would ever be forgotten, and none would ever be erased. I panted like I was hyperventilating. He took hard breaths and stroked and stroked and kissed and panted and kissed. The connection was powerful, electrifying. It felt more than sexual. It felt dangerous. It felt like madness. He kept a steady stroke. We had found our sex groove and moved around the king bed, trying a dozen positions. It was coitus to end all coitus. The people in the room next door banged on the wall.

I felt spasms. Wonderful convulsions. I was engulfed in a spine-tingling contraction, a set of contractions, and I made the orgasm sound, made the face that told him I was on a wonderful journey.

He thrust, stirred me, and as he moved he whispered, said endearing words, told me how tight I felt, how good I made him feel, talked dirty, and in between my sex noises I told him how good he felt inside me, told him that his cock was big, that his cock was perfect, and I talked dirty for the sake of talking dirty, said things that motivated him to please me like he'd never have the chance again.

We complimented each other as lovers do, whether it is the truth or not. We were civilized savages, intellectual fornicators in the throes. We were beasts with manners. We were kind liars.

He suckled Tina, then licked Marie, multitasked as he stroked Susan and held my callipygous butt, held what many saw as part of my African heritage, gripped both cheeks of the booty nicknamed Ophiuchus, gave me the dance of all dances. I danced with him, and I was so high. Susan sang because there had been so much clitoral stimulation from his tongue, and now she was open and felt so much vaginal stimulation from his LSD. My sex hadn't been massaged like this since . . . ever. I was over the moon, beyond Mars. I had an outburst of passion, a sudden rush, was besieged by a thousand tingles and spasms. This was better than ten years of masturbation. My heart beat faster. Involuntary rhythmic rapid muscle contractions and more spasms made me hold on to him like I was falling. The heated feeling from those tingles spread to other parts of my body. I was manacled by euphoria. Feral desires magnified. Those desires handcuffed me as well. Muscles tightened. My breasts felt like they had doubled in size, and my nipples were so tender, so fat, so erect. My face, neck, chest, all of my skin was flushed. Susan felt alive, wet, engorged. Every noise I made was power, reflected the pleasure I was experiencing, and expressed how good he was making me feel. The expression on my face revealed to him how good I felt, just as the expression on his face told me the same. He looked like being inside me was better than being in a suite in heaven. I touched his face. Wanted to stare at him, study him, remember this moment, remember what this felt like forever.

11:11 P.M.

Well lubricated. There was no pain. It just felt so damn good, because I was so well lubricated. First I had been reluctant; now I wanted more. I didn't pretend that I didn't want him. I professed that I wanted less, that I wasn't that turned on; I played the you-can't-control-me sex game, became that chick who challenges her lover. But he knew. The more he gave, the more I wanted, and I wanted more of him over and over. I wanted as much of him as I could have before the night, before this stolen moment, ended. I was in the zone. Grunts. The headboard moved. The expensive bed squeaked. Skin slapped, kissed skin. I gasped at times. Heard that wet sucking sound. My legs opened, separated as far as they could go.

"You're tight. So damn tight."

"You like Susan?"

"Susan is driving me crazy."

He stroked like he was addicted, like he was half-crazy, like he was overexcited, like he wanted to ask me to marry him, like he didn't give a damn about unplanned parenthood, like he was about to emancipate himself from his load too fast. But he hesitated. Winced. Took sharp inhales, swallowed.

I asked, "Did you just come?"

"Almost. But no."

"You okay?"

"Give me a moment."

"You come, I get cheesecake."

"Be quiet."

"Don't be rude."

"Will you shut up?"

I laughed. My vagina pulsed around his cock, felt good as I laughed.

A few sharp breaths later he restarted his ingress and egress.

Our sex was beautiful.

I let go and went with it. Did it because this wrong felt so right.

Many men lack the knowledge and the concern for the woman of the relationship, for the woman they are making love to, for the woman they are with in bed. Their thoughts are always stuck on their own satisfaction, chasing their own orgasm and nothing more. They grow hard, become lions, but unfortunately many have sex like a lion: fast, and done in the time it takes to set free a good yawn, done as the lioness lies there in agony and roars. They sex fast, but unluckily not as often as the king of the jungle. Some men never mature in bed. All have dicks, but not many work well, and most men are about their own pleasure. That makes a woman sexually disturbed, leaves her impatient, and that yields an ill-fated relationship, a dreadful marriage. He showed me that he was not one of those weak, inconsiderate men. He showed me how he sexed his wife, and God knows he showed me well.

I was jealous and angry; jealous that she had this, and angry because I didn't.

He had given gentle fingers and an educated tongue, a tongue that had a PhD from at least ten universities and possessed an honorary degree in porn. He had eaten me without overworking my clit, without leaving it sore and tender, only anxious and aroused, very stimulated, smiling at orgasm, and then he took me as if he were trying to prove a point, treated me like he wanted to educate me and grad school was in session. He handled me like he wanted me to know he was a man among men. I treated him the same, wanted him to know that I was a good woman, a smart woman, a keen woman, a woman who had known only a few men but knew how to please, a woman who was worthy of the best of the best of men, a woman who, despite setbacks and pain, would always be a woman among women. This was my thesis, my proposition put forward for consideration. My upward thrust met his downward stroke, and with vigor I defended my position. We pulled away from each thrust in a sweet rhythm and my up met his down over and over. I sexed him like I was always the one who loved more, that being a blessing and a curse, and I deserved two hundred dozen roses and just as many cheesecakes simply for being this damn awesome. He was remarkable, too, damn remarkable, so he had me and I had him. With each stroke, the passion effloresced, and I met each thrust, be it deep or shallow, fast or slow. I showed up and met each thrust, showed him I was a participant in this affair from beginning to end, not a lady lover, not a blowup sex toy, not a warm place to come in the latex barrier between us. I wondered how this would feel bareback. It felt awesome, incredible, but I wondered how he would feel, wondered what his wife had felt. Winter felt like spring, and everything bloomed. It bloomed inside me, the sounds and faces and the way my body responded, how it rolled as he thrust, how I breathed as if I had a respiratory disorder, letting him know that soon I would come. The tingles were strong, and bit by bit my orgasm bloomed. It felt sleek at first, but it grew; it fattened itself, became impossible to hold back. Nails in his skin, I whimpered. Good sex makes me whimper, and those whimpers were a song that was sweet and young and innocent. Each whimper was as erotic as it was fuzzy. He hit my spot and that made me tense, made me sing a song I hadn't sung before, and I sang it like it was the national anthem. Oh say can you see that an orgasm was on the horizon. It came closer with each stroke, grew in size with each stroke. Orgasm ran its finger up and down my skin, each finger filled with electricity, each touch, each stroke making me jerk, making me move and fight back, making this battle for cheesecake the best battle ever fought. He made sweet sounds of suffering in my ear. That excited me, empowered me, thrilled me, made me respond. He stroked faster, and still didn't lack in smoothness or continuity, steep rises and smooth drops that were never broken. It was a beautiful poem. It had rhythm, was never curt. I was close to another orgasm. His cock was so nice, and he kept telling me how tight I felt, how good it felt to be joined with me. He had size and made me feel like I was tighter than O.J.'s leather glove. He was on a journey, going deep, searching. Going in and out and so deep and hard that I was close to tears. I tried to hold back, but it came without warning, and I became vocal. Told him not to stop. I came again. I came and he didn't slow down. He rammed me for a moment, was rough, and gave me pain, a sweet pain. His thrusts were rhythmic and varied in speed and depth, which gave my body a stirring that was unexpectedly good, and with all the foreplay I had endured, kept me in a blinding fog of light, kept me in a trancelike state with my mouth wide open, hoping there were no flies in the room. That was not the type of protein I was craving. My orgasmic song was elongated, echoed, very telling. His sexual movements were smoother than warm butter, creative, musical, and right away he became a conductor who directed the performance and moans of his one-woman orchestra with his dick. I sang like a choir. He switched up, inserted an unexpected harpsichord solo between Bach's two movements. Already I was breathless, but my song continued as I moved against him. I mimicked his dance, learned his rhythm, and what I gave was so intense he stopped moving as I performed my own damn solo. I rendered a wicked, toe-curling solo that made him tense, stop breathing, then set free a long groan. He closed his eyes tight, grabbed the sheets. I didn't ease up. I became the director. My one-man choir tensed and made a guttural sound, the solo of all solos. He held the edge of the condom and removed himself from me. He surrendered. I wasn't done, but he had disconnected, sweet and intense agony in his breathing and on his face. I thought he was about to pull the condom off and come on me, maybe on my breasts. Thought he was going to anoint me, and was prepared to curse him if he did. He disconnected, made me want to holler and bite and kick his sexy ass. He wheezed a hundred times, then got a grip on himself. He apologized for the *coitus interruptus.* He was enjoying himself too much, relished me too much, and he needed to slow things down or he would burst.

He trembled, managed a red-faced smile, and said, "I don't want to disappoint you."

I quivered, legs restless; I felt delirious, like I was resurfacing from a fifteen-hour dive, and in puffs, as I moved through the haze he had created, I replied, "You're. Not. Disappointing. Me."

"Give me a moment."

"Okay. It's not me, is it? Am I doing something wrong?"

"You're distressed."

"Very aroused right now."

He went down on me, ate me, slowed things down for him and kept them going for me — or actually sped them up. He gave me more stimulation, had the time of his life on my sensitive clit. Only for a few seconds, not even a minute, but he tortured me, and then he was back in control, back inside me, slow stroking, singing his own song. I was glad he didn't come. My toes curled. My butt tightened. My muscular contractions magnified the experience of aurora borealis. My hands tingled until I became aware that I had hands, and then I felt numb, cramped, felt the discomfort up my forearms. My eyes opened wide. He was in motion, still chanting in his own handful of genres, but he was chanting solo, singing his own song. I was in bed with a man I had just met. I was in bed with a married man. I had never been comfortable the first time I had had sex with a new lover. There was an adjustment period that took place over the sessions, over time. As trust grew, I opened up, changed from a caterpillar to a butterfly.

Tonight it felt like I was with a lover I had been with many, many times. He treated me like he knew my body by heart. With kisses he had made me make honey. He made me make so much honey.

Then it changed. Changed from the intense, pleasurable, relaxing feeling. It became completely overwhelming. A surge of pain hit my muscles. I didn't want to stop, but what I felt was too much, like having every nerve touched at once. I tried to endure, to ride it out, and I mewled and refused to scream. I gasped and moved with him, became very aggressive, showed him what happened when I was that turned on, but I held on to the feeling of being completely overwhelmed for as long as possible.

I asked him to stop.

He didn't.

He was so into me, so deep into the moment, so into a new world. Trembling, breathing in short spurts, I put my hands on the sides of his face, looked in his eyes. Asked him once again to stop.

He shuddered, caught his breath, asked, "I do something wrong?"

"No, not at all."

"Tell me what I did wrong."

"It's not you."

"I'm not doing it right?"

"Oh, you're doing more than right. You're hitting spots right, left, and center."

"What happened?"

"It's too good."

"Too good?"

"You are very good and I . . . I just got too excited, overexcited, and I think I was flexing my muscles very hard, and now they're cramping a bit. Just need a second to relax; have to relax my hands."

"You're not having a heart attack, are you?"

"No. I'm not having a heart attack."

"This happened before?"

"Few times. But it hasn't happened in a long time, not in three years. I just have to wait a moment, or it can spread to my legs. If it does, I'll be cramped up in a ball and I'll be a hot mess."

Then we heard them. The sounds. The applause. The intrusion.

It sounded like a murder of crows. A crowd was congregated outside our hotel room door.

They applauded, laughed, and then raced down the hall laughing and imitating my sounds.

I chuckled. "Oh my God."

"Perverts. Eavesdropping perverts."

"Was I that loud?"

He yelled toward the door, *"This is a respectable hotel, assholes."*

I laughed. "If only it allowed respectable people inside."

"And they have perverts in the hallway?"

"They heard me."

"Us. They heard us. You made me make noises I never knew this body was capable of making."

"Dammit. Wonder how many assholes were out there?"

"Should I get up?"

"No. Stay there. I'll be fine in a moment."

He asked, "You're not done?"

"You're done?"

"No."

"Really? The way you move, you can keep that pace? I thought you'd be done by now."

"You were uncomfortable, so I assumed you were done."

"You didn't come?"

"Not yet."

"Then, no. Not done."

He said, "Okay."

"Sorry I wrecked the flow."

"It's okay. Guess the perverts in the hallway think we're done."

"I'm embarrassed two times over now.

249

Them and you."

"No need to be embarrassed with me."

"We have a fan club."

He asked, "What should I do?"

"Kiss me like you did in the parking lot."

He raised up on his elbows and took his weight off of me, and we laughed, chuckled, rubbed noses, played like kids, chased tongues, and eventually kissed, and just like that my body started to relax, and a half minute later I was fine, was moving my ass as a signal for him to restart the party, and soon we were chanting together, talking dirty again, back where we left off. I couldn't remember the last time I had talked and laughed during sex. This was nice. This was fun. Wonderful.

I sucked on his neck, made him squirm, then asked, "What's your addiction?"

"I told you, I don't do drugs. Not anymore. I was a teenager then."

"Not what I meant. What are you addicted to? What's your obsession?"

"Outside of work and trying to keep my marriage from dying, I don't have one."

"Everyone has an addiction."

"What's yours? Tattoos?"

"Used to be buying Barbie dolls."

"That's every little girl's addiction."

"Yup. Every black girl has to have a white

Barbie doll. Black girls will get a black Barbie, but they have to have a white Barbie. The black Barbie never really seems like a true Barbie, not like the queen. The black Barbie is sold for less than the white Barbie. Identical dolls, except for skin color, which is telling the world she is less, that she is cheaper, that she does not have the value of the one with blond hair and blue eyes. No one wants the cheap doll. No one wants to look like the cheap doll."

"You really need to seek help. You probably dream in black-and-white as well."

"I dream in black."

He chuckled. "Would think you'd dream in colored."

"Don't make me sit on your face."

"I'd like that."

"But let me say this: White dolls outsell black dolls, always have and always will, and that's because black parents are more likely than white parents to buy their children dolls of a different race. You don't see little white girls with a basket of black dolls. You don't see little white girls putting black angels on their Christmas trees. You're brainwashed from the first breath. It carries on into adulthood. Black women race to dress up like Wonder Woman, get the Wonder Woman symbol tattooed on their rear, wear Wonder Woman negligees, but you rarely see a white chick . . . whatever. Yeah. I digress."

"You probably dream in colored while you sing Negro spirituals and eat cabbage."

I laughed. "What's your addiction?"

"Tonight, it's you."

I smiled. "Is it this nice with your wife?"

"No. We don't have moments like this. At least not with each other."

I asked, "You make love to her this good? Is this why the distraught woman is so jealous?"

"We don't . . . we don't have fun. I didn't lie. Nothing I said was a lie."

"Why put up with it? Sounds like she married you for the sake of being married."

"Marriage is hard work, and you have to show up in hard hat and boots every day of every year."

"Yeah, but everybody who shows up on the job ain't necessarily working. Some are just showing up to get a check. People come to work to not work, and if you ask them to work, they get an attitude."

"I guess that's true."

"Everyone wants the job, the title, but no one wants to roll up his or her sleeves and work."

"Very true."

I said, "They want to delegate. Bunch of reality-TV-watching wannabes trying to be like the fake bitches on television. They want the wedding, the ring, and the gifts the same way people want the job, the benefits, and the vacation days, but don't want to do any more than they have to do to maintain it."

He shrugged. "We choose the people. The choices we make are seeds to our misery."

"Guess I'm a freakin' farmer."

"We're all farmers, reaping what we sow."

"Yeah. That's true."

"Things have changed. They changed a long time ago."

I kissed his injured face. Kissed his face and masturbated him slow and easy.

My cell vibrated again. His cell did the same at almost the same moment.

We kissed, again lost in ecstasy, and chuckled.

He took to my breasts, sucked Tina and Marie like he knew them well.

I squirmed, held his head, said, "You really want me to sit on your face?"

"I do want to continue my chat with Susan."

"Be careful what you ask for. She's loquacious and will talk to you all night."

"Bring Susan to me. Tell Susan to come

have a discussion."

"Seriously?"

"Seriously. I want to tell her how I used to want to visit every country in the world."

"Even Greece?"

"Never been, but would go if invited."

"Don't get any ideas."

He laughed.

He made himself comfortable on his back and I climbed him, straddled his face, adjusted Susan, and leaned toward the headboard so I could keep my balance and stay in control, so I wouldn't fall on his nose. Right away that tongue began to wiggle. He concentrated on the ten and two o'clock marks on either side of my vagina. His wicked tongue found a spot that made me ride and grind and bite my lip and close my eyes tight and give up intense sex sounds. He made his tongue dance back and forth across my folds. He was on two hot spots.

There was a knock at the door. The licking stopped. The intense sex sounds faded, but didn't die all at once. Skin flushed, pupils dilated, parts of my body shaking, in slow motion I fell away from his face. He sat up, mouth wet, dampened by the honey from sex. My legs shook and I pulled at the sheets. *Coitus interruptus* caused sexual agony, but the removal of a tongue at the moment when I could've climaxed created a special kind of throbbing and annoyed me on a new level. I set free an aggrieved cooing sound that came from not making it to ne plus ultra. I had almost reached the pinnacle, was ten licks from going over the top. I made my hands into fists to keep from touching myself to get the other side of the pain. Vibrations escaped my lungs and I was unable to breathe. Soon I coughed like I had Middle East Respiratory Syndrome. I grabbed his hand, was about to use his fingers like a toy.

He said, "Your fingernails. Ouch. Your nails."

"Sorry sorry sorry."

I put his hand on Susan, made the tips of his digits rub her, caress her, stroke her.

Whoever was outside thumped at the door again. Then I let his hand go, was able to catch my breath, was able to open my eyes. I panted and frowned and glowered at the entrance to our fornicave. Our phones had sounded like danger signals; now someone was kicking the door. The two actions felt connected. Someone was hunting for someone. Someone had found whomever he or she was tracking. They banged with urgency and anger. We regarded each other. His eyes were wide, his jaw once again tight, as if he questioned whether it was Chicken and Waffles. My eyes questioned if it was his distraught wife.

My heart raced, faster than before, and I trembled, now with fear. Our escape from the real world, our amoral escapade, was over. The knocks on the door made me realize how wrong this was. This unapproved adventure that had given me happy endings was about to have a very ugly ending.

11:29 P.M.

There was one demanding bang after another at the door.

"Security," a voice called out. "May I have a word with you?"

My lover took a deep breath, then called out in a stern voice, telling them to hold on for a moment.

I had to lie there, had to tremble, had to open and close my eyes.

I missed that feeling, his tongue being inside me.

The man from Orange County asked, "You okay?"

I panted, said, "Assholes. Couldn't they just call up here instead of banging on the door?"

He stood up, his breathing labored, his erection strong.

I said, "Maybe I should go to the door. You could stab somebody."

He looked down at his condom-covered

penis and agreed.

I found a robe, tugged it on, hand-combed my dreadlocks, wiped my face with the palms of my hands, and staggered to the door. I cracked it enough to see her face. She was a heavyset East Indian woman who didn't have an East Indian accent; she sounded very Californian, meaning she was born here in America.

She asked, "May I speak to the priest?"

"The priest?"

"The one in charge of the exorcism."

"You've got jokes."

"People are complaining about the noise."

"Are you freakin' serious? We just started."

"Thirty minutes ago. We've had a dozen complaints for at least thirty minutes."

"Nobody was that damn loud. What, are we on a floor filled with celibate haters?"

"Just finish what you're doing so people can stop ringing the front desk."

"We'll finish when we finish; that's when we'll be done. If you knock on this damn door again and disturb my groove, you'd better have a venti one-pump caramel, one-pump white mocha, two scoops vanilla-bean powder, extra-ice frap with two shots poured over the top, apagotto style, with caramel drizzle under and on top of the whipped cream, double cupped. Have a Merry Kiss-

My-Ass, bitch."

I closed the door, laughing, pulling my fingers through my damp dreadlocks, once again prancing, dancing like I was in Pharrell's "Happy" video. Orange County was on the bed, laughing as well.

He looked so handsome, so much younger, so yummy, so likable, so devoid of stress now.

He said, "How dare she?"

"Fat as butter and breath that stinks like durian."

"A cream-faced loon, no doubt."

"Wait. Are you a priest?"

"Afraid not."

"Too bad. Was going to ask you to pray for me."

"You're weird."

"And confident about it."

"Do that dance move again."

I stopped and tap-danced like Shirley Temple. Then I went old-school, did the freak, spank, and bop, then threw in a little Cabbage Patch, Running Man, and Dougie. My body parts bounced and bounced. He watched Tina and Marie move with my groove and loved the show. I threw down some Iggy Azalea rapping "Fancy," then went Beyoncé on him, did an amalgamation of her smooth moves, dropped it, brought it back up like a single lady. He laughed and clapped. His smile was broad, now that of a playful kid. Not long ago he had looked like a man incapable of laughing. Now he looked like a man who seized every risible moment and lived to arouse laughter, enjoyed provoking laughter, a boy trapped in a man's body.

I stopped performing, moved my dreadlocks from my face, and stared at the door, concerned.

"I'm glad that wasn't your distraught and jealous wife."

"I can tell you've had a lot of dance training."

"Your distraught and jealous wife would have been really upset when I opened the door."

"Love the way you dance. Never would have imagined you could move like that."

"Stop ignoring me. You hear me talking about your distraught and jealous wife."

"I'm too busy admiring the way Tina and Marie jiggle while Ophiuchus bounces to ignore you."

"Love the way you put it down. You make me want to apologize for things I haven't done yet."

"You make me want to do a lot of things. You make me realize that the obstacles in our lives are self-created. Most of the walls we face are the ones we've constructed. We author most of our pain."

"Stop being philosophical. I'm dancing naked."

"I digress. You were saying?"

"That would've freaked you out if that had been your skinny, distraught wife banging at the door."

"Or if Chicken and Waffles was standing out there holding a plate of chicken and waffles."

"If Chicken and Waffles had been at the door holding the Obama Special from Roscoe's, yeah, that would've freaked me out."

"I would've handled it."

"He would've kicked your ass back to Colorado and up a ski slope."

"Don't underestimate men from Vail Valley. Many have and ended up surprised."

"You said you beat up the guy who slept with your high school girlfriend?"

"Kicked his ass, broke the windows out of his Mustang, smashed his headlights, and left the car on four flat tires, with a touch of graffiti spray-painted bumper to bumper, then had sex with my girlfriend's friends."

"You're a monster."

"I went on a rampage."

"You need to practice self-control."

"When provoked, we're all animals; we all are capable of becoming monsters."

"This animal has an uncontrollable desire to dance. Dance with me."

He rose to his feet. Came to me. Surprised me that he could dance. It was a dirty dance. A sexy dance that I wished I could've recorded for posterity. We danced about a minute before we were too turned on. He pulled me down on the bed, aroused, his erection strong, eager to be inside me.

I told him, "Before that come shooter gets too close, we've made a pit stop, so change condoms."

"Okay."

"Let me do it."

I removed his condom and dropped it on the soft carpet, then grabbed another rubber from the nightstand, opened it with my teeth as he massaged my ass, put the cock sheath in my mouth, amazed him once again as I put it on him, then kissed him after, made him taste what I had tasted.

He said, "You're torturing me, you know that?"

"I want my cheesecake before you go home and Donkey Punch your distraught wife."

"Be warned. Now it's going to be hard,

intense, not nice, and you will surrender."

"I should put on a helmet."

"Elbow and knee pads, wrist guards, a mouthpiece, and a parachute, too."

"Whatever it takes to win the cheesecake."

He sucked my neck and asked, "What's Donkey Punch?"

"Something we will not be doing because that is where I draw the line."

11:38 P.M.

Then I was on my back, the soft mattress again giving under my weight, again with my legs open, his penile weight again in my hand, guiding him back inside with him in control, in the position of male dominance. When I was a young girl, we called the act of a girl putting a boy's penis inside parking a car in her garage. This time he pushed deep. I know the people in the next room heard. They heard that uncontrollable sound I made upon penetration, and it was a din like no other din. The way it echoed, reverberated, was beautiful, because in that moment I felt more than beautiful. I was perfect. It was my song, sung in my voice, in three octaves, my call to the gods. Being opened up and filled with firmness set me on fire, made me jerk and whimper as if he had never stopped being inside me. He was intense when we first started, and he was just as intense as we continued. His husky grunts kissed my din and that turned me on. I was still wet, but tender, tingling, and again he shocked my system. I felt the fire come back, flames on high. His phone buzzed once. A text. Or his wife had hit him up on Facebook or WhatsApp. Then my phone buzzed. Chicken and Waffles had made my phone tremble like it was having an orgasm.

I fell into Orange County, into the cadence of his mean stroke. My body moved, my hips thrusting up into him as I held on, refused to let him go, and he kept up with me. Aurora borealis began again. My sighs, my purrs and soft cries, bloomed, and soon I gasped for air, jerked, covered my mouth. He yanked my hand from my mouth. I pulled my lips in tight, clenched my teeth, cursed and swore. When that wasn't enough, I put my head against his shoulder, tried to bite him and control him the way a jockey puts spurs into a horse. I tried to show him who was in charge. He rebelled, went deeper. We fought like that, fought each other as we both fought the need to come. The bright lights of aurora borealis went on and on.

He took control, turned me over, became aggressive, now a caveman in bed. I was waiting for him to beat his chest and yell in monosyllabic grunts. He was behind me, had his hands on my waist and was going in and out of me slowly. Slowly. Nibbling. Whispering. Teasing. He tortured me and I sang, arched my back, raised my head, looked through my fallen dreadlocks and saw the red digits illuminating the time. Tonight I was stealing the time of another woman. I was a thief, robbing as I had been robbed more than a handful of times, maybe as I had been robbed on this same day. The universe timed us while other lovers waited on us. I had thought that we'd be done with this and gone within an hour, but Orange County had made me his summer home during the wettest winter. He went too deep. My eyes rolled into the back of my head and I called out to God and Jesus. I collapsed from my knees and lay flat on my belly. He asked me if he had hurt me. I told him to not stop, not to slow down, to give it to me like that, to give it to me like that, like that, like that. He was intense without being brutal. He gave it to me like that for a while, for as long as he could endure that pace, then went back to gentle stroking, kept a steady rhythm. Like that, like that, like that. The feeling of falling owned him. He had no self-control, no composure, no sophistication. Then, all of a sudden, he slowed, then stopped moving. I assumed he'd had a quiet, secret orgasm.

I asked, "Did you finish?"

He struggled to breathe. "Not ready to come yet."

"You can if you want to."

"Don't want to."

"Are you trying to kill me, or convert me into being your mistress?"

He ached to get to his happy ending, but he paused to smirk.

I said, "Not going to happen."

"You're terrible."

"And you're married."

Part of me wanted to end this torture. His breathing was so ragged, his body so reactive to touch. I loved what I was capable of making him feel. I moved underneath him, but only for a few seconds; I was tempted to make him lose control, but I only made him suffer, made his sex sounds rise, made him grab the sheets. It was hardboiled, gritty, intense, action-packed, the way I like it in bed. A moment passed and he started again, breathless, his pulse pounding. He moved like he wanted revenge, released an underlying current of aggression balanced by an appreciation for the beauty he saw in me. He gave it to me like he wanted to bend me, not break me. He moved like he wanted to win all the cheesecake.

The way he was in bed, I knew who he was. He was a frustrated man who had no control at his job, no control at home, a man pushed around and taken for granted, and now he got to be the boss, the boss of a woman like all the women who had ever walked by him and never offered a second glance. He got to release his frustration. He gave it to me like he had studied the art of sex, like he was an educated man who had been a horrible lover when he was younger, was ridiculed for coming too fast, had been sexually incompetent, then studied how to not come so fast, had studied his own body, had studied the makings of a woman, had studied the art of foreplay, how to excite a woman, how to make love, and now his mission was to make it last, to not embarrass himself, to conquer and prove to a woman like me, a woman who represented his every rejection and failure, that he was the alpha male among all alpha males. He gave it to me without pause, and I reciprocated, moved my ass, danced under him, sang under him, put my nails in his flesh, strained, became overwhelmed, and came. My orgasm was his victory. He needed me to come to feel validated. I felt like I came many times. I kept going. Had to. Wanted that cheesecake. We changed positions a dozen times, variations of missionary, variations of woman on top, variations of doggy, variations of being side by side, and as he put me through some sort of flexibility test, I pulled a pillow to my face to smother my never-ending chant, and all I could think was that my lame boyfriend would have come by then, would have finished long before then, when the timer was still in the single digits. This lover was a beast. The more he gave the more I asked for, as if there would be no pleasing me. He put a finger inside. He slid a finger inside my ass effortlessly. He took it to a new level, one that was twisted, dark, and very compelling. I loved it. I announced that I loved it. Every part of my body trembled, and I said things that would never get me into heaven.

My hands slapped down and grabbed the sheets, my curses and whimpers filling the room.

He showed me what he was made of in bed, showed me what he could do when unleashed. He took me through positions, advanced sexual positions. He carried me, my legs wrapped around him, and moved in and out of me, stroked me as he walked around the room. He took me to the bed, put me down gently so we were side by side, giving and taking, stroking and humping as Heatwave sang "Always and Forever." That smooth, outré dance music set the pace. He rubbed between my legs, squeezed my breasts, sucked my fingers, repositioned me, had me on my back, one leg up, the other open, going deep, going for deeper penetration, going for the cheesecake. I sang a song that had Jesus's name in many verses, but due to the profanity would never be heard on Easter Sunday. I was the contortionist; he was the acrobat. It was exciting. Not knowing what he was going to do excited me. He was on his back and then pulled me over, had me on my back touching his chest, my legs bent back. He held me and did the thrusting. Soon I was on my back, my hips arched, and he was on his knees between my legs, again thrusting deep inside me. Songs changed and we changed positions: Stevie Wonder singing "You Are the Sunshine of My Life." By the time that song started, I was standing on the carpet, one foot on the ground, the other high in the air. I held that position. Surprised him with my flexibility as he took me like he was taking a ballerina, a prima ballerina assoluta. From there, I was on the edge of the bed, my feet on the carpet, and he was on his knees, between my legs, moving in and out

270

of me, whispering provocative things to me. I scooted back on the bed and he kissed my body, rested on his side, had me on my back perpendicular to him, my leg over his hips, and he was sideways, like a cross, going in and out of me, crucifying me with pleasure. Then I took over, wanted to be back at the edge of the bed again, this time with him sitting on the edge, me straddling him leaning back, my upper body off the bed. He held me, had me suspended in air, in a position of trust, and he did all the work, his dance so sweet and without pause, thrusting, stroking, doing me well until we lost balance, and he tried to hold me, and I tried to grab for him. I fell to the carpet. I fell and he tried to hold me, but fell to the soft carpet with me.

Still aroused, severely aroused, I didn't miss a beat, and kissed him, kissed him, kissed him. Was going to mount him, ride him, and earn carpet burns, but he stood up. He reached for me and I reached for his hand, let him pull me back to my feet. I stood up too fast and became dizzy for a moment. He held me until I was steady. Not until then did I move my dreadlocks from my face and laugh a little.

"Guess I really should have put on a motorcycle helmet."

He laughed.

I said, "Not funny. At least I didn't queef."

"Glad you didn't have cabbage."

He laughed harder and so did I.

Like I was a dominatrix, I pushed him back on the bed, made him get back on the edge because I loved that position. I sat on him and wrapped my legs around him, put him back inside me, put all of him inside me, moved clockwise, rode his cock clockwise, then changed the course, rode him widdershins, rode that cock counterclockwise. The laughter stopped. He was flabbergasted — a good flabbergasted, speechless, but not soundless. Once again, he was in awe. Cheesecake was on the line.

We faced each other, kissing, caressing, and I moved up and down on his power. He tensed, held me, and enjoyed the ride. Soon, keeping him on the edge of the bed, I turned around and gave him the lap dance of all lap dances, one much better than the weak one Nicki Minaj gave Drake. I danced on his anaconda while I sang "Romping Shop" by Vybz Kartel, sang his explicit part and the part by Spice, was wining my bubble against him like a Jamaican in heat. He couldn't stand the wickedness of incendiary dancehall moves. He was on some new shit now. His eyes rolled and he moaned like an old man. I danced until he cursed, growled, grabbed my hips, and took control, made skin slap against skin.

"How do I feel inside you?"

"Indescribable."

"Never in my life have I felt anything like this. Never in my fucking life."

"Merry Christmas, Baby. Merry Christmas."

His strokes were deep, unexpectedly good, and sent me into a blinding fog of light.

The more he gave the more I asked for, as if there would be no pleasing me.

I murmured, "I'm coming."

"Are you?"

"Yes."

We moved around the bed and soon I mounted him again, sat on him, took charge of depth and speed and rode backward, reverse cowgirl at the pace of a drunken turtle. I tortured him. He set free more protracted moans, sensual whimpers that felt like flashing colors, and he squeezed my slow-moving rump. Biting my bottom lip, then sucking in air, I rode him backward so I didn't have to see him, didn't have to witness orgasm rising in his handsome face, and didn't have to see his sexy eyes. But he felt damn good inside me. His rod, his staff, it comforted me. This handsome man, this married man, made me feel good. In this position every man had made me feel good. Men had lit up my body, had set me on fire, but few had illuminated my memory, so most were forgettable, unremarkable. Again, instead of coming, he paused, pulled out, gave me his mouth, his heated breath, his tongue.

He whispered, "You like that?"

"I like that. I like that a lot."

His hands cupped my breasts and I closed my eyes, closed my eyes and licked my lips.

His tongue found its way to my belly and then moved back between my legs. He moved his tongue back and forth, left to right, until I couldn't take it anymore and held his head on my sacred spot.

As he licked me, his hands cupped my ass. Soon he moved his hands back to my breasts and pulled at my nipples. My nipples were strong, powerful, dual epicenters of my arousal.

Forbidden fruit. He savored me as if I tasted like the sweetest forbidden fruit.

He was very accommodating, like he really wanted to please and then be pleased.

I said, "I want you to come."

"Not yet."

"I want to look in your eyes and see you

come, want to feel what it's like when you come."

"Soon."

I pushed his face away and straddled him, my back to his face, and held him, guided him, as he entered me again, filled me up again. I moved, determined to make him come.

I asked, "What does it feel like to be inside me?"

"Warm. Tight."

Our melodies became Gregorian chants that intertwined like a sacred hymn.

He asked, "What do you want, most of all?"

"What?"

"Out of life. What do you want?"

"An unencumbered life."

"Let me help take care of you."

Then I turned and faced him, looked into his two-colored, my blues rising and becoming smoky and guttural hums, like it had been a long time since I'd allowed a man to taste me, to ease inside me, and I owned the fear of both creating attachment and becoming emotionally involved. This man didn't know me and I didn't know him. But now we were familiar.

He asked, "What can I do to make your life less encumbered?"

"My dutty wine makes you want a concubine."

"I want more than this."

"You want to be allowed to use my body as you see fit, then discard me when you're done."

"I want you."

"You want to be with me for the same reason men go to see Scarlett Johansson in movies."

He talked like he wanted to be my hero, to become my personal Lone Ranger, the honest man in the Wild West, the one who rode in on a white horse and saved the day. He said things, sweet things that men say when they are enamored by what they feel, enthralled and a slave to what they desire.

Again, like we had done in the beginning, we were negotiating for goods and services.

This time he was the liar, the one coming to me with the con. An affair was nothing more than a con. An affair was nothing but false promises. For one person in every affair, it was nothing more than rocks in a box. And the fool who disagreed was doing nothing more than conning him- or herself.

He was as much of a good man as I was a good girl in this heated moment, him being inside me proving both points. The time when there was a clear line between a good man and a bad man had become as blurred as the lines that showed the difference between being a good woman and a bad woman.

This was a world that loved the bad men, the bad women, and praised the home-wreckers.

I tried not to, but I moaned and it sounded like a fifth of Jack Daniels was in my blood. He was louder and twice as inebriated. We created a drunken sermon together. My body craved seeds. It took control of me, something that I couldn't be in command of. I felt it coming and it felt so good, the hollowness inside my belly, a rising savage-ness, a sensation of hunger that I wanted to run from, yet embrace; control, yet submit to; and all I could do was squirm. I wanted that excitement. I wanted to dance and revel in its passion, but I didn't want to get burned. And I hummed a melody that sounded like an age-old liturgical recitative, a sweet single pitch, and his syllabic chants rose to meet my every sound, and our desires married. Our sounds, our chamber music was so intense, so fucking beautiful. Eyes closed, naked, imagining I was in the seat of love, the elegant warmth of orgasm, the best bad feeling ever, a feeling that I could hardly stand, a happiness that I desperately needed, embraced me.

Those waves refused to set me free, kept rolling through my body, kept me anchored where I was. He forced me back to missionary, back to the position of dominance, to the position where gravity worked in favor of his overweight orgasm, one that had been to the edge many times and never released.

I said, "I want you to come. I need you to come for me."

"Why?"

"My ego."

He grinned and asked, "Is your heart strong?"

"It's been broken beyond repair, but it's strong."

"No history of heart attack in your family?"

"Oh, is this about to get that serious?"

"It's going to be that serious."

"Don't talk about it; be about it."

With fervor, with desperation, with what felt like crossness, he controlled me. My mouth opened in the shape of a scream, but no sound came from my bruised soul, not then. Soon my will dissolved. I surrendered. As rain fell against the world and drunks passed by our suite singing Christmas carols, my face wrinkled in pleasure. He took the lead, his strokes deliberate and as consistent as he was aroused and firm. Three times this way, three times that way. He danced inside me. He lost control. He began pounding like there was house music jamming inside his head. We were delirious. He worked me so well I had to stop moving, had to surrender as my dreadlocks swayed with the power of his strokes. He grew harder, longer, sang louder, stronger, set free groan after groan. He stroked me and I was floating over Barbados, Venezuela, and South Africa. He took me through the clouds and around the world.

His orgasm was going to be intense. So damn intense. His pelvic thrusts were rapid, as if he had lost control, as if the need to reach a thousand little deaths owned him. Each stroke tested me. Each stroke created a new song at a new octave. Each stroke tried to dominate and domesticate me. He had me. In that moment, I was tamed. I would have become his slave for twelve years.

His heart beat strong against my chest, his breathing in and out, fast and furious.

"I'm coming; I'm coming."

"Come for me, come for me, come for me."

He was in his own world and pushed deep, so deep I thought he was trying to crawl inside my body. I called out. He held it there, held all of him inside me, tensed, took hard breaths, gave in to what he felt and became a roaring lion. Again he gave short thrusts, like he wanted to perforate my soul. He started to come. Again he shuddered like an enormous number of nerves had been touched. When I thought he was done, he began stroking again, stroking to get the last drop of orgasm out of his body. He used my body to satisfy that itch. It was a struggle for him to empty himself. His stroke devastated me. He gave it to me like he was an ex-criminal, ex–taxi driver, ex–club bouncer, and ex-marine.

The way I made him feel was good for my ego. My response was good for his.

I thought he was done. He was in my core, and I was giddy, on another planet.

He stroked me again, and I wondered how much come he had had stored in his nuts, wondered when was the last time his wife had pleased him, wondered if he made love like this each time.

I looked at him, at his face, at a face that was tight, veins in his neck standing out, so much power.

"Come for me. Get it; get it all out of you. Come for me. Get that nut."

Being sexed like this was uncanny. In a

good way, it was uncanny.

He strained, closed his eyes, opened his mouth, looked enraged, looked so damn sexy that it turned me on, made me feel like the queen of queens. Again he roared like a lion, roared and arrived at his own personal heaven. As he arrived, I held on to him, closed my eyes, legs wide, and again he lost control. His muscles contracted and jerked with his spasms, and he pushed, pushed, pushed inside me.

He hit my spot. He hit my spot and orgasm woke up inside me.

I'd thought I was done, but he had irritated that sweet spot again.

I ached. I itched and I ached. The itch was so damn powerful.

Nails digging into sweaty skin, body straining, my face tight like a fist, I called out.

"Don't stop, don't stop, right there, don't stop."

It wasn't me talking. But it was my voice.

He had an out-of-body experience and pushed, pushed, pushed.

Each push hit my spot and I trembled in a way I had never trembled before.

Dreadlocks fell into my open mouth, but I was no longer here, no longer alive.

Stars twinkled behind my eyes. Emotions

erupted, and there was a fireworks show.

I wasn't prepared for this. I wanted to feel good, to escape, but I wasn't prepared for this.

My face, neck, everything was warm. I was going to cry.

I was out of control. All I could do was hide my face, hope he didn't see me.

I felt so many damn emotions, some good, some amazing, some bad, some horrible.

It doesn't take long to commit a crime. Doesn't take long at all.

Chest rising and falling, a dry cough in my throat, tingles dancing between my legs, radiating through every part of me, I opened my teary eyes for a moment, opened my eyes and wiped my face with part of the ruffled white sheets, wiped more emotion from my eyes on a pillow and glanced to the side, to the table, where I saw his wedding ring in the glow from the television, and once again I closed my damp eyes.

The clock glowed: 12:15.

I blinked twice and it was 12:18.

Then it was 12:19 in the city of lost and fallen angels.

12:19 A.M.

He came like a flash flood. He came and the floor shook as the bed slapped the wall.

He created so much power, and the orgasmic explosion was brief. Hard, intense, but brief and strong enough to disrupt the San Andreas Fault and cause Southern California to drop into the Pacific Ocean. That final moment, as he controlled me, as he dominated me, as he became barbaric and came, when he behaved like electric shocks were being sent into his body, I wished he could've maintained that desperate pace, could have kept that level of hardness, that passion, could have given me that level of pain and pleasure until the day after Christmas. His orgasm had triggered another orgasm inside me. That relentless pace, being taking by a caveman, had made me come, and I had quaked and waned until I couldn't quake anymore. Sinning had been beautiful. But it was done. He had come, and it was done.

I had come, and the appetite to orgasm, to obtain pain and pleasure, only grew. It had to be horrible to be a man. A man's orgasm is so much shorter than a female's, leaves the man satiated and the woman ravenous. The journey for a man is maddening, but doesn't seem to be quite as euphoric when all the huffing and puffing has ended, when the hard work is done, when the sweet violence is over. I had lost control, had given in to the sensation and come as he was coming, had experienced another slice of heaven through his burst of orgasm, through his much-needed violence, an orgasm that felt full and powerful, a million shards of explosive energy that delivered a load that could have painted every wall in the room. As he grunted and the sperm soldiers rushed and charged into a new land, for a new egg, they were captured at the border by the enemy: latex. They were captured; the penis was still hard, but no longer moving with urgency. I was still in need, still holding him, bringing my body against him, still humming and experiencing waves. Our duet had become a desperate solo, the spotlight on me. He came and it looked like he had gone numb. He had rocked my world. Now I was flabbergasted.

He had given numerous combinations with the right doses of grittiness, softness, and tenderness, had been explicit, had been comprehensive, and the orgasmic violence had opened my heart, my emotions.

He was still on top of me, still inside me, shrinking, but I contracted, felt him.

His phone rang. My cell rang. Our sirens continued while I let out a whiny, simpering love song that had no place in this room. I took deep breaths. I had to, to calm myself, to bring myself down. His phone rang again. In my mind I cursed his wife for being so goddamn rude.

He grabbed the base of the sheath and eased out of me, our sexual scent perfuming both of us.

We disconnected. It ached. Being filled, then vacated, that abandonment never felt good.

I glanced toward his wedding ring. Again I glanced toward the clock and saw that we had been here too long. I expected that he would stand and get dressed right away, kiss me on the forehead, leave.

My tears had stopped. My body was warm, was kindling.

I couldn't raise my head now, couldn't be coy, couldn't be assertive and make eye contact with the man I had slept with. He had been inside me, and I smelled like him and Hubba Bubba bubble gum. I had experienced him, and he smelled like my honey and the same scent of chewing gum. I hand-combed my curly dreadlocks, walked to the thermostat, and turned the heater off. Back on the bed, body still tingling, baby-making music still playing, now Gladys Knight on a midnight train to Georgia, I scooted closer to him, but stayed about three feet away, three feet that felt like I was three rooms away. But I held my foot close to him, in case he wanted to touch after sex, the same thing I would do with my boyfriend. I didn't know if this lover would be guarded and want to get away, or feel amorous and want less space between us. Having this wickedness with a married man was tragic. But it was wonderful.

Coming with him, that last moment when we were uninhibited and clung to each other and sucked tongues and sucked fingers and bit flesh and moved like we were severely intoxicated, while we percolated, murmured, groaned, and made odd sounds like we had clogged sinuses and bad allergies, it had been like no other moment to date. He inhaled, reached down, and checked the condom.

I asked, "Condom still on the ding dong?"

"Still there."

"Didn't break? You got pretty rough. That was one helluva stress test."

"Didn't break. Sorry about that."

"I liked it like that. You came a lot."

"I know."

"When was the last time you got some?"

"Long time. Told you."

I asked, "Don't you jack off so you don't end up with blue balls the size of coconuts?"

"I don't masturbate. Always seemed pointless."

"Saving it up like that is bad for the prostate."

He said, "Well, thanks for the relief."

"No wonder you were so testy. Maybe that will get the thorn out of your foot."

"Same for you. You make love like you were starving, undernourished."

"I came like a tornado, and the way you come should have a flashflood warning."

"It was good."

I said, "You're a perfect fit."

"Like a glove."

"Damn good."

He said, "The way you respond to me — it's like I've never been with a real woman before."

"Stop lying."

"You make every other woman I've met, every woman I have touched seem . . . dull."

The man with impeccable sartorial taste, the great stylish dresser who was now nude and still fine as hell, went to the bathroom to flush his prophylactic filled with semen. He came back, eased back onto the bed. Then I went to the bathroom, went to see if I could urinate, then used wipes and cleaned myself before going back to the bed. And now I had that awkward after-first-time-sex-with-a-stranger feeling, that not-knowing-what-to-do-now feeling. As a function of the sympathetic nervous system, apperception of dignity is impossible while sex is in progress. Dignity doesn't exist when a person is aroused. But after, that need to feel dignified creeps back. That's why people leave abruptly after having sex. Dignity. Embarrassment. I felt the downside of arousal. Didn't know if I should cover myself up now. I didn't know if I should make the first move, gather my things, shower, and leave. Or wait to see if he wanted to try to go again. Or turn the TV on and watch reruns of *The Golden Girls*. He had been in my garden. We were hidden from the world, in a room, Adam and Eve. I didn't know who he would be now. Didn't know how close I should get to him, if closeness was permissible. He scooted closer to me, closed the gap, his warm skin next to mine.

A twinge of guilt rose.

But I had another issue, a self-esteem thing. The last time I had been with Chicken and Waffles, it had been disastrous. While I rode him, I heard him snoring. It sounded like someone was inside his chest starting an asthmatic tractor-trailer. I was on him, moving, and he was calling hogs. I fell away from him. That humiliation had never happened to me before. I sat on the bed, questioning myself. I had questioned my ability to be that kind of a woman, the way I had questioned my being a mother.

I'd redeemed myself. I was desirable, and I was capable.

He asked, "Were you drifting again?"

"Just enjoying the moment."

I pulled up another part of the sheets and wiped my eyes again. I didn't want to ruin the moment. He reached for me and I scooted closer to the man from Orange County. Anxiety melted. I belonged here. For now, for the next few minutes, or the next hour, I belonged to him, not to pointless regrets. He rubbed me. The slightest touch could restart the fire inside me. He could whisper and have me again, if he wanted. Wanting me again would be more about satisfying my ego.

He said, "You're catching a cold?"

"A little stuffy."

"Getting sick?"

"Allergies."

I went to the bathroom, blew my nose, rinsed my nostrils, wiped the insides of my nostrils, making sure all was clear and nothing embarrassing was left behind, then went back to him.

He played in my dreadlocks, toyed with my strength, and I relaxed. His breathing was no longer labored; his body was relaxed as well. Again I caught a glimpse of his wedding ring. I pulled my lips in.

That uneasiness made me jerk. He felt the change and rose up on one elbow.

He asked, "Did you enjoy that?"

"That was freakin' fabulous."

"Are you sure?"

"Anything past five minutes deserves a gold medal and a key to the city."

He asked, "You timed me?"

"Don't be a narcissist. I timed me."

"You timed yourself?"

"Almost broke my personal best."

He glanced toward the glowing numbers on the clock and said, "Damn."

"You have to leave. You need to tend to

your distraught wife."

"Not that. I didn't make it to the hour mark."

I slapped his backside and asked, "You timed us?"

"I timed me."

"Well, I'm glad that I happened to be up under you while you did."

"You said you wanted me for an hour. I wanted to give you an hour."

"Damn. Aren't you considerate? You were holding out all that time because I said that?"

"Was that okay for you? I don't know what you're used to. I'm sure men have given you all types of pleasure. I was trying to make sure I'd be remembered, wanted to outdo any lover you've ever had."

"I don't behave like this. I might dress like I'm free-spirited and have tattoos like I belong in Woodstock and in the era of free love, but I don't sleep with strangers. Never kissed on a first date. I don't let strangers do to me what you have done to me. I don't let strangers stick a finger in my bum and twirl."

"We're not strangers anymore. As they say in the Bible, we now have known each other."

I said, "You're lucky to get to know me."

"How so?"

"Six weeks. It would take at least six weeks to get me in bed, and that's if I really liked you."

"Six weeks?"

"Ten cups of tea and muffins at Abbot's Habit in Venice; a day trip to tour the Universal Studios back lot; three Jamaican dinners at Will's in Inglewood; three hiking trips — one up Runyon Canyon, one up to Griffith Park, and another up Escondido Canyon, to the waterfalls — then a day at the aquarium in Long Beach, and another at Santa Monica's open-air mall and down at the pier; a trip to Tijuana and San Diego; one trip to Roscoe's Chicken & Waffles on Pico, another to the one on Gower; six dozen kisses in public at both parks and movie theaters later; a field trip to six bookstores; and at least three plays."

"And then?"

"Then you might get to feel on Tina while you licked Marie."

"Guess I got the e-ticket tonight. I made it to the front of the line."

"You caught me when I was most vulnerable, when I was lonely, frantic, and a little on the emotionally weak side, which is rare, and you made me feel secure, made me realize that my world wasn't at its end, and that was before sex. You made me like you. The sex, this swive, well, you just made intercourse feel new. Like it was my first experience. It was magical. The way you held me was magical. I felt like a princess. I want to wake up with you. I want to stay in this room with you and never have to leave."

The room phone rang. The ring made me anxious. Sirens and ringing phones were unnerving.

Again we were a bit undone. Only the guilty are anxious. We were the guilty.

The phone stopped ringing, and right away it started ringing again.

I said, "Dude, you're in trouble. I think a distraught someone is looking for you."

"Maybe. Maybe not."

"Wonder if the 7-Eleven thing has become a big deal."

"Probably has become the talk of Hawaiian Gardens, if nothing else."

"You left dude out cold. He could have a concussion."

"Or be dead. He could be at that Disneyland in the sky."

I whispered, "I hope there is a Disneyland in the sky. I really hope there is one."

"I hit that guy as hard as I could."

"I hope he's not dead."

"That would be on the news, too."

293

"Afraid not. If he is, he ain't white, so it won't be a big deal on the news."

"He got what he deserved. You commit a crime, there are occupational hazards."

I said, "I'm just glad his thug friends didn't have guns."

"Damn phone won't stop ringing now."

"The call is for you. Maybe someone saw your car, got your plates, told the cops, and they tracked your charge card to the hotel, and now they're calling here looking for you, for us."

"If it were the cops, they would knock at that door."

"I'll bet that's what happened. We were on the camera at 7-Eleven."

"In that case, I wish we had gone to a fleabag motel and put the room in your name."

"Love it when you talk dirty, but *fleabag* is just plain filthy. Dude, you crossed the line."

My lover slapped me on my ass four times and I crawled toward the ringing phone.

I said, "If it's the police or the sheriff's department or the CIA or the FBI —"

"I'll get dressed, pour another glass of wine, go downstairs, and greet them."

"If it's your distraught wife —"

"End the suspense. Answer the phone."

I crawled across the bed, an anxious

hunter chasing the irritating noise, and grabbed the receiver, answered in a soft voice laced with the deepest sarcasm, "We're done. I insincerely apologize for the noise that he made me make. Oh, and tell the people in the hallway to stop eavesdropping. Tell whoever is in the next room to stop hating. It's a hotel, for Christmas's sake. People come to this fornicave to stain white sheets. Look at the clock on the wall. This is the hour when people get busy. So now that we've had our round of who's your father, we'll sit quietly and chat about global problems, such as drug addiction, corruption, violence, racism, discrimination, and xenophobia. Or maybe we'll talk about how so many non-tax-paying assholes are allowed to come to America and live off the taxpayers' dime. From another country, never paid a dime in taxes here, drop a baby, your kid is American and entitled to benefits I can't get unless I get pregnant out of wedlock and live on Skid Row. Hate that part of America. Anyway, we're done with the intense pussy eating and hardcore sex for now. Merry Kiss-My-Ass, and have a good night."

Then I hung up the phone, smiled at the exhausted man sprawled across the bed.

The phone rang again. I answered again.

The caller heard my attitude and hung up.

He asked, "Who was it?"

"Probably the jealous bitch at the front desk calling back to have a word."

He said, "That was some rant. You're a very intelligent girl."

"Not really. I get bored. I take risks, like I've done tonight. I dress in a way that lets you know I color outside the lines, if there are any lines. I think with my heart, which will be my downfall."

"That is another thing we have in common."

"I fail to see anything we have in common, and that is a serious compliment, trust me. I've made more mistakes than people three times my age. I have a hard time following rules. I don't work well with others, which was why I did the rocks in a box alone and didn't have backup. I change my mind a lot. I hated you, then I called you, hated that I had called, and now I've slept with you, and to be honest, I'm still not too sure how I feel about this, but I did enjoy you, only wish I could have known what it would have been like without actually doing it. People tell me I'm eccentric. I dream big, but plan small."

"I see a lot of qualities in you that I wish existed in me."

"Is that your slick way of saying I have that crap called Hood Disease, Mr. Affluenza?"

"I'm saying you're a wonderful human being. And I don't suffer from affluenza."

"Looks like you've made much better choices. Nothing wrong in your world that a quick trip to divorce court, a trip to Paris, two hookers, and three bottles of red wine can't fix."

"Serious. You're very intelligent. We should have met a little earlier in life."

"Depends on how intelligence is being measured. My sexual intelligence is much greater than my moral intelligence at the moment, and my commonsense intelligence does not exist right now, and all of those pale in comparison to the problems plaguing both society and Mother Earth."

"Are we really going to chat about racism, discrimination, and xenophobia?"

"Not before morning. Never talk about that crap, jingoism, or the ever-widening gap between the rich and the poor, or about how imperial dominance is established by means of cultural imperialism. Never have those kinds of talks, or bring up the rights of women, or mention that never-ending dark-skinned versus light-skinned black woman battle in Hollywood. Never mention any of the aforementioned nonsense before the second grande, quad, nonfat, one-pump, no-whip mocha, plus a doughnut and a Red Bull."

"What do you and your boyfriend chat about after sex?"

"We don't talk after sex."

"Really?"

"No. Not anymore. The first couple of times he did. That was back in May. It's December now. Guess we've talked about all there is to talk about. Now, guess he's used to me. It's a typical pattern, one that always leaves me feeling as if I'm being taken for granted. After he's been at my place a few minutes, he'll tell me to get naked. Or if I'm at his place, I go in, kiss him on the lips once or twice, undress, get in the bed, and he gets undressed, puts a condom on, and we do it, and then I wash and dress myself when we're done. I get dressed because he flushes his condom and cleans his dick, then pulls his underwear back on, which is like cleaning your gun and putting it back in the holster, and when you holster your gun, you're about to leave the firing range. Then he pulls his shirt and pants back on."

"You just fall on your back and he falls into you?"

"He's a doggy-style guy. Sometimes from the beginning to the end."

"Impersonal. Not face-to-face. Objectifying."

"You did the same."

"I started with us face-to-face. I looked into your eyes. I gave you respect."

"Yeah. You did. Hmm. Wow."

"Doesn't sound too romantic."

"This was romantic. Wow. I guess that's what's felt different all night. You didn't just bring me to the room and hop between my legs. Waiting for the moment was intense. The way you treat me in bed is a new experience for me. He pumps a few times and he's done. I'd get more good pumps in a venti half and half, ten pumps vanilla, extra whip. Every pump you gave me was a pump that struck oil."

He said, "We must be doing something wrong."

"Cheating on them?"

"No, shortchanging ourselves. You with Chicken and Waffles. Me with my wife."

I said, "The fool and the idiot savant."

"More like two foolish idiot savants."

"Being with each other is cheating on them, but being with them is cheating ourselves."

He said, "After being with you, after he

experiences you in this wonderful fashion, you said that he goes to play juvenile games. And after being with me, my wife rushes to play Candy Crush."

"You told me that. I don't believe it. Not the way you throw down. You made me squeal."

"Well, the way you throw it back, I can't imagine him doing anything but wanting more."

I grinned. "Jesus, you're so damn good in bed. You actually made me squeal. I never squeal."

"I'm following your lead. Trying to keep up."

"I'm trying to handle that LSD and keep up with and beat you to get my cheesecake."

"LSD?"

"Long, sweet dick. Long, strong dick."

He laughed. "I guess Susan and LSD are compatible."

"Yeah. My body is so attracted to your body that it scares me. So compatible it's scary."

"I haven't even shown you half of what I want to do to you."

"I haven't shown you half of what I'd like to have done before I do you the way I want to."

"Swive? Is this another challenge?"

"Stop bluffing. LSD is now a limp, snoring dick."

He smiled, chuckled. "How do you feel at this moment?"

"That salad at Denny's did not do it for me. These thighs are hungry."

He reached for the hotel phone. Asked me to hand him the menu. I told him that food here was very pricey. He pinched my booty and asked me again to hand him the menu. It was hard to move, but I did. He took a deep breath, took control again, ordered food, then hung up and came back to me.

I asked, "Are we on a date now?"

"Yeah. I think we're on a date."

"Fourth date."

"Fourth? This is our fourth date?"

I said, "Gas station was the blind date, Denny's was the second date, then the movie theater, and of course the dramatic date at 7-Eleven."

"Then this would be the fifth date."

"So I kissed you after the third date?"

"Yeah. After the movie. Took me three dates to get some of that tongue."

I laughed. "Surprised we lasted this long."

"Me, too. Thought that thing at 7-Eleven would have sent you packing."

"Surprised we made it past Denny's. You say some of the rudest things."

"I'm surprised we made it to Denny's. You and your con game."

We enjoyed smiles and a moment of silence. It was beautiful. It was so peaceful.

I asked, "Want to watch television? Want to see if we made the news?"

"I just want to look at you. Right now I need you."

"Jesus. I need you, too. Right now, I need you, too. You're the only art I want to see."

"Oh, so now I'm art?"

"You are definitely art."

I went to my bag, came back with two mints. He sucked on one and I sucked on the other, then we lay side by side, facing each other, touching lips, French kissing as we talked and sucked sugar from each other's tongues. There was no noise inside my head, no train running around my brain.

I asked, "What does it feel like to be rich and be able to have everything you want?"

"I don't have everything I want."

"Compared to me, based on what I have seen, you have options, right?"

He nodded. "I have options."

"Then you have everything."

"I'm not happy."

I said, "You can control your destiny."

"Some things are beyond anyone's control."

"You can be unhappy in Dubai or Italy. I have to be unhappy in my one-bedroom apartment. I have to be unhappy on an empty belly, and you can be unhappy at an all-inclusive resort in Barbados."

He said, "I won't argue that, not with your perspective."

"I'm wrong? Fancy car. Boat. Business. You have the things people kill to have."

"A man can have access to everything and still have nothing."

"That's sad."

"That's true."

"That's tragic."

He said, "Only takes meeting one person to turn your life around, good or bad."

12:28 A.M.

He asked, "Do you come with your boy-friend?"

He mentioned Chicken and Waffles and a chilly, nippy sensation crept into my bones.

I took a breath and said, "Nah. I have to play with it after and come."

"He doesn't make you come?"

"Sex isn't always about having an orgasm. Sometimes it's just the closeness that's needed."

"Don't make excuses. You stay with a man who doesn't satisfy you?"

"Lots of women do the same. Lots of women don't come from penetration."

"You came with me."

"That surprised me. I never come with a guy the first time. Usually I'm too tense. Too worried about pleasing him. That last moment, that was intense, both of us coming at the same time."

"Yeah."

"You make your wife come?"

"She orgasms."

"Bet she loves it. Bet she's loved it since you dicked her down on your boat."

"My wife isn't as expressive as you are."

"She talk dirty?"

"She'll get vocal toward the end, but nothing decipherable, nothing that wakes the dead."

"She's a dead fish, then starts to flop a little bit during the third act?"

"Not a dead fish, but she's not that dynamic. With me, she's very reserved."

"Aristocratic sex."

"She's not that bad."

"You put her in a frenzy and make her have spasms, have convulsions, throb like you did me? Do you make her curse and want to take it any way you want to give it? Tell me the real deal."

"This was a new experience for me, this level of sexual compatibility."

"Is she boring in bed?"

"I don't think I've ever motivated her beyond missionary and an occasional doggy. She's never there with me, not completely. It's like being with a whore more concerned with the time on the clock."

"I can't believe that. You are the bomb. Well, tonight you're the bomb."

"You're inspiring. Arousing. You make me want to do so many things."

He closed his eyes in a way that told me he didn't care for the conversation. It was different now than when we were strangers at Denny's. What people are willing to reveal always changes after sex has been put into the equation. I kissed his lips two more times, each kiss an effort to measure where we were now, and when he didn't respond, I moved away. He reached for me, pulled me back to him, pulled me close. I understood where we were. We were where we didn't have to be afraid of silence, a tranquil place where many couples never arrive. Comfortable, I cuddled up to him, closed my eyes for a second.

I was at Kenneth Hahn park, chasing Natalie Rose through the grass. It was an eidetic memory, and I recalled every sound, every color, and every word. I sang, serenaded my child. She looked back at me and laughed. I loved the way she called me Mommy. I smiled at her, wondering what she would be like when she grew up, where she would go to university, who she would marry.

There was another knock on the door, and Natalie Rose went away.

I sat up, jerked like I was being burned by a cigarette, ready to scream for Natalie Rose to come back to me. Woke up boohooing and panting like I was in labor. The human body can tolerate up to forty-five units of pain. When a woman gives birth, she tolerates up to fifty-seven units. That is like twenty bones being fractured all at once. That is the excruciating level of pain a mother endures to give birth. We take ourselves close to death to give life. That's why a mother's love is so strong. My love was powerful. Since losing Natalie Rose, some part of each day had been at level fifty-seven.

That was how much I loved my child. No man would ever be able to understand my angst.

I wanted to see her again, wanted to tell her that Mommy would be with her again.

I ran across the carpet and opened the door, the bright hall light shocking my eyes, making me think I had opened the secret door to heaven, and I stood there looking for her, expecting her to be there. No one was there. My eyes adjusted. It was just a long hallway, a very long and empty hallway.

Still, I said her name. Whispered her name three times.

Felling overtired, I went back to the romping shop, went back to the comfortable bed.

The man from Orange County sat up all

of a sudden, said, "What was that?"

"Nothing."

"Was someone at the door?"

I kissed him. I contemplated him and my pupils expanded.

He eased out of the bed, stretched, went to the bathroom, closed the door.

The water in the sink came on. I took that to mean he had to go potty real bad.

I went back to the door, looked out the peephole. I had wanted Natalie Rose to be there. I wanted my child to come back. I wanted to sit with her and watch *Kirikou and the Sorceress* again and again.

I fell into a trance.

Remembering Natalie Rose. Feeling my daughter's presence.

It was Christmastime. The time of year when people get ready for and celebrate Christmas all over the country. Since Natalie Rose left me behind, this has been the hardest time of the year for me.

Until I saw her again, this would always be one of the hardest times of the year.

We were supposed to spend many, many Christmases together. Not just six Christmases. Not just six Mother's Days. Not just six birthdays. Her father had moved on, and I yearned for her.

Nude, I looked out the thick window,

stared at the rain. The man from Orange County came up behind me. The man I had only just met, the stranger I didn't know from Adam, took soft steps across the carpet. He crept up on me as I stood in a trance, as I was unaware. This was dangerous, trusting him, being here. My eyes readjusted, moved from the rain, and I saw his reflection in the darkness of the glass. I saw the shadow of a stranger. The man who could have been a serial killer came up behind me, and by the time I saw his reflection, saw his horrible intention, it was too late. I was unable to move.

It was too late to run, too late to duck, and screaming would do me no good. His hand rose up high, and then it came down fast and hard, delivering a blow to the back of my head.

12:36 A.M.

It burst wide open. It felt like my head had burst wide open.

He attacked me. While I was naked, vulnerable, distracted, he attacked me.

I screamed and bent over, grabbed my head, my fingers drenched.

I cried out that I was going to kill him, and he found my sudden anger funny as hell.

The lights came on and he stood a few feet away laughing, colorful water balloons in each big hand. The balloons that I had left in the bathroom — he had filled them with water. He had commandeered my water balloons and attacked me like a child. Warm water dripped from my dreadlocks.

I yelled at him, "You hit me in the head with a water balloon? You wet my hair?"

He threw a purple one and hit me on the back. It exploded, sprayed against the curtains.

I yelled, "What, are you twelve? Put that down. I'm not playing. Put that —"

The next balloon burst on my hips as I covered my head and turned away.

I raised two middle fingers at him and said, "Oh, this is about to get serious."

He threw another water balloon, but not hard, and I caught it.

I threw it back at him, made it explode against his chest.

I said, "Where are my balloons? This fight is on now. This is on and popping."

He had filled up a baker's dozen of balloons, filled them all with warm water.

Like two children, we ran around the suite, laughing, having an all-out war.

I played with him as if he were a child, a little boy. We ran around our imaginary world like we were chasing aliens, monsters, and demons. Soft screams. Muffled laughs. I was once again a rambunctious little girl with wild hair, the child of a man who married a woman with fine hair, then was pissed off when his daughter didn't have the highly approved complexion of the woman he had married. One night, when he thought I was sleeping, I heard him grunt and tell my stepmom that I might be beautiful if I had the same flavor skin as my mother, that if I had fine hair like my mother's mother, if my hair had been less powerful and more delicate, like that of the European women generations before me, or more like the Guyanese, or like the manes of West Indians, then I would have been as beautiful as I was smart.

I thought of all of that in a flash, and two blinks later it was all gone, and I was focused, with a man who treated me as if I were the most beautiful girl in the world, a man who now behaved like a little boy. I saw the well-traveled and privileged boy who used to play with G.I. Joes and other action figures. I saw a strong man with high intellect, yet a fragile heart, a man who was raised and had two unhappy-yet-together-for-life parents who stuck it out, a boy who wasn't shipped across waters to live between two countries and two houses and two families and forced to spend time in noisy and crowded houses that never felt like homes with family that never felt like a real family. He was a man who had had better guidance. He was a man who hadn't procreated out of loneliness, hadn't had a baby because, in the end, even if the Las Vegas–loving, poker-playing, chain-smoking, herb-puffing, highly functioning alcoholic father of my child was a bad choice, and I knew he was a bad choice before he had entered me the first time, knew that after he had given me a two-inch scar on the crown of my head, a mark hidden by my dreadlocks, I knew that we were doomed, and if I stayed with him, in the end, I would be doomed as well. Still, there was a need. I wanted to have a child to love. I had chosen him because he was there. He had promised to stay, to support our child, but he had other women, so I knew that was a lie. His child had become unimportant. What I had needed was larger than anything he would offer. I wanted a child to give and receive unconditional love. The love I had inside me, I had to give it to someone. I had given it to her. I had felt whole. I had wanted to have my own family, even it was just us. I was a grown woman. Once you are paying taxes, you are grown, and your daddy has nothing to do with the perpetual fucked-up-ness in your life, not anymore. I was in charge of my own destiny.

I was in control.

The water balloon fight had us running like heathens, chasing each other, and having a ball.

It only took a couple of minutes, but soon there were twenty more water balloons, ten for him and ten for me, and we were going at it, balloons exploding, water splashing

against lamps, mirrors, some bouncing off
the art on the walls. Colorful bits of exploded balloon decorated our romping shop.

I ran to the bathroom, turned on the
faucet, and filled a plastic cup with water,
then chased him, splashed him, and wet the
television. We were soaked, holding each
other, naked, skin sticking, sliding.

We laughed so hard we could barely stand.

I went to the bed and grabbed pillows.
The war between representatives from
Orange and L.A. counties wasn't over.
Laughing, he ran to the other side of the
king bed, tried to grab his ammunition.

Then we had a pillow fight, a war that
lasted no more than another minute, thirty-
nine minutes shorter than the Anglo-
Zanzibar War that was fought between the
United Kingdom and the Zanzibar Sultan-
ate. But we fought with a playful fierceness,
and like the war between China and Viet-
nam, both sides claimed victory. We were so
juvenile. He never hit me hard; he mostly
took soft swipes at my ass. He let me grab
his pillow and beat him across his shoulders
and head as hard as I could. He grabbed
me in a frisky hug, lifted me up as I play-
fully kicked my feet in the air. He put me
down on my tiptoes, and I stayed on my
toes as I faced him, pulled his damp body

to my bosom, and nibbled his bottom lip.

Our smiles were broad as we stood and rocked, gazing into each other's eyes.

We put on hotel robes and ran down the hallway to the bank of elevators and summoned one to our floor, and when it arrived and its doors opened, we jumped on and pushed the buttons, illuminating each floor before laughing and running back down the hallway toward our room, along the way stealing DO NOT DISTURB signs from every doorknob on the floor. Then we doubled back, *tap-tap-tapped, tap-tap-tapped, tap-tap-tapping* on doors hard and fast, like we were that irritating Sheldon on *The Big Bang Theory,* and called out that we were from room service, room service, room service, then hurried away, hands over our mouths to muffle our childish laughter. He made it to the room first and locked me out.

I banged on the door, again like Sheldon. *Tap, tap, tap.* Asshole. *Tap, tap, tap.* Asshole. Then I changed and started singing that song from the movie *Frozen,* asked him if he wanted to come out and build a snowman, or ride our bikes around the hall. He let me in, but not before a dozen pissed-off people on the floor had peeped out of their doors. He thought locking me in the hallway naked except for the hotel robe was ingenious and hilarious. He had a lot of frat boy in his blood. When I marched by him and complained about him leaving me in the hallway, a water balloon hit me in the lower back. He had hidden one; the sneaky bastard. Our laughter was loud, reverberated. The guffawing and snickering was infectious. It felt like we were two people who had met on a dreary night and become the happiest in the hotel, in the city, in the county, in the state, in the country, in the world, in the universe. The dystopia that had darkened our souls had been replaced by joy, and that joy was like the sun at noon over the West Indies.

The energy between us felt so sincere and intense, or maybe that was what existed inside me, once again radiating outward, but even if I was projecting, his actions, his attention, his focus, the energy was so profound. I gazed at him the way Eve must've stared at Adam in those first moments.

I looked at him as if I'd never seen a decent man before in my life.

Aretha Franklin sang a little prayer and we danced in the suits of our birth, swayed, turned, and he dipped me like we were in the movies. He had the moves of a jungle cat, and now he looked devastatingly handsome. He had become Idris, Denzel, Blair Underwood, Michael Ealy, the guy who plays Thor, the guy who plays Captain America, Prince, Bruno Mars, and Brad Pitt. Then the room shook and we stopped moving like we were Ginger Rogers and Fred Astaire, and as the jolt from the angry earth rolled through our naked bodies, I held him tighter, in love's embrace, and he held me as if he wanted to protect me. The jolt came and went in less time it takes a man to have the best orgasm of his life.

The tremor wasn't bad, just enough to know that it was undoubtedly caused by fracking. Hydraulic fracturing of the earth was the big thing now. Fracking earthquakes were happening almost every week, would probably cause California to sink like Atlantis, but the sounds of both of our phones vibrating at almost the same moment was more powerful than any earthquake ever recorded. Others demanded our attention, but unwanted intrusions were ignored.

The digital clock glowed, but I refused to acknowledge that time was against us.

I used the imaginary powers inside me, tried to suspend time. This was a new road for me, an abnormal road that was traveled by others, but my lane remained unpaved. Unpaved, untraveled roads are always lined with life and flowers. I wanted a bubble placed around the space in which I existed.

I said, "On the bed; get on the bed."

He did and we held hands, jumped up and down, up and down, up and down.

It wasn't New Year's Eve, not for some days, but before it was time to check out of this room, we would have to check out of this affair. Therefore we would have to sing our own version of "Auld Lang Syne," the song they belt out as the ball drops, as a farewell. When we stopped comforting each other during this period of darkness; when it was the proper, awkward moment to end this recklessness; when the sunset to sunrise of this moonless sexual affair, this romantic encounter, took its last breath and sent us back to the lives we had before gaining knowledge of each other; when this fun, this feast, this party for two in a world of billions, this intense indiscretion lost its power and revealed its secrets and the sun fought through rain, smog, and marine clouds, then made it to both knees and rose above the horizon, there'd be a good-bye-forever song rendered on behalf of all that had been done, a misdeed not to be celebrated. He held on to me the way I held on to time.

We took towels, dried each other off. He used a towel to dry my dreadlocks the best he could, then we held each other and laughed. No words, just laughter; pure laughter, joy, and happiness.

LSD woke from its nap. He put a condom on. The laughter stopped.

Susan smiled an impatient smile. Tina and Marie rejoiced.

The doors to the church opened.

12:47 A.M.

His other hand moved down between my legs, and he rubbed me, strummed where I ached. We kissed and panted and kissed and grunted and kissed and made love like we were animals. I thought of it as love. Something had changed, something inside me, and I thought of this tryst as love. A new addiction was trying to get its claws in me. I'd tried cigarettes, alcohol, prescription painkillers, ADHD medication, antianxiety medication, cocaine, and twenty kinds of marijuana, and none of that made me feel as good as I did with him inside me. Each stroke moved me further from free will and good choices.

When it came to love and sex, my brain was wired the way an addict's brain is wired for heroin.

He sweated, suffered. Then I was on my back and he had my ankles on his shoulders at first, then bent my knees until they were at my ears, then I rested the bottoms of my feet against his chest. He was going for the positions that allowed him to go deeper. The rhythm of him going in and out of me, of opening me, allowing me to close and then opening me again — it was madness. He grabbed my ankles and held my legs wide, and he plunged into me, stroked and stroked and stroked, used all of his weight and came down on me and plunged and gave it to me like he wanted to break me in half. I welcomed the pain. Wanted this to go on until Jesus called me home. With each stroke he was closer to coming, and with each stroke he became rougher with me, became as savage and powerful and desperate and unyielding as men do when they are in those final moments of madness. I made noises and said so many things. If security knocked on the door, I didn't hear. If someone was in the hallway listening, I didn't care. Where I was, in that state, I wanted to stay there forever, wanted to suffer forever, wanted to be as far away from pain, heartbreak, loss, and fear as I could. But it would end. He had to come, had to get it out of his body. It felt like he wanted to break me, but he couldn't break what was already broken. I sweated and choked up, suffering from nirvana as well, the orgasm that I held at bay my only reprieve. He gave it all to me and I called out to God. I cursed. He did it over and over, gave me his all. I was free. I was alive. Then I moved, challenged him, and showed him I was the type men loved to bed, but never would be able to handle. He represented men like him and I represented women like me. I showed him that women like me, those underappreciated, those underrated, were simply amazing in all ways. I closed my eyes again, sang the blues, my lamentation rising over and over, and moved my head from side to side, amazed at the sensation, almost overwhelmed by a fiery aurora borealis. Every nerve in my body was alive, on fire, and his erection massaged my spot over and over. I clasped his ass, clasped his ass and massaged and caressed his ass every time he rose and fell. Then another aurora borealis was on the horizon, the tingles again like fire on my nerves, shortening my breath. I hooked my ankles around his calves and he kissed me and we moved with desperation, the melody strong, our sinful hymn profound, feverish murmurs, frenzied woos. We moved like we were both on fire, everything so manic.

We battled as if we were in the middle of an unholy, sexual war.

The room phone rang. It rang and rang, and I thought it wouldn't ever stop ringing.

He slowed for a moment, wheezed, made faces like he was about to burst, then continued his stroke, resumed his measured ins and outs. The phone yelled again, but my cooing, his curt and repetitive grunting, our spiritual chant drowned out every intrusive noise. He went too deep, deeper than any lover had been, and the LSD hit new real estate, forced me to sing like Shakira; made me belt out a stream of trembling *ay, ay, ayes* and more *oooh*s and *ahhh*s than I had said since never. His laments told me that he was near climax; the grunts told me the climax was going to be a monster, and the way he pumped and pumped told me the severity of the sensation he felt was crucial. My noises. His sounds. It was a beautiful symphony. We harmonized, became a choir of two. He came. He came hard, like the volcano in Pompeii. He came with so much force it both terrified me and made me proud. He tensed and strained and used my body to get the last of his orgasm out of his body. He strained. Then he was done. The flash flood ended. Within seconds he slowed. I wanted to go on and on, but he had lost his urgency, so it was time for me to lose mine. Still aroused, I held him. He lessened and began to wind down.

Soon I reached down, made sure the condom hadn't slipped off.

The LSD was still covered. That made me happy. That gave me relief.

We inhaled and exhaled in spurts, then lay there like victims after a car accident.

He was the first to try to stand. I focused on the rise and fall of my chest, then looked at him, looked at his condom-covered penis. The condom looked like it was loaded with a frothy liquid, the same texture and color of spume resting on top of most of the drinks served at Starbucks.

I remained aware of my nakedness. I remained equally aware of his.

He would flush his seed and leave now. It was time for me to walk away.

He struggled to find his equilibrium, and asked, "You okay?"

I struggled with the same breathing and balance, groaned, "I'm fine. I'm great."

"I came fast that time."

"So did I."

I looked at his penis, stared at that cyclopean monster and grinned. Condom dangling on penis, he staggered to the bathroom, moved like a man who had drunk one bottle of Jack Daniel's too many. The toilet flushed. My eyes closed. I focused on breathing. I heard the water running. He staggered back with a wet towel. He cleaned me. That was thoughtful. He tossed the towel on the floor, then turned the lights off, only the glow from the television on our dank, bare skin now. The baby-making music on the television could be heard once again. He put his hands in my hair again, massaged my scalp, and we exchanged energy. We heard a headboard slapping the wall. Soft taps that became rapid. Lovers next door. It was their turn to entertain the people on the floor. Orange County moaned a fake moan. I did the same. We moaned louder and louder until we were sure the people next door heard us competing with them. We laughed at our silliness and then we smiled. A short kiss later Adam led Eve back to the bed in their Garden of Eden. Lust danced with curiosity and this felt profound, like we had a deep friendship blended with a strong emotional and physical connection. I wanted all of him, but I knew that I could have none of him. Again I closed my eyes. I wondered if he would cut my hair if I fell asleep, wondered if he would become like Delilah and do me like she had done Samson, cut my hair, and steal my power while I was dead to the world. I tried not to sleep. I tried and failed. Again my body pulled me into a soft sleep. It was the first time in a long time it didn't feel like a mean sleep. There were no sirens in my mind. No fire trucks. No scent of burnt flesh. I was at ease. My mind wasn't racing. We had tranquility. In a world gone mad, for ten seconds, we had tranquility.

Then demons from hell broke free and banged on the door.

12:56 A.M.

First I jumped like we were about to be raided by the FBI, then I realized where I was, heard the soft taps again, shook the man sleeping next to me, watched him open his eyes, saw the panic that gave him sudden consciousness. I cleared my voice, stood, and called out, "Yes. How may I help?"

"Room service."

"Room service? I think you're at the wrong door."

"You called down an order, right?"

I looked at the time. Minutes had flown by. "Oh. Right. Food. We ordered food."

He sat up, looked around the room, whispered, "Guess I should go hide."

"Why would you have to hide? They know what's up. I'm sure they've been invited into rooms where a lot more was going on than two post-sex people hanging out buck naked with funky breath."

"Well, let me step out of the room until they leave."

"Okay. Just send the naked lady to the door."

He headed for the bathroom and again I hurried to the closet, rushed to throw on the white robe, checked the peephole, and saw a woman in a white shirt and black pants in front of a cart. I opened the door and gave her greetings in the name of our Lord Jesus Christ, and she raised a brow and chuckled.

She said, "Permission to enter?"

"Please. Come on in. The snake has been put away."

I clicked the lights on, the sudden brightness a shock to my body.

As she rolled in our order, I heard Orange County in the bathroom taking a powerful leak.

Dishes rattled as she pushed the cart by me. "Heard there was an exorcism up here."

"Sure was. Reverend Long Dong Silver tried to get the devil out of Mrs. Jones."

"I was outside and waited about five minutes before I knocked."

"You were outside the door?"

"Well, you sure have made a mess of the room. Rearranged the furniture, too."

"Look at you. Trying to judge me, trying

to be all high and mighty, and look at you."

"What?"

"Look like someone sucked the devil out of you last night. Like a damn leech."

"This morning. As much as she could. Trying to hide the damage my new girl left behind."

"Take some toothpaste, rub it over the monkey bite, and allow it to sit for about an hour."

"Really? Toothpaste will make it go away?"

"Really. Toothpaste. Or you can put a spoon in the freezer and rub circles on it until the spoon is warm. Or try using a cube of ice in a spoon, rubbed in circles. Or check this out: You can use eye drops to get the redness out. If that fails, go to Target and buy a turtleneck that comes up to your nose."

She looked at the room, at the dishevelment. She smirked, shook her head like we were insane.

She said, "You're having a damn good time."

"We worked up an appetite."

"Shrimp salads. Seared tuna. Blackened fish. Calamari. Tuna Calabrese. Lobster-tail salad. Linguine. Downstairs they joked that you ordered food like Jesus and his homies were up here for the sequel to the Last Supper. I told the people in the kitchen that an exorcism burns up a lot of calories. They dared me to use that exorcism line when I came up here."

"Security used that line earlier."

"She stole it from me. She was in the kitchen when I said it first."

I read her nametag, paused, signed the six-hundred-dollar tab, and added a fat tip to the charge.

She said, "Aren't you a comedian?"

"Wow. Was. Twice in one night someone has recognized me."

"I saw you one night at the J Spot. Saw you again at the Laugh Factory. Last time I saw you was at Comedy Emporium when they were filming *The Leonard DuBois Story.* That was on my birthday, and the fair-weather lesbian I was dating at the time took me up there. You were funny as hell."

"That was a long time ago. You hang out at comedy clubs?"

"Not anymore. Had a bad experience."

"Jokes were that bad?"

"Last time I went to one, after the show Johnny Bergs shot the comedian right in front of me."

"You were on Sunset Boulevard when Francine was murdered?"

"Three feet away, trying to get an autograph. Actually, I wanted to get her phone number, too."

"That was an unforgettable night. I was inside the club, about to go onstage."

"I saw the whole thing. Will never go to a comedy club again in my life."

"Sorry to hear that."

"But you were real funny."

"Yeah. At one point in my life, I was pretty funny. I laughed all the time."

"Well, you're not laughing tonight. Don't look like nobody is up here telling jokes."

"You've got jokes."

"I'm funny from time to time, but I ain't got the nerve to get onstage like you do."

"Let me see the receipt again. Let me tell you a big joke."

She handed it back to me. Now nervous, she thought she had taken her jokes too far. At first I had given her 30 percent. That was a lot of money to someone like me. I raised her gratuity to 50 percent.

She looked at the receipt. She looked at it two or three times.

Her bottom lip trembled and she gazed up at me, her face blanketed in disbelief.

She asked, "Is this for real?"

I nodded. "Merry Christmas. Hope that helps keep the lights on. Or gas in the car."

She cried. Just like that, she cried. She

turned her head away from me, ashamed.

She said, "My mother has cancer. I'm trying to take care of my little brother and her."

She smiled a lot, laughed a lot. A woman who laughed a lot had a lot of pain.

I asked, "Your mother . . . ?"

"They give her six months. This is going to be our last Christmas."

I put my hand on her shoulder. A moment went by with us standing like that.

The television played music as the shower ran inside the bathroom.

In a broken voice she said, "I really needed this money. God bless you. God bless you."

My eyes watered, too. I looked back at the room, the disheveled romping shop, my escape.

I was here to escape the inescapable. I had tried to not think about it as much. I had needed a day away from the memory. A day away from fire. I needed to block it all out. I had to keep moving.

The waitress read the receipt again, eyes red, tears falling, lip trembling.

She said, "No matter how much noise you make, nobody is going to bother y'all. I'll see to that."

I stood there with her as she wiped her

eyes, tears falling down across her chain of hickeys.

By then I had to wipe my eyes, too. It was the season to be jolly, and I missed my little bundle of joy. She was never far away. I knew that. The waitress wore a nametag. Her name was Natalie.

John 11:35. Jesus wept.

For a minute, so did I.

When Hickey Girl left, I locked the door. Then I wiped my eyes, pulled away my robe, and tapped on the bathroom door. He asked me inside. I opened the door and he was in the shower, soaped up.

I said, "The feast is ready, my lord from the county of oranges."

"You can start, my lady from the county of riots and drive-by shootings."

"You're not eating?"

"I'm going to eat before I leave."

"I'll wait, then."

"You said you were starving."

"I want to eat with you, not alone."

"You need me to bless the food again?"

"You've got jokes."

"Jesus wept."

"Shut up."

I watched him the way I used to watch my husband. I stood the way I used to stand in our overpriced apartment in the Valley, leaning in the doorframe, watching him. I blinked a few times and reality adjusted itself. He was washing me away. I saw the memory of us being scrubbed from his skin. This meant he was leaving soon. The new sun wouldn't touch us. Daylight would never touch us. I'd be back to my car, to a child seat I couldn't let go, to Barbies I'd never throw away.

He motioned for me to come join him. It was the motion of desire, approval, and acceptance.

I grinned. Simple gestures do big things to a harsh mouth and a tender heart.

I put the child seat and the Barbies back into their mental compartment.

Then I was in the shower with him, his hands soaping me up as well, his strong hands rubbing my breasts, my ass, cleaning between my legs, even washing the bottoms of my feet. He took to his knees for a few seconds, and I held the wall and balanced myself with one foot on the edge of the tub. I wished I had my phone to photograph this moment, at least take a selfie of my face, of my expression. This was a first. I had done many things, but this was a first. I rinsed my face and prayed for God to make that hard Cali water be holy water and wash away each and every one of my peccadilloes, but there wasn't that much holy water on the planet. And running bathwater and bathing seven times like I was in the River Jordan wouldn't do me any good, either, not tonight. Since Beyoncé was on my mind because my one-time lover — a delusional man who would only rate her as a six — had mentioned her tonight, I sang a jazzy version of Beyoncé's "Crazy in Love" without realizing what I was saying, sang and bounced my ass and danced with him under the waterfall, trying to do lead vocals and backup vocals at the same time. Then I switched up and rolled my hips smooth and easy and sang a slow and sensuous version of "Drunk in Love" while he held my dreadlocks and sucked on my ear.

I said, "Bite my neck."

"Like this."

"Harder."

"You want me to become a vampire and draw blood?"

"I want you to give me a dozen hickeys."

"Your boyfriend will see them."

"I want twenty. Give me thirty."

"Why?"

"I want to feel the pain right now. I need to feel alive."

"Are you okay?"

"Bite me. Give me forty hickeys."

"Okay."

"Bite me hard. Give me tattoos."

He removed all the metal dish covers and I inhaled the aroma of the food. My belly growled and I applauded. Outside of all the things Hickey Girl had said were on the menu, there was Pacific snapper with oak-grilled vegetables and cilantro sauce. Mashed potatoes. Apple pie and ice cream. Another glass of wine. There was a healthy fruit salad of papayas, berries, and mangoes, a carafe of orange juice, and a carafe of black coffee. Honey. Brown sugar. Whipped cream.

I said, "You're going to have me leave here looking like the Michelin Wo-Man."

He sighed. "I don't want to leave. I want you to know that. I want to stay here with you."

"We need to get to Skid Row and give some of these leftovers to the homeless."

"I want to stay until we eat every crumb."

"Wish I could see the sunrise with you.

Wish you could stay until the rain ended, then ride down to Venice and walk out to the sand and watch the sun come up, then get tea from Abbot's Habit."

"I have to leave."

"No sunrise for us."

"Sorry."

"When a married man parks his car in your garage, he can't let the engine get cold."

"You're cool with it?"

"Dude, I'm a big girl. I made a choice to let go and be crazy tonight. Made a choice to get me some strange with a sexy man I'd just met. Was fun. It was great. No illusions about the outcome. I'm cool with it. You have obligations. I have a boyfriend. I have a boyfriend who likes to play video games after he gets a nut, and you have a wife who likes to play Candy Crush after you get yours."

We ate like Egyptians. He fed me. The glow from the television made our shadows move like hieroglyphics on the wall. Simply Red sang that he was holding back the years. Orange County filled his mouth with fruit and kissed me again. Light and gentle. Over and over. A man I thought should be exhausted and sleepy was once again aroused. That power nap plus those five cups of coffee had him alert like it was ten in the morning. Me, too. Another wave of passion made parts of me wetter and parts of me swell. He gave me just enough tongue, fed me just enough fruit, made me just wet enough. Then he opened the honey, drizzled it across my breasts, put fruit on the honey, and ate from my flesh.

He said, "I heard you brushing your teeth when you showered a while ago."

"When I first got here. What's wrong? Is my breath funky?"

"Not at all. Where is your toothbrush?"

"Why? I hope you're not going to use my toothbrush."

"Where is it?"

"Bathroom. In my bag. If you use my toothbrush, I am going to scream."

He went to the bathroom, came back with my electric toothbrush. He turned it on. It hummed. He turned it off, then detached the section with the bristles but kept the motorized base in his hand. He took a shower cap from the bathroom, placed the base in the shower cap, covered it, turned it on.

I asked, "What do you think you're going to do with that?"

As the Philips Sonicare electric toothbrush

vibrated on CLEAN, he placed it on my vagina.

I died.

He pushed the green button, made it move from CLEAN to SENSITIVE to MASSAGE, and I died a thousand little deaths over and over. I would never see my toothbrush the same way again. I could only handle that for a short time, but he had turned me out. He stopped. Sucked my nipples while I lay there in awe, trembling. Soon I could hear again. Susan hummed along with the song that played in the background. He took a tongue filled with honey and kissed me again; soft, unhurried kisses. This was like Bogey and Bacall with honey and fruit and whipped cream spread from neck to vagina. Cary Grant licking and eating Grace Kelly until she became a princess. Orange County kissed my cheeks, caressed my face, then moved back to my lips, back to my tongue.

He whispered, "Guess I got carried away."

I laughed again. It was a laugh of amazement, a laugh of irony.

He said, "What's so funny?"

"You joined Club Adultery."

"My ongoing journey toward the center of hell amuses you."

"A cheater like Jacob, with an apparent

temper like Peter, having an affair like David, getting me drunk like I'm Noah, as insecure as Gideon, and as depressed as Elijah. That's hilarious."

"That's not funny."

I calmed a bit, rubbed my hand across his back, smiled, asked, "Is adultery a new sin for you?"

"You asked me that."

"I think you lied. You're smooth. Showering. On the bed with your dick all fluffed. Taking control. You're a man who has had many, many women. We've done it, so it's okay to tell me the truth."

"It is my first time being with another woman since I got married. It felt awkward. When I was in the shower, it felt awkward. Was hoping you had bailed on me. I was uneasy. Nervous."

"Are you sure?"

"Other things were on my mind."

"Things that would concern a married man."

"Deeper things."

"You seem to be so good at this particular sin, like Jordan doing a slam dunk."

"I can't say it's my only sin, but it's the latest to add to the list."

"Me, too. I've stolen. Coveted. Even slept with a friend's boyfriend once or twice.

Long story. She was a bitch. She deserved it. Don't judge me. But this is my first time committing adultery."

He moved back to the food, ate a little. "You didn't commit adultery."

"I didn't?"

"You're not married."

I stayed on my back, my fingers touching where he had put honey and fruit, but not feeling sticky, not at all. He had licked away every drop of sweetness.

I said, "Oh, is that how it works? I have to be married to be an adulteress?"

"Yeah."

"So I'm just a chick who crept on her boyfriend with a married man."

"That sorority has many members."

"You sure I'm not qualified to join the Adultery Club? That club has elite status."

"You won't be the criminal in this crime, unless you were in the Middle East, and then you would get stoned. But here in America, you're not the one at fault. You broke no laws, just went against the laws in the Bible. Bible says you're a horrible witch of a woman and should be stoned to death."

"Bible thumpers who get divorced and eat shellfish and eat meat on Fridays and work on Sundays and shave their hair and wear more than one kind of material and plant more than one kind of seed and aren't virgins are going to take the time to stop bashing same-sex marriage, judge me, and pick up rocks?"

"Stop it."

I laughed.

He said, "You're artistic, can sing, know politics on a global level, are particular about English, work as a part-time con woman, and you know the Bible."

"All except the part about adultery. Wasn't on my bucket list."

"Why are you laughing now?"

"You're a cheater, mister."

"You corrupted me."

"I feel like I've popped your adultery cherry. Kinda proud of myself."

"And you cheated on your boyfriend. You cheated on him and joined that sorority."

"I'm not married. You are. Why, oh, why do married people do such things?"

"For some, marriage exists at an altitude so high that it's almost impossible to breathe. It's suffocating. Or maybe because after a few years of trying to work it through with the unhappy wife, being honest and up-front about one's physical needs and desires, she just flat out ignores it or shoves your angst under the rug and basically points the finger and blame at the husband, so what is a guy supposed to do?"

"Or you're a total ass. Stop trying to intellectualize everything. It gets to be exhausting."

"Why do women cheat on their boyfriends and husbands?"

"Sometimes it's easier to cheat than to break up. Some people just don't want to deal with the drama of breaking up, and creeping is the easiest way to get back to feeling good, or having self-worth. You cheat and you feel competent, you feel worthy, you feel proud, you feel alive, you feel self-conscious."

"Ego. Then it's about ego. You kill someone else's ego to feel better about yourself."

"It can be about ego, or just being tired of being in bed in the same position with the same person."

"Why not just move on?"

"Same reason people don't quit jobs they hate — again, too much drama. You're married, so that would be infinite drama. You have money. You have security. Money is a glue for her, possibly."

"Really. So that ego-chasing and perpetual lying and engaging in misdirection leaves me feeling as if I am incompetent, neglected, ignored, underappreciated, and at fault."

"Some things are beyond your control.

She could sleep with you twice a day, and maybe that still wouldn't be enough to stop her from wanting to sex someone else. Just like a woman can give her man sex like a porn star and he'll still put his dick in the next free hole. But this is about you, so let me stay on point. She might love being the bad girl. Cheating could be her character. Or it could be about revenge."

"No, no reason for revenge."

"She could just be an unhappy person."

"Are women ever happy?"

"Not even when we're sleeping."

"Why is that? Help me unravel that mystery."

"Started with Eve. She was the unhappiest of us all."

"Eve? We're back to picking on her again? How was she the unhappiest of the unhappy?"

"She didn't have shoes. A woman can't be happy without shoes. Only had one man to choose from. How much fun is that? One cock, and there were no malls. She wore a leaf. *Scandal* hadn't been invented. Adam didn't have a car. She had two sons, and one was a psychopath. You want the list?"

"Men get unhappy, too. We have shoes and we're unhappy."

"Have you seen men's shoes? Hideous and

come in two decent colors. What's to be happy about?"

"Good point."

"Do black men feel guilty about being with a white woman?"

"What is your obsession with race? Is this the sixties? Let me check my calendar."

"I know sisters who date white men, but never take them to a black area, always leave their tribe and venture into the white world to have their fun. I know a lot of black women who will never date a black man, only white men. They fantasize about private-school and half-breed babies with good hair."

Then he went down on me again, licked me a hundred times in a few seconds.

He said, "Until now, I have never cheated on my wife."

"You've only been having sex with one woman."

He licked me. "Until you, only her."

I squirmed. "You've been having sex with one woman more than a monk sleeps with."

He licked me a dozen times. "And you've never cheated on your boyfriend?"

I squirmed more. "Never cheated on Chicken and Waffles until tonight."

He tried to come back up, but I gripped his head, pushed him back down.

I clenched my teeth and panted. "Don't do that and leave me hanging like this."

My hips moved. I grabbed his head, began to grind on his tongue, held his head, and positioned him where he needed to be to make this happen again. He centered on the bull's-eye. Arousal erased our inhibitions. I owned him, was his master. When I let him go, he came up, kissed my lips, put his palm between my legs, facing up, and his finger slipped inside me, gave me the come-hither motion, tapped on my spot. He knew where it was now. He tapped my spot over and over. Soon he moved his finger away, put the tips of his fingers on either side of my vagina, slid his fingers up and down.

He went down on me again. Ten licks. Pause. Five licks. Pause. Twenty licks. Pause. That rhythmic licking came first; then came the humming. He had my Sonicare humming in his hand again. Those vibrations. After he played with me, he ripped open another condom. He was ready to go again.

I had to pause my breathing, had to stop moving and surrender.

The intrusion was saccharine. He separated my lips, parted me, divided me in a sensual way. I made honey. He made me make honey. Again I opened for him, the flower bloomed, went into full bloom, and I sighed and felt myself stretching to accommodate his length and girth, wondered how tensile I could become, how much of a man I could take when I was severely aroused. His dick had recuperated and had come back strong. Unyielding. Now he had to go harder to be stimulated, to make it rise like it had risen before. In my mind I saw the blood flowing through his veins, rushing to fill the meat that protruded from his body. For a moment he struggled, vacillated between hard, then soft, then pumping hard to raise the dead once again. He apologized. I told him it was fine, said I understood. The condom stole sensitivity, made it so he was inside me, but never really felt the true me. For a few dozen strokes, I felt the condom, and that made it feel like an inanimate object was moving in and out of me. I was aware of the intrusion, aware of his every breath. But soon it felt better. Soon reality began to fade. Soon I stopped watching the rain as it fell on the other side of the darkened windows. Soon we no longer felt like two bodies, but one working together, a beast with two backs. He tensed and made a sound that reminded me of sorrow, only it was the opposite, so that meant it felt better to him. So he gave it to me, gave it to me good to make his erection reach its potential, then once it had filled the condom, he tested me, tested to see how much of him I could handle, see how much I could stretch, how deep he could go before I broke and begged him to back off, and when he was satisfied with his power, with my whimpers, my confessions that came as whimpers and coos and mild screams and calls to God, he resumed a pace that told me he wanted to coast for a while. I wanted it all, tip to balls. I wanted him to lose control, stroke me like he wanted to break the condom. Wanted fast and hard and deep. I wanted to prove to be a woman and take it all no matter how he gave it. I wanted to be better than all his other women, than all the women he thought about when he made love to his wife, and I wanted to be better than his wife. His stroke was a sweet punishment, and it all but paralyzed me. I held him like I was trying to keep from falling and he stroked me, an evil bastard who wanted me to come for his entertainment. Then I turned him over, sat on top, reached for a pillow, pulled the pillowcase free and wrapped it around my waist like a belt, then had him hold both ends of the pillowcase like they were reins. It was time for me to ride. It was time to show him what I could do.

He held the pillowcase tight, held it so I couldn't get away, and I rode him rough. He made all the noises. This time I did the riding and the choking and the slapping. I read his face and saw the pressure build inside him. My easy rise and fall made him grit his teeth and grip my hips. He wanted to thrust, but I didn't give him the range. I was in control. He realized that, backed down, took deep breaths and looked like he was about to explode. His eyes lost focus, like the world had gone blurry. My world was just as unclear. I moved, moved and I was there with him, was underwater, and was in the place of good feeling. My contractions, that achy feeling in my stomach came, and I was at the point of no return. I growled and moved faster. For me it was going to be an orgasm like being hit by a train. He made sounds like he was drowning in the same feeling. It was like he was going into convulsions. I was on top, in control, but he was pumping me from the bottom, prodding me with a fat cock made of steel. He grew inside me and heat traveled from his cock inside me. A doorway was opening, one I struggle to keep closed, one that guards my emotions. Euphoria arrived. Again I made enough noise to alert the living and raise the dead. The itch. The itch. The sweet itch. I moved up and down, scratching that itch. My eyes rolled to the back of my head and I grabbed him as an anchor. The tension in my body demanded to be unchained. I cursed. He grunted. I sang. He shouted, tensed, strained, became so damn powerful it excited and frightened me. His cock grew more. He told me he was coming. I bit my bottom lip, whimpered, put my hand around his throat, squeezed, and rode him harder. Skin slapped skin. This time, no matter how he tried to hold out, no matter how hard he tried not to, he was going to owe me a lot of cheesecake.

1:29 A.M.

Soon I fell away from him, exhausted. Staccato breathing. Skin dank. He rolled away, spent; the world had been removed from his shoulders. Sounded like we both needed oxygen and albuterol. Coming down was intense. I wanted to cry. Emotions had been opened up. Aftershocks made me twitch, yet I felt peaceful, happy, drained, the fire slowly burning itself out. Slowly. Soon, I watched him. Watched him in his post-orgasmic state. He gazed at the illuminated time like it was a warning, made a sound like a soldier who had been mortally wounded on the battlefield, then collapsed on his back like he was knackered from his toenails to the tops of his eyebrows. He licked his lips, coughed, and blinked.

I laughed. "You look the way Loki did after the Hulk slammed his ass in the concrete."

He caught his breath and said, "That was

intense."

"Baby, in bed I am the truth. And you can't handle the truth."

"You win the cheesecake. Damn. You win a Cheesecake Factory."

Thirsty, I dragged myself to the edge of the bed, reached for my glass of wine, sipped three times, and then sat up and pulled a pillow to my lap, again covering myself. He looked back at me, his smile not as strong. I hated that look, the appearance of a man who had to be somewhere else, somewhere more important. Negativity covered me. That was the awkward, impatient look Chicken and Waffles would give me at ten thirty. If I didn't understand that expression then, I knew for sure what it meant now. It hurt. It upset me. Seeing that expression on the face of this man, on this strange man's face, stung. Coming out of denial wasn't an easy thing to do. I sipped more wine.

I said, "I know. It's cool."

"We're good?"

"Hit the shower again. Go wash the condom smell off your thingamajig. Go wash my smell off of your hot body. Out of respect, I'll send you home smelling as close as possible to the way you did when you left. And when you get home, take another shower, so you go to bed smelling like your soap."

"You seem to be the expert."

"I'm the expert on being made the fool, not having the upper hand. It's disrespectful for a man to come back home and his dick smells like his outside woman, like the pussy from a strange cat."

"What happened to you?"

I paused, imagined the inside of my VW, the mess, the mess that had been there since it happened. Then I rubbed my shoulder, rubbed the roses on my right shoulder, and exhaled slowly.

I said, "Nothing special."

"Are you crying?"

"We have to be more careful whom we choose to love. My love is very intense, and I have to do a better job of choosing whom to love. I'm damaged. I'm not mad. I'm just cognizant of who we are, of what we have done, of what you have done with a woman you will wake up at home tomorrow and probably remember as being no more than a wayfarer. You're anxious now. You can't keep your eyes away from the clock. You've been looking at the clock all evening, like it's counting down to some grand event. Like it's New Year's Eve. I see the conflict in your body language. You want your wife now. You want to go home. So let me make it easy. Now. Go wash your distraught wife's dick and go home."

"I love you."

"Baby, go wash your pecker."

1:31 A.M.

The man from Orange County took to the shower again, but didn't invite me the second time. Shame. Emptiness. Possessiveness. Annoyance. Relief. I felt it all. I fought every emotion. I wanted to get up, gather my things, and leave while he showered, vanish as suddenly as we had met, but I had left my bag in the bathroom. I should have showered first, then vanished while he washed away my scent. But I also felt exhausted. I wanted to go to sleep, but I needed to stay awake, needed to get dressed and leave the romping shop and walk out of the hotel with him, go back to my car, part ways, get back to my side of town.

I found the energy to move and checked my phone.

Chicken and Waffles had called four more times. He had sent a dozen text messages and just as many to Facebook, Twitter, and WhatsApp. I'd never been MIA before. Had always answered his calls, responded to his texts, to his whims. Like I had been his wife. Like I had expected him to behave like he was my husband. Not tonight. I'd gone too far to turn back. This journey had to run its course.

I put my phone down. Felt a little nervous. Felt a lot tired.

I fell asleep. Natalie Rose was waiting for me. I saw her, saw her darling, breathtaking, angelic face. She crawled on me and I smiled for her, kissed my little elf on her chubby cheeks, kissed her wide mouth on the lips, pinched her cute little nose and told her she was my honey bunch, sugar-plum, pumpy-umpy-umpkin, cuppycake, gumdrop. I sang her the Strawberry Short-cake song.

She laughed. I heard her laugh. The best laugh in the world, the laugh of a happy child.

I will never understand how a mother could harm her own children.

The man from Orange County sat on the bed, and that jolted me from my dream.

I jumped and said, "Fire. The Christmas tree is on fire."

"The food. You just smell the food."

Disoriented, I sat up and looked for Natalie Rose. By degrees, the room became recognizable.

By degrees, then became now. The clock told me only a few minutes had passed. He had showered and dressed in record time. Again he smelled fresh, like the hotel's soap, not like me.

He asked, "What's wrong?"

"Nothing. Was dreaming. Was just dreaming that . . . a Christmas tree was burning."

"High cheekbones, apple cheeks, widest eyes. Graceful neck. Good posture."

I almost asked him if he had seen her, but he was touching me, describing my face.

He was memorizing my features, using words to make that memory concrete.

I said, "High cheekbones, apple cheeks, widest eyes. Best laugh in the world."

"Your laugh is beautiful. It is the best laugh in the world."

"Runs in the family."

He collected his clothing. And I memorized his sturdy build, prominent chin, and deep-set eyes, his beautiful eyes, memorized how his eyebrows slanted down like Christian Slater's, committed to my mind the features of a handsome man who broods, laughs, and loves like a demon.

This was over. There was a bittersweet feeling.

I said, "Let me take a quick five-minute

shower, and we can leave at the same time."

"Stay."

"You sure?"

"It's late. You've been drinking."

"You look pretty exhausted yourself."

"I'm fine. Stay. Have them change the sheets if you want. Enjoy the room."

"Thought you'd be ready for me to get out of the room when you left."

"Stay. Room's paid for. No need for both of us to rush out into the cold."

I pulled my lips in, felt the alcohol and overtiredness hold me.

I said, "I'll chill out another hour or so."

"Room is yours until noon. Probably can relax until one or two if you get a late checkout. Wake up. Get breakfast. Watch the news. Make sure you watch the news. See the news and traffic."

"I can't stay that long."

"Up to you. It's paid for."

I whispered, "It's paid for."

"What?"

"Nothing."

I pulled the sullied sheets up to my neck, pulled the covers over my body. I felt so naked in front of him now, after the sex, after the orgasms, after the shared sex sounds, after the incredible thrusting and riding and licking and groaning and boning. During his adultery I'd felt empowered. It was as if I had risen to a place high above the laws of man or God, a place where I had ruled everything around me. After his adultery, I felt embarrassed, no longer a member of the Upper Room. He seemed different, too. I had no idea how a married man felt after sex with someone other than his wife. This was new territory for me, a onetime visit. I only knew that a man with empty nuts always behaves differently than a man with full nuts. He had had powerful orgasms and come down off of his lust-sponsored high.

He had come down fast, like a skydiver. I was floating to the ground on the back of a feather.

I didn't know who I would be after sex with a married man. Usually I was different after I had an orgasm, softer, more agreeable, more hopeful, more girly, and too vulnerable.

He pulled the sheets down, looked at my bare form, played with one areola, then the other. I quivered, rubbed my legs together, and became a purring cat. My reaction made him grin. I ached, and he enjoyed making me ache. He enjoyed making me arch my back and sing like Idina Menzel.

He said, "Guess it's a good thing I pulled

off the 605 and stopped to buy gas."

"Good thing it was the night I got up the nerve to try to make a fool out of somebody."

"And you don't believe in destiny."

"I don't believe in fate. Not anymore. I don't believe some things are destined to happen."

"So some things could be avoided."

Then he touched me again, my breasts, my nipples, outlined my hips with his fingers.

I asked, "What are you doing?"

"Remembering. Memorizing. Absorbing."

I rubbed where his bull's-pizzle rested, massaged the sleeping giant.

I tingled, bit my bottom lip, tried not to move, but I wiggled with his touch.

He asked, "You okay?"

"What do you mean?"

"With what we've done, here, now, tonight, are you okay?"

I nodded that I was fine. "Thanks for the wonderful evening."

He nodded, stood to leave, but curiosity and insecurity made me pull him back to me.

I said, "Tell me about her."

"Tell you about who? The first woman to break my heart?"

"Your wife. Tell me about the woman you're about to leave me for."

"Are you angry?"

"Your wife. Tell me about the intellectual model with the degree in international law."

"Where are you going with this?"

"Do you swive with her like this?"

"Like this?"

"You go two times with her? You rock her that long?"

"No and no."

"You used to?"

"It's different with her. It's not like this. Never has been like this."

I said, "Okay."

"Do you please your boyfriend like this?"

"No."

"Why not?"

"Well, for starters, he's not as good in bed as you are. He's half a Snack Pack pudding, and you're crème brûlée. Compared to the way you throw down, he's whack in bed. And the real reason we do it doggy style, why we do it mostly *coitus more ferarum,* the true reason we have sexual intercourse in the manner of wild beasts, since you were so concerned with our positions, is because even though he's a big man, he's not a big man. Can't really feel him the way I feel you when he's on top, and he is painfully aware of his shortcomings and his fast coming, but I never complain, never damage his ego, so he gets it from the back, doggy style. I do that for me, to make it feel better, do it for me to make the vaginal canal as short as his dick, and it's good for his pride because then he can act like he's so deep and feel like a big man and make me whoop and holler like he's going where no man has gone before, but we all know that the penis can penetrate deeper into the vagina that way, when you're doing the congress of the cow. To be technical, the dick might make much-needed contact with the posterior of Susan's wall, like yours did as soon as you put it in, but that doesn't make him a good lover."

"Why are you with him?"

"Why is anyone with anybody? Jesus. Not everybody gets the best partner. Most are lucky to have a partner. Some girl has to get the guy with the little dick, or the guy who comes fast, or the guy we pretend is better than he is. Or the weirdo who asks her to sit in a tub of ice so she can be as cold as a corpse, and then wants her to be on her belly and be still and play dead while he screws her. Someone gets the weak or weird partner. Someone gets the asshole hooked on symphorophilia or autonepiophilia, or she realizes when he says he's an animal lover, he's really an animal lover. Anyway. Look. Sex is nice, but you can't base everything on how ten minutes of up and down makes you feel. You just can't base it on a few orgasms. The other twenty-three hours and fifty minutes have to be considered."

He nodded while I rambled, said nothing, the end of my diatribe leaving me feeling strange.

I said, "There is something that I have always wanted to do to a good-looking man."

"What's that?"

"You've been very kind to me. You've been more than generous, so you deserve it."

"Are you going to tell me or do I have to guess?"

"Let me show you."

I went to him, tongue out, showing him my tongue piercing, showing him what had aroused him from the start, and then I pulled his pants back down, welcomed him inside my mouth. Wanted him in my mouth. He became my toy. The warmth and wetness of my mouth sent him to a place he had never been before, to the place good angels went after they had died in heaven. The hard ball on my tongue moved around and teased his cock. His fingers massaged my head, grabbed at the dreadlocks, at the history that aroused him. On the television the Isley Brothers began singing about a voyage to Atlantis. While they crooned, I used my mouth to massage his balls while I stroked him out of that state of detumescence, and when he was a little beyond flaccid, I took him inside my mouth and worked on the restoration of that organ to a workable size. Gave him eye contact, let him see my lust, my hunger, my power. My hands and mouth worked together. He gripped the chair and panted, stared down at my rhythm in amazement. I sucked him well. He chanted, grabbed my dreadlocks. I made him call for Jesus and his father to come and save him from my evilness. I sucked him until my jaws hurt. He was stubborn. I was persistent. I was in control. I was empowered. He tried to get away, he tensed, he pulled my hair harder. I sucked and made him roar and come. I stole the orgasm he had hidden in the back room of his testicles. He was oversensitive, tried to push me away. Then, as his hands let go of my dreadlocks, I rose to my feet and looked at him for a moment, tempted to kiss him, but instead went to the bathroom, closed the door, spat his soldiers into the toilet, and rinsed my mouth, first with peroxide, then with the hotel mouthwash. I left the bathroom barely able to saunter. I passed by him.

He lay collapsed on the floor, his pants and underwear at his knees.

1:43 A.M.

He could barely move. He could barely breathe. Sweat dampened his forehead.

Again he was Loki slammed into concrete.

I asked, "So how much does being mansion-smart matter now?"

Again he sat next to me. I put two fingers inside Susan, then put her taste inside his mouth.

I whispered, "Go find your wife. She's distraught. Go to the hospital and comfort her."

"What's going on with you?"

"It's her turn to feel good. Go drive your wrecked car to your wrecked marriage. Go forget me."

"Do the same with your boyfriend. Get your good-night orgasm with him."

"Now who's jealous?"

"You'll probably be with him as soon as you leave me."

"Wouldn't want to end up in bed with two

guys within twenty-four hours, or the same week, so I might have to put him on hold for a change. That would be ironic, me putting him on hold. He'll be back. I know he will. I'm a smart woman. I am a good-looking woman. I'm having a hard time, but this too shall pass. You know how I give head. You know what I can do on top and from the bottom. You know there is good-good between my legs, so he'll be back. They all come back, or at least try. They wander the streets looking for better, realize they had the best of the best, then come back scratching at the door. You won't be able to do that. Once you're gone, you will be gone, as if you never were. Even though we used condoms, I'll still go to the doctor to make sure all is cool before me and my boyfriend hook up again."

"See me again one day."

"No."

"I wish I could see you again."

"I already have a boyfriend."

"He's not good for you."

"And what, you think you'd be better?"

"You wouldn't be in the streets trying to hustle rocks in a goddamn box."

"You have a wife. What could I gain from being with you? Absolutely nothing."

"I just wish that I could see you again."

"You're ridiculous, and this is crazy, and it's getting a little bit too intense."

"And you're not intense?"

"Take it down a few degrees toward reality."

He put his pointer finger inside me. His digit slid into me like I was hot butter.

He made that come-here motion over and over, while his thumb rubbed on my spot.

Then he used two fingers.

He made me grab the sheets.

Made my back arch.

Made me want to howl.

1:47 A.M.

His fingers. Each finger was like a new penis.

The things he could do with those digits.

I said, "No more."

"What did I do wrong?"

I pushed down on his hand, squirmed to get him to stop, but he didn't ease up.

The fire came back and all I could do was ride the waves of agony. Love wanted to come down, and I wanted love to stay where it was. I contracted around his two fingers. He finger-stroked me.

"I want to see you again."

"Stop, stop, stop."

He gave me the right amount of pressure. That was my G-spot, the epicenter of madness. He knew how to make me act like a fool. Then he leaned in, and while he worked his fingers, he put his lips on me, sucked me from the outside. I wanted to kill him, wanted to marry him. It was that wicked.

He said, "I want to be with you."

"Stop. Don't do this."

"I want to see you again."

He took to his knees and his tongue joined his fingers.

"Run away with me. Let's leave all our problems and go on the run."

"You're going to make my love come down again."

"Tell me I can see you again. Tell me I can have you."

"Oh God. Oh, Jesus Christmas."

Again, I held his head, put my fingernails in his flesh, wanted to mark him, and I sang.

When the song ended, he came back to my face, kissed me again.

I bit his bottom lip, sucked his tongue, bit it hard, bit it like I was evil.

He pulled away. "Ouch. What was that all about?"

"I told you to stop."

He said. "You want me again, and you know you want me to fuck you again."

"I don't want to be fucked, not all the time. Look, I love good sex to help get rid of all the tension. I need to ease the stress. I love to be pleased in bed, or on the floor, or on a chair, or put up against the wall so I lose it, fire all cylinders. Make me work, make me sweat. I want to be in the zone and lose control, but I never want to feel like I was fucked. I don't want to have sex and feel like I was conned."

"This was your idea."

"I know. You wanted some of this from the start. But you didn't con me into bed."

"So you liked this or didn't like this?"

"How can you do that? Pick a woman off the street, not know her, make her laugh when she hasn't laughed in forever, and then make love to her like that? What kind of mess is that, that you can show up and talk to me like you know me, and have me like you know this body, like you have a right to this body, like we've been lovers for weeks, for months — how can you do that? I don't know you, and just like that I told you I'd sleep with you. Is that what you do?"

"You want me to fuck you without fucking you, and to make love to you without it being love."

"Jesus Christmas, I've said too much."

He shook his head. "I don't understand you."

"How did we get here? I was trying to rip you off, not end up ten toes up, ten toes down."

"Misery. Depression. Desperation. Maybe they weakened our orbit, our values, knocked us off our trajectory, and when an object loses its trajectory and approaches a larger object, what feels like it could be happiness, or what could be love, or just lust, that object pulls that lost object into its orbit."

I said, "Why won't you leave? Is it so hard for you to leave?"

"I could love you."

"What?"

"I could love you."

"Don't say things like that."

"I'll be honest. There is a connection. It feels like I do love you."

This was no longer fun. It had become dangerous. Now I needed to escape.

"Let me repeat what I have said many times tonight. I'm not mansion-smart."

"Neither am I."

"You're married, with a possessive, jealous, distraught wife waiting for you to go comfort her."

"I know my situation. I am aware of what's waiting for me when I leave here."

"You don't know me."

"You have shared your body with me. You have shown me part of your soul. You have laughed with me, have accepted me as I am, have taken me to your bosom, and for that I could love you. The world is a messed-up place, and being with you, tonight, I forgot all about that. Love does that."

I pressed my fingers against his lips.

I said, "Anything beyond this, my spirit would suffer, and if we had an affair, a real affair, and I was the second woman to a married man, if I went against my core values . . . That may sound hypocritical at the moment, but this is not who I am, this is not who I want to be. What I have done tonight, if I stayed on this course and went down this road with you, my mental health would suffer, and this thing would never have the assumed perfection that it has had tonight. We would have pain day after day after day. I like you. I do. A lot. Obviously. On the real, if you ever get a divorce, look me up. Not separated, not legally separated, I'm talking divorced. And after your body and mind have handled the withdrawal of divorce, and there is a withdrawal period, find me."

"How will I find you?"

"The universe put us together tonight. If the universe wants us to meet again, it will make it happen, when it's ready for it to happen, however it wants it to happen."

"Give me a number. Give me a way to contact you."

"Go tell your sorority-girl-condo-smart-intellectual wife you finally bedded the type of girl you always wanted to bed, a girl from north of your county line, an underachiever, the type who is equal to the dude who had sex with your first love — tell her that. Tell her you had your fantasy. Tell her how you made me come, how you went down on me, and how I went down on you, how I drove you mad."

"You're jealous."

"I'm so freaking angry."

"Why?"

"Guilt. For allowing this to happen. I just sucked some married woman's husband's dick."

"You're not married."

"But you are. I don't have sex with married men."

"Just with guys who don't give a damn about you."

"I'm like every other honest chick. I sleep with guys who lie and say they're single. Things happen. Almost every guy seems to have a chick on the side. I deal with whoever until I find out I'm being played. But I have never, never, *never* entertained a conversation or had sex with a damn married man."

"I popped the dreadlocks-wearing, tattooed woman's don't-do-married-men cherry."

"Fuck you."

"You're a bitch."

"We're not having sex; that game is over. So, disgusting asshole, don't talk to me like that."

He said, "Sure. It's late. We're tired. We're both tipsy and punch-drunk right now."

"You'd better watch how you address me."

"Everything was nice between us."

"And you had to keep talking and kill the moment."

He asked, "Why the sudden stress? Why feel guilty now?"

"People don't feel guilty about things they haven't done, asshole. They feel guilty after. This is after. This is after all that feel-good cunnilingus and fellatio and doggy style. This is after you were better than I had anticipated, after realizing I don't want you to leave, and I don't want you to stay."

"Is it really guilt? Or do you feel something for me?"

"Don't flatter yourself."

"Let's face it. You're smart, but you're in the streets doing rocks in a box. That tells me you have no motivation. You're smart, but you have no drive, not until you're down to your last bread crumb. Then you will get up off your ass and do something that's nothing more than a temporary fix, or could get you locked up, and you probably would love being incarcerated because you'd get a taxpayer-sponsored place to sleep and a few free meals to boot. I exist at a level, in a place you may never be."

"You don't know me. You don't know my story, just like I don't know your story."

"Your story is both obvious and cliché."

"I'm getting a little past being a little bit angry now."

"Now who can't handle the truth?"

"Don't appreciate you calling me a bitch."

"I see the real you now."

I snapped, "I see who you are, too. I see you."

He backed away. "You're mad because I'm leaving."

"Dinner. Money. Seeing you jump to go home after all this, after using a damn electric toothbrush to make me come. You penetrated me with a damn toothbrush. How am I supposed to feel after you do things like that to me? Now I feel like I've been bought and paid for and screwed and discarded."

"That's ridiculous. We entered this not as

a barter, but as consenting adults, as two people, as two human beings who had a strong curiosity, two people with a strong attraction to each other."

"You're a repulsive half-breed. Yeah, I called you a damn half-breed. I'm saying to your face what the rest of America says behind your back, or tweets, which is basically the same thing. You are not in touch with the reality of the people, just the reality of the rich, which is not reality at all."

"I see why your boyfriend treats you the way he does. I see why he treats you like you're a blowup doll, fucks you like a dog, gets his nut, then goes back to playing his games. I understand it now."

"You're just an asshole. I know, same insult. I'll think of something better to call you."

"The mind of a woman."

I said, "Be careful where you travel. The mind of a woman is a labyrinth that ends at the truth."

"You mean maze, not labyrinth. A labyrinth only has one path. A maze is complicated."

I whispered, "Fuck you. Smart-ass asshole. Leave. Just leave. Get out of my life."

"I will, but not until I understand what happened. Why the change in attitude?"

"I'll go home, or go to my boyfriend's place, and you go home to your wife. Pretend you've done no wrong, that you're as innocent as Joseph, and I'll go home smelling like alcohol, cologne, and latex."

"Yeah. You meant maze. The mind of a woman is a maze inside of a maze inside of a maze."

"It starts as a fun night. It starts off as just sex. Wild sex. And we set fire to the rain. We burn. We consume each other in the fire. And we connect. We're human. Some feelings are there. We enjoy it. Want more. It turns into a fling. Feelings take over. We catch feelings, and that fling is now a clandestine relationship we hide from our lovers, from wives and boyfriends. We want them and we want each other. Like the selfish, we want it all. And in time, things get out of control. It becomes a big mess, a big emotional mess. And I went in knowing from the top that you were not good for me. It's not about you being married. I'd wish that I'd never met you. Or that we had ended it right here, before Christmas. I'd wish that we didn't go on into the New Year, didn't go on until there was no good way out. Let's pretend we've had a long relationship, that we have had months of fun, that we have hurt other people, that we've made your wife's life a living hell, that we've shouted and cried, that we've come to our senses, and now let's end it."

"Ah. The truth shows."

"What truth?"

"You lied."

"You're not worthy of a lie."

"This isn't your first time being with a married man."

"You don't have to jump in a fire to know it burns. Sex was the easy part. Naked was the easy part. We talked. I opened my soul to you. You saw me emotionally naked before I undressed."

"Still a maze."

"Leave. You had your swive. I had my swive. Your sacs are dry. Let the curtain fall. This concludes our social experiment of a destitute con woman and despondent married man, an experiment of opposites having sex, of strangers having passionate sex like they were in an unrecorded Masters and Johnson experiment, so take your obsession with girls on this side of the county line, women like me who reject guys on the other side of the tracks, guys like you. Take your strange and creepy late-night obsession with women who aren't mansion-smart, women you underestimate, and leave before this goes too far and I fall for you, and without warning I become the woman who shows up on your front porch to smile a bitter smile at your wife and tell her I'm sleeping with you, who would feel so much envy that I would do my best to ruin it all, would look her in her eye and tell her we'd been having an affair since this night, a night she was distraught and at a hospital agonizing over a family friend who was close to death, and do my best to destroy what you have with her and hope that drove you back to me, so just get out of my life."

He said, "You have a dark side."

"Almost as dark as yours. The way you hit that guy at 7-Eleven, that was a tell."

"I released my demons at 7-Eleven, just like you released yours here."

"Go back to the woman with whom you have a nonspiritual yet legal contract, a contract between moneyed and ambitious spouses, or, in your case, between educated fools. Go honor that pointless legal document that establishes rights and obligations between you and the woman who plays Candy Crush after sex. Why are you still here? We've done what we came to do. Why are you still here?"

"Because you are upset. This isn't the last memory I want to have of us together."

"I knew this was too good to be true. I knew this was another goddamn mistake."

1:54 A.M.

I jumped up from the bed, head spinning, and bumped into the food cart, knocked over my glass of wine, stubbed my toe, cursed, limped, picked the glass up, set it on the nightstand, wiped my wine-stained hands on my breasts, and started turning on lights and grabbing my things.

He said, "No. No. You had a lot to drink. More than me. I'll leave."

It took a moment, but I sat on the bed, dizzy, embarrassed, my back halfway to him.

He turned the lights back off. Dark souls stood in silhouette.

Earth, Wind & Fire sang about writing a song of love. I sang along with each song, and he listened without interrupting me. I sang, and my lower back tingled as my curiosity took control.

I asked, "Your wife is white?"

"Does that matter? I have a rich back-ground, but why should that matter? Is that the alpha and omega of your concerns? Can I not simply be seen as a human being married to another human being?"

"Is the bitch black or white?"

"Which works better for you? Which would make you feel more victorious or at ease?"

"Bet she's pretty, like a top-shelf Barbie doll."

He touched me. I pulled away, shoulders tense, eyes wide, teeth clenched, hands in fists.

He said, "What was that?"

"Thought you were going to hit me."

"What kind of relationships have you had?"

"Brief ones followed by briefer ones, and this will be the briefest of them all."

"I'm serious."

"With men who didn't wear expensive suits and didn't have wives waiting up for them all night."

"Men have hit you?"

"Don't try to be nice to me."

He said, "So we're like that now?"

"What do you think?"

He leaned in. Tried to kiss me. I leaned away. He followed. I moved across the bed. He chased me across the bed, grabbed my ankle, his grip firm, and pulled me back to him. Traced his fingers along my tattoos. I moved away. He pulled my ankle again. Sucked my toes. I stopped retreating. Stopped and gave in to that sensation. He kissed up my legs, over my butt, came closer to my belly, kissed my belly as he held my breasts. Sucked my right breast. Squeezed my left breast.

"Jesus. You touch me and a damn vibrator hums inside me. I'm sensitive, and you touch me, and it starts to wake up the monster I want to go to sleep. You touch me, and I want to come again."

He said, "You want me back inside you."

"I want you to leave and go back to your hell in Orange County."

He brought his tongue back to my nipples, suckled again. "Calm down."

I held his head as he continued to nurture my breast. "Don't you dare tell me to calm down. Don't think because we had sex that you're the God of me and now can tell me to calm down."

"Let me eat you again. Let me taste you again."

I pushed him away. "No. One swipe of your tongue, it would change into another swive. No more sex. No more cunnilingus. I'd go crazy and want you until I died. See? You've got me talking crazy as hell."

I twitched, felt waves roll though my body, the effect from him sucking my breasts continuing despite my having pushed him away, and I cursed, cursed him, struggled to control myself. When it was done, not until then did I escape him, shaking. I felt as stable as Venezuela, felt weak at the knees.

I slapped him. Slapped him hard. It sounded like a gunshot, or the slap Mudbone had received from a big old collard green–eating bitch down in Tupelo, Mississippi. That slap hurt me from the tip of my fingers up my shoulders. I screamed with the shock from the pain. Orange County grunted like he had been stabbed, held his face as if he expected half of it to be slapped up against the wall.

Slaps like that start fistfights that end with someone in a body bag.

1:56 A.M.

My voice trembled with anger and fear, and I snapped, "I said stop. I told you to stop. Stop doesn't mean finger-fuck me. *Stop, stop, stop.* Stop doesn't mean keep eating my goddamn pussy like you've lost your freakin' mind. Stop means to stop. Respect me. If you don't stop, *you don't freakin' respect me.*"

I jumped up and went to my clothes, took out the money he had given me, threw it at him.

"Money doesn't mean you own me. Because I let you swive me once doesn't mean you have the right to swive me twice. Who do you think you are? Take your goddamn money. Take your gift back."

He stared at me, standing naked, hands in fists, chest rising and falling.

He whistled, then rose slowly, shaking his head like he was ready to rip my limbs from my body.

In the next second, I held my box cutter in my hand, the blade exposed.

Then I was afraid. Afraid because I had seen what he had done to that man at 7-Eleven.

Now I was at the wrong end of his anger.

I said, "Just let me go. Just let me get my things and go, and there will not be a problem."

He stared at me, at my weapon, at my anger, at my vile expression, at the money on the carpet.

He said, "The honeymoon is over."

"I hate that I slept with you."

"Should've ended this at the parking lot after Denny's."

"At the damn gas station *before* Denny's. Jesus. I let you fuck me."

He said, "And I see it now. I see it. The bleakest of all blackness, mixed with the hardest of hard times and the deepest frustration. I see what has made you the bitch of all bitches, and you are a bitch."

"Do you want to leave your wife? Did you get married and realize you made a monumental mistake and now you have buyer's remorse? Do you see happy couples, couples happier than you, and that has made it worse? Did your soul shift in a new direction? Did her soul shift and now you're beneath her standards? Sex like this, in a room with a stranger — this is how you hide from problems, not how you cure problems. Nothing has changed for you, and nothing has changed for me. Same shit is still waiting for us."

We stared. Most of the questions I had asked, I was really asking myself, diagnosing myself.

I said, "Face it. You haven't got a clue, have you?"

We stared.

"Same damn thing over and over. You did it with your wife. I did it with my boyfriend. We did it with each other. Started off with false assumptions, revealed some of who we were, some truth rose, some lies, then lust had you, lust had me, and we chased orgasm. And after orgasm comes ugliness. We have had an entire relationship in a matter of hours. The mayfly has been born; now it has to die."

We stared. I had no smile, just the face that shut everything down.

I said, "You made me come. Let me tell you what that means. Let me tell you why that is horrible. It means I am responding to you, means that I am interested in having a relationship with you. If I didn't orgasm, it would have been a better sign, better for me. This is not good for me. So it would not be good for you. We have to stop. This would lead to more of this, and soon I'd want to feel you, or you'd forget a condom, or a condom would break, and then there would be an accidental baby."

Eventually he shifted. His anger was strong, apparent. He wanted to peel my skin.

"We fornicate until it's too late to turn back. My belly is swelling, and I don't do abortions, so a few hundred bucks can't fix your new situation. Three seasons later, I'm asking for medical expenses, putting all our business in black and white and filing with the court. Gets real ugly. Your wife has to know now. You stand on one side of court and I'm on the other side holding a baby that has your unique dual-eye color and my attorney is telling the judge that I'm entitled to income from your side of the table. Poor bitches are snickering at you and giving me a high-five because in their naive eyes I have come up. They don't see a baby, or destroyed lives, or broken families; they only see dollar signs and imagine that I will now be in a boss crib wearing boss shoes while a woman who can barely speak English cleans my house, and to them, all the stressful crap I have to go through is worth getting a check at the end. You become the government that sends me a check once a month. I get your money without having to work to get your money. I don't have to pay taxes on child support. That's a gold digger's victory. Your wife will be on your side of the court, there to protect her financial interests. Having to send my kid away on weekends to a father who never wanted it from the start, not out of love, but to lower his child-support payments, because that is the law, because he has more money. Then your wife deciding that you should take my kid, and since you have the money and the power, you do it. We fight the way we used to have sex, same energy, different form, still passionate. You'll live in court. Or your wife decides to leave you and wants to take everything you have. Y'all go from sucking and sexing to cursing and fighting, and you wake up day after day wishing that we had never met each other. So let me save you. Take this for what it is, what it was — a good time, a moment in the sun, a few orgasms that will be forgotten — and please go home to your wife."

A moment passed. Vanessa Williams and Sting were singing to Sister Moon.

He asked, "Done? Or should I wait for the sequel?"

"Was actually hoping you would interrupt

me, not let me ramble like a fool."

He headed toward the door, pulling on his suit coat, adjusting his tailored clothes so he would look proper, pausing, wanting to look back, but not surrendering to the urge, like an actor leaving the stage.

I said, "Wait."

He turned and looked at me.

I threw him the base of my electric toothbrush.

I said, "A keepsake. Use it on the jealous wife. Might help her stop feeling distraught."

He looked at it, looked like he was about to toss it back, but dropped it in his pocket.

He said, "I have a gift for you, too."

"Okay."

"There are more black men in prison or on probation than were slaves in 1850. That's what is in your blood. Not the blood of the kings and queens from Africa, but the blood of the bottom-feeders created by America. America took kings and queens and did its best to make them all bottom-feeders. Don't hate me. America hates you, and now you hate yourself. You buy into the hate that they feed you and feed that hate to your kids, teach them the same hate you have, and no one will ever rise up. You're smart. Do better. Do better than trying to be a criminal. I don't know the stats for black women, but the number incarcerated has to be high. Just keep that in mind, con woman. From inside a jail all you'll be able to do is have sex with a guard and have his baby as a way of trying to get some leverage."

"What the hell do you know about being black? I mean, the real struggle of blackness?"

"I have been black every day of my life. This is what was assigned to me without permission."

"I mean, two-black-parents black?"

"Does that make it any better for you? Does that make you feel better about yourself?"

"You think you know everything about everything. What, giving me stats made up by white folks as a way to convince me you're smarter? Richer? Yes. Smarter? *Never.* Don't you dare talk to me about being black. I am all the way black, and you are only halfway."

"You're an idiot. You're a biased, low-class, influenced-by-the-bean-pie-pig-feet-and-forty-ounce idiot. This was beautiful. You have no idea how badly I wanted this entire night to be perfect for us. For most of the night, it was the best night of my life, was a fantastic journey, a hegira, one that I needed, to escape from an undesirable situation in my life. This has become *worse* than a marriage."

"You made me realize something just now."

"Which is?"

"You know why people are honest with strangers on planes?"

"Enlighten me. You're the smartest one in the room, so please, enlighten me."

"Because that stranger can't judge them. People can take off their masks for a while. They can relax, breathe, reveal who they really are. That's what a one-night stand is. Sex with someone who can't criticize you, and if they do, you don't give a damn because you're too busy judging them as well. We've dropped pretenses. You took your mask off. I took mine off. We undressed. We experienced each other. We unloaded orgasms. We took away the pressure that we walk around with every day."

"And we talked. The big thing was that we talked."

"We did talk. You said things to me about your wife that I know you will never tell her, and I have told you things I'd never say to any man I've dated, and not to the chicken and waffles guy I'm seeing now. We know each other in ways our deceived lovers never will. We've peeped behind each other's masks. So all that bull you said, dude, I don't give two poots. You're already in your prison. Criticize me. Judge me. Judgment is cancer, and when you judge people, walls go up. My wall is touching the sky right now."

"I know you. I know you better than you know yourself."

"You know my sense of humor, what my kisses are like, how my breath smells, how kissing turns me on, how I react when a man sucks my ear, when a man sucks my neck, how I love to take my time and get in the mood, and when I am in the mood you know how I swive, how I fellate, how I laugh, how Susan tastes, how I can make it vanish, how I climax, how I lose control, and how I tend to get so loud they want to throw me out of a hotel room; you know how I do all of those things tonight, and a few other men already know the same, but in reality you have no idea who the hell I am. You don't know my go-to karaoke song or my biggest fear in life or if I had to moonlight a job what I would choose or my daily mantra or which song I wish I had written or my childhood nickname or the craziest rumor I've ever heard about myself or what I want to do before I die. You don't know how I feel about life and the inevitably of death. You don't know how I feel about funerals, if I attend or avoid. Understand? You've never even heard me burp or fart or smelled what it's like after I take a good dump. You've never woken up next to me when I've been cramping all night, or seen me with morning crust in my eye, or heard me snore, or saw too much hair growing in my nostril, or saw me with the flu. We're not past the point in a relationship where I would leave to drive an hour to get home or sneak away and drive to the closest mall to use the toilet because I wouldn't want you to know I needed to have a damn bowel movement. I'd want you to think of me as being perfect. We're not at the taking-a-dump phase. You know nothing true or profound about me. Sure, you know the sexual part of me that I keep hidden away from the world. You know a finite subset of me, you know a secret that's not worth keeping, a secret that I can admit to or deny, the same secret a few others know, but you do not know me, not the real me, not the whole me."

"I had a one-night stand once, long time ago, in my early twenties. I treated her badly, screwed her like she was one of those plastic dolls with a hole, finished, and tossed her like she was a used rag."

"What are you saying?"

"College days. Nice girl. I used to feel bad about that. Now I don't regret that one bit."

"You're an idiot. You're a dumb, sexist idiot in a nice suit."

"I'm not the first married guy you've been with."

"Why are you so insecure? You're too rich to be insecure."

"Because . . . I am a human being, and because I am hurt and insecure and I need to feel special."

"See, in one sentence I know who you are. I know your weakness."

"I'm not afraid to be weak. That is what makes me strong."

"You're weak."

"A man admits he's not perfect, doesn't know the answers, that he's afraid, and he's weak."

"You're weak."

"Am I the first? Am I the first married man you've been with? Or did you lie?"

"Would that make you feel better, or jealous? Would it confirm how you see me?"

"Am I the first?"

"No, you're not. I've been with a married man. But you will be the last."

As soon as I told him that lie, I wanted to recant it. The married man I had been with had been my husband. A technicality. I had been left with a beautiful daughter, the only thing that made that horrible relationship worth the ticket, and then that had been snatched away in the blink of an eye.

The man from Orange County, I remembered how he had made me feel in the parking lot at Denny's. How he had made me feel had made all the other things possible.

He had touched my goddamn hair. That was how this had started.

With his hand, his curiosity, his energy had infiltrated my hair.

He said, "About five this morning, she had gone to the gym, was gone when I came home from my trip. She had rushed out and left her iPad sitting on the kitchen counter. I was making tea, about to start my day, and the alerts were blowing up. About ten in a minute. I thought it might be an emergency, some reason I'd need to contact her at the gym and pull her out of Zumba. I looked because it was buzzing over and over. Each notification was an explicit message from him. Certain things are so appalling. Certain things are triggers. Certain things hurt. That was the anger that started my day."

"You've had a very interesting day."

"This has been both the best day and the worst day of my life."

"Your wounded hand and that bruise on your eye."

He admitted, "There was a confrontation."

"He kicked your ass."

He asked, "How does a man's life end up like this? This damn convoluted."

"Shit happens. It's part of living. Shit happens to you, to me, to everybody. Shit happens."

"I don't deserve this."

"You get what you get. You married who you married."

"Your boyfriend, he's a loser. You deserve each other."

"Just like you and your loser wife deserve each other."

"Just when I thought my wife was the bitch of all bitches, I met you."

"You and that distraught bitch can catch the express train to hell."

"I lowered my standards. Wish I had never put my dick inside you."

He unlocked the door, eased it open, but he paused.

He said, "This had nowhere to go."

"It never had a chance."

"You're not mansion-smart. You'll never exist on my level. You'll never get more than a worm's-eye view of a man like me. From a bird's-eye view, you're small. You're insignificant. You're nothing."

"But I'm not dumb enough to let a man mess me over the way your wife has messed you over."

He eased the door closed. Footsteps faded down the hallway.

I whispered, "When I was finished, I tossed him like he was a used rag."

This time it wasn't me. It wasn't me leaving a man's romping shop before sunrise, tipping out early in the morning before his nosey neighbors woke up, wasn't me going out into the rain alone. The man from Vail was the one taking the dreaded Walk of Shame. He was the one the people at the front desk would see leaving in the middle of the night, checking his watch and putting on his wedding ring. The whore always left the room. The whore was always the first to go, wearing the same clothes worn the night before, disheveled, hair sticking out in all directions, face greasy, makeup half gone, wearing unchanged undies, or with her stained and funky undies hidden in a pocket or her purse.

2:06 A.M.

I shoved the food cart to the side. Sat down. Rocked. The walls in the room talked to one another.

There was no applause. The show was over, and there was no clapping.

I whispered, "I met a man and saw the colors of the wind and flew too close to the sun a long time ago. The love ended badly; the pain was unbearable. This time, I flew, but I didn't go that high, was in the clouds tonight, but not high enough to melt my wings, not high enough to fall like a fool. I crossed the line, but I turned and came back down on my own, not like a meteor crashing to the earth from outer space."

Time slowed down. Something changed in the universe. I felt the change.

My phone rang, the ringtone of a man who loved Roscoe's chicken and waffles. He had been harder to find than Bigfoot all day, and we were now deep into the hours when last-minute, clandestine sexual liaisons were arranged. I had gone missing like Flight MH370. I picked up the phone and held my finger over the green button, but I pushed the red button.

That's what it felt like to be ignored. That's what it felt like to be rejected.

That's what it felt like to not know what someone was doing in the midnight hour.

He called right back. I pushed the ignore button right away.

We did that stupid dance five times in a row, like he was poking me on Facebook, like he thought this was a freakin' game. Then he stopped calling and began texting.

He didn't fulfill my hierarchy of needs, didn't give me anything physiological, nothing regarding my safety, no love or sense of belonging, nothing for my esteem nor my self-actualization.

Yet he would come to my apartment for sex, eat my food, and use my toilet without hesitation.

Sitting in the darkness, I remembered every question Orange County had asked me about my boyfriend, heard every tough question and saw the light — or at least edges of the light. But this boyfriend really wasn't any different from the boyfriend before him, or the boyfriends before him.

When you repeat the same mistake twice, it is no longer a mistake; it has become a decision, a pattern.

My cell buzzed again. Chicken and Waffles in search of his runaway girlfriend.

And his neglected girlfriend was tripping out over her runaway lover.

My mind was on the man from Orange County. I pulled at my dreadlocks until I felt pain.

I whispered, "You said you love me. Don't say things like that to me. Just don't."

The Orange County man who had wooed me and spanked me was gone. The tall, dark, and handsome man who had excited my spirit and made me feel that I was adored was gone. I needed the rain right then. Deep inside I am a lover of rain; rain gives me joy and peace of mind.

I watched God cry.

I'd never learned how to cry, not like that, not so freely, have never been able to allow tears to cleanse my eyes so that I could see clearly. I grew up in a world where crying was for the weak.

But I wanted to shed tears.

If I could've cried, I would have created a new Lake Superior.

2:08 A.M.

Phone in hand, I went on Facebook and changed my status from *In a relationship* to *Single.* That's code on social media saying either he has been busted cheating or I have been unfaithful.

As soon as my status changed, Chicken and Waffles called again. We had mutual friends, and I guess that update had made his phone explode. Within seconds, guys filled up my in-box asking if we could go out. The sharks smelled blood. I changed my status from *Single* to *It's complicated.*

It's complicated said it all.

Chicken and Waffles kept blowing up my phone. He had ignored me for hours, had made me a low priority when I needed him. Six months, and he had never said he loved me. Now I was visible to the man who had never asked me about Natalie Rose. If I answered, he'd hear in my voice that I was upset, and my tongue would become a

406

blade and try to slice him a hundred ways, but he would also hear that I was living on cloud nine, my voice having that husky after-sex sound; he would hear in my voice that I had been well-fed and well-fucked, that I had waited on him to be available for the last time, and he would inhale and know that I smelled of anger, dinner at Denny's, and blueberry-flavored condoms.

I burped, sat up, told myself to shower, dress, leave, go pay my rent, and return to my real world, but this room was free from hardship and more comfortable than anywhere I had slept in a long while.

When I got up to use the bathroom, that was when I saw it. The glow from the television and its love songs lit it up. A rectangular slip of paper had been left on the nightstand.

It took me a moment to realize it was a personal check, made out to *Cash.*

I glanced, squinted my eyes, saw that it was a check for another four hundred dollars.

I whispered, "Four hundred dollars."

The amount he would have paid a whore for a trip around the world.

He was a man who probably saw all women in the same light.

His name was printed across the top of

the check. He had a very nice name; a sexy name.

A well-dressed, clean-cut black man from Colorado with a name as sharp and smart as he.

And he had had sex with me and left me a check.

It was a reality check.

It was a tip for services rendered, a job well done.

"Disgusting, married asshole."

I had no idea when he had found the time to write me a check.

But he had. When was inconsequential, what mattered was it felt premeditated.

I held the edges, was going to tear the check up. But I didn't.

It was money. There was no such thing as bad money in this world.

It was all good when it was time to pay bills, no matter how it was obtained.

Services rendered, funds received. With my luck the check would bounce to Zimbabwe.

I lay back on the bed, first rubbing my temples, craving a ton of Advil for my headache, then rubbing my tats, touching them as he had touched them, stroking my arms as the heater in the room kicked on and hummed, then caressing my arms to comfort myself, touching my breasts and taking cathartic breaths, rubbing my belly, feeling wet, knowing I was wet, knowing I was wet for him, imagining his stroking, how he had gone deep, touching where my legs joined with my palms, touching with the tips of my fingers, touching. I imagined Orange County, before it went bad, the deliberate sucking on my clit, the languid cunnilingus, the kind with the right pressure, the kind that made an orgasm gradually reveal itself, the kind that didn't make my vagina hurt, the kind with no teeth, the kind that was methodical, and I remembered how he had gone fast, hard, and deep, remembered how he had taken this pussy like he owned this pussy, like he loved this body, and I responded in a strong voice, felt waves, felt the start of waves, of a tsunami, and without realizing what I was doing, I imagined his hands, missed his hands, and with watery eyes I touched and touched and played with myself, squeezed my breast, and played with the tingles he had left behind, the traces of heat and orgasm he had left behind, and the tingle magnified and I jerked, let my breast go, tugged at the sheets with my left hand. I chased the tingle, wanted to feel the fire again. With my small hand I imagined his larger hand as I remembered it, imagined his grayish-blue eyes. It felt like he had been gone twelve years. I remembered his best feature; I remembered his tongue.

Then I lay there, the room feeling too hot, love music from the television now too loud.

Janet Jackson sang about how making love in the rain made her feel.

I wiped my eyes, blew my nose, whispered, "Who the hell am I kidding?"

I looked at the clock, at the red glow, at the system created to measure the length of our existence. It told me how long I had made love, how long I had been blissful, and now it measured my life in another way. It measured the downside of the wrong kind of love. Time. A system used to measure how long we had endured, survived, or conquered. It also measured both happiness and misery.

I ran to the door, naked. After I undid the lock, I looked out into the hallway.

I called for him. I yelled for him to come back.

I yelled that I was sorry.

The hallway was silent. As if I were the only person in the swank hotel.

I grabbed my clothing, then dropped it because time wasn't on my side, but I pulled on my purple Timberland Nellie Chukka

410

Doubles and raced back to the door, opened it, ran out into the hallway, then ran back and caught the door before it closed and turned the deadbolt, made it protrude so I could close the door without the lock engaging, and not be an idiot and lock myself out, then ran down the hallway, naked, the laces from my Tims slapping my calves and shins, holding my breasts, sprinting toward the bank of elevators like it was the finish line at the end of the L.A. Marathon.

He was already gone.

I used the wall to hold myself up, panted and waited.

He'd come back. He had to come back.

I whispered, "Orange County. Why didn't you just buy the stupid computer and leave? Oh, right. There never was a MacBook Pro. You were to learn a lesson, but ended up being the teacher."

I touched my breast.

I cursed, whispered, "I'm sorry. I was mean. I was jealous. My life has been so complicated. There is so much about me you don't know. I adore you. Don't judge me. Just don't judge me."

A second went by with me looking at the elevator doors, waiting for them to open.

I said, "Come back. I'm sorry that I started tripping. Let me make it up to you.

Let me show you how to get through this maze. It's not as complicated as it seems. Okay? Come back. I will give you the truth. I will give you my real name. I will . . . I will . . . tell you about my car seat . . . the Barbie dolls."

I rubbed the back of my neck the way Aladdin rubbed that mythical lamp.

"Come back to the hotel. Somebody up there make the rain fall hard and force him to abandon his car and catch a ride with Noah and hop off the ark back at this forni-cave and come back to this come-stained romping shop. Are you there, God? It's me. No, it's not Margaret. I'm Jackie Summers. Yeah, the actress-slash-comedian-waitress-substitute teacher-grifter-slash-whatever brown girl with the white-girl name. Like, oh my God, are you, like, in Venezuela trying to deal with madness? Are you, like, looking for the missing brown girls? Okay. You have a bigger call on line one? Fine. I'll hold."

Head spinning, I sat down on the carpet, rested in front of the bay of elevators.

I said, "You didn't save Natalie. You allowed her to die a horrible death. You allowed her to burn like she had been sent to hell. I cursed you. Hated you. I'm still mad at you now. What did my child do to deserve the death penalty? What did she do in your eyes to deserve to be taken away from me?"

I sat and sang part of the Strawberry Shortcake song, rubbed my nose, let go of the thoughts of fires and funerals, and like a puppy waiting for master to come home, I waited for the man I had met earlier that night, waited and tugged at my dreadlocks, dragged my fingers over my tattoos, the ones on my shoulders and forearms, the one across my lower back, the one that ran from my left ankle up above my calf, over every inch of the inked skin that philanderer, that Just Cavalli–scented adulterer had held, sucked, licked, praised, craved, nibbled, and possessed. I needed him again. Withdrawal kicked in strong and I was on the edge of suffering — what the French call *avoir le mal de quelqu'un,* a sickness that comes from missing someone so much your body becomes physically ill, and it felt like I was suffering from someone-sickness for a man I hadn't known existed during my last breakfast, one sunrise ago. I looked up. The digits on the elevator were changing. Someone was coming up.

I grinned away all the negative energy that had glued itself to my soul.

"Miss me and come back. Need me like I need you right now. Feel what I feel."

The moment I made that wish the elevator stopped rising.

There was a soft *ding.*

The elevator door opened.

2:13 A.M.

The woman saw me. Her face contorted in shock.

She was a Latina with a wide forehead, and pointed chin, face in the shape of a beautiful heart, the face of a trustworthy woman with a playful face that had been shocked at the sight of me. She had a sexy Rubenesque figure, full and curvy, but not obese. She held her room key in her right hand, her big overnight purse over her left shoulder. Her hair was shades of brown, gold, and blond. She stepped off the elevator, but did so in a way that suggested she'd already started moving forward before the doors had opened. The now-anxious woman wore a jogging suit and makeup, but no jewelry. Her nose crinkled when she saw my nakedness, my tattoos. My guess was that she was an escort coming to meet a client. That assessment, that parade of thoughts, lasted no more than two blinks and a sigh.

I said, "Seventeenth floor?"

She looked down at her encased keycard to verify the floor, and then nodded.

I said, "Sweetie, you have the right floor."

I left her in shock as I walked away, tugging at my dreadlocks, head down, back toward the room, the sound from my Tims being absorbed by the carpet, my laces once again slapping across my shins and calves. I passed a half dozen people along the way, people heading toward the elevator.

Everyone looked. I came upon a group that looked like bad stereotypes. Chris Browns, Lil Waynes, and a handful of whooty girls who could pass for Twiggy, January Jones, and Kate Hudson.

A guy imitated Nelly and chanted, "It's getting hot in here, so take off all your clothes."

Their speech sounded like the result of perennial drunkenness or laziness.

"She's finer than Freema Agyeman *and* Anika Noni Rose, but bro, she's wearing Tims."

"What that mean?"

"She's in *Tims.* Means this one is a lesbian, dawg."

They laughed. A series of clicks and flashes followed, the sound of phones snapping photos.

The Latina said something, insulted them, defended me a woman, and there was a disturbance.

They exchanged words and I moved on, my hands covering Tina and Marie.

Even when the thugs and their whooty girls ran for the elevator, I never looked back.

The wine had me high. I needed to get back to the room, in case he called.

He would call. He would miss me and call before I checked out tomorrow.

I'd stay as long as I could, ask for late checkout, and wait for him to call.

Or come back.

But I knew he wasn't coming back. I knew there wouldn't be a call.

Fingernails dragging along the walls, I was lost.

The Latina asked, "Do you need assistance?"

"I'm fine. Thanks for running the wolves away."

The hall had seemed shorter on the way out. I didn't know how far I had run to arrive at the bank of elevators. I went from door to door, searching for the one I had left open. I looked back. The guys were definitely gone. But I wasn't alone on my journey from sanity to madness and back to the fringe of sanity. The Latina. She was walking two rooms behind me, her hand in her heavy bag, not watching me, too busy looking at the hard-to-read numbers on the rooms, looking for hers. I was nude, wearing only Tims and hickeys. I didn't look back again. Felt embarrassed.

Then she was one room behind me.

I said, "Looking for my room. I think they moved my damn suite. Wait. Found it."

I pushed the door. It didn't open. Wrong room.

She passed me, then looked back and saw me pushing on the wrong door.

I went to the next door. Pushed it. Wrong room again.

Behind me, doors opened and people looked out, asked what was going on.

I pushed two more doors, then a third, which flew open. While others asked why I had tried to open their doors, I pushed the door open wide and walked inside, laces still lashing my calves and shins.

The Latina said, "Is that your room? Are you sure that's your room?"

"I hope so. If not, it better be somebody's birthday."

The television glowed like a soft fire. I stopped moving, paused, fell into its glow.

I whispered, "Fire."

Music greeted me with open arms. L.T.D. sang about holding on when love was gone.

The door didn't close behind me. The lights came on.

Startled, I looked back.

The Latina had followed me into the room and stood with her hand on the light switch.

She asked, "Are you in the right room?"

"That light is bright as hell. Do you mind? Are you an employee of the hotel?"

"You didn't have a key, and I want to make sure you entered the right room."

"If I walked into the wrong room like this, it would look like Free Pussy Night."

It felt like I had walked into someone else's room. For a moment I expected to see naked people wake up screaming. Or smiling. There were no naked people. There were no people at all; just a disorganized room. I looked at the mess. The bed was disheveled, and there was so much leftover food.

I said, "This is my joint. Those are my clothes. If not, someone has had the nerve to buy clothes that look just like mine. Joking. Those are mine. Folded right where I left them. This room is mine. Well, it's the room they gave him when we checked in. He's gone home. So it's mine until morning."

Then someone tapped on the door.

She jumped. I did the same, only a big smile came across my face.

I said, "He's back. Guy I'm with, he's back. Black guy, not a white guy. Well, not black-black, just half-black. Or half-white. Guess it depends on how you feel about it. All-the-way-white guys are always coming at a sister, and they do it in public. Always telling me how beautiful I am, and that is good for the self-esteem. All-the-way-white guys always want to invite beautiful brown skin into their world."

She inspected the mess we had made in the room. It looked like rock stars had opened a playground. The door pushed open and it wasn't the man from Orange County. It was hotel security, a big black guy who looked like a bear with a goatee. He had a filmy vulture eye.

I said, "Dude, you are so in the wrong room. Edgar Allan Poe is not in here."

He saw that I was nude and averted his eyes; I pulled a pillow in front of me to hide my nakedness.

He asked, "Is there another problem up here?"

The Latina said, "I thought she'd locked herself out. When I exited the elevator, she was in the hallway as she is now. Guys were giving her too much attention. She was going from door to door, and I needed to make sure this was her room. And she has assured me that this is indeed her room."

I said, "Yeah. That. I had a moment. I am fine now. Thanks for your concern."

He said, "Guys came down to the lobby and said that there was a woman on this floor with a —"

The Latina interrupted, "With no clothes on. The men came out of some room up here and were in the hallway taking photos of her like this. At that moment, I encouraged them to stop."

Then her cell rang. The ringtone was Cee Lo Green singing "Fuck You."

She didn't answer her personal siren, and her ringtone almost made me scream my lungs out.

It was the same one I had assigned to my ex-husband.

That ringtone ignited another unwanted memory for the umpteenth time tonight.

I snapped, "Everything is fine. Y'all can go. Thanks. Get out. I need to go to sleep now."

Security backed out of the room, and the door closed.

A dozen deep breaths went by before I moved my dreadlocks from my eyes and looked at the door. I expected to see her there, but the Latina was gone, too. She had gone with security.

I knew she was on the other side of my door because her phone rang again, again ringing out Cee Lo's vulgar angst. The music faded as she hurried toward her room, toward her lover.

It was her turn. Let people bang on her door and eavesdrop the rest of the night.

This show was over. The curtain on my tête-à-tête, on my one-night affair, had fallen.

Silence returned.

Silence screamed.

I went to the wall, slapped it until I found the switch, turned the lights back off.

Again I stared at the glow coming from the television, listened to L.T.D.

Purple Tims heavy on my feet, I collapsed on the comfortable bed, the softness sucking me two feet closer to hell. Dreadlocks across my face, I observed the room, the aftermath of what we had done. I wanted to call the man from Orange County. I had deleted his number from my phone.

I had thrown away his business card. He no longer existed in my world.

2:18 A.M.

Rubbing my neck, I got back in the shower. I was going to drink all the wine I could, then raid the minibar and drink and eat this buffet until I passed out. I thought I heard a sound, like metal against metal. It was an abrupt bump. My heart raced. I paused, turned the shower off, and listened. I stepped out, wrapped myself in a towel, and went to the room. No one was in there. The door was still locked, the deadbolt on, the security bar in place. I looked at the door. Wondered if that bump was Natalie messing with her mommy from the other side. I looked out the peephole, wished it was a fisheye that allowed me to see her in heaven, but I only saw the hallway. Saw no one. Then I cracked the door in case she was there. She wouldn't be tall enough to be seen. No one was in the hallway. I dropped the towel where I was, scratched my head as I headed back to the bathroom, and stepped back in the shower. My neck. I saw my necklace. I had almost forgotten about the red circle of hickeys he had given me. They ran from ear to ear and would look fantastic with a cream-colored pearl necklace. When I was naked in the hallway, the Latina who had left the elevator in shock, the fools rapping and taking photos as I headed back to my romping shop, the security guard who had come inside my room — all of them had seen the bite marks left over from my exorcism. I went to the bathroom, slipped on a housecoat, put on lip gloss, then returned to the room, turned the lights on, retrieved my cell phone, pulled the covers up to my nipples, and took two dozen selfies. I needed to remember this moment, this night, when I wasn't tipsy, when it didn't feel like a dream. I posted two on Instagram, knowing they would automatically appear on my Facebook account and link to Twitter. Chicken and Waffles was a friend and a follower. I wrote, *I've been drankin, I've been drankin'* on the post. Then I changed it. *La petite mort. La petite mort. So many little deaths visited me tonight. So many orgasms. I've been nasty. I've been nasty. I got filthy when good wood got into me. I'm a grown woman, a single lady, can do whatever I want, with whomever I want, and I've been drankin' with a nice, long, strong surfboard. Graining on that surfboard from Orange County like a mofo while Gladys Knight sang he was the best thing that ever happened to me. Nice to be with a handsome man who has a slow hand and knows how to make a grown woman come. La petite mort. La petite mort. So many little deaths. Until I die again, I will live with a smile.*

I broke all my own Facebook etiquette rules. Wanted the world that knew me to see me now. I made the happiest face in the universe. I took a photo with the food tray and wine behind me, one where you could see the disheveled post-sex bed, one where you saw my clothing folded, and one where you saw my overnight bag in the frame. I let my dreadlocks down, had the housecoat where it barely revealed the darkness of my nipple. I took that one in black-and-white, very artsy, very erotic, and posted it. *Stop calling. Game over. Moved on to a better surfboard. Should've offered me more than chicken wings and waffles and been a real man and put a ring on it because I have done an upgrade, so to the left, to the left.* That was out of character and daring. Every woman on my page clicked like and sent high-fives and told me to get mine. Tommie McBroom posted a haiku on my page.

Unhappiness is a sorority with many members. I put my business on social media. On a page called Natalie's Mom, a page that had hundreds of photos of my child and me, a page where I had always been a respectable single mother who had lost her child, I had a moment that couldn't be taken back. Social media is not erasable. The wine I had been sipping was using me as a mouthpiece. That's what the sex and orgasms had done to me. When that was done, the smile went away. I sat there waiting like a lonesome queen.

I had met Chicken and Waffles online. We had found each other on social media, had been in the cesspool of information that reveals how people really feel on the inside, where people go to reveal their true selves, a place where much of what is shared is negative, vindictive, and hopeless, where we learn to be racist in 140 characters or less. We broke up the same way: in less than 140 characters.

We were so advanced we'd found ways to be together without ever being together.

We'd learned how to create false connections to maintain false relationships.

The night with the man from Orange County had been filled with words.

We had talked. Shared ideas. Agreed.

Disagreed. Had sex. Loved. Argued. Fought.

We had broken up. We had had a full relationship in a matter of hours.

I missed his voice. I missed his smell. I missed his touch.

I missed a man I barely knew.

Broken balloons were all over the room, stuck to the furniture, to the mirrors.

Maybe I'd clean my car. Maybe it was time.

The child seat. The plethora of Barbie dolls. The food on the floor mats.

I heard her laugh. I smiled. Thought about her. Almost went to the door again.

The money. I stared at it for a while. With that money, I could've taken her to Disneyland, stayed at the hotel for three days, ridden all the rides and eaten candy and hot dogs until our bellies burst.

Mommy was supposed to get rich for her, travel the world with her.

I picked the check up as well. Stacked it on the desk.

I sat the reality check on top of the money.

Not only was his name on his check, so was his home address.

That was stupid. His stupidity told me a lot.

He'd never had an affair before. A seasoned adulterer would never leave a paper trail. Never give your mistress your bank information or your home address. It was a sign of a man who was too trusting.

I looked at the four-hundred-dollar check, squinted and read his information, printed across the top, and picked up my phone and keyed his address into Google. Thanks to Google, all I needed to do was put an address into the Google browser, and the home or apartment or building would pop up in 3D. I saw palm trees, nice cars in long driveways, and the uniform bland color of the community's architecture. I could click arrows to walk through the entire neighborhood. I zoomed in, came so close I could see the fancy handles on his double front doors.

2:25 A.M.

This was the address on the check, and I assumed that it was the man from Orange County's home address. I didn't want to be curious, but now I was throbbing, inquisitive.

I wanted to see where he lived, wanted to see how he was living.

Wanted see where he was going after he pleased me and left me enamored.

Like a teenage girl, I was jealous.

I went back to the browser and thumbed in the property address again. Property valuation, names of owners, and a heading that read FIND OUT WHO LIVES AT the address popped up. Another link took me to a real estate sight for Anaheim Hills. Jackpot. A description popped up, along with a virtual tour. Google had taken me to his front porch; now another site was letting me inside his home. This was a criminal's tool; how burglars could tell what you had and what room it was in, even see what type of security system you had. It made it easy to plan a break-in. Either the house was on the market or he and his wife had just bought it. Single-family home on Foxhollow Drive in the hills near Disneyland: four bedrooms, three and a half baths, three thousand square feet on a lot of more than five thousand square feet. Built in 1998. I took the virtual tour through thirty photos, looked at the double doors that led into the home and the impressive two-story ceiling over a formal living room that opened into the formal dining room, which in turn led to a grand wooden staircase.

The kitchen was boss. Spacious, with granite counters and a work island in the middle, and it had a breakfast nook. Next was a large family room with a fireplace. I was staring at my dream home.

There was a bedroom on the main floor: The master suite, where booties went to do doggy style, was oversize, with a private retreat, a space that looked like it could be a sweet fornicave, a place for all sorts of kinkiness, and there was a luxurious bath with dual vanities, an oval tub, and a separate shower.

I sat there grinding my teeth and rocking. Mansion-smart.

If that was only house-smart, I would hate to see what his idea of mansion-smart was.

The house cost three quarters of a million.

Google is a stalker's best friend. Everything is on the Internet. That was why I never gave anyone my address. Or made sex tapes with anyone. The one who claimed to love you today would get pissed off and not hesitate to betray you tomorrow. My apartment had a living room, a kitchen with small gas stove, a bedroom with a twin bed, dull walls, and gray carpet that the landlord would clean once every six months, but wouldn't replace. Orange County's home was impressive. Compared to Leimert Park, his neighborhood was Beverly Hills. I could put his address in MapQuest, go to Orange County, sneak behind enemy lines. I dropped his name in the Google search engine.

His picture appeared, followed by the story of his life in black and white.

I whispered, "Oh. My. God."

Then I sat with my head between my legs, panting, overheating.

Then I closed my eyes. Searched for Natalie Rose.

I needed to know that she wasn't alone.

All I found was darkness, a deep, peaceful

darkness.

It felt beautiful.

I slept.

A key card was placed in the door. I jerked awake. It was placed in the wrong way, taken out, flipped over, put back in. Then the sound of a click, then the sound of metal against metal as the latch brought the opening door to an abrupt stop, a sound like an exclamation point in deep font. The door handle turned and was pushed forward. It was the same abrupt sound I had heard when I was in the shower. Someone had tried to come into the room before. I think I heard them again while I slept.

3:47 A.M.

I called out, "Hi, rude person on the other side of the damn door. I'm available right now so you can speak to me personally. Please tell me what the hell you want this time after the beep. *Beep.*"

There was no reply. But someone was there. My heart thumped.

While I sat there in shock, a keycard was placed in the door again, and the door was shoved open, but was again stopped by the security bar. That terrified me. I jumped up and grabbed the box cutter.

Maybe I could cut somebody six ways to Sunday. Maybe I could.

I called out, "Yes? Are you deaf? Jesus Christmas, what's the issue now?"

"Are you okay?"

"Who is it? Is this a wellness check by a deaf person?"

"It's me."

"Me who?"

"Guy from the gas station."

"What guy from what gas station?"

"Guy you slapped so hard he saw the light."

He'd come back.

I asked, "What's up?"

"What do you mean?"

"You sound angry."

He said, "It's been that kind of night."

"Thought you'd gone to your distraught wife."

"I forgot my wedding ring."

"Wow. That's it? You came back for your wedding ring?"

He said, "On the dresser."

"You left in a hurry. Hope you made sure your drawers were on forward and not inside out."

"Well, are you going to let me back inside?"

"Hold on for a second."

"Why do I have to hold on?"

"Let me get dressed."

"You're joking."

"I'm serious."

I grabbed my clothing, dressed. He'd come to put me out. He'd come back to put me out.

Once I'd pulled on my clothing, I opened the door, and he held up a plastic bag.

I asked, "What's that?"

"Cheesecake."

He looked at me. I looked at him. It felt like the first day of spring.

With his left hand he touched my neck, touched the hickeys he had left behind.

I whispered, "You went out into the rain and bought me cheesecake."

"From Pure Cheesecakes. Supposed to be the best cheesecake in L.A."

"You drove in the rain to find cheesecake for me?"

"You're worth it. The moment I left here, I wanted to turn around and come back."

"I missed you."

"I missed you, too."

"I'm sorry."

"It's fine. I'm sorry, too."

We kissed, a soft kiss with lips touching, then with the dancing of tongues.

And that ended the fight.

I wanted to get undressed again, to get on the bed, sip wine, eat my treats.

But that was when I saw that he wasn't the same man. He was the man I had met in Hawaiian Gardens, but he wasn't the same man. He smiled, but it was a different smile. This smile was heavier. Distraught. It had been robbed of something. The energy had changed. The same went for his complexion. Not until that moment did I see him clearly. He looked sallow. Broken. He looked the same way I had looked, the same way I had felt when I gave my child back to the earth. He looked like he had seen death.

My tone shifted, filled with fear, anxiety, and I asked, "What happened?"

"Before it was too late, I wanted to bring you the cheesecake, like I promised."

"What happened?"

Bad news came with the good.

He said, "My wife called."

"Does she know you're with someone?"

"She suspects I've been in this hotel having the time of my life."

"So what does that mean?"

"She was leaving to come here."

"Here?"

"Here."

"In traffic?"

"In traffic."

"She's pissed."

He said, "Traffic and rain would not stop anger and jealousy from reaching their destination."

I paused. Looked at the room. I saw the insane fun we had had. I saw all we had shared. Heard the laughter. The time on the clock glowed. He gave me a tight hug, the kind that lifted me off my feet. When it was done, I went to where he had left his wedding ring, picked it up, took the circle that symbolized forever to him, put it on his finger as if I were asking him to be mine, then kissed him again.

In the softest voice I told him, "I should leave before she gets here."

In a softer voice he said, "She's already downstairs."

I said, "She's already here? Your distraught, anorexic wife is here?"

"Already here."

"She's in the lobby?"

"No, in the garage. She's in my car."

"How long has she been there?"

"Not long. Not long at all."

I didn't want to know how it came to be that she was downstairs in his car.

Now I was sober.

I said, "Can you get the room cleaned, pretend you were here alone, maybe rent another room if they have one, take her to a fresh room, and then . . . Wait, can you tell her that you didn't want to drive home in all the traffic and the rain? Can I do something to help you . . . to help not make matters worse for you?"

"Things were done before I met you."

"Let me get my things. I need to get out of here."

"Stop."

"Your wife is here. This is done."

"We'll leave here together."

"You said that your wife is in your car, and you want to leave here together?"

"I want to leave here the way we came in."

"I don't remember arriving here in a hearse."

"I want to leave holding your hand."

"Are you mad?"

"You said you wanted to watch the sunrise at Venice Beach?"

"You said your wife is here, so I doubt that is going to happen."

"There is more to it."

"What more could there be?"

"Sit down."

"No. I'm not going to sit down."

"Let me tell you something."

"Something happened."

He nodded. "Something happened."

"Just say it."

"Okay. But it's bad."

"How bad?"

"Bad."

"Dude, is this regular bad, or police bad?"

"Police bad."

"How bad police bad? Are we talking tickets or handcuffs?"

"Sit."

"I'm not going to . . . not going to . . . what is that?"

That was when I saw the damp spots on his suit coat, on the lapel. I thought it was more rain, like the raindrops on his shoulders. But when I touched it, the tips of my fingers came back bloody red.

Then I understood that his wife was waiting in his car.

My world shifted. I felt like a drop of water floating in space. Felt like there was no gravity. Felt like my body was losing its form.

Anxiety had him in its clutches and he couldn't get free. His lips curled in. He quivered. His shoulders slumped. He broke, and he trembled, and it felt like he was about to implode, collapse in on himself, and leave nothing more than a crater where a strong man used to be. I had been that way that day. I had imploded, collapsed, had had no one to support my angst. I put my arms around him. I held on, tried to keep him from tumbling in the wrong direction, tried to hold the big man up straight. My strength came alive. I couldn't stop the implosion, but I held him.

In a voice that was barely there I asked, "What happened?"

"Before this night, some things were already inevitable."

"What did you do?"

He said, "She noticed my missing wedding ring."

"What do you mean?"

He held me and rocked, and hummed.

He said, "Can we cuddle for a moment?"

"You want to cuddle?"

"I want to cuddle with you."

"Now?"

"This might be the only chance we get to cuddle."

I paused, touched the side of his face. "What have you done?"

"I just want to cuddle right now."

"Sure, we can cuddle."

"Clothes off or on?"

"You decide. I'll let you decide."

"I want to undress you."

"Okay."

"I wanted to undress you earlier."

"I would've liked that. No man has undressed me in a very long time."

3:56 A.M.

I dismantled him.

The man who wore the suit that symbolized achievement, I dismantled him.

I eased away his suit coat with care, with patience. I paused and cupped the sides of his face with my hands. Gave him eye contact. This was trust. This was honesty. In silence my actions were louder than words, told him I was with him. My eyes said that I wasn't leaving him. I kissed his cheeks, his lips. I undid the buttons on his shirt, pulled its tail from his trousers, undid the buttons at the sleeves, and helped him out of his shirt. Then I pulled away his white undershirt. I paused then, rubbed his neck, his shoulders, and his back. I made him sit and I took away his shoes, the right then the left, and then his socks, the left then the right. I rubbed his feet, and looked at his face. He touched my hair. I told my hair to take away all of his energy, to take the negativity that he couldn't bear and bring it to me. I had been through days worse than this before. Soon I undid his zipper, unbuckled his belt, and pulled his pants away. I had him stand and I pulled his boxers down to his ankles, kissed his legs, his thighs, memorized him before I had him step out of them, then added those to the pile of things he had worn, to the invisible pile of things he had carried throughout his life, a complicated life I had taken for granted.

We kissed. We kissed and tried to erase dystopia. We tried to make time go in reverse.

He stopped and faced me, looked me in the eye. His eyes took me in like he'd never seen me before. He looked at me and gave me small kisses on my lips, kisses of endearment. I became a high priestess, and he worshipped me as if this were the start of our night. I felt his passion. It remained. In his weariness, in the middle of his crime, his passion for me was stronger. He turned me around, stood behind me and pulled my hair up, kissed the back of my neck, kissed me softly, ran his hands over my curves as if he were meditating, memorizing this moment, then put his face to my neck, tasted me, captured the sight, sound, taste, and smell of me. He reached under my sleeveless dress, eased it up and over my body, over my hips, shoulders, and head. He put that to the side and unsnapped my bra, pulled it away, left shoulder first, then the right. He kissed my bare shoulders and my fingers reached back and touched his face, his hair. He moved in front of me and pulled away my jeggings, then my thong. He kissed my navel, then he picked me up, carried me to the bed, laid me down on my back.

He kissed my tattoos, kissed every tattoo, put his invisible marks on top of what was there. My hands came up, touched my neck, touched the circular tattoos he had already created. I touched my new necklace like it was made of pearls.

We embraced, hugged, rocked to the music coming from the television, held each other close in an affectionate manner, hugged tenderly and nuzzled in the darkness, beneath a solemnness that was eager to descend and reveal all that I didn't want revealed. I wanted now to last until I needed something different. But we don't get to choose. The things we cling to can be taken away. So I would cling to him while I could. We nestled into our pain as the inevitable approached one breath at a time. There was no fondling. We had moved from the childish and juvenile stages of an affair and into the adult stages of a relationship. Somewhere after dusk and before dawn, we had grown in ways unseen to us both. We sought something that lived beyond lust and on the other side of love. We looked for what we could imagine existed in the movies, but would never be able to find.

Skin against skin, I expected to hear a knock at the door, a demanding knock. But there was silence in the hallway. So we continued as we were. Sought warmth and affection from each other, without the quest for sexual gratification. This was an art form, like kissing, like sex, like love.

I turned my back to him and he snuggled up behind me. We became two spoons in a small drawer. My head rested on his chest, my dreadlocks forming a pillow underneath his head. One of his arms was up high, around and under my neck, his other hand around my body, the palm from that hand on my breast, resting over my heart, not massaging my breast but feeling my heartbeat, feeling the life force, feeling the thumping that signaled that this existence continued as it echoed inside me. My hand was on his hand and I felt his heart beating against my back. His life force thumped against my back, sent his vibrations into me.

Our energies intertwined. We enjoyed the closeness, the honest affection, and for a moment the cuddling broke the negativity and our curt and troubled breathing eased, and there was the sound of happiness. This is why we cuddle. Cuddling releases a hormone that reduces stress and anxiety. Cuddling is good for the mind.

We didn't talk about racism, discrimination, or xenophobia.

We didn't talk at all.

No sirens.

No ringing phones.

No one banged on the door.

No longer masked in lust.

Living in trust.

I allowed his demons to find a resting place inside my hell.

My darkness enveloped him, became a safe haven for his troubles.

He said, "Houghmagandy. My wife has a membership to Houghmagandy."

"What are you talking about?"

"I mentioned a place called Houghmagandy to you earlier tonight."

"The country club."

"*Houghmagandy* is an ancient word that means 'fornication.' "

"Am I supposed to guess the significance of that?"

"Houghmagandy is the name of an underground swingers' club up in the Valley."

"You're swingers?"

"I'm not a swinger."

"You just said you were members."

"She's a member."

"And you're not?"

"I'm not a member."

"You gave her permission to join?"

"She's been a member for years. I just became aware of the place this morning."

"When she left her iPad on."

"I saw all the messages about Houghmagandy and Decadence."

"And what is Decadence?"

"An exclusive swingers' club in the Bible Belt."

"That sounds like an oxymoron. Or at least like hypocrisy."

"I travel abroad a lot to do business, and when I'm out of the country, she always says she's going to South Carolina to visit a girlfriend from college. She's been going to at least two swingers' clubs."

"Alone or with her girlfriend?"

"Not alone. She has a special male friend. He takes her to both."

"Wait. You're telling me your wife not only has cuckolded you, but she's a swinger?"

He said, "She's had an entire other life outside our marriage."

"One more interesting than playing Candy Crush."

His voice thickened. "She's a member. She and the older guy are members. They have joint memberships, on his card. It was paid for on his personal American Express Centurion Card, so it never showed up on our accounts. They have been members for over five years. I found out this morning."

"She's a well-educated woman living in

the upper echelon of society, right?"

"Very accomplished and sophisticated."

"I thought that intelligent people were more likely to remain faithful."

"Scholarly people are just better at hiding the immoral things they do."

"What kind of guy was she dealing with?"

"Older guy she's been sleeping with has two PhDs and used to run three companies."

"Sounds like a regular Neil deGrasse Tyson. You know who the older guy is?"

He frowned at his wounded fist. "I know who he is."

"Who is he?"

"Family friend."

"You're joking."

"He's always been a friend of the family."

"A friend of the family? How close?"

"Was like a second father to me."

"That's pretty close."

"He also stood in for my wife's father in our wedding."

"When did you find out about your wretched wife's extreme ratchetness?"

"Told you. This morning. I took her iPad, took the evidence and went to pay him a visit. I was going to e-mail the interactions to him, but I wanted to look in his eyes and show him his own words."

"You had a fight before the sun came up."

"The fight was unexpected."

"What did you think was going to happen?"

"Had no idea. He got the first blow in. But the last belonged to me."

"With a racquetball racquet?"

"No. He attacked me with a racquetball racquet. He came after me with his favorite GearBox Max1 170 Teardrop Racquet — the racquet I gave him last Christmas. Same type of racquet I used when he and I hit the courts together every second and fourth Sunday."

"Are those strong?"

"The most powerful, durable racquet ever designed by GearBox."

"He hit you with a racquetball racquet like he wanted to kill you."

"He hit me like I had been the one sleeping with his wife for the last six years or more."

"What did you use?"

"Baseball bat."

"Damn. I was at Chick-fil-A having a number one, and you were fighting for your life."

"He attacked me. Then I lost it and beat him with a baseball bat we had bought at Dodger Stadium. We went there to celebrate when Magic Johnson became part of the front office up there."

"Your distraught wife is panic-stricken because of that fight."

"So am I. I drove away from the scene, and she ran to the scene."

"That's the older guy who has been on the news all day."

"Same guy. He was my friend. He was one of my closest friends."

"He was an older dude."

"And because of that, at times he was like a father to me as well. Gave me much counsel during my college days. He was the adviser to my fraternity, was a part of my wedding, and was part of my life."

"He slept with your wife."

"He ate dinner at our home. He brought his wife, when he was married. He was good with deception. I didn't see that one coming. My wife always said he was like a second father to her as well."

"That's sick."

"I loved him, too. Like he was my father. Like he was my friend."

"Wait. That makes no sense."

"I can connect the dots. Where did I lose you?"

"You told me you had met her at Barnes & Noble. You said she was coming up the escalator like an angel. Now you're telling me she already knew the people you knew? She already knew him?"

"I was at the bookstore with the older guy and his wife."

"You left that part out."

"I know. I think she was coming to see him. I didn't know they were involved. His wife was with him. I ran into them, then ended up strolling with them, and went to the bookstore to buy a Harry Potter book. I felt that she was coming toward me, but maybe she was going toward him and I got in the way and introduced myself, then introduced her to my friends. She revealed nothing. He revealed nothing."

"They acted like they had never met?"

"Like they were total strangers. She chatted me up; sat with me talking about Harry Potter, flirted with me while her lover and his wife were at the next table drinking tea and eating muffins. My friend's wife kept staring at her with a strange smile on her face, and she had become cold and unfriendly, but I assumed that was an older woman's jealousy sparked by undeniable youth and beauty. Some women hate what should be celebrated. They left us there, left us there talking and getting to know each other. I was unaware, but like I told you, his wife, his ex-wife, was always mistrustful. My wife was never able to look his wife in the eye. Never could."

"I know what happened. I don't believe in coincidences, so I know."

"Tell me."

"Her jealous ass was following her lover, then happened to meet you."

"I guess she was following him. Maybe she wanted to size up the competition. Or maybe, like me, she was just passing through The Grove, saw him, and followed him, initiated some sort of lover's game."

"She knew he was there. That's why she was alone. I'm a woman, and I know the heart of a woman. She followed him and wanted to see what his wife looked like. She wanted to see how they interacted as husband and wife. She wanted to see if their relationship lined up to whatever lie he had told her. She didn't like what she saw. What she saw let her know that he'd never leave his wife and be with her. My guess is that's why she was so receptive to you out of the gate. She rubbed it in her lover's face. You were the ultimatum. He hated her being with you but couldn't open his mouth or do a damn thing about it."

"You've drawn an interesting scenario; complicated, yet very simple and direct."

"She slept with you the next day."

"She did."

"I bet she gave him twenty-four hours to make up his mind. He couldn't leave his wife. She was envious of her old guy's wife, and she wanted to hurt his heart, too. I'll bet he knew she was going on a date with you. If you didn't tell him, she did. He couldn't say anything, of course; plus, it might've helped to quell his wife's suspicions. Your wife, before she was your loving wife, she had you to anger him, to force his hand. No man likes being backed into a corner. No woman likes to feel like the fool. That probably put a rift between them, but at some point they went back to hooking up. You dated her and made it possible for them to be seen together in public and draw no suspicion. Hey, are you all right? You don't look too well."

"I've moved from denial to anger to bargaining to depression."

"Acceptance? How far away are you from acceptance?"

"Now I accept it. I have no other choice but to accept it. Again, I'm the idiot savant. I can start a business, can run a business, raise capital, assemble team members, develop marketing strategy, but with women . . . it's like I'm good at algebra but have been given a problem in physics. I hate to admit it, but maybe I have what some call situational stupidity. Emotions take root and obstruct my ability to reason, and because of that I can be indistinguishable from a person who is just plain stupid."

"I guess we have something in common. You are with women the way I am with men. I get emotional, and because of that, I, too, am an idiot savant. They were in your face, and you had no idea?"

"You wouldn't look at them and think anything. He's older than her goddamn father."

"If you say so. But I know you've heard of Viagra. That blue pill keeps old players in the game."

"He may have been like her father, but she was in bed with him like he was her husband."

I said, "That's disgusting."

"With me, I thought her sex drive was low, or I didn't please her whenever we did have sex, which was a rare occasion, but I guess it was anything but. She preferred someone else, for whatever reason."

"She knows you and him got into it?"

He said, "She ran to that sonofabitch as soon as she heard he'd gotten what he deserved."

"His being attacked came on the news, and she ran to him." I asked, "Does she know you did it?"

"She knew. She knew that it wasn't a home invasion. She knew she had been exposed. Took six years, but she was exposed. Her iPad was unlocked, went missing, she saw my bags, so she knew."

"Wow. Text messages and instant messages don't lie."

"She tried to purge everything on the Cloud, but it was too late. She came back from Zumba, or wherever she was, called me a hundred times, saw the special report on the news, probably received two dozen phone calls about the old man people saw as her second father, and ran to the hospital."

"All of that, and she had the time to be jealous?"

"She was like that."

"Again, ratchetness."

"I'll tell you everything that happened tonight."

"I think I know."

"Actually, you have no idea that you are sitting in the eye of a storm."

"What did I miss?"

"You were almost murdered."

5:44 A.M.

It was an hour before sunrise.

When the sun rises in one place, it always sets in another. And when the sun sets somewhere, someone is experiencing a sunrise. Darkness gives way to light as light gives way to darkness.

Life will always be that way.

There was a marine layer along the coast that helped decrease visibility to about a quarter of a mile, a rolling fog that made everything from the 405 to the ocean look like it was being accosted by London fog. After I loaded up my VW, I put a Barbie doll in the passenger seat, buckled her in, and followed Orange County through traffic to Venice Beach. He had taken Lincoln Boulevard, avoided the freeway, but there was still traffic, moving slower than cold molasses flows. A group passed by us in the rain, all on Fatback aluminum bicycles, bikes that cost around four grand. Then a man in a Santa Claus suit passed by pushing a shopping cart overloaded with plastics, cans, and bottles. This is common; this is life in the beach areas. It is a culture inside a culture wrapped around another culture; professionals surrounded by slackers and sipping coffee with bums and weirdoes as gang members spray-paint coded gang signs and encrypted messages of death and terror on dull stucco walls. It is a world that fascinates me, one I love and hate at once. We pulled into a pay lot and drove to the far back corner, away from the entry, to a spot that was empty. It was going to be another rainy winter day, now a mixture with fog. There wouldn't be a wild crowd. The chainsaw jugglers and dancers and joke-tellers and henna-booth vendors might skip half a day. At the malls, at coffeehouses, at twenty-four-hour gyms, the die-hards might get up and feed their addictions. But there wouldn't be a crowd here for a while.

I told him, "I want to meet your distraught wife."

"I don't want to show you."

"I want to see her. I want to see who was going to kill me."

He nodded and opened the trunk of his damaged car.

I said, "Jesus."

"You okay?"

"I saw her at the hotel."

"And she saw you."

There was a gash in her head, and a tile sat on top of her body.

The tile was broken at the corner.

I asked, "What happened?"

He told me that she had been getting off the elevator in the hotel lobby when he had come back with the cheesecake. She saw him at the same moment he saw her. An incredulous moment. Christmas songs were still playing, the Christmas parties and the inebriated now in overtime, the rappers in the lobby as well. She made a scene. He was at a hotel. There was lipstick on his collar, and my perfume was on his suit. I had bitten his neck as well, had put at least half a dozen marks on his neck. She saw the signs of betrayal, all the things I would have looked for, the same signs I had seen on the functional alcoholic I had married once upon a time in Las Vegas.

He looked at me, evaluated me as he told his tale, then said, "You're not freaking out."

"Have you ever seen the body of a dead child after a fire? Ever lost all that mattered?"

"No. I can't say that I have."

I left it at that, and with mild sarcasm said,

"Looks like you Donkey Punched her."

"Snapped. Anger. Frustration."

"Lack of sleep."

"That, too. All of that mixed with irresistible impulse."

"I guess it's too late for you two to engage in conscious uncoupling."

"Way too late."

"She was in our room."

"So I heard."

"She was in the room and left."

"Just be glad she did."

"Is she dead?"

"She could be dead. Maybe. Maybe not."

"Jesus Christmas. She was so jealous, so hot-blooded she was going to kill me."

"She was. After what I had done to her friend, I was on the hit list, too."

"I need you to back up. Slow down. Tell me this from the hotel."

"I can only tell you what she told me when she was ranting, when she was making threats to divorce me. She'd seen you. She saw you go back to the hotel room. She walked behind you, already knew the room number, but was surprised when she realized that was you in the hallway, as if you had been waiting for her to get off the elevator. Then you walked away from her, leading her toward the room like you wanted her to follow you, like you were going to fight her in private. It threw her for a loop."

"I was waiting for you."

"I don't understand."

"What's to understand? You left, I was sad, I missed you, and each second felt like an hour."

"Why were you in the hallway naked? Did you get locked out?"

"I had on my boots, so technically I wasn't naked."

"What she told me made no sense. She told me that she had seen my wedding ring. She had been in the room, had seen the food, the bed, and had seen the wedding ring I had left on the dresser. She told me the exact spot where I had left the ring. I thought she had done something to you."

"She was close enough to touch me. How did she know which floor we were on?"

"She's authorized on my card."

I said, "You checked us in as husband and wife."

"So she went to the desk, simply said my name, our surname, showed her identification, smiled, didn't cause a fuss, and they gave her a key. She was smooth with it. Maybe the staff's shift had changed; maybe whoever was covering the reception desk was asleep at the wheel, or just didn't care."

"So she showed up, went to the front desk, and showed them her identification."

"They gave her a room key and the room number. She had a room key when she came across me. Like I said, I was walking into the lobby, and she was getting off the elevator."

"She drove here from the hospital."

"No. She called a car service. She'd been dropped off."

"Jesus. How much did she know?"

"She told me I bought gas in Hawaiian Gardens, knew how much I had spent at Denny's, knew I wasn't there alone, knew the time I paid my bill based on the charge, even knew that I had charged a haircut in Santa Monica. She had basically traced my steps from the moment I left Orange County."

I moved my dreadlocks from my face, whispered, "We were face-to-face."

"She came to the hotel armed and angry."

"For me? I just met you, don't know her from Eve, and the loon was coming for me?"

"For you, for us, but you were in the hallway. Why were you in the hallway?"

"I was in front of the elevator when she got off."

"She said you were *naked* in the hallway."

"I told you, I wasn't naked. I had on

462

purple boots."

"Made no sense. She described you, your dreadlocks, your tattoos, your weight —"

"What did she say about my weight?"

"Nothing that matters. And your purple boots. She said purple boots, and I knew she had seen you for sure. She saw me and wanted to go back up to the room."

"You're joking."

"She wanted me to bring her to you. She wanted to have it out in the hotel room."

"What happened? Why didn't she bring it? Why didn't she come back?"

"That's when I told her that I had a Christmas present for her and it was in the car."

"You're kidding."

"She heard I had a present, and she paused to find out what the gift was."

Just as there had been an outburst of entertainment in the two-star Denny's in Lakewood, there was an outburst in the lobby of the five-star hotel, one that made high-class people have less class than rappers. But when he had mentioned there was a present for her in the new car, she wanted to see the present. As hotel staff and security had looked at them without intervening, they had left the hotel lobby together and gone to the covered parking lot. They argued, and their voices echoed.

I said, "Wait. Back up. She came to the hotel, and just like that she wanted a Christmas present?"

He told me that he said the word *present* and the arguing, the screaming, the cursing stopped.

He said the word *present* and there was a Pavlovian response, like she was a child at heart.

He had hickeys on his neck, and she cursed him for that, said vile things, but she wanted her Christmas present before they continued the fight. His wife was a woman with unwavering priorities.

I asked, "What type of woman did you marry?"

"A very ambitious, jealous, and materialistic one."

"Damn. So, you told her that you had a present, and . . . ?"

"She followed me to the parking lot."

"She's cheated on you for years, a man has been beaten to death's doorstep, you're in the hotel with me committing adultery, and she pauses the madness because she wants a Christmas present?"

"She stood in the parking lot complaining, arguing, making so many threats."

"Awww. That's so sweet. So she didn't

forget about me."

"I yelled at her, argued about the old man she was seeing, and she yelled at me, insulted you."

"Then what?"

"She saw the car. She saw the new car that was going to be her big gift this year."

"What did she do?"

"She changed gears, jumped up and down, screaming. Until she saw the damage."

"Bet that was a downer."

"While she went off about that, I put the cheesecake on the roof of the car, opened the door, took out the MacBook Pro you sold me. Everything else is fuzzy."

"The tiles? How did she end up in the trunk with a gash in her head?"

"I handed her the box. She ripped open the seal. Ripped up the flaps. Took out the tiles."

"Okay."

"She handed me one. You had glued the image of an open MacBook Pro to the tile, but it still looked like a tile. She held it up, looked at it like it was supposed to change into a MacBook Pro."

"I can't believe that. You're kidding me, right?"

"She tapped the tile with her fingers,

tapped it like it was the touch screen on an iPad, then turned it on its side and looked for a switch, for a power button, shook it, stood there trying to make it come on."

"Are you serious?"

"I told her I'd bought the MacBook Pro from a nice girl at a gas station. Told her that the nice girl worked for Best Buy and had done a run and found one computer too many left in her care. Told her while I had pumped gas, a girl wearing a wig, a yellow polo shirt, Dockers, and a Best Buy badge had stepped out of a truck and asked me if I wanted to buy it before she sold it to someone else. I told her that I had paid two grand for her second-tier present."

"Then?"

"She called me stupid and kept trying to make it turn on. She called me stupid, just like a self-centered girlfriend did a long time ago on Christmas morning — the selfish woman who'd been unfaithful since before I put a Garrard eighteen-carat blue sapphire–white diamond engagement ring on her finger, the woman who'd worn her wedding ring and gone to swingers' clubs and did God only knows what . . . she called me stupid. There was no remorse, not one tear, no apology."

"She was angry because she had been

exposed."

"My wife called me stupid after having an affair with a man older than her father and coming home smelling like old-man come, while she held a kitchen tile, trying to make it power up."

"She got to you with one word. She knew how to get to you."

"She called me stupid and I went back in time, back to the girlfriend from Vail, the one I had given a present to and she had insulted me, back to all of them at once, and I realized that I had dated the same woman over and over, that I had married that same type of woman, and I was furious, angry at myself, at my choices, incensed at the way I had been a fool, and rage, the rage came on so strong. The rage came on so damn strong."

"Jesus."

"I wanted to destroy them all. And for a moment, she looked like all of them at the same time."

"Jesus Christmas. She complained and ranted and you went old-school Bible and smote her with a tile. Like in the Bible, in Numbers, where God gave death to all those who complained."

"She called me stupid. She had an affair with my friend, my mentor, her father figure, was a member of at least two swingers' clubs, had done only God knows what, and she snapped at me, called me stupid; stupid because I loved her too much to see the signs? Stupid for marrying her?"

"How did that make you feel?"

"It made me feel like I was less than a man. What I felt was indescribable."

"I'm sorry, but that mischaracterization of your masculinity, that low blow, was her objective."

"She stands before God, marries me, cheats on me, and the slut of all sluts calls me stupid."

"Your wife came to find you. You beat up her lover, then she came to deal with you."

"She didn't respect me. The guy she had the ongoing affair with, he didn't respect me, either."

"Did she love the old guy? Did she love him, have him for sex, and marry you for money?"

"Ask her."

"Kinda late to do that."

"She had an affair for years, and then rushed to confront me after she saw I was at a hotel."

"That's how a guilty conscience works. She figured you were here getting your revenge."

"I have no idea."

"She didn't come after you until she knew you had checked into a hotel."

"I guess not."

I shivered. "She was standing behind me, and you're telling me she had a gun."

"You were naked. She saw the food. Saw my wedding ring on the dresser. The messy bed."

"And my neck. She saw the love bites on my neck."

"She saw your neck, too."

"She had a gun, but security came in."

"If that's what happened, then that's what happened."

"That is what happened. Security came knocking."

"I guess that's what saved your life."

"You didn't answer me before. How did she find you? How did she find us?"

"I told you."

"Tell me again. This is . . . shocking."

"Whenever I use my charge card, it sends an alert. E-mail goes out for every transaction, no matter the amount. It's that way for fraud prevention. Had an incident in the past. People can do many small transactions, under the radar. So the moment there is a charge, no matter the amount, an alert is sent to both of our phones. She saw that

I had gotten a room, knew where. The card leaves an electronic trail."

"Your credit card is your snitch and needs stitches. In that case, before all that happened, she knew you had bought gas in Hawaiian Gardens, might have known you had bought condoms at 7-Eleven."

"And she was alerted again when I paid for the room service."

"Well, she knew you weren't alone if she saw that bill."

"She knew I wasn't alone at Denny's."

"Technology is a beast. Now everyone can pretend they are Big Brother. Everybody can stalk everyone and never be seen. She knew you bought condoms and wine at 7-Eleven."

"She knew. She cursed and told me she knew."

"They can do that? Send a message stating everything you bought? Rhetorical question that time."

"She was alerted again when I left and bought the cheesecake."

"She knew you had left the hotel."

"Yeah. That last alert was how she knew I wasn't at the hotel, and maybe that gave her the confidence to go up to the room, see how it had been left, and wait for us to come back."

"Or see if I was still there. A woman always wants to see what the other woman looks like."

"I was gone. She knew I had gone in search of the best cheesecake in Los Angeles."

"She probably assumed I was there with you. Or that we'd be back."

"Probably."

"You knew that she would know everything you had done tonight."

"It didn't matter, not anymore. I told you that at the start. I know what she's done as well. What I did was a drop of water. What she's done has been an ocean. What I did doesn't compare."

"She went to some place called Houghmagandy."

"And Decadence."

"She doesn't look like the type. She looks so wholesome, so Procter and Gamble."

"The sneakiest whores look like the girl next door."

"She was a beauty queen?"

"She was Harvest Queen in her hometown."

"Why didn't she just divorce you?"

"Ten years. She needed to be with me for ten years. After ten years, in the state of California, she would have been entitled to

471

much more than she'd get from a divorce now."

"She was a well-dressed and educated scavenger in it for the long con. She was playing you for the long con better than any hood rat puts a man in a trick bag and gets him for eighteen years."

"I guess so. Whatever you just said, I guess so."

"You said the marriage was bad. Why didn't you divorce her?"

"My parents never divorced. Thought it would get better. Thought I was doing something wrong."

"She came to kill me."

It played again in my mind.

I had seen her. When I was in the hallway, naked and at the bank of elevators, she was the woman who had exited on my floor. The elevator doors had opened on my angst and inebriation, and then she had stood there, disarmed. She was behind me, coming to our fornicave, to my romping shop.

I had passed rude people and gone into my room. He told me there had been a gun in her purse. I blinked, numb, still in a state of disbelief. I tried to remember those cloudy moments.

I had passed others in the hallway. She had passed others.

So she had let me return to the room.

She had entered my room after I did.

She had closed the door.

Then security had come on her heels.

She had to make a choice.

I assume she had to make a choice whether to confront me, fight me, and kill me.

If she had killed me, she would have had to kill the security guard as well.

She could have sent me to play in God's sprawling Disneyland with Natalie Rose.

I tried to process what I had missed, what had happened right in front of me.

When the hallway was clear, she had come back, had returned when I was taking a shower.

That's what had happened. What had happened off-camera revealed itself in my mind.

His jealous wife made her choice and left, but she came back when she thought the coast was clear. She had to be ready to take it to the next level, but she pushed the door and couldn't get in.

Then his wife had hurried away, retreated from the battlefield when she realized I was awake.

She had used her electronic key to open the door. She might have heard me in the shower then.

But before, maybe she thought I was so drunk I had gone back to the room and passed out.

Now it was clear to me that I had heard her open the door and try to rush in before she was seen.

I had heard the latch catch the door and create the sound of a big, bold exclamation point, and that exclamation point had been a shock that caused an adrenaline rush inside both of us. Mine had sent me to the door to investigate, hoping he had come back. I guess that had triggered her overwhelming flight-or-fight response, and in that moment, exposed, she had chosen flight, and her adrenaline rush had made her legs move and sent her running away, running fast to the elevators, maybe hoping she hadn't been exposed. I could have been playing with my daughter right now. We could've been together again.

It wasn't my time.

My unseen enemy had been cunning. She was smart. I never would have looked at a woman as put together as her and seen my own death staring back at me. She could've sold me rocks in a box.

She had pulled off the best capitalistic con in the world. She had done well for herself, better than most, had married a man for money, but I guess that hadn't been enough. She had an affair with one man while she was married to another one.

She had come for me. She had been inside my room.

I said, "Your jealous, distraught wife had a gun."

He nodded to confirm what he had already told me more than twice.

I said, "Damn. I think I know what happened when she got off the elevator."

"What?"

"She pulled her gun, maybe brandished her gun when the guys were in the hallway."

"You saw her pull her gun?"

"She was behind me when I was walking back to the room. I passed by a group of prairie dogs in sagging pants, and I wasn't paying attention."

"Group of prairie dogs?"

"There was a coterie of Lil Wayne wannabes in the hallway acting out and heading for the elevator."

"Thugs."

"The kind that rap the N-word, think they're Jay-Z or 50 Cent, and are poor-man rich. Sagging pants and fitted caps tilted to the side. That kind of swarm of ignorance came up on us unexpectedly."

"They would've scared her. Just their look

would've terrified her."

"They were calling me names because I was naked. I remember that now. She was actually trying to protect me from those guys. I think that's what she was doing, until she realized who I was."

"Why were you in the hallway naked?"

"Not important. Trying to remember. Was so spaced out. Jesus Christmas, I think she went NRA on them and brandished her gun like she was working a neighborhood watch program down in Florida. She was probably intimidated by them and showed her gun. I would've done the same. Probably. Not a gun person. Anyway. They ran to security and snitched. That's why security came upstairs so fast."

Despite her wrongs, despite his point of view, be it reliable or not, she had been coming for her man. She had been coming for her husband. She had been coming for whomever he was with.

The most jealous and insecure are the ones who are guilty of betrayal. The ones who are the angriest are those who are pulling cons themselves, only to find out they're being conned as well. A thief hates to be robbed, and a cheater always wants you to be loyal while they are being unfaithful. When suspicions arise and the questions start, they are always defensive, always volatile. A thief takes being robbed personally, the same way a player falls apart when he finds out he is being played.

She had returned, had come back to my door when we should've been in bed sleeping, naked, vulnerable. And she had a key. She could've walked in and done whatever. She had on sweats and trainers. She was cute, but she had come in the clothing of a high-end warrior. The bitch had come back to fight, at the very least. Emotions were high. The man from Orange County had beaten her lover, and then made a mockery of her infidelity by having me. It was as if the gods had their hands in this cruelty.

She wanted revenge on so many levels that it was scary. We fight for what we love, what we feel we own, right or wrong. No matter if I was right or wrong, I still would have kicked her ass.

Or died trying.

I said, "She's not white."

"You're obsessed with race."

"Because I'm a true American. I am the mirror and mouthpiece of everything that is going on in this country. I've been programmed. I have been ridiculed and underappreciated. What I am is what America has made me, and it hurts to be this way. Do I like it? Hell no. But this is my reality."

"You're like a one-woman, Negro Tea Party."

"You're from Colorado, where the girls put on condoms a little bit too late."

"I'm a cheater like Jacob, with a temper like Peter."

"Only when you've been motivated."

"That's my weakness. I can only take so much. Then I lose it."

"Irresistible impulse."

"I'll keep that in mind when I consult with a team of attorneys."

"Anyway. She's not white. At least not all the way."

"Portuguese, African, Dutch, Indian, and British."

"She looks Latina."

"She's not. Lots of people assume she is when they first meet her, but she isn't."

"You lied about her ethnicity."

"Never lied. You assumed and delved into racial profiling."

"I know who you are."

"Do you? Based on whom I married, you think you know me better?"

"I'm being serious. I looked you up online. You lost your business."

"It's not gone. It's being downsized, like the postal service, like Barnes & Noble, like

Sears, but I'm holding on like a warrior."

"What I read online said you will lose it, and three thousand people will end up without jobs."

"Things will change. I might end up sleeping on Crenshaw."

"Will you have to come off the hill and live among the colored folk?"

" 'Colored'? Didn't being colored go out with Donkey Kong?"

"Glad you still possess your sense of humor."

"After this one day in my life, I will need that, and a good team of radical attorneys."

"This is your wife."

"This is the one I chose. The one who chose me. Though she is no saint, I'm sure she'll be portrayed that way by the media. You pushed a lot of buttons tonight. You asked me hard questions."

"You did the same for me. You made me realize a few things."

"I try not to say too much about the woman I chose. This was the one I chose. Never have chosen a good one. Not since Colorado. I seem to get the same woman over and over. Until you."

"Damn. Sorry to hear that."

He nodded. "I'm not sure why she married me in the first place."

"You're rich."

"Stop saying that."

"That's why she rushed you to the altar."

"She had lovers. I don't see why she made such a big deal out of getting married."

"Because it's expected. Because it's pushed on women from the moment we're ejected from the womb. That's the way women are taught to hunt. And we do it, follow the programming, and it turns out bad for most. Not saying it's a bad thing, just saying only a few win the lottery."

"Very few end up like my parents."

"Most people just skateboard from unhealthy relationship to unhealthy relationship."

"That has been my journey, without the skateboard."

"So. Your wife."

"What about her?"

"She had an old man for a lover, and he has been there from the start."

"I don't think being monogamous ever occurred to her. She was upset tonight. She'd given me an interesting life, and now she couldn't handle the idea that I was engaged with someone else."

"But you said all of your credit cards were set to alert both of you to charges."

"They are. The personal credit cards that

we share are set on alert."

"So you knew she'd know you were at a hotel."

"I knew."

"You wanted her to know."

"I did."

"You were spitting in her face."

"I was. Does that make me a bad person?"

I shrugged. "Makes no sense to me."

"Because you're sane."

"Glad someone thinks so."

"You have to be crazy to understand crazy."

"Or crazier than the crazy you are facing."

"She drove me crazy. In the end, she drove me crazy."

"You've had a hell of a day."

"I have."

"Guy she was seeing, you went to confront him."

"That was where it all went to hell. Never should have gone up there."

"Tell me. Tell me what they're not saying on the news."

"How much do you want to know?"

"All of it. I want to know all that was going on, and I had no freakin' idea."

"He made love to my wife countless times, then attacked me with a racquetball racquet."

"Insult to injury."

"I was angry, but only wanted to talk. He denied everything. Denied it all until I showed him her iPad. I yelled, began reading the exchanges. I shouted her words. I screamed his words. I yelled how he loved for my wife to suck his dick. I read that to him. He became outraged, yelled, and acted like I was the criminal for invading his privacy. Everything was twisted, and it got out of hand real fast. It happened so fast, the energy was so high, that even now it's blurry and I have to piece it together."

"I've seen you angry. It's nothing nice, especially when you have something in your hand."

"He grabbed his racquet and hit me."

"That explains the head blow."

"He tried to take me out. I swung at him and missed."

"You hit the wall."

"Yeah. I clipped the wall. But I got the best of the old man. I knocked him across a table and he fell down, got up, and charged at me. Then I saw the Dodgers baseball bat, a bat for his grandson that had been personally hand-signed by Yasiel Puig, saw it leaning against the wall, a bow around the middle, one of the kid's Christmas presents."

"You beat him with an autographed bat? That's blasphemy. Have you no respect for the sport?"

"I didn't care if Babe Ruth had autographed that bat after he had hit his first home run at Yankee Stadium back in '23. The old, arrogant fool had lied, then hit me with a racquet. He was sleeping with my wife more than I was sleeping with my wife, was sleeping with my wife like she was his wife, and he hit me. He attacked me. He drew first blood. There was no remorse. He was taking my wife to swingers' clubs, was doing only God knows what to her in front of other people, probably was sharing her with others, and there was no remorse."

"You didn't just walk in fighting."

"No. I was there a few minutes before the

fight started. He was surprised to see me, but let me in, asked me if we were supposed to play racquetball, thought he had the days wrong. We walked to his kitchen, and I sat on a bar stool, powered up the iPad, and told him I needed to talk to him about something important. He had coffee on and poured me a cup. I was calm. I was rational. I didn't go there to fight."

"Okay."

"Then I presented the evidence. The e-mails, the *I love you* messages from Skype, the messages from Tango, the flirtations on WhatsApp, the sexy photos, and the picture of the dick he put in my wife. She used an app to track her period, and she kept track of her weight, body temperature, and when she was intimate. With that app, she put in the days she had had sex. I stood in front of him and read him the information from the damn Pink Pad app, told him the exact moments he had fucked my wife."

"What did he say about all that?"

"Asked me why I had broken into my wife's private accounts."

"What?"

"Then he shook his head like I was pathetic. Told me to get over it. That did it for me."

"When I met you, you were coming from

committing a crime."

"Revenge shouldn't be called a crime. Revenge is the response to a call; the answering of a bell."

"It should be an entitlement, but it's a crime."

"A small crime in the name of love, honor, and ego, and showing an old fool that I was a man."

"No wonder you were angry."

"It was like being that high school kid in Colorado again. Same feelings had me again. Opened an old wound. Their affair had been going on from the start. This morning I found out he was with her before I was with her, during his marriage, during my marriage, during his divorce, until now. We took vacations together, to Tel Aviv, Tokyo, and Stockholm. His wife never interacted with my wife. Never. I never understood why his wife didn't like my wife, why she despised her, why she was jealous, but now I get it. She could look at them and see beyond the father-and-daughter facade they put on in front of me and others."

"Why couldn't you tell?"

"I didn't think twice because I trusted him, like he was my second dad. When I went away on trips, he would go by and check on her. I was in Dubai, in China, in London, in Australia, in Barbados, in Ireland, in Denmark, in San Francisco, in Hong Kong, in Memphis. I was all over, working my ass off, trying to get this company to go international, and when I called home, exhausted, he was there checking on her. I asked him to go by in the evenings to make sure the house was safe. I would be gone two weeks at a time. Once or twice I was gone for a month. He'd stop by every day. We'd talk on the phone while he was in my house. Then I'd hang up, and he'd drink vodka and undress my wife, then take her to my bed or call a car service run by some guy they simply called 'Driver' and have him chauffeur them both to Houghmagandy."

"That was in the messages?"

"It was in the messages."

"You showed him the messages? Is that what you said?"

"I sat in his kitchen, cup of coffee in front of me, and used her iPad to pull up many of their recent exchanges, show him the lingerie photos she had sent to his multiple e-mail addresses. She had sent thousands of erotic photos. And I showed him the photos of his dick. I stood in front of a man showing him a photo of his own dick. He gritted his teeth, sipped coffee, and I showed him indisputable truth."

"It wasn't password protected? She'd gotten real comfortable."

"She didn't expect me to come home and had left it unlocked."

"Lucky you. She left you access to her entire life."

"She said he made her pussy meow. They discussed buying vibrators. They created a world where I didn't exist. She sent pictures of herself in her underwear and told him her legs were missing having him between them. *He sent pictures of his dick.* They watched porn. Yesterday morning I sat in my kitchen, shocked, looking at pictures of her naked, looking at photos of his damn dick. I was so damn angry, and read it like it was a cheap eBook. I went to the car I had bought for her, was going to drive it back to the dealership and get my money back, but I got in and headed north, went to have a face-to-face with him regarding my wife. I went to see him about the woman he would lovingly refer to as his daughter. I went to his front door, went in to sit down and read every line. I repeated all the vulgar things he had done to her, and read all the things he had promised to do to her before the end of the year. They were going to get together Christmas Eve. He was going to take her to a hotel."

"Which hotel?"

"The one we were in. The same one we just left."

"They used that swank hotel for their affair?"

"Would have been their first time there. Based on what I read, that would have been their next fornicave and their next romping shop. She had picked the spot. I beat her to the punch."

"Jesus. You knew she'd see that on the card. You rubbed it in her face."

"You led me to that area. It was strange. It was as if you knew. So I pulled up there. Part of me wanted to see where they would've gone. I wanted to see where they would have had room service."

"Then exchange presents and semen."

"That was their last exchange. I went to see him. Wanted to verify his intentions. Don't have sex with my wife behind my back for the duration of my marriage and act like I'm the crazy one."

"She was your Clara Bow, your Pamela Anderson, a woman with a trustworthy face like Nancy Reagan, but behind closed doors, she was someone else. She was his little Lolita."

"She did a lot more than Lolita ever did

with Humbert Humbert."

"You beat his ass, then you went to a barbershop, got yourself a fresh haircut."

"I did. Put that on my charge card as well."

"To look good in your mug shot."

"No, this is my haircut day."

"Creature of habit."

"Not even a little anger, betrayal, or death should steer us away from the important things in life."

I asked, "Did you do a good job covering it up?"

"No. Not really."

"Did you clear your prints? Check for cameras?"

"Not as good a job as you would have. Was high on emotion. Rage took over and it got out of hand, fast. He didn't respect me. She didn't respect me. She had used me. He had betrayed me. I had had enough of the disrespect. I barely remember what went down. I just remember him being down on the floor, looking broken. Then, after it happened, I dropped the bat and felt incredibly calm."

"Like after a man has had an orgasm."

"I just know that I felt relaxed. He was on the floor, and the house was quiet. I sat down, finished my coffee. Had a second cup. I was unflustered because I understood why my marriage was the way it was. I understood what my marriage was. I knew that it wasn't me. For years, since we married, I'd felt like I wasn't doing something right. Now I know it wasn't because I wasn't a good husband. It was her mind games, her reverse psychology that had me feeling like I wasn't competent in so many ways."

"Who found him?"

"I finished my coffee, then called nine-one-one and sent the authorities to the home of her soul mate."

"Why would you do that?"

"He used to be my friend. He was a brilliant businessman who gave me good advice."

"You had a soft spot for the old guy who had been with your wife behind your back?"

"I didn't want the asshole to die. He never should've attacked me with that racquet. When things happen, it gets to a level where it's no longer about the woman. It was about one man betraying another. I went to see him more about that than about my wife having an affair. I expected more from him than I did my wife. I expected remorse. I expected full disclosure. I expected him to fall on his knees and beg for forgiveness. That is a different kind of pain than a woman betraying a man. Man betraying man, it sparks wars. She should've chosen a stranger. She could've cuckolded me with any man, and most men would have been glad to have her. But she chose my friend. My mentor betrayed me with my wife. How do you process that? Knowing that was in your face and you missed it, how do you? That destroys a man."

"You got the best of him. Since he went for your head, it could've ended up the other way."

"But when it was done, when I was winded, when I dropped the bat and looked at him, when I saw what I had done, there was regret, there was instant regret, but it couldn't be undone. I had struck him many, many times in rage. I knew that he was on the next train to that Disneyland in the sky."

"Jesus. Your wife was your ultimate betrayer. She makes Cleopatra sound like a saint."

"She didn't act alone. They were complicit. Both betrayed me. He was a Benedict Arnold and she was another Doña Marina. He had my wife and me on his Slipstream yacht, and when he divorced he brought his girlfriends to party on mine. You're looking at me like *that*. You really should leave now."

"You had a lot of cash. When I met you,

you had a lot of cash on you."

"I took his money and hoped it would look like a robbery."

"His cash? You gave me his walking-around cash and rushed away with a box of rocks."

"Now you know why I gave you that wad of money so freely."

"You gave me blood money."

"I show up with two grand in my pocket, and you appear out of nowhere, telling me you have something worth two grand. At that moment, I thought you knew. Then I heard all the sirens."

"I don't know what to say about that. I don't believe in kismet, try not to, and for my own sanity I have to not believe that all things, good and horrible, are already written, but that's weird."

He said, "He's been on the news all morning."

"Now I know why you were avoiding the news. That's why you jumped when you heard sirens. That's why you didn't call the police when that guy did the hit-and-run. That's why you were jittery when the police came into Denny's. That's why we rushed from the 7-Eleven. That's why you reacted the way you did when security knocked on the hotel door. You expected the police to come for you."

"Thought they were coming for me. I knew they'd show up at the hotel."

"Is he dead?"

He paused, choked with emotion. "His brain isn't responding."

"Will they be able to do anything?"

He took a few breaths, tears in his eyes. "You should go now."

"Why?"

"I don't want you to be here when they come for me."

"I'm not calling the police."

"This car has GPS. The police are smart. Maybe someone saw me leave. Maybe a camera inside his home recorded it all. I'm sure a fingerprint was left somewhere. I don't think I cleaned the coffee cup. They'll find this damaged car and me. And now they will find her, his mistress, in the trunk."

"Sirens."

"I hear them. Leave."

"No."

"You have responsibilities. Think about your kid."

"How do you know about my kid?"

"You're a mother."

"How do you know I have a child?"

"I know you."

"How do you know me?"

I repeated, "How do you know about my kid?"

"I assumed you have a child because you have mild stretch marks."

My hands went to my belly. "You saw?"

"I saw them. I kissed them. I kissed them all. They give you character."

"They're not that obvious. I stayed in the dark."

"The television had a nice glow. Enough to see a child's face is tattooed on your arm."

"She's drawn as roses and angels. That's my daughter."

"Her image is beautiful. You shouldn't ever cover it up."

"You made out her face. You didn't say anything."

"Wasn't sure what to say. Wasn't sure it was what I assumed."

"When were you sure?"

"Just saw inside your car. Barbie doll buckled in the front seat."

"My road dog."

"Plus, there is an infant safety seat in the rear. You definitely have a child."

"Had."

"Had?"

"Died. Dropped out of college when I was pregnant. Was never good between her dad and me. I thought I could fix him, and ended up destroying myself. Anyway. Long story. He never really did anything for her. I had a job. As an actress. Had to be gone a few days. He kept her. It was his first time taking her for the weekend. Then there was . . . the accident. I felt so guilty. Dropped out of life when she died."

"An accident?"

"Started by a dried-out Christmas tree. Her father had bought a cheap Christmas tree, had had it for two weeks, maybe longer, and never watered it. It dried out. It caught fire the night she was there."

"Jesus."

I wiped my eyes. "Damn. I don't want to cry in front of you. Sorry."

"It's okay. It's okay."

"Should've told you about that."

"No, it's fine. I hear the pain in your voice."

"Guy I'm seeing now . . . was seeing . . . I talked about Natalie Rose too much with him. We talked about her online, when we were on Skype, or on WhatsApp, and when we met at Roscoe's. I could tell it became too much for him, and I tried to abstain, but Natalie Rose is in my heart and at times all I can talk about. I guess, no matter what, it seemed like all conversations would lead back to my daughter. Soon he just ignored her. He couldn't relate. He acted as if she never existed. He let her go. I guess that was his way of saying that I had to stop talking about her. The only way to *not* talk about her was to try to not start talking about her. It was so hard to . . . to pretend that . . . she was . . . here but not here."

"You have family?"

"I have a brother in Florida. Johnny Parker. Parker was my maiden name. But we aren't close. He's had a bad marriage, too. Runs in the family, I guess. He was seeing a nice white girl named Jennifer for a while, but that didn't work out. Anyway. I don't want to call him crying all the time."

"You need to talk about Natalie Rose. Never stop. You stop, and she dies for real."

"Doing it now. I always need to talk about her. Some days I can't get out of bed, and I have nights when I can't sleep. When I sleep, sometimes I wake up crying. Not hard, just wake with tears in my eyes. I lost my child. I've had days and nights when giving up was all I thought about. Wanted to start cutting myself. Doctor wanted me on pills, but I wasn't taking anything to mess with my head."

"What did you love the most about being a mother?"

"Serious?"

"What did you love the most?"

"Why do you ask?"

"I haven't had the chance to be a father. Maybe that will never happen for me. I thought that it would have happened at least five, maybe six years ago, but it didn't. The wife didn't want children."

"Our kids would have been the same age."

"What did you love the most about having her in your life?"

It took me a moment, and for a moment I thought that I was going to break, that it would be like one of my tougher days, thought the emotions were about to pull me to my knees and make me scream to the clouds and try to make sense of what made no sense at all, and for a moment my bottom lip trembled. I shook with anxiety and I knew the next battle would be fighting back tears, and then wishing that the day she died they had tied me down and injected me with a lethal dose of pentobarbital so I could leave with her and take her on to the next part of this unknown journey. I almost broke down because after that day, every day was a nightmare, a nightmare when I was sleeping, a nightmare when I was awake. But on the heels of sadness came so many happy memories, and those memories dripped on me like rain, and that rain took me to the moment she was born, carried me from the moment I was so excited to introduce myself to her as her mother to the day I had to let her go, to the days I was no longer a mother, but still had the scars from childbirth, and I shoved the bad feelings away, discarded hatred, and focused and thought of the first days of her life, saw smiles and laughter, and my face lit up with each raindrop.

"I loved so many things. I think teaching her new things was my favorite. Watching her mimic me and try to do things on her own was so amazing to see. She came out of me unable to do anything but poop and cry, and I watched her on her journey to becoming a whole person. Every day was amazing."

"Was she like you?"

"She was too much like me. She came out

of me ready to have an argument about the umbilical cord being cut too soon. She was having too much fun inside me and wasn't ready for the real world. Just like her mother. I laughed the most when I saw my personality or sassiness come out in her."

"Bet she was the best kid ever."

"Just being able to be there for her when anything was wrong gave me fulfillment. I was supposed to be there. Nothing bad was supposed to happen. Nothing. We used to watch a few TV shows together, all the kiddie stuff. She would have loved *Frozen*. She would've tried to sing along to it all day. I read to her all the time, and when I worked out, she would mimic me, and we would be on the floor of my little apartment exercising together. I wanted her to be older so we could sit in spa chairs and get our nails done. She was like my little partner in crime. She was going to be all I ever needed. Yeah. She mimicked me. She wanted to do everything I did, and I wanted to teach her everything I knew."

"He should've been there. The guy you're seeing, whenever you talked about your daughter, no matter what time of day or night, he should have listened to every word. She was taken away too soon."

"I've been angry ever since. Lost. I can't

take her things out of my car. I have tried, but I can't. So I guess she rides around with me. When I do bad things, I hide it from her Barbie dolls. Last night I put them on the floor before I stole the truck and did the con game. Silly, I know. I keep thinking they're going to tell her that I've been a bad mommy or something. Sounds really silly saying that."

"You leave her stuff in the car. It's like you're keeping your daughter with you."

"In some ways. I can't part with her toys. One day. Not yet. I left them where she left them. I left the mess she made in my car the same way she left the mess. She stays in my heart."

He let a moment pass. "It's time for you to go. You should leave."

"I have nowhere to go."

A chilling rain dampened our faces as we looked at his wife.

I said, "She's pretty. She's way more than pretty by the standards of mainstream America."

"I wish I hadn't done that. I'm so sorry that happened. This isn't what I wanted."

"I know. I can tell."

"Leave. I don't want anyone to think you were involved, or this was because of you."

I put my fingers in her blood, then

500

touched the damaged tile, left my finger-prints along with his.

He said, "That won't change anything. I've been caught on video all night at many locations. You weren't in the hotel lobby when I ran into her; you weren't there when I escorted her to the covered parking lot. Cameras might be there too. I will assume they have cameras. They'll know."

"But I am standing with you now. I'm standing with you until the end."

"This isn't like the movie theater."

"I know."

"Not like 7-Eleven."

"I ain't going anywhere."

After that symbolic gesture, I closed the trunk of his car, inhaled glacial air.

I sat down next to him, held his hand, and rubbed his cold fingers until they were warm again.

I said, "You love your wife. This hurt you. Loving her gave you great pain."

His voice trembled. "I do. Even if she's dead."

"Loving someone who is dead — nothing wrong with that."

"Not at all. Some people are easier to love that way."

"If a man's wife dies, he's called a wid-ower. If a woman's husband has died, she's a widow. When children lose their parents they are orphans. Why isn't there a name for a parent who loses a child?"

"Because you will always be a parent. Even when children have left, or have died."

"I'm still Natalie Rose's mom."

"And you will always be."

"Thanks. I needed to hear that."

Police sirens wailed in the distance as the rain started to fall again.

Sirens. Sirens. Sirens were far away, but would not stay far away, not for long.

Sirens screamed and Christmas songs were being played all over the land.

I watched the man from Orange County, examined his worry, and touched his chin.

He grinned at me.

He was a well-groomed, honest man who had been dealt an interesting hand in life, a man who would give up his seat to a lady and who told the truth even when it wasn't nice because it needed to be heard; a well-read man who knew how to listen; a man who frowned when he was angry and smiled when he felt joy, and probably cried in private; a romantic man who told me he didn't know all the answers, not even to this mess, but he wasn't running away. He was a man who had learned something every day but hadn't learned everything. Intelligent and still naive, like the rest of the world. He hadn't hardened like me, hadn't learned to never trust anyone.

I'd been served an interesting hand in life as well. I was a big cup of the best of the best covered in hopes and dreams, difficult at times, and smart, very smart, not as smart as Einstein, but I had made my own mistakes, mistakes worse than forgetting to put your pants on, larger than marrying and then divorcing. I read, was trustworthy, was romantic, but had been on the wrong road.

Thump.

I looked back at the trunk of the car and asked, "Did you hear that?"

He was in another place, reliving his own agony; I held his hand and listened.

Sirens. Sirens. Sirens.

I had a feeling that this time they would approach, but they wouldn't pass us by, and the wave of wails wouldn't recede. I stuck my tongue out, caught a few raindrops, water mixed with the smog.

I said, "We could both use a good night's sleep and a lot of laughs."

"I have something better."

"What do you have?"

"Well, maybe not better. But just as good."

He took out the bag of cheesecake and forks. There were ten kinds of cheesecake.

I said, "Still, it was the best night ever."

"Didn't want it to end. Not going to pretend. Not the sex, but the connection."

"It's not over yet."

"Where do we start? Cheesecake. How do we lay out the food?"

"Smorgasbord."

We opened all the cheesecakes and put them in front of us like a buffet.

I said, "I want the caramel-pecan piece first. I won that slice first. That slice is all mine, Buster."

"Caramel pecan. Chocolate chip. Cherry. Blueberry. Chocolate chip–cookie dough."

"Key lime. Pumpkin. Oreo."

"Red velvet and Reese's cheesecakes."

"You kept your word."

"I did better than my word. Ten kinds of cheesecake."

"You went all out."

People began to appear on the boardwalk. Spanish-speaking people who would always be called and considered Mexicans, no matter where in the world they were born, appeared and started hustling umbrellas. He bought one. He bought us a big umbrella. We sat under it, shoulder to shoulder.

He said, "Starbucks in Ladera Heights, the one not too far from where you live."

"Used to be the black Starbucks."

"Must you grade everything in black and white? Didn't MLK want that nonsense to stop?"

"I was there early this morning. Was avoiding my landlord. Was stressed, plotting how to get quick money. That's where I saw the MacBook Pro box sitting on an outside table. Someone had left it."

"I should've been there, too, instead of going to Santa Monica. I should've stopped there and cooled off, maybe evoked slow thinking over quick thinking. Would've been great to see you walk in."

I asked, "Would you have hit on me?"

"Would you have been receptive to a half-breed, pissed-off man in a suit?"

"Who is playing the race card now?"

He said, "You started it. Would you have been interested in me?"

"Every gold digger's alert would've gone off as soon as your new ride hit the parking lot, and they would've been rushing to grab you like you were on a table at Walmart the morning after Thanksgiving. People will kill over a toaster, and I know they would've been ripping you apart. The Gold Digger Alert goes off at a pitch that only dogs can hear, so bitches would've been breaking their necks to get to Starbucks."

"Would you have been interested in me?"

"I'm not a gold digger looking for a wish-granting factory that walks on two legs and has a baby-making dick made of wood and comes in gold. If I were, maybe my life would have been a little bit better. I've never been an ass-for-cash kind of girl. I didn't want Natalie Rose to have an ass-for-cash mother."

He asked, "Would you have been interested in me as a person, as a man?"

"Only if you would've been interested in a girl who frustrated the workers and held up the line by ordering a tall, half-skinny, half one-percent, extra hot, split quad shot, two shots decaf, two shots regular latte with whip, then realized she didn't have enough money in her pocket to pay for the inconvenience."

"Is that a yes?"

"That is a yes. We could've had a nice first meeting. Might've been boring compared to the last twelve hours, but nice. We could've taken it slow. Kissed on the second date. Sex on the fourth."

He said, "Sex on the tenth."

"I'd have to wait ten dates to get some of that?"

"Takes more than chicken and waffles to get into these boxers."

"Whatever. I'd wait. You're worth it. That

LSD would be worth the wait."

"You stood up with me at the movies."

"Yeah. I did."

"That was the moment that did it for me. It made me want to kiss you."

"Really?"

"Yeah."

"Might've been the moment that did it for me, too. You went all caveman."

"I went too far."

"God, wish I had met you early this morning at Starbucks."

He smiled.

I said, "Everything would have been perfect if we had been in line at the same time, exchanged smiles, and you had said something nice, and we had started up an intellectual chat."

"We could've started out like this."

"Could've had more than one night."

He said, "But we had a fun night."

"Kicked out of the movies. Kicked ass at 7-Eleven. Had sex like rabbits. We had the best night."

"What was the best part?"

I laughed. "The water balloon fight."

"Hell yeah."

"Knocking on the doors like Sheldon."

"Pushing the buttons on the elevator."

"We were out of control. Surprised we

didn't get thrown out."

He said, "The sex was amazing."

"Yes. The sex."

"Best sex ever."

"When was the last time you had sex?"

He said, "Thanksgiving."

"You were clogged up."

"You? When did you last chicken-and-waffle until the sprinklers came on?"

"Not answering that."

"I'll bet it was since Thanksgiving."

"Not answering."

"Doesn't matter. Who you were with, when, why, it doesn't matter."

I said, "You're my first great lover. This feels like my first great love."

"I enjoyed every moment."

"Every kiss."

"Especially every kiss."

"You dropped me on my head."

"That was funny."

"It was funny. You were grabbing for my ass to catch me."

"You have a body like an ecdysiast, and move it like one, too."

"We were all over the room."

"We messed that room up."

I laughed. "Like rock stars on a world tour."

"Like children free from every problem in

the world."

I smiled. "We had a lot of food."

"Now we have a lot of cheesecake."

West Coast weed heads staggered like zombies in search of the nearest 420 shops. The hungover passed sober men and women rushing to wherever they worked. The homeless pushed overloaded shopping carts and collected cans and bottles while they checked messages on their cell phones.

He said, "I want to see photos of your daughter."

"For real?"

I took out my phone, handed it to him, and showed him the best thing I'd ever done.

"She's beautiful."

"Thank you."

"Her father's not black."

"No, he isn't."

"Hypocrite."

"At least he's not white."

"Still a hypocrite."

"I'm still black, no matter who I sleep with."

"Post that on Facebook."

"Whatever."

"You have secrets."

I said, "Can I tell you something?"

"Yes."

"You're the first black guy I've ever slept with."

"Half-black."

"Same difference."

"Well, welcome home."

"Halfway home."

We laughed.

He looked at a few more photos of Natalie Rose, then handed me my phone.

Thump.

Thump.

Thump.

I heard soft thumps from inside the trunk of the car.

Thump.

Thump.

Thump.

6:19 A.M.

Thump. Thump. Thump.

Then all I could hear was ice-cold water falling from skies darker than the racial history of America. Maybe I hoped to hear endless thumps. I was pretty sure I heard thumps, and not the echo of an old man's heart still beating under the floorboards of one of the apartments in the distance. I hoped. For him, I hoped. Maybe I hoped for her as well. I didn't have any feelings of hatred or resentment for the woman. But I did feel for him. His journey with me was ending, yet it was only beginning.

He said, "Sorry about your daughter."

"Natalie Rose. Her name was Natalie Rose Summers."

"Wish I could have met Natalie Rose."

"Thanks for saying that."

"No mother should ever have to lose a child, and not like that."

"Shit happens. As long as I can believe

that shit happens, as long as I can imagine that all of this is random, I won't take it personally. A plane filled with adults and children goes missing. Mudslides kill people in Oso. Tsunamis. Poverty. Injustice. Rape. Molestation. A bad marriage. A little girl dying in a fire for no reason is something that I can't comprehend. Maybe someone has a bad sense of humor and this nightmare is just a prank. A sick joke. If this is intentional, if this pain is intentional —"

"It's okay to let it go."

"Why give her to me, then take her away like that? What kind of plan is that?"

Tears mixed with rain. Not many tears, but they were saltier than the sea.

He said, "Did you get the present I left you?"

"Present?"

"I left it next to the bed."

"Oh. The check. That was kind of you."

"Hope you didn't mind."

"I got it. Thanks for the extra four hundred dollars. I really mean that. You've been so kind."

He repeated, "Four hundred dollars."

"The extra four hundred will come in handy."

"Four hundred dollars."

"Will need it sooner than you know."

"Can you read?"

"Of course I can read. I read better than that asshole who was texting at the movies."

"I don't think so. Put your glasses on."

"Why?"

"Look at the check again."

I did. I saw a mistake. I saw an extra word. After the word *hundred,* there was an unnecessary word. The word *thousand* was after the word *hundred* and before the word *dollars.* I paused. My checks always stopped *after* the word *hundred,* so I hadn't read any further than that. The word *thousand* sitting there after *hundred* looked strange; it looked lost. It looked unreal. It looked like a mistake.

I asked, "Is this supposed to be for four hundred dollars?"

"No."

"Four thousand dollars?"

"Read the check. Read it the way it is."

"Four hundred . . . then . . . the word . . . *thousand* . . . then the word *dollars.*"

"That's it."

"No."

"Yes."

"No way."

"Way."

I asked, "Are you for real?"

"You didn't read the check at the hotel?"

"I read the word *four* and the word *hun-dred* and then stopped and put the check down."

"Now add the last word."

"I can't take this. I'm not even going to say that amount out loud."

"You can."

"This is a lot of money. This is, like, ten years of money."

"Fifty if you work at Walmart."

"Four hundred thousand dollars? What would I do with that much money?"

"Go to Dubai and get a suite at Burj Al Arab. Stay at one of the world's tallest ho-tels."

"No."

"Yes."

"I don't have a passport."

"No excuses. You can go down on Wilshire and get one the same day. Two days from now you can be there, in Dubai, with Bar-bie dolls, with the memories of your daugh-ter. If you rent a room that costs about three thousand a night, they will send a private helicopter to pick you up from the airport."

"I can't do that."

"You can."

"You can't go with me."

"No. I can't go with you."

"Then I can't go."

"Some journeys have to be taken alone."

The sound of sirens added depth to what he was saying, to what he was doing.

I said, "Four hundred thousand dollars."

"Merry Christmas to you. And Natalie Rose."

Then I couldn't breathe. For a moment I couldn't breathe.

I put my glasses away, wiped my eyes; my voice cracked as I said, "This isn't right. This isn't fair."

"It is fair."

"Good things don't happen to me."

"Good things do."

"Bad things shouldn't happen to you. Not to a guy like you."

He whispered, "Shit happens to the good, to the bad. It happens to everybody. It's just my turn."

I put the check in my pocket. Tears ran down my cheeks. This was bittersweet.

I asked, "Is this for real?"

"Yes."

"I mean, is this for real, for real?"

"Yes."

"You're not a cop, are you? Is this some form of entrapment?"

"Sure is. You're under arrest. You have the right to remain silent, which I know you won't do."

I whispered, "Dude, I so love you."

"You don't know me."

"I love you for this. I love you for who you are. I love what's in your heart."

"Thanks. You're an amazing woman."

"I have to get up out of this black cloud and do better."

"I want you to do better. No more rocks in a box."

"Okay. I'm done. I promise. No rocks in a box."

"No stolen trucks."

"No stolen trucks."

"Do better."

"I'll do better."

"Get back on track."

"I'll get back on track."

"For Natalie Rose."

"I stumbled. I fell."

"Time to get up and dust yourself off."

"I'll get back on my feet, get on track, and make her proud of me."

"Keep your word."

"A man attacked you, a wife betrayed you, and you'll go to . . . go to . . . this ain't right."

"I've been in prison a long time. Mine was a bad marriage. We create our own prisons."

Eyes filled with tears, I repeated, "We create our own prisons."

"You open the door and let the problem in. I opened the door. I fell for the illusion of perfection. We all have problems, and I created mine. But it's time for you to get out of yours."

"Are you okay?"

He grinned. "Not sure. I'm afraid. I feel like I'm a six-year-old boy, and I'm afraid."

"You could run."

"I'm not running. Not from the inevitable. It would bring more shame on my parents."

I wiped my eyes with the backs of my hands. "I'd run away with you."

"I wouldn't let you."

I took his hand, calmed him, and did my best to keep him with me. I had been his unexpected lover. Now I was his friend. We sat like we were very close friends who were not just a part of each other's loins, but part of each other's chests, part of each other's hearts.

We sat like we had known each other for years.

I asked, "Still thinking about every woman you've ever loved?"

"You. Only thinking about you."

A naked man ran by, wearing only tennis shoes and a Santa Claus hat.

We laughed at the ridiculousness, and then watched a few drowsy women taking the Walk of Shame.

Not many members of that before-sprinklers-came-on sorority were out.

Not many in the city formerly known as the Town of Our Lady the Queen of the Angels on the River Porciúncula were out at all. Los Angelinos feared rain the way most men feared real emotions.

Too many are afraid of falling water. Too many have pluviophobia.

And too many are afraid of the darkness. And smog. And traffic. And being open.

And being vulnerable. No one wants to feel powerless, susceptible, impotent.

Man or woman, it doesn't matter; we are all fragile, delicate, weak, ailing in some way.

And our weaknesses come from our pores, like water vapor, and rise to the skies, create condensation, and fall again, mixed with the rain. Love from broken hearts escapes through fissures and rises, becomes clouds, and the heaviness from the one true emotion saturates us all.

Love never goes away.

It goes up, spreads around, and comes back down, sometimes in the oddest places.

I said, "Best first kiss ever."

"You have witchcraft in your lips."

Again I imagined that I heard a thump.
Thump. Thump.

He asked, "How do you feel?"

"Susan is sore. Tina and Marie are wide awake."

"You're too much. Now I have a question."

"Okay."

"A serious question."

"Okay."

He asked, "Would there have been a chance for us?"

"As long as you like kisses and chatting about racism, discrimination, and xenophobia."

"I would have boiled you eggs for breakfast."

I smiled. "I would have made you an omelet."

"Well, you're an extremely hard act to follow, too."

"Wish I had met you first."

He said, "Me, too. Before everyone."

"Wish I had met you and taken a different trajectory in life. But I loved my daughter. I'd never undo her being born. I'd take every mistake ten times over, would redo everything I did up until she was born. No — just until she was in my belly and we were both sharing the same body for a while. We were roommates for nine months, and I couldn't wait to meet her and be her mother. Then I would want you. If you would have wanted me then, if you'd have wanted us, I would have wanted you, too."

"I would want both of you."

I asked, "What would you change?"

"If I had known you existed, I would have waited to meet you. We could've been a great team."

I frowned. "Wait a second."

"What now?"

"Are we breaking up? Are you dumping me twice in one night?"

"Are you going to slap me again?"

"If we're breaking up, yeah. Hell yeah. I will slap you."

"I guess we're not breaking up."

"Maybe we're beginning."

He said, "Yeah. We're just beginning. After all my past relationships, I can truly appreciate how great this is."

"I love you. I love who you are. I love feeling that I can really love you."

"I'm disgusting."

I said, "Be quiet. Don't spoil the moment."

"I love you, too; love who you are. Wish I had spent the day with you. The whole day."

Sirens wailed as red and blue lights moved through rain and the marine layer.

Came closer.

As the police sirens grabbed my attention, cold winter rain fell, ice water dripping from cubes in the sky. His breath fogged as he touched my chin, pulled my attention away from the sirens.

Closer.

He pulled my attention away from the red and blue lights. He pulled my mind from lights that looked like fire. He smiled at me. My lips curved upward, driven by my heart, by my emotions.

I said, "Only takes meeting one person to turn your life around, good or bad."

In my mind it was a bright and sunny day. There was no rain making splashes in the Pacific Ocean. I could smell the Philippine Sea as well. We were on Saipan's Forbidden Island. I was dry, wearing a sundress, purple cowboy boots, and a fedora like in the "Happy" video. He had on shorts, sandals, a Kobe jersey, and Ray-Ban shades. In the distance I heard Natalie Rose laughing, singing the Strawberry Shortcake song. We were high on a hill, blue waters as far as we could see down in my favorite archipelagos. It was just the three of us. In my mind, it was the most perfect day in the universe.

Closer.

I took out my Samsung. I took a dozen rapid selfies. I cried. Tears fell, but I smiled and held my phone at arm's length, took selfie after selfie. Then I posted two on Twitter and Facebook before I put the phone away. Let the world see our story. Let the world judge us. Let the world decide.

I took a forkful of cheesecake and asked, "What do we do now?"

He took a forkful of two types of cheesecake and replied, "I want to hear your life story."

Closer. Closer.

I said, "Okay. Starting where?"

"From birth in Saipan."

"I'll tell you my life story. I was an actress. A comedian."

"That explains a lot. Your acerbic wit is a force to be reckoned with."

"I played volleyball in high school. I went to UCSB, up where they had the shooting, only long before. I was a biology major, wanted to be an anesthesiologist, but changed to English because it was easier. Then one night, I went to open-mic night, and a friend dared me to get onstage. I did, got a few laughs, and was hooked on Hollywood. I'll tell you all about it."

He said, "And I'll tell you all about me and my thirty-two years on this planet."

"I have one brother, Johnny. He's ten years older. We don't talk to each other."

"You said that already."

"Sorry."

"Explain the wedding ring."

"I was married to Natalie Rose's dad. My ex-husband's a cop."

"That's why the cops at Denny's were staring and whispering."

"Yeah. Sorry about that little lie. One of the guys knows the man I married."

"You're divorced, or separated, or an adulteress?"

"Divorced at twenty. Met him when he pulled me over to give me a speeding ticket."

"One look at you, and there was no ticket written."

"Let's just say it was a cleavage day."

"Really?"

"Was on the way to audition for Hazel Bijou. Tried to get a part in a sci-fi movie."

"Mom. Actress. Comedian. Dancer. Singer. Grifter."

"And substitute teacher."

"Is there anything you don't do?"

"I'm a Jackie of all trades, master of none."

"Your name is Jackie?"

"My name is Jackie. My mother named me after Jackie O."

"Jackie."

"Yep. My name is Jacqueline Francesca Parker-Summers."

"You've been keeping secrets, Jacqueline."

"I'll tell you all about my failed marriage and Natalie Rose, if you want to know."

"Then what?"

"Whatever you want."

"Whatever I want?"

"I'm yours. Whatever you want, because I'm yours from the inside out."

"I'll want to touch your beautiful dreadlocks again."

"Oh, Lord. Then what?"

"You have more mints?"

"I have more mints."

"Might get up the nerve to ask for another kiss."

"You don't need a mint to kiss me. You can kiss me whenever you want."

"Is this our sixth date?"

"Seventh. This is our seventh."

Closer. Closer. Closer.

I glanced at my phone. It was 6:31 A.M.

He leaned over, kissed me like I was the love of his life, then said, "We could always . . ."

Who wants that perfect love story any
way, anyway?
Cliché, cliché, cliché, cliché.
— Jay-Z, Ft. Beyoncé, "Part II (On the Run)"

Never had room service all night . . .
Never had a love affair so tight . . .
I've never felt a feeling so right.
                    — Maxwell, "Fortunate"

ACKNOWLEDGMENTS

Psst. Hey, you. Yeah. *You.* All of you. Come closer. Closer. Closer.

Not that damn close! Pop a mint, please. Not calling any names, but pop a mint.

LOL.☺

Whassup, peeps! I was just reading messages and laughing as Hulu supplied background noise. My good friend-poet-mom-cook and Bajan extraordinaire Rebel Glam calls me Dickster. I think she started that at a poetry slam near the sea one night in Barbados. And up here in America, over in ATL, my buddy Carey calls my readers the Dickey Nuts. ☺Not easy having a surname like . . . mine. I think he in-boxed me that yesterday, and I'm still laughing. Actually, Bajan Rebel Glam in-boxed me after she finished reading *A Wanted Woman.* I have great friends and fans, but since my surname seems to inspire giggles and blushes in the West Indies, I'll just keep calling myself EJD, and I'll keep calling you guys my readers.

I keep hearing Snoop Dogg's voice in the back of my head saying, *"Dickey Nuts."*

Let me get on with it. It's time to chat about the creation of *One Night.* Pull up a chair. I won't take long. Ready? Cool. Taking a deep breath. I had just finished writing a pretty intense novel, *A Wanted Woman,* an exciting tale that moved around the globe, destroyed a lot of property, reduced the population in the name of revenge, and probably had the most exciting heroine I'd ever created. On the heels of that wonderful madness, I wanted to create something smaller, less populated, a novel that used fewer locations. Did my best to leave out the guns. I did. I promise. I really tried. The start of this novel, the short con, was written (a version of it, that is) years ago, at least a decade back, and I think that initially it was how Dante was supposed to meet the original Scamz. Way back the idea was dropped, and the scene sat in my computer and had a party with other scenes still waiting for a chance to make it into a novel one day. Well, this particular scene sat on a floppy disk, the 8-track of storage, then was rediscovered and reentered into Word along the way. It changed from Dante (*Thieves'*

Paradise) doing the con (using a heavy television) to Panther (a different version of the same character that ended up in *Naughty or Nice, Drive Me Crazy,* and *An Accidental Affair*) doing the con with a lighter flat-screen television. Technology changes with the times, but the con remains the same. Rocks in a box is still alive and making money as I type. After I had taken everyone on the wild ride from Florida to Memphis to California to Trinidad to Barbados with Reaper, I revisited that scene. Like I said, I wanted to write a tale that had few characters, preferably only two, and started writing the interaction between the two main characters. I fell into the *what if?* zone, and soon there was a rugged flow. I really enjoyed where it was going and decided to attempt to make the entire story take place at dusk and be done before sunrise. That was the concept. I hadn't thought about it at the time, but I've always been a fan of "talking" movies like *Before Sunset* and *Before Sunrise* starring Ethan Hawke and Julie Delpy (I haven't seen *Before Midnight*), and the way the tales move moment to moment and gradually reveal who the characters are. (I'm also a huge fan of tales that are done in less than three days.)

It's been a long day, so I'd better hurry

up and get to thanking people.

I always have to thank the people at Dutton. Brian Tart, here's another one. I hope it's worth the killing of a few trees, a thousand times as many downloads, five movies, and ten sequels.

Much love to my editor, Denise Roy. Once again, thanks for the great edits.

You're awesome. The story has wings.

Emily Brock and everyone in publicity, thanks for all the hard work and making the tour for *A Wanted Woman* a great success. Time to do it again!

Matthew Daddona, same to you: a million thanks for helping keep this boat afloat.

To my wonderful copyeditor, JoAnna Kremer, you are truly (awesome* Pi)^5. I mean that. You have really helped smooth out this bumpy road. Speaking of bumpy roads, shouts to Barbados!

I just glanced at the time on my MacBook Pro, and it's 9:34 P.M. I'm on the bed, and *The Good Wife* season 2, episode 14 is playing in the background as I call to mind all the rest of the wonderful people who took part in this journey. The Dicksters. LOL. Still laughing. Laughing at Carey, too.

Pilar V. Arsenec, thanks for the wonderful interview on the last novel, and thanks for reading about the "Love Birds," as you affectionately called them. You read page after page as the scenes were being created and changed, as I added, deleted, and shuffled everything around. You read the original, much longer version.

Same to you, Jacqueline Bouvier Lee at Books-A-Million. Thanks for the support. I think you were the first to read the complete version, the version before this final edit. Thanks for your time and your interest in this project.

Jackie Parker-Summers (JPS) and the man from Orange County thank both of you ladies for being both beta-readers and flies on the wall, and not calling the front desk when JPS became a little too spirited through the night.

No one has read this, or any book that I've written, more than my agent, Sara Camilli. Thanks for being there since the nineties. Time flies when you're writing books and traveling. Tell Ray and Stephen I said thanks as well! How many novels before I get to one hundred? Need to write faster. Trying. But well, there's Netflix and Hulu and Facebook and Twitter and. . . . Kidding!

To the readers who have been hanging out with me as bookstores opened and closed, as we moved from bricks and mortar to the digital age, to all of you who have been here since the days when people wrote letters and mailed them to one another with those things called stamps — thanks for sticking around. Many hugs to you and yours. And to the ones who just discovered my work, welcome aboard, and thanks for giving this kid from South Memphis a shot. Riverview Elementary, Middle School, Carver High, U of M, shouts to all of my peeps. Dreams do come true. Stay motivated. Hope you enjoy the ride, be it long or short. I hope you enjoyed reading the novel you're holding in your hand, be it made from what used to exhale oxygen, or as decoded 1s and 0s on your handy-dandy electronic device.

Thanks for taking the time to come and support me on the book tours.

Hope to see you on the next one. Until then, see you on Facebook, Twitter, and wherever we go next.

To all the writers out there, put your butts in the chair. Write. Write. Write. No excuses.

And in case I forgot anybody, it wasn't intentional. So break out the pen and let's make sure you're included with the usual suspects. This novel wouldn't be possible without the help of _____. They stayed up with me at night, made themselves available on Skype and Facebook, and brought me green tea to start my day.

Peace and blessings from a member of the '06. Ice, ice, baby.

Carolyn's only son signing off . . . still laughing at Rebel Glam and what Carey said . . .☺

Eric Jerome Dickey
Tuesday, July 29, 2014, 10:25 P.M.
73 degrees, 0% precipitation,
humidity 50%, Wind 3 mph
Back in the USA; *Latitude:* 33.800057;
Longitude: -84.517211
Gray shorts, faded sky-blue Argentina
T-shirt, clean-shaven, fresh
conservative fade, and shoeless.
Dickster is leaving the building.☺

ABOUT THE AUTHOR

Eric Jerome Dickey is the *New York Times* bestselling author of twenty-two novels, and is also the author of a six-issue miniseries of graphic novels for Marvel Enterprises, featuring Storm (X-Men) and the Black Panther. He also penned the original story for the film *Cappuccino,* directed by Craig Ross Jr. Originally from Memphis, Tennessee, Dickey graduated from the University of Memphis, where he pledged Alpha Phi Alpha, and also attended UCLA. Dickey now lives on the road and rests in whatever hotel will have him.